A LOVE OF INNOCENCE

ROBIN JENKINS

EDINBURGH

B&W PUBLISHING

1994

First published 1963
This edition published 1994
by B&W Publishing, Edinburgh
© Robin Jenkins
ISBN 1 873631 48 0

British Library Cataloguing in Publication Data:
A catalogue record for this book is available
from the British Library.

Cover photograph by kind permission
of the Hulton Deutsch Collection

Printed by Werner Söderström

A LOVE OF INNOCENCE

ROBIN JENKINS was born in Cambuslang in 1912, and educated at Hamilton Academy and Glasgow University. He taught English in Scotland, Spain, Afghanistan and Northern Borneo and has written twenty-three novels. As well as novels set in Scotland, including *The Cone-gatherers*, *Guests of War* and *A Would-Be Saint*, his extensive travels have provided the backdrop for other highly-acclaimed work, such as *Dust on the Paw*, based on his experience of Afghanistan. Robin Jenkins lives in Argyll.

Other B&W titles by Robin Jenkins

A WOULD-BE SAINT

For Colin

One

After twenty years of being in charge of the Home, and after innumerable but unforgotten failures, Miss Montgomerie had still not admitted to herself that it just was not possible for the one smile, the one tone of voice, the one form of dress, and the one human body to combine the two roles of mother and paid official. Though she loved the children in her charge, she had also to respect her obligations to society which employed her to look after and discipline them. Of the matron's uniform in which she had so conscientiously assumed her duties, years of elimination had left only the white collar; for the rest she wore what their mothers, had they any, would have worn; or so she imagined, her taste in off-duty dress having been, even in her probationary days, peculiar. Years of experimentation, too, had resulted in a kind of smile and a certain warmth of voice that might not immediately endear her to a child but would not intimidate it either; rather they left the way open not only for trust, which in almost every case entered later, but also for love, whose entry was never quite so easy.

It depended on the circumstances of a child's admission, and also on how long he or she stayed. Some were admitted crazed with terror, or numbed with brutal neglect: these she could restore if she had them long enough; but too often, at the outset of her patient efforts, they were taken away to foster-parents, who might or might not continue the restoration by carrying out the recommendations she always sent.

One thing she had always reminded herself to be utterly necessary; indeed, her predecessor had given it to her as the most important piece of advice she had to offer: never to have favourites. A real or obstetrical mother could perhaps afford such a risk; she dared not. Yet this evening, in budded April, as she sat in her office listening to the cries of the children at

1

play outside, she confessed that in the case of John Sneddon she had probably broken the sacred rule. No one else knew it, none of the staff, and certainly not John himself. On the contrary, her reaction had been to be towards him a little stricter than to most. She had compensated him for that by being particularly patient with his young brother Tom, whom she rather disliked, or would have if her sense of duty and fairness had allowed her to dislike any orphan of six, no matter how ungrateful and snivelly.

There were, God knew, extenuations.

Crossing to the window she watched for the two brothers among the thirty or forty children. In spite of the similarity of dress—navy-blue jerseys and dark-grey shorts for the boys and dark-blue frocks for the girls—she soon picked out John, racing after the ball and seldom reaching it, but when he did kicking it with glee if little skill. After him ran his brother, no doubt whimpering as usual, and seeking reassurances that no one in the world, not John even, could ever give him.

There were certainly extenuations.

Tom Sneddon had been only an infant of three when, three years ago, he and his brother had been brought to the Home. In the tiny kitchen their father had killed their mother, striking her with a hatchet that had been kept in the bunker for chopping sticks. He had been mad with jealousy. Neighbours had testified that he had always been a quiet, hard-working little man—a cobbler—devoted to his children, although it was whispered that the younger boy, Tom, wasn't his. Mrs Sneddon, a dyed blonde, had considered herself too good-looking for the wage he earned, and so had become nothing better than a prostitute. In the end it had come to murder in the gas-lit kitchen two days before Christmas, with the walls, the ceiling, and the coloured streamers splattered with blood.

The two children had been asleep in the other room; or so at any rate it was hoped. Certainly Tom, only three, must have been; but it was thought possible that John, six then, might have been awakened by the screams, and, creeping through, had seen the dreadful climax among the decorations. The authorities, accepting a plea of insanity, had considered it

2

unwise to question the boy; but the sergeant of police, with whom Miss Montgomerie had discussed it, had given his opinion that John must have seen something. He had been wide awake when neighbours had rushed in; and when the police had arrived to take away the gentle murderer, the boy, now in a neighbour's house, had kept nodding, though no one had been asking him anything.

Out of a midden flowers grew. Why then be astonished that from such a sordid environment so admirable a child as John Sneddon should have grown? Cheerful, uncomplaining, and helpful, it didn't matter in the least that every teacher found him slow at his lessons; in fact, Miss Montgomerie was inclined to think this a blessing, because had he been a clever child he might have brooded to his own disaster on the terrible thing he had seen. At the same time, she often wondered how, if he really had seen it, he could remain so free from black moods, apprehensions, subconscious resentments and nightmares; and even if he had seen or heard nothing, he had surely been old enough to know afterwards what had happened: that his father, whom he had loved, had savagely killed his mother, whom he had probably loved too, and was now an incommunicable ghost in a criminal asylum. There were times when, watching the happy boy, she had been convinced that inimical forces, deep within him, and gathering invisibly without, were waiting with hellish patience to surprise him one day with what he already knew, and torture him with its consequences. Though she went with her charges to church every Sunday and made sure they knew and observed the Commandments, including the fifth, like most people she found it hard to understand why a child should suffer for what his father or mother had done; but she had been brought up as a child herself to believe it, and now, as a devout woman, still had to.

After tea that evening, in half an hour or so, she was to take them to her sitting-room, where she would tell them, as considerately as she knew how, that it was their turn to be severed from the Home. Foster-parents had applied for two boys, brothers, one about nine, the other about six. The

3

selection was never hers, but she was always consulted; and in their case she had consented, thinking that if they went to live on the island of Calisay, where space and light were so abundant, then those forces of darkness threatening John might be overcome. She had suggested that his foster-parents, whoever they might turn out to be, should not be told about his background. Authority had demurred, but finally had agreed. As for the nearest living relative, their father's sister, she had hysterically insisted on signing, free, a deed of renunciation, and not once had she come to visit them. A stupid woman, anxious to protect her own family, she had seen in her nephews a perpetuation of the crime. At first a neighbour or two had visited them, bringing fruit and sweets, but latterly no one had come. Thus they were, in a way, as free as birds to fly from the doom-laden, conscience-ridden city to the innocent and beautiful island.

She, who had warmed their nest and fed them, must be content to sit with her wings folded.

As far as she knew, there were already a number of boarded-out children on Calisay; none, however, was from her Home. Had any been she would have visited them during her holidays—unofficially, of course, as she had done with the two larger islands, Mull and Tiree. She took presents with her, and always, so she hoped, was welcome; though naturally some of the children had almost forgotten her, and a few, the happiest, seemed to associate her with the fear troubling them constantly, that some day the authorities who had hired them out would take them back again.

On her way down to the dining-room she visited the nursery; but first, on the wide marble staircase, she paused for a few moments to look up at the painting of Alexander Macrae, a former Lord Provost, who had bequeathed this great mansion for its present purpose. In his white and crimson robes of office, and with his gold chain round his neck, the old, sly-smiling, child-loving man seemed to her to be nodding approval, as if he not only watched her at her patient ministrations but also read her thoughts, and, deeper still, divined the ambitions of love she strove so hard

4

to achieve. He had also stated in his will that the grand and expensive furniture should be left in the house for the enjoyment and consolation of the orphans, but it had been decided long ago that such opulence and luxury would make ridiculous the work of charity that had to be carried on there. So it had been removed, and now the furnishings, in the children's quarters at least, were appropriately plain and useful. By some oversight, or through some official's strange decision, two white plaster busts had been left to adorn the staircase, one of Sir Walter Scott and the other of the Roman Emperor Augustus. Some imaginative children would, if allowed to, have seen these as ghosts, and dreamed about them. Miss Montgomerie's method of stopping that was simply to set the small would-be neurotics the task of dusting the pale eyeless heads with a feather-duster, herself standing by. When a former Sister had suggested that it would be kinder to have the busts removed, Miss Montgomerie had refused. You could not, she pointed out, get rid of terror by hiding it, but only by demonstrating that, when bravely faced, it was harmless. At the same time she had been severe on past jokers who had daubed the Emperor's nose with red ink, and pulled a regulation jersey over the Laird of Abbotsford's neck.

Outside the nursery she walked with particular quietness on the brown linoleumed floor, so as not to disturb any baby that might be in a restful sleep, after an hour or so's fractious crying. That she sometimes caught one of the young assistant nurses in neglect of some duty was incidental. This evening, for instance, when she glided in, she found Nurse Greer feeding a baby as it lay on its back in its cot.

'You know as well as I do, Nurse,' she said calmly, 'what the proper way is. But I shall show you again.'

Nurse Greer, seventeen, new, lipsticked all ready to go on duty in an hour's time and meet her boyfriend outside the cinema, tried not to giggle indignantly as she watched the splay-footed, grey-haired, hypocritical besom lift the baby with remarkable expertness, considering she had never had any of her own, and, holding it in the right position, feed it with the bottle. The performance, like everything else the

5

sweet-smiling tyrant did for children, was just too perfect: no one looking at her then would ever have mistaken her for the baby's mother, or, remembering the grey hair and swollen stomach, its grandmother.

'You may take him now, Nurse.'

'Her, Matron.'

'Of course.' The Matron smiled. This baby still had no name, but it did have a sex; the more, perhaps, was the pity. It had been brought in three days ago; one of lust's throw-aways, it had been found by a street-sweeper.

She walked round, making little adjustments. There were eight cots; one had its side down. She drew the other young nurse's attention to it.

'You realise how dangerous such forgetfulness can be, Nurse?'

'I didn't really forget, Matron. He's only six weeks and—'

'So in his case you think it does not matter if you forget?'

'I've had my eye on it, Matron. As soon as I had finished feeding little Bobby I was going to fix it.'

'Much honester to admit you were careless, Nurse.' She paused to tickle briefly the pink cheek of a crowing infant of about twelve months. Another baby, still to be fed and fretting sorely, she passed by.

At the door she turned: 'As I've said so often, we must show these unfortunate children more care than their own mothers would.'

When she was safely gone, Nurse Sutherland, small and pert, moved the hand that was holding the baby until she had her finger at her snub nose, pointed towards the door. 'Their own mothers!' she cried. 'Would they be here if their own mothers had shown them any care at all, old Flannel-pants?'

'Old Flannel-pants!' repeated Nurse Greer.

Both girls laughed hilariously. One of the babies seemed to join in. The fretter, though, went on crying. One or two slept, and one or two lay and watched the ceiling.

'Ah, poor things!' cried Nurse Sutherland. 'We're not laughing at you.'

'How can she possibly love them,' asked Nurse Greer, blushing a little, 'when she loathes what brought them into being?'

'But it isn't right, Mary, to have babies and just abandon them.'

'No. But better that than never having any at all.'

Nurse Sutherland, replacing little Bobby in his cot, shook her head.

Meanwhile the Matron, smiling, proceeded to the dining-room. She rather liked the two young nurses. If they were a bit too slapdash in their work, their fond-heartedness made up for it. They were too young to appreciate how very heavy was the responsibility of working with, not typewriters or pots and pans or shop merchandise, but small children, with the potentialities for good or evil, happiness or misery, budded within them. Probably they would never be old enough to appreciate that; few women were. Most were at their limit in looking after—often irresponsibly—the few fragments of their own flesh. Theirs was, to speak the harsh truth, an excluding kind of love, for all that concerned them was their own wombs' fruit. Nature had made the ordinary mother like that: her breasts were private. A woman like the Matron, on the other hand, who had never given suck and never would, had been made differently; she was able to love and cherish children who, being nameless, could truly be said to belong to God.

In the dining-room she was awaited. Sister Strachan, who was in charge, hurried along.

'I've put the Sneddon boys at your table, Matron.'

'Thank you, Sister. And who else?'

'You said you'd choose the others yourself.'

'So I did. Well, let me see.'

The thirty-three children were quiet. Some turned their faces away. They knew Matron was about to choose two or three of them to sit at her table with Johnny and Tommy Sneddon. They knew also this meant that the Sneddons were to be warned that evening that it might be their turn next to be sent away. In spite of their awe, some kept peeping to

7

where Johnny smiled and wee Tommy looked glum. After tea Matron would take them by the hand and lead them, not to the office where punishments were handed out, but to her own sitting-room, where there was a fire, and where she would let them take a sweetie out of the big glass jar. Then she would tell them. It had happened many times before. It might happen to anyone of them. Almost as terrible was to be made to sit at her table to keep the doomed ones company. Even a greedy boy like Fattie McColl would find it hard to enjoy his tea there, and tonight was Tuesday, when they got fried egg and sausage.

'Whom would you suggest, Sister?'

Sister Strachan didn't answer. The Matron knew every child in the Home better than anyone else, or so she thought; and no one cared to advise or contradict her. Besides, the Sister was married, with children of her own. In some way that made her judgment, in the Matron's view, unreliable.

'Nancy Brown, please.'

Nancy, a chubby-cheeked girl of eight, jumped up too suddenly. She had been whispering: 'It'll be me, it'll be me, oh goodness, it'll be me.' She banged her knee-cap against the leg of the table, making dishes and cutlery rattle. It was very painful; had she been in a home of her own she would have cried.

'Now, Nancy, you needn't be in such an awful hurry. I'm sure John Sneddon won't eat everything.'

A few who were nearest laughed.

'Please go to my table, Nancy, as quietly as you can.'

Trying not to limp and to keep tears out of her eyes, Nancy walked to the white-clothed table. She had been chosen before, and hated it.

Miss Montgomerie made what she knew was a brave, loving, but experimental decision.

'And Jean McDonnell, please, will you go with Nancy?'

Jean, yawning and sleepy, had to be dug in the ribs by her neighbour before she became aware she had been chosen. Grinning rather triumphantly, she got up and clumped towards the top table. No one had expected her to be called.

8

Red-haired and tough-spirited, she was the tomboy of the Home. Miss Montgomerie wasn't sure yet whether she was merely mischievous or bad. It could scarcely be held against the child that she had been returned a few months ago: her foster-parent had died. But it might not be easy to find her another place.

'Not so noisy, Jean, for goodness' sake. You're like a little cart-horse.'

'It's the tackets in my shoes,' explained Jean.

Sister Strachan tried not to smile. 'I don't think she's well,' she said. 'She's been looking very tired.'

'She's such a wild one, Sister. I saw her playing football with the boys hardly more than half an hour ago.'

'She's got a grand little spirit.'

'Yes. Well, Sister, I think we could have grace and then begin. Whose turn is it?'

'Well, it should be Peggy Morrison's.'

Matron was disappointed, but tried not to show it. Peggy usually made such a mess of saying grace that the rest tittered.

Her mouth was always full of saliva. She was not, however, by regulation standards, an imbecile; had she been, she would of course have been in a different kind of Home. But she was not normal. Three foster-parents in turn had sent her back. It was a pity she was so glaikit, for at first sight, with her lustrous black hair and mild eyes, she was an appealing little girl. Though she was illegitimate, her parents were known: her mother had been an Irish servant, now dead, and her father a docker, since decamped to Australia.

'Shall we skip her?' asked Sister.

'No, no. We mustn't ever do that. They all know it is her turn. We mustn't put the poor child more at their mercy than she already is. Besides, Sister, there is a purpose in having each one of them say grace.'

'Yes.'

'So Peggy it must be.'

The Matron went and sat down between the two Sneddons. Every head was bowed. Grace was said sitting, to avoid upset and clatter.

9

Peggy had to be whispered to by Sister. Up she got, clutching her spoon for comfort. Eyes tightly shut, she slobbered the grace at a great speed. A stranger would have made out only the last five words, uttered with startling clarity: 'For Jesus Christ's sake, amen!'

Rather moved, Matron gave the sign for the food to be served. The maids, Nelly and Agnes, helped by a few of the older girls, got busy. Top table was served first. All helpings were generous; the kitchen staff forgave the Matron a lot because of it.

Miss Montgomerie improved the arrangement of the daffodils on the table.

'What are these flowers called?' she asked.

'Daffies,' answered Jean promptly.

'Daffodils, you mean, Jean. Please take your elbow off the table.'

Jean had hardly been aware she had been leaning on her elbow. Now she clasped her freckled hands in her lap. She couldn't help yawning.

'Yawning is very rude too, Jean. At least cover your mouth.'

'I think I've got a sore froat.'

'No doubt you've been shouting far too loudly, as usual. Another thing you've got is dirty hands.'

'I washed them.'

'Not well enough, my dear. Please go and do it again, thoroughly this time. If you don't hurry your food will be cold.'

Sturdily the little girl marched down the room. She showed her hands to two or three acquaintances, as if to demonstrate that they were clean enough to satisfy anyone in the world except Matron. The rest of the children, either waiting or eagerly eating, watched with that kind of frightened glee that comes from apprehension justified: nearly every time Matron came to tea with them somebody was ordered to go and wash his or her hands. Sometimes she got so angry she stopped them all eating and inspected their hands; then lots of them had to troop out. If it was corned beef for tea, it didn't matter; but if it was fried egg and sausage, it was terrible, because these

10

got cold and greasy. This evening, however, there was to be no general inspection.

Serving was resumed.

'And now,' said Matron brightly, 'will someone tell me what happened at school today?'

Nancy Brown and John Sneddon looked at each other in dismay. Nothing had happened worth speaking about, but Matron wouldn't accept that. Besides, to talk about school would spoil their tea even more.

Tommy Sneddon went on eating, noisily and messily. He used fingers oftener than knife and fork. Bits of food were picked out of his mouth and examined suspiciously; one he flung down on the floor, the rest he pushed back and ate. For John's sake Matron refrained from scolding.

Her children attended the local corporation school. She knew the headmaster well; every day she telephoned him to inquire about their behaviour.

'Well, what happened?' she repeated.

'I think,' said Nancy cautiously, 'I think Jean McDonnell got the strap.'

Miss Montgomerie frowned, not merely because a child from her Home had evidently misbehaved, but also because Mr Massie that afternoon had answered, with his usual jolliness: 'All doing fine. No trouble at all. Wonderful bunch of children, Miss Montgomerie, absolutely wonderful, considering their disadvantages. You know what I mean, Matron. Of course they're lucky, very lucky, to have landed in your care. We often say to each other here, nobody could possibly tell just from looking at a class who in it were the state orphans, as you might say, and who were mummy's pampered darlings. Not just because your kids are so clean and nicely dressed, but because they're every bit as chirpy as the rest. You're doing God's work, Miss Montgomerie, true enough. No, no, rest assured. Nobody's given the slightest trouble. On the contrary, your kids have brought us their share of joy.'

Garrulous, lying, pompous, old fool. One would have thought, after his forty-odd years as a teacher, he would have learned that, particularly when dealing with children, the truth

11

must be utterly respected; and what was still more important, they must be shown that it was being respected, even if the showing had to be painful.

'I'm no' in her class,' whispered Nancy, 'but they telt me.'

'Who told you?'

'Girls in her class.'

Then Jean came marching back. As she got up on to her chair she remarked: 'I like daffies, but I like them better when they're growing in the grass, no' in a red jug.'

The jug was a beautiful vase Miss Montgomerie had brought from Venice. She let the blunder pass. Never in her life would Jean McDonnell be appreciative of beauty.

'What's this I've just been hearing about you, Jean? Did you get the strap in school today?'

Jean put out her tongue briefly at Nancy, her unhappy betrayer; but she had to hurry with her food, now tepid. 'Aye.'

'You mean?'

'Yes.'

'May I ask what you got it for? Please stop eating when I'm talking to you.'

'But it's getting cauld, Matron.'

'You should have remembered that when you came in with filthy hands. What were you punished for?'

'Sums, just. I got two wrang. Some had mair than two wrang, and they didna get the strap. Miss Thomson said mine were untidy.'

'Untidiness deserves punishment.'

'But I hadna a rubber and nobody would gie me a lend o' one, so I had just to rub it wi' my finger. It made a mess.'

Miss Montgomerie sighed. Jean was incorrigible. No child in the Home was more rigorously disciplined, but she never seemed to benefit. It was inevitable that she would grow up to be like her mother, a slut with three other illegitimates; who her father was, only God knew.

'Well, John,' she said, 'and how did you get on with your sums?'

'I got four wrang, but I didna get the strap.'

'I should hope not.' She had been about to say that honest

12

incapability ought never to be punished, but realised in time that the child might be hurt. He was unpredictable in his sensitiveness.

'Mr Smith's a good teacher,' he said. 'He only gies you the strap if you're careless or lazy. Jim Murgatroyd—' he looked for him in the room, a small crouched boy with dangling feet—'gets a' his sums wrang every day, but he never gets the strap.'

'Strap? Goodness me, is that all school is? Getting or not gettin the strap?'

'That's a',' said Jean.

'Nonsense. Most children today like school.'

'I'd like it better,' admitted Jean, 'if when it was finished I could go hame like Milly Baxter.'

Matron winced. 'And who is she?'

'My best pal. She's in my class. She's got a room o' her ain, wi' a big doll's cot.'

'In the playroom here there's a far bigger doll's cot than Milly Baxter's, I'm sure.'

'But it's her ain. And when she goes hame her mither gies her a piece wi' bramble jeely.'

'I'm sure you get all the bread you need with bramble or any other kind of jelly or jam.'

'But we've to wait. She gets it just when she asks. And she's got a baby sister.'

'Well, upstairs in our nursery, haven't you got have baby brothers and three baby sisters?'

'They're no' mine.'

Miss Montgomerie gave up. She would wait until she had John in her sitting-room. In the meantime she contented herself with admiring him as he ate, and found herself slipping into a state of mind not unlike Jean's. He was an adorable little boy, with his fair hair, pink clear skin, and frank blue eyes; but only in an unsatisfactory way was he hers.

Two

A colleague once said of Margaret Mathieson, Child Welfare Officer, that as a substitute mother she made a good discus-thrower; but even he had to admit, with wonder, that she was remarkably efficient at her delicate duties. Tall and strong, she strode out like a man, and wore thick brogues with big visible tongues. She was shrewdly garrulous, and on her inspection visits to foster-parents, actual or prospective, no kind of deceit could escape her copious interrogation. She was especially sharp at sniffing out mercenariness as a chief motive. People found themselves disconcerted into frankness by her unexpected handsomeness, for she had a proud head, fine auburn hair, and the complexion of a girl of ten. Children took to her quickly. She used to say they were grateful to her for never for a moment pretending to be their mother; with an instinct profounder than any animal's they realised that too many attachments, broken one after the other, must leave the heart ravaged and empty.

She was a puzzle to her friend, Helen Montgomerie. No one respected truth more than the latter, but she also believed that it was sometimes difficult to distinguish, so mingled and secret a person's motives could be. Margaret, on the other hand, used to declare that she could recognise it in any circumstances, no matter how distorted; and once recognised, it must be disclosed without hesitation or subterfuge. Conceal-ment constructed labyrinths: she preferred to walk boldly and know where she was going. Whether that magnificent claim itself was true Helen had never been able to decide. Early in their friendship, Margaret had announced: 'About love I have no confessions or revelations to make. No man has ever jilted me; none has left me tormented by his memory. I am not a virgin. I like children ready-made.'

One morning, towards the end of April, she telephoned

Matron at the Home. 'Just to let you know, Helen, I returned last night from Calisay. I interviewed the McArthurs, and I'm going to recommend them. I couldn't do otherwise. They're good people. The Sneddons will be well looked after. The island itself is a paradise for children.'

'When will they be going?'

Margaret laughed. 'Don't sound so doleful, Helen. I'm sure we're leaving you plenty. I should think in about a fortnight.'

'Your report will be accepted?'

'I see no reason why not. Do you?'

'No, no. Could you come and have a talk about it, Margaret? You know I'm always interested in hearing about the people to whom my children are sent.'

Margaret consulted her work diary. 'Tomorrow morning? About eleven. Only for half an hour, I'm afraid.'

'You should be able to tell me a lot in half an hour, Margaret.'

'Oh sure. I ought to have been an auctioneer.'

'You know I didn't mean that.'

'Why not? Sometimes I feel like one. "Now here's a couple of small boys, in recognizable human shape, in good health, and if not highly intelligent at least not imbecilic. Pedigree admittedly hardly of the highest." '

'Margaret, please! . . .'

'I know, Helen. But I do feel like that sometimes. I want to spit in humanity's big, crass, conceited face.'

'Are these McArthurs crass and conceited, then?'

Margaret paused to recover breath and faith. 'No, they aren't. They're good people. They'll be kind to the boys.'

'What is Mrs McArthur like?'

'Look, Helen, I've simply got to run. I'll answer all your questions tomorrow.'

'Very well. Be sure and come.'

'If I can't I'll phone.'

'No, no. You must come.'

'All right, Helen. I know what it means to you. I promise.' Then, after a pause filled surely with pity, she hung up.

Miss Montgomerie set down her telephone with a hand that

15

had begun to tremble. For the first time in years she felt about to weep. Resisting, she heard a voice within speak, clearly and viciously: it told her not to be a sentimental fool, to remember her stoutness, her thin grey hair, her flat silly feet, her wrinkles, and her duty. Then it relented. Be content, it said, if they trust you. You have learned you cannot inspire love in them, and you have ordered your life accordingly. Don't derange it now. Deep in you there has always been a suppressed hysteria; God knows what it is compounded of; keep suppressing it, otherwise it might well shatter you into a pitiable wreck. Be realistic, acknowledge that even John Sneddon prefers Sister Strachan to you; that they all do. They prefer Agnes the maid, though her tongue's as coarse as her hands. Let him go to Calisay, and if you wish to remain in his life do it by prayer. Remember the children still in your charge; those unfortunates Peggy Morrison, Jim Murgatroyd, and Jean McDonnell. Remember the child to be brought in between now and the going of the Sneddons, at this moment still in the womb of time, as Christ Jesus once was.

She was calm when Margaret came. It was raining and rather cold, so she had a fire in her sitting-room, and Cook had been instructed to send up coffee and biscuits ten minutes after Miss Mathieson's arrival. Margaret wore a tweed costume and a hat that didn't seem to match. She was in a hurry, and said at once she couldn't spare a minute more than half an hour.

She sat upright, with her big golfer's hands on her knees. Her handbag lay at her feet like a large brown dog. Before they had got to the end of the usual trivialities about weather and acquaintances she suddenly plunged, tore open her bag, lugged it up on to her lap and, rummaging in it, brought out an envelope containing a photograph.

'Your successors, Helen,' she said, and handed it over. 'Mr and Mrs Donald McArthur of Calisay.'

Miss Montgomerie took it with a hand that remained steady although in the photograph she was seeing an amazing thing: Mrs McArthur was so like her, they might have been sisters; the other woman was perhaps a year or so older, but

16

she too was stout, with stomach more prominent than bosom, and she stood tranquilly on feet pointed outwards. So uncanny was the resemblance that Mr McArthur himself seemed very familiar. He was a tall, droll-looking man, smoking a pipe and holding a scythe. A dog lay at his feet. Hens interloped. Roses grew. The sun shone. The sea glittered beyond.

Miss Montgomerie could almost hear the larks sing overhead, and smell the wild flowers of the machair. How sweet to stroll there, with John gathering her a posy!

Margaret did not seem to have noticed the likeness.

'There's a daughter too, about twenty-five, and a son about twenty. I was particularly taken by the girl. At first I wasn't— she seemed with her big watchful eyes and glossy black hair like the usual wander-witted Deirdre you often get on those islands. But no, she turned out to be very intelligent and quite passionately good-hearted. She works at the hotel. You see, Helen, I was on the look-out for somebody like her to confide in about the Sneddons' history.'

Shocked, Helen looked up from the photograph. 'But it was decided, Margaret, no one was to be told, in the children's own interests.'

'I know, Helen, but I didn't agree with the decision. No child should harbour anything in his head that his parents— even if they're only his foster-parents—don't know about. How can they protect him if they don't know what it is that threatens him? You and I have been in this business long enough to be aware that it isn't only illness or hunger or neglect that children have to be guarded against.'

'But, Margaret, in my experience most children have secrets.'

'Such as letting nobody know the toy soldier they like best? Helen, we're talking about the most hellish secret on earth. It's just not right they should be asked to bear it alone. I hope Flora McArthur's got the guts to help him carry it.'

Then there was a knock on the door, and Agnes came in bringing the coffee things. They had to wait until she'd gone.

'She seemed the most likely. I had a talk with the schoolmistress. She's all right, a shade close, a bit too sensitive about

17

her teeth, which stick out rather, but firm-minded enough.
Still, she hasn't got it. Flora McArthur has, unless I'm much
mistaken.'

'Hasn't got what, Margaret?'

'Don't ask me to name it. I couldn't. It's not pity, though
there's pity in it.'

'Is it love?'

'No, it isn't, though there's love in it, too. Whatever it is,
the Sneddon child's going to need it when, as you and I are
sure is inevitable, the whole damnable thing comes shrieking
up out of his memory. Pray God he gets it.' Briskly she glanced
at her watch, and changed the subject. 'Counting the Sneddons,
there will be twelve children at the school. Of these we shall
have supplied eight. So what it amounts to is that we're really
repopulating the place. High time, too. The school records
show that in 1910 there were fifty-five pupils, in 1930 thirty-
one and now twelve; take away those lent, four. And yet,
Helen, if there's a more glorious spot on God's earth for
children than the Isle of Calisay, I don't know where it can
be. It's got everything: sandy beaches, where the seals bob up
and yabble to you; cliffs with guillemots, kittiwakes and
puffins; dozens of caves; hilltops with eagles; trees; skylarks.'

For a moment the Matron felt the clean, tangy, liberating
air of the island bathe her soul. She smiled and shivered.

'But, Margaret, it's people that matter. Tell me about the
people. This Mrs McArthur, for instance, what kind of a
woman is she?'

'Comfortable and homely, I would say; the lucky kind,
Helen, that children don't have to be bribed or coaxed or
bullied into loving. As for Mr McArthur, I don't think I've
been treated with finer courtesy in my life. Often it can be
damned embarrassing for people, being interviewed; but not
for the McArthurs. Not for a moment did I ever feel they were
trying to hide anything.'

'The fact remains, Margaret, they are doing it for payment.'

'They need the money. It's as simple as that. But the most
important fact is that these children are going to get a kind
home, in a beautiful place. They deserve it, Helen. We ought

to be glad.'

'I'm sure I'm delighted, Margaret.'

'You're really fond of this pair?'

'I hope I'm sincerely fond of all the children entrusted to me. Did you speak to the minister?'

'Yes. It's usually very profitable to speak to the local reverence. If you're speiring for information about character, he's the best clype you can get. This one, though, wasn't very helpful; in the first place he came to the island only a few months ago, and in the second place he was more interested in talking about the boat he was making, with his own hands. He has forearms like a boxer. Shavings were flying all over us. But he was enthusiastic about the McArthurs; it seems Mr McArthur knows the island waters better than anyone else, and Mrs McArthur makes the best pancakes. He was bellowing hymns to himself as I approached his boat-shed; made them sound amazingly cheerful, too. Small, burly chap, about as theological, I would say, as a Glasgow tram-driver.'

'Did you meet his wife?'

'I did, for a few minutes. She was sitting happed up by the manse fire, though the sun was blazing outside. She's just recovered from a miscarriage. Poor thing, she looked like a cat whose kittens have all been drowned.'

'How old is she?'

'About thirty-five, ten years or so younger than he.'

'She still has time.'

'Apparently she hasn't. Next time would kill her. I think this last one nearly did. Pretty woman, with eyes like a brave panda. Oh, and I met Mrs Morton-Home, the laird's wife. She stopped me on the road and introduced herself. My God, Helen, nobody would ever call her bonny. I thought at first she was some eccentric Englishwoman who'd taken up shepherding. I'm supposed to be odd in my taste; so are you, Helen. But compared with Mrs Morton-Home we're Dior's favourites. She had a tartan skirt at her knees at the front, and damned near her heels at the back; and a cardigan of orange angora wool, like a fuzzy caterpillar. In a voice that could have been heard across in Jura—I noticed sheep running—she

19

informed me there weren't finer people in Scotland or out of it than the McArthurs.'

'Has she any children of her own?'

'No. And never will have now.'

'The whole island seems to be full of childless women: the schoolmistress, the minister's wife, the laird's.'

'And there are others. The woman whose husband keeps the shop has none; and Mrs McGilvray of the hotel hasn't any either.'

'So it would be safe to say there's a lot of maternal affection going begging?'

Margaret sprang up. 'Yes, Helen, I think it would be. But I'm afraid I must rush off now. I've got a woman to visit who's been reported by her neighbours for cruelty to her own children. They send me on such jobs because I'm big. By the way, as I'll be taking the Sneddons to Calisay, I'd like to get to know them a little better. I thought I might take them out on Saturday afternoon, if you've no objection?'

'Why should I object to an act of kindness?'

'Some matrons do. They resent interference.'

'Tell me, Margaret, before you go, how does one get to Calisay?'

'By train to Gourock; steamer to West Loch Tarbert, through the Kyles of Bute; bus to East Loch Tarbert; steamer to Calisay, calling at Jura and Islay. You arrive in the dark. There's no pier, a motor-boat comes out and takes you off. It seems as if the whole island's there to meet you on the jetty. Of course the steamer calls just twice a week in summer; once in winter. It's a beautiful journey.'

'It must be.'

As soon as Margaret was gone, Miss Montgomerie took down an atlas and opened it at the map of Scotland. With her finger she traced that journey to the western islands. Beside her was the photograph of the McArthurs, representing for her, as they would for the two boys, the end of the journey.

She kept staring at it until she began to imagine that she was this pleasant-faced crofter's wife with the sunlight on her hair, and Miss Montgomerie, the Matron, was someone else.

Even the finger resting on the little island grew more and more unfamiliar as she gazed at it.

Three

Since the train left the Central Station at 8.29 a.m., they had to set out from the Home at eight o'clock. Breakfast on weekdays was usually at that very hour, and Matron had at first refused the staff's request to delay it for a few minutes. She sympathized with their wish to be free to wave goodbye, but had always considered that only if routine was adhered to could these frequent partings be prevented from causing demoralization. The Sneddons had been in the Home longer than any other child, and the bonds in their case might be especially painful to break; wiser, therefore, to have all farewells over with the night before, leaving the boys themselves undazed for the long journey and for the confronting of their stranger parents. But to everyone's surprise, she relented and gave permission for the brief postponement, so that when the morning came, sunny and warm, staff and children were getting ready in a laughing, tearful excitement, while the two principals, in new suits, were having breakfast with Matron in her own quarters.

Since he felt there was nothing else for it, Tommy ate sturdily. Now and then he paused, stared at his brother, who was quietly crying, pushed out his lips, tried to squeeze out some tears himself, glanced stealthily at Matron, who looked grim, sighed, felt in his pocket to make sure his Dinky model of a tank was safely there, and resumed eating. It needed a little more boldness to turn and peep behind him at the sideboard on which, beside a photograph of a young woman in a nurse's uniform, stood two parcels wrapped in fancy paper and tied with coloured string; but once or twice he ventured. They were, he felt sure, presents for him and Johnny; the Matron always gave presents to those being sent away. He hoped his was another tank; with two you could have a battle. Johnny would prefer soldiers, especially knights in armour, on horseback. One parcel was bigger; it would be for Johnny, who was bigger too; that was fair. Matron couldn't be very angry with them or she wouldn't be going to give them presents, but she wasn't very pleased either, and when he let a bit of ham fall on the clean table-cloth she scolded him in the way she always did. But he was lucky, for it was at Johnny she kept looking most of the time, asking, in a quiet voice, if he wanted more ham or more milk or more toast. Tommy would have liked more ham himself, but she didn't ask him and he didn't like to say.

Once some water ran out of her left eye. She quickly dabbed it away with her hankie from her sleeve, but he had seen it first. The same thing happened to him if he was outside in a cold wind. But in here there was no wind at all: it was so still he could hear the clock on the wall croaking like a little frog, and the sun was shining, as another glance at the window showed him. For a moment he tried to think about the journey, but he couldn't.

That Johnny kept crying troubled him, and he stopped eating once to think what he could say or do to comfort his brother; but he could think of nothing. Even offering his tank would be no use, so he just had to go on eating. He knew Johnny was sad because he had to leave the Home. Last night he had cried, and Tommy had cried too, but only to keep him company: he himself wasn't very sad that he was going away. He didn't like Matron much, not because she was always giving him rows, but because he thought she didn't like him. The other woman, the big one that laughed like a man, had told them that the place they were being taken to had hens and a dog; she wasn't sure, but she thought there was a horse too. There were no hens in the Home, and once when a wee black dog had slunk in the gate Matron had got the gardener to chase it out again with stones. He had asked the big woman if at the new place they would sometimes get cream cookies for tea. She had said they would, but she hadn't seemed very sure about it. She had said they would get pancakes; well, he liked pancakes but he preferred cream cookies.

Johnny's crying suddenly got worse.

To the smaller boy's astonishment and fright, Matron got down on her knees, and nearly dragged Johnny off his chair. At first Tommy thought she was punishing him for crying, and then he saw she was cuddling him. She was crying too. It was the first time Tommy had seen her cry. He was amazed and alarmed. He hadn't thought she could cry, and now here she was, quite loudly, and telling Johnny she oughtn't to let him go but she couldn't help it. She had a brooch on her breast which must have been sore on Johnny's face, so Tommy wasn't surprised to notice his brother moving his head away from it. Once when Agnes the maid had cuddled him— Tommy—her hair had got into his nose and made him want to sneeze.

Just as suddenly as she had got down on her knees she rose again, very stiffly, and going to a mirror wiped her face fiercely with her handkerchief. When she turned she was looking angrier than Tom had ever seen her before. In a harsh voice she said it was time now for them to get ready. Did they need to go to the lavatory? They would have to go anyway to wipe their hands and faces. They mustn't be long, for the car that was to take them to the station would be there any minute. What worried Tom, as he slid off his chair, was that she might change her mind and not give them the presents after all.

Johnny, though, seemed better. He was smiling again and his grip was reassuring as he took his brother's hand. As they went out, Tommy glanced back, really to look at the presents, but it was Matron he saw. She had her face covered with her hands. Sometimes Jean McDonnell did that to him, but it was in fun and she keeked out through her fingers. Matron didn't.

The washroom was thronged with boys naked to the waist, washing hands and faces under the supervision of Nurse Greer. For a moment they were all quiet when Johnny and Tommy went in. Then they shouted at once.

'Hae you had breakfast wi' Matron?'

'Did you get ham and eggs?'

'Did she gie you anything for going away?'

'Did she tell you to wipe your nose?'

Nurse Greer, putting her fingers in her ears, yelled to them all to be quiet. She had noticed that John was in tears. When she had got silence she was sorry she had: there was then only the sound of taps running that had been left on, the wheezy breathing of Robert McColl, and John's sobbing as he bent over the wash-basin. The others watched and listened with an intensity that made her afraid: she could not be sure whether they were enjoying their friend's grief or were appalled by it.

A small boy with thin determined face approached Tom. 'Do you need your tank?' he demanded.

Tommy nodded and put his hand on his pocket. For weeks Jackie Cameron had been trying to get his tank. He had wanted to exchange two Jap soldiers for it; one couldn't stand and the other's gun was bent.

'You'll no' need it. Jim Ballantyne telt me they wouldnae let you play wi' it where you're going.'

'Jim Ballantyne said nothing of the kind,' cried the nurse. 'Didn't you, Jim?'

Jim, hair sticking up, soap on his ears, nodded and scowled. Aged ten, he had recently been withdrawn from foster-parents who had turned out to be unsuitable. 'They never let me,' he muttered.

'For goodness' sake,' cried Nurse Greer, 'why have you all stopped? You'd better hurry up if you want to wave to Johnny and Tommy going away.'

They noticed with dour satisfaction that there were tremors in her voice, and when they stared at her trying to hide her face in a fierce busyness as she dried Jackie's neck, they knew she was nearly crying herself. Those who had had experience of foster-parents began to discuss them; on the whole, they were unenthusiastic.

A gentle tapping on the door silenced them utterly. Even before they looked, and before she spoke, they knew it was Matron.

'They are rather noisy, Nurse.'

'They're excited,' the young girl answered, unable to control her impatience with that calm authority. Is it my fault, her tone implied, if children aren't animals, to be sold here

25

and there, without a cry at least of protest?

'All the more reason for you to set them an example of calmness. The car has arrived. John and Tom, you must come now.'

For the last time Tommy shook his head. 'I canna gie you the tank, Jackie,' he said. 'If they don't let me play wi' it, I'll hide it.'

Johnny seized his brother's hand. 'We're ready,' he said.

'We'll hurry up, Johnny, and wave to you,' they cried.

'Make sure, Nurse, they give themselves a proper wash.'

'Yes, Matron.'

'We mustn't let discipline slip altogether, you know, though it is rather a special occasion.'

The nurse looked up sharply: had she actually detected a hesitation, as of sorrow, in Matron's voice? If so, she was too late to catch it on her face; there was the usual tight-lipped strictness, so difficult to understand and bear, because no doting granny's face was ever more plump, pink and soft. 'But, Mary,' Nurse Greer's mother had said, 'the woman's got a very difficult job to do. You wouldn't expect her to show her feelings like an ordinary woman, would you? She wouldn't last long if she did. She'd be useless; the one thing children in their position need is someone they know will always be firm.' If that was so, Nurse Greer had thought, then the sooner I get out of it the better. Now, as she bullied them into hurrying, she was ashamed of herself. She would certainly get out of it as soon as she was old enough to be accepted by a hospital; but she saw now that she would leave with considerable respect for Matron, as one who had not only stuck it for many years but had helped to make it as successful as it could be.

In the hall Margaret Mathieson formally took custody of her charges. In addition she tweaked Tommy's ear and patted Johnny on the head.

'No use prolonging it, Helen,' she whispered to her friend. 'We might as well go right away.'

'You still have a minute or two to spare, Margaret. I believe the staff and children wish to say goodbye. Breakfast has been put back to 8.15.'

'I see.'

'Normally it is against my principle to give an opportunity for painful scenes—'

'A wise principle, Helen. I must say they seem to be taking it very well.' She remembered children who had had to be carried into the car. 'The little fellow seems quite composed.'

'If he gets his meals regularly and has a place to sleep, Tom won't mind.'

'A stoic?'

Matron was surprised. She had always thought of Tom as a cry-baby, even for a six-year-old. Had she misjudged him? And had he only cried in her presence because she had not paid as much heed as she should to his involuntary craving for love? 'His brother is much more sensitive.'

'Well, he's a good bit older. He knows what's going on.' As she looked at the fair-haired boy clasping his small brother's hand, her heart was moved by the effort at courage and resolution so visible on his face. Yet, she thought with gladness, where he was going was far better for him than here. Poor Helen was fond enough of the children in her Home, but though she were to strive with all her heart she just couldn't persuade them to love her: circumstances were against it; whereas the moment they set eyes on Mrs McArthur tonight on the jetty at Calisay they would embrace her like sons.

Agnes the maid came swaggering forward, carrying two small parcels.

'God bless you,' she said to the two boys, in her tough affectionate voice. She ruffled Johnny's hair with her hand as rough as a man's. 'You've been an example to us a', son. When we hae thought we were gi'en too much to put up wi', one look at you has made us feel black ashamed.' She laughed. 'Aye, wherever you are, Johnny boy, you'll be a' right. They've no' crushed you yet. Don't let them. For auld Agnes's sake, don't ever let them crush you. Here, this is frae us in the kitchen. And here's for you, Tommy wee laddie. They say you grumbled, but Christ knows if ever a bairn had cause to grumble, you hae had. Good luck to the baith o' you.'

27

She bent and quickly kissed them.

More circumspectly, but just as sincerely, the others of the kitchen staff came forward and took leave. Tommy began to whimper: he seemed to think all this affection had some kind of menace in it.

The nurses on duty said goodbye too; the others had said it the night before.

'Well, boys,' said Miss Mathieson, 'time for the troops to march. Lead the way, John.'

She drew back to let him make his own exit. He looked up at Matron, stared round at all the others, tried to say something, couldn't, swallowed hard, made sure he had a tight grip of Tommy, walked a few paces backwards, and then, turning, almost ran out.

The children were gathered round the car. Some clapped, and one or two squealed when the Sneddons appeared. The driver stowed the parcels and luggage in the boot beside Miss Mathieson's tartan bag. Everyone watched him. He had already made himself popular with the children; it wasn't the first time he had done this job. Then at last he was holding the door open.

Margaret had a final word on the steps with Helen.

'I should be back on Thursday night,' she said. 'If I can I'll drop in on Friday morning to let you know how things went.'

'Please do that, Margaret.'

Then Margaret hurried straight into the car. Some of the children clapped her. Tommy was about to clamber in too, but his brother suddenly restrained him and pulled him back towards Matron.

She smiled down at them.

'Goodbye,' said Johnny. 'And thanks very much.' He nudged his brother.

'Thanks,' said Tommy, although he was sure he had already thanked her for her present.

'Don't forget us, boys. We shall all remember you. Try to write and let us know how you are getting on.'

'I canna write,' said Tommy anxiously.

Some of the children laughed.

'I'll try to write,' said Johnny, and tugged his brother towards the car.

Before they reached it someone came running from amongst the girls. It was Jean McDonnell. She took a bunch of flowers from behind her back. They were daffodils, plucked, most illegally, in the Home grounds.

'They were a' I could get,' she said. 'Some o' them are withered.'

Most of them were. Johnny took them, puzzled as to why this girl should have put herself into more trouble just to give him and Tommy some flowers that weren't even pretty, and had no scent. Looking at her through them, he saw, to his embarrassment and still deeper puzzlement, that tears were tumbling down her freckled cheeks. But she was grinning too.

'I wish it was me going on a boat,' she said, and turned and fled, not just back to the other girls but beyond them into the sunshine.

They got into the car. Miss Mathieson, who had been cracking her knuckles in an effort not to express impatience, whispered to the driver to hurry. The children had fallen silent. Some were still staring after Jean McDonnell running into the sunshine; they knew she had a secret place among the daffies. The rest were looking at the car. When it began to move they waved, but, though they had meant to, they did not cheer, they found they did not want to.

Seconds later the car had disappeared round the corner of the drive. They listened and heard it bump over the bad bit at the gate. Then it was gone.

Four

They passed the school. Eagerly Tommy pointed out his room. His teacher, he said, had given him a box of coloured crayons; it was in his case. He was to draw a picture of his new place and send it to her. If it was good she would hang it on the wall. Maybe he would draw the dog, if there was a dog; he hoped there was.

'Yes, there's a dog,' Miss Mathieson assured him.

'What colour is it?'

'I think it's black and white.'

'Has it got a white tail, or a black tail?'

'I'm afraid I don't remember. You saw it yourself in the photograph.'

'It was sitting doon. It'll be easier to draw it if its tail's white, because there's a white crayon, but I don't think there's a black crayon. Is there a black crayon, Johnny?'

'No.'

'So if its tail's black I'll maybe just need to make it white. Miss Ramage willna ken I've done it wrang, because she's never seen the dog.'

'No flies on this one,' chuckled the driver.

'If you hadna put the parcels under the lid, mister,' said Tommy reprovingly, 'I could hae looked to see what was in them.'

'Well, that's easily mended.' The driver stopped the car.

'Are you sure we've time, Bob?'

'Time enough for this, Miss Mathieson, even if I've to drive you all the way to Gourock to catch your boat.'

He was back seconds later with the parcels. 'And here's a knife too, if you can't untie the knots. Don't cut your fingers.'

'Knots break your nails,' said Tommy. 'Here's yours, Johnny.' He held them out, but his brother shook his head.

'Johnny will look at his later,' said Miss Mathieson. 'You

30

see what you've got.'

Grinning, Tommy cut the string of the parcel Agnes had given him. Under the brown paper were two little boxes; in each was a tank. There was also a card with 'Love and Kisses from Agnes, Nelly, and Cookie'.

'Tanks,' he said, with satisfaction so complete it couldn't have been loud.

Both Miss Mathieson and Bob were moved. The former scratched her leg vigorously.

'Wi' three tanks I can hae battles,' he added. 'You open yours, Johnny. Maybe it'll be knights on horses.'

'Are all boys fond of such things nowadays, Bob?' asked Miss Mathieson. 'Seems odd, in this era of hydrogen bombs.'

'You should see our kitchen when my two get theirs out. Bobby's got a bridge, like the one over the River Kwai, and Alec's got a Wild West fort. You canna take a step but you're upsetting some attack or ambush. I don't think it does them any harm.'

'Fattie McColl's got a Foreign Legion man wi' a flag,' said Tommy, 'but it's made o' tin and its heid's aff. Will I open yours for you, Johnny?'

'If you like.'

Tommy at once opened it. Inside were two knights, visored and armoured, carrying shields and lances; they were mounted on splendidly caparisoned horses. Tommy bounced on his seat with glee. 'Look, Johnny, just what you said you wanted.'

To please his brother Johnny took a knight and admired it.

Miss Mathieson picked up the other. 'They were brave, those knights of old,' she said. 'You'll be too young to have read the story called *Ivanhoe*.'

'We read it in a comic,' said Tommy.

'Well then, you'll know how brave they were.' Suddenly she felt ashamed of trying to force the comparison on the child. Those stalwarts of battle and joust never had to face the agonies that this nine-year-old boy had had to endure since he was six. Shutting her eyes, she prayed: 'Christ, protect these children.' When she opened her eyes and saw that they were

31

now driving through the busy streets of Glasgow, she felt dismayed; confidence flowed out of her like blood. What treachery, what desertion, was she being a party to, taking these small Glaswegians away from their native city, famous all the world over for its warm-heartedness? If it was felt by the authorities, themselves Glasgow men, and by her, also born within the beloved city, that these boys' problem could not be settled here, where it had arisen, was it not deliberate self-deception on all their parts to believe that the simpletons of Calisay, with the help of the sea, a dog, and a few sheep, could do it? Or rather, since everyone knew in his heart what he was about, was it not simply cowardice, dishonesty, and a shuffling-off of responsibility?

Tommy had disclosed the contents of the parcel Matron had given him; it was a blue pullover, with white bands round it. He wasn't disgusted: he had been trained at the Home to appreciate useful presents like clothes; but he wasn't thrilled either.

'Is it cauld in this place we're going to?' he asked.

She couldn't help laughing. 'Not very.'

He opened his brother's parcel; it too contained a pullover, hand-knitted. Matron had done it herself.

'Whit are we going to do wi' Jean McDonnell's flowers?' he asked. 'They're a' withered. Look.'

'But it was nice of the little girl to give them to you,' said Miss Mathieson.

'She would get a row for pu'ing them. Matron didn't like her.'

'Now I'm sure that isn't true, Tom. Matron likes all the children at the Home.'

He made a little polite groaning noise in his throat that made Bob almost choke with laughter.

Then they were at the station, driving through the tunnel right on to the platform. Within a couple of minutes Bob had them and their luggage installed in a compartment.

'Wait a minute,' he said. 'I'll be back.'

'He'll need to be,' observed Tommy, 'because he's left his car.'

Very soon Bob was back, with comics and sweets. 'Share these wi' your brother, Tommy,' he said.

Tommy nodded. 'Thanks.'

'That was kind of you, Bob,' said Miss Mathieson. She leant out of the window. 'I'm a bit anxious about the older one. It was the younger one I was warned about; he was said to be an awful whiner. But he's doing fine, isn't he? It's his brother who's the worry.'

'Oh, he'll come out of it. The older they are the harder it is. They know what's happening to them.'

'Yes.' But Bob didn't know just what it was that Johnny Sneddon knew.

The whistle sounded. She felt her jacket tugged.

'Let me see the man wave his green flag,' said Tommy.

She made way for him. He saw the flag being waved, and was pleased. He waved at Bob, who waved back. Then he sat down on the seat beside his brother, and began to look at one of the comics.

It seemed to Miss Mathieson that one of her fellow-passengers, a shrewd-faced elderly woman, was looking at Johnny too curiously, as if she had jaloused from his pale unhappy face that he was some kind of prisoner. Perhaps, too, she had noticed that the car in which they had arrived had the Corporation crest on it. Such glances were common in Miss Mathieson's experience. If they weren't followed by impertinent speirings, she let them pass; but if they were, she subdued them with what was known among her colleagues as her Amazon-Queen scowl. The trouble was it tended to subdue her charges too, just when she wanted them to be at their brightest.

Luckily the inquisitive woman got off at Paisley, and the other two passengers, a young man and woman, evidently sweethearts, held hands and noticed only each other.

By the time they got to Gourock, Tommy had his brother explaining to him what some of the pictures in the comics meant.

At Gourock Johnny brightened in a way that pleased Miss Mathieson, but also caused her a flicker of apprehension.

33

Though there was plenty there to rouse any boy out of depression—the red-funnelled steamer, the keen-eyed gulls, the wide water glinting with sun, and the craggy hills of Argyll on the far side—still, he seemed to her to change too abruptly, too mechanically, as if something outside his control had clicked into place in his mind, so that now he was interested and predictable, whereas a few minutes ago he had been downcast and remote. She told herself not to be a superstitious old wife before her time, but she could not quite shake off the fear that in the human mind disaster waited side by side with happiness, and often accident decided which should be chosen.

Now why the hell, she told herself angrily, should I turn gloomy just because the poor child's cheered up? She looked at them chatting excitedly by the rail. She wanted to go and join in, but decided she had no right to until she, too, felt cheerful and could contribute her share. So she smoked one of the three cigarettes she allowed herself per day.

About an hour later, when the steamer was approaching Rothesay, she sought out her two charges. Again, though, they were so happily engrossed with the rowing-boats being warned out of the way by blasts of the siren, and with the promenaders on shore, that she was able to stand close behind them, unnoticed, and listen with amusement to their chatter. She had been listening for almost a minute before she realised that, children though they were, without a home or relations, they still had a right to be private; but just as she was about to slip away they began to talk about their parents.

'Did you ken this isna the first time we've been to Rothesay?' said Johnny.

Tommy shook his head. 'I never was here before. I never seen the sea before.'

'You were just a baby in your pram at the time. You used to paddle your feet in the sea.'

'Did the big woman bring us?'

'No. It was our ain dad and mum.'

'Before they were deid?'

'Aye.'

34

Tommy glanced up at the blue sky, his gaze travelling across it as mindless as a bird.

'Dad took me oot in one o' those rowing-boats. I can mind that. There was somebody else in it, some other boy.'

'Was it me?'

'No, you were just a baby; you couldna walk.'

'How could I paddle my feet then?'

'Somebody held you.'

'Was it you, Johnny?'

'Sometimes.'

'And who else at ither times?'

'Dad.'

'Did my mum hold me too?'

'Sometimes.'

'Whit was mum like, Johnny?'

'I've telt you before.'

'Tell me again.'

'No. Some ither time.'

'Did you oar the boat, Johnny?'

'Just wi' one oar. I was too wee for two.'

'Will they hae boats in this place we're going to?'

'I think so. It's an island, wi' the sea a' round, so they'll need boats.'

'Will they let us oar them?'

'When we're bigger, maybe.'

'Will we be in this place till we're big, Johnny?'

'It depends.'

'What does it depend on, Johnny?'

'If the folk like us.'

'But maybe we'll no' like them. The big woman said we would, but maybe we'll no'.'

'We'll just hae to try to.'

'You used to tell me to try to like Matron, Johnny, but I couldna. I think I like the big woman. Do you like her, Johnny?'

'She's all right.'

It was at that point that Miss Mathieson realised she was intruding on their privacy. Yet she did not want to go; here,

35

where these children chatted, was somehow hallowed; to go would be to suffer an exclusion, a deprivation of grace. Nevertheless, she crept away, and at the opposite rail, facing the water, found herself trembling.

A seagull sailed past, its hooked beak rather than its yellow cynical eyes reminding her of old George Gilliespie, a senior colleague in the Child Welfare Service. 'You mustn't get callous, Meg, but you can't stay tender, either; either way you do harm. There's a state in between where you can tell the kids what's got to be told and yet keep your self-respect; but I don't know anybody who's ever reached it. Talk about climbing Everest, or driving a car at five hundred miles an hour, or sending a man to the moon! Here's something very close at hand that's a damn sight more difficult to do, aye, and more worthy of doing. But if you succeed, don't expect to find yourself in the headlines.'

For a morning the quiet little man who had given John Sneddon a shot with one oar had appeared in those headlines.

I can see myself ending up as a grim, hard-hearted, self-deceiving old bitch, she thought. Poor Helen Montgomerie's going that way, though she doesn't know it. How could she possibly know it, when all the time she thinks she's lavishing love on every child in her Home? It seems it just can't be done. If you're callous you can get on with the work and do it efficiently enough, even if you harden the children too; but if you try to remain tender they misunderstand you, and you destroy yourself.

She considered bitterly the criticisms often made against her and the other conscientious spinsters in her profession. Their wombs being fallow, they were inevitably at too great a distance from children. Intelligence and compassion could not compensate for the lack of maternal instinct. But, for God's sake, was that instinct worse when curbed than when distorted? Such distortions, as she was in a position to know, were far from uncommon. She recalled the little woman in the Cowcaddens whom she had visited a few days ago, to investigate reports that she was being cruel to her own children. It had been a futile and exasperating interview.

Invincibly stupid and indulgently vicious, yet with a hideous kind of grinning humour, the long-haired, pale-faced creature had produced from a drawer cuttings from newspapers, all to the effect that there was today too much official interference between parent and children. She had also asked if Margaret was married. Many married women these days, she had granted, didn't think it worth their while to wear wedding rings. She didn't herself, look. Then she had hinted, with menacing cackles and horribly interpretable winks, that what Margaret and other interferers like her needed was to sample the joys of motherhood, particularly the one at the beginning. Of course, when Margaret had spoken to the two crafty-eyed children themselves, they had defended their mother; or at any rate had refused to attribute to her the bruises on their faces and bodies. These, they muttered, they had got playing. She had gone off, furious but helpless. No doubt it would come to a court case when some injury requiring hospital treatment was inflicted; but in the meantime the children were left in the cage with the tigress that had given them birth. The whereabouts of the father were unknown; the bastard, so his mate had snarled, had slunk off, leaving her with all the problems.

Miss Mathieson awoke out of this horrible reverie to see that the steamer had left Rothesay Pier and was heading for the lovely Kyles of Bute. Everywhere was loveliness and clarity. She took several deep, grateful breaths of the clean air, and at the same time thought of the McArthurs on Calisay. Refreshed, and with pessimism overcome, she went off to look for the Sneddons, to take them to lunch.

Five

At lunch Tommy, impressed by eating at the level of the sea, displayed a gravity and correctness of table manners that surprised Miss Mathieson, who had been warned by Matron that he was an untidy and greedy eater. When she pointed out the Maids of Bute—figures of women painted in red and white on stones on the hillside—he paused with his soup-spoon halfway to his mouth, and admired the celebrated spinsters with wide-open eyes, without spilling a drop. Then at Tignabruaich, steep and green with trees, and vivid with rhododendrons, when he was told that the Gaelic name, which he couldn't pronounce, meant 'the house on the hill', he wanted to know which of the hundred houses was the one; it was his brother who tried to explain that. Going round Ardlamont Point, with the great sandy beach as white and desolate in the sunshine as Crusoe's, the three of them discussed that most famous of castaways, about whom Tommy and Johnny had read in a comic. Then across Loch Fyne, renowned for herrings—fish which had too many bones for Tommy—they sailed into East Loch Tarbert, where many yachts waited for the season, and a number of drifters with names like *Juno* and *Stella Maris* and *Bonny Jean* lay at the fish-pier, in a fine smell of fish and a snowstorm of gulls. In the bus taking them across the isthmus, Miss Mathieson told how this was the same route by which the Viking chief a thousand years ago had had his longboat dragged so as to be able to claim that he had sailed round the Mull of Kintyre. Assuring himself and the two others that he was only joking, and knew that the boat with the dragon's head wasn't there any longer, Tommy kept staring out and seeing it in this field or that, among those whins and hidden in these woods. Aside, he reminded his brother that one of the boys in the Home, Jim Murgatroyd, had two Vikings, with wings in their helmets

38

and garters round and round their legs.

At the pier on West Loch Tarbert the sturdy little steamer *Locheil* waited, and soon it was heading down the long sunny fjord, past the Isle of Gigha, where seals basked on rocks, and then out among the racing white horses of the sea towards the Sound of Jura, with the mountains of that island and of Islay dominating the western sky.

Hours later, after sunset, they arrived at Port Askaig, in Islay. There most of the passengers disembarked. On the pier, buses and cars waited for them. Many greetings in Gaelic rang out as friends met. It fascinated the two boys to choose someone, watch him or her stagger down the gangway with luggage, be welcomed at the foot, exchange handshakes or kisses, chatter excitedly, laugh happily, and all the time keep moving towards a car or bus, enter it, and soon be driven away to some house in the dark hinterland of the island, where, as Tommy said, between yawns, they would get their tea and go to bed.

At last, after all those meetings and departures, when the pier was quiet again, with swallows swooping about in the dusk and seagulls screeching forlornly—as if, Johnny whispered, their friends hadn't come after all—the steamer cast off and made over the darkling sea for Calisay, still two hours away.

Tommy, in the midst of vowing that he was going to stay awake until they arrived, fell sound asleep, and had to be stretched out on one of the padded benches in the saloon. Johnny too was tired, but shook his head when asked if he wanted to lie down; he preferred to go up on deck and watch the lights of Calisay come closer. Only four other passengers were bound for the island, English holiday-makers who were going to stay at the hotel. To quench their curiosity Miss Mathieson had told them she was taking the boys to live with relatives; now that the island was so near it did not seem untrue to claim that relationship for them.

With Johnny beside her at the rail she watched the island draw near, or rather the two islands, for close to Calisay, separated from it by the great tidal strand, was Orsay, with its holy ruins. She told him how Columba during his flight from Ireland had vowed not to build his church in any place from which his native country could be seen. He had gone ashore at Orsay, climbed the hill there, and had seen Ireland in the distance; so he had gone voyaging farther north to Iona. But afterwards in his memory a priory had been built under the hill on Orsay. Today it was a roofless ruin, but those who had visited it said that it was still a holy place. She understood that when the tide was out it was possible to walk across the mile or so of sand from Calisay.

To the south now Islay lay behind, and in the east, with the moon already shining on the tops of its high hills, loomed wild Jura. Only the Atlantic, with the sky above still flecked with sombre red, could be seen westward. To the north, far away one minute, close the next, and far away again the next, was Calisay, with its low hills and mysterious lights.

Then came the moment when, as Johnny shut his eyes, slept on his feet for a minute or so, and opened them again, the islands suddenly were there, so near that white breakers could be seen and heard on their rocks. Orsay was still dark, but the lights on Calisay came from houses. Yonder was a jetty, with people waiting. Soon, making for the ship that now, with a clanging of bells, came to a stop, a motor boat could be seen.

Miss Mathieson put her hand on Johnny's shoulder. She felt him shiver, and knew it was with anticipation as much as with cold. Trying to imagine what he must be feeling, she suddenly realised that her gesture had surely been masculine: hand on the shoulder, firm squeeze, nothing spoken. There, with the air at last of Calisay fresh and cool on her face, she made an admission about herself. Every gesture of encouragement or affection or consolation she made towards children could be called masculine. She never wept, no matter how many tears they shed, never embraced, never fondled, never used pet names, and never misrepresented out of kindness; in short, never behaved as a woman would have been expected to behave in the circumstances. Yet the little boy Tommy had said he liked her, and Johnny's 'She's all right' would now, she was sure, be replaced by something more enthusiastic. Her tactics were reasonably successful, but why had she adopted them? Had she done so consciously, considering the masculine attitude more official and so less likely to provoke emotional complications? Was she by nature mannish, as she certainly was in her way of walking, in her fondness for thick-soled shoes, and in her appreciation of a fine-looking woman. Was, for example, her liking for Helen Montgomerie quite normal, as between one intelligent woman and another, or was she Helen's nearest approach to a man to love, and Helen not her friend but her sweetheart? Had she not often wondered why, being the younger, she had tended to dominate Helen, and why Helen, so domineering with others, had appeared to acquiesce?

She was recalled, bewildered, by Johnny tugging at her arm.

'Should we no' go and get Tommy?' he was asking. He seemed to have asked it several times.

'Yes, yes of course. It's time now.'

But it was one of the crew who picked Tommy up and carried him down to the door opened in the side of the ship. Below, the motor boat rose and fell as ropes were tied.

In the motor boat were two men, one a youth of about twenty who eagerly got ready to help the passengers to make the jump. First came the holiday-makers, thrilled by this adventurous way of disembarking; as one remarked, you might be landing at Tristan da Cunha. Then the lad in the thick jersey was reaching up to take Tommy.

'Careful, please,' called Miss Mathieson.

'Surely. Visitors for the McArthurs?'

'Why, yes.'

'Don't you recognize me, Miss? I'm Hector McArthur. And now for—John, is it?'

'Yes, please,' whispered Johnny. 'I think I can do it myself.'

Hector laughed. 'Right you are, then.' He appeared to step back, but was really ready to catch the boy if necessary. It wasn't. 'Oh, grand!' he cried. 'You've got a sailor's legs all right.' To Miss Mathieson, whom he now assisted, he said: 'Mother's on the jetty. They're all there, Uncle Angus too.'

His laugh was peculiar as he mentioned his uncle; and she

remembered that all the smiles evoked by the absent Angus had been odd too. Either they were ruefully proud of him, or fondly ashamed.

'He's the one I didn't meet,' she said.

'No, he was at Oban; but you'll meet him now.' Again that odd grin. 'We'll not be long; just as soon as we get some of this stuff unloaded. The wee fellows will be ready for their beds.'

She watched him as he helped to take on board all kinds of merchandise, including, she noticed, bread from Glasgow. It occurred to her that perhaps the island was scarcely the paradise she had made it out to be to Helen. Bread from the city suggested unworthy dependence and degeneration. This young man, too, so eager and obliging, was soon to emigrate to Canada to join his relatives there. On the island were children under fourteen, and adults over forty-five; hardly anyone in between, except Flora, lucky enough to find work in the hotel, and the minister's wife, who somehow didn't seem to count. Of the hundred or so inhabitants, at least a dozen were over seventy.

'We'll need to make another run,' said Hector to her, as he stepped past to untie a rope. 'There's a great lot of stuff for the hotel and the big house.'

Soon the motor boat was making for the jetty. One of the English holiday-makers whistled 'Over the Sea to Skye'; his companions laughed. Johnny Sneddon had his arm round his brother's neck; Tommy was asleep. Hector steered, while his colleague tended the engine. Miss Mathieson noticed in the western sky a star sparkling, and suddenly, confusing and rather humiliating her, the thought broke into her mind that perhaps she ought to take to wearing jewellery of some sort, such as ear-rings. She had some, in a drawer at home. When she got back she must try it on and this time not be in too big a hurry to laugh at its silly effect on her. Perhaps, too, she ought to make an effort, if not to captivate some man, at least to allow herself to be captivated.

Six

As she waited in the little ante-room of the hotel Mary McArthur wished Elspeth and Morag hadn't insisted on accompanying her to receive the two boys; they had come because they were her friends and wanted to help, but they should have known this was a matter for her and her family, alone. The latter, though, had deserted her for the time being: Donald, her husband, was already at the jetty having a crack with some friends; Hector would be preparing the motor boat with Andrew Galbraith; Flora was busy helping Isa McGilvray of the hotel to get things ready for the guests expected off the steamer; and Angus, her brother-in-law, was lording it in the hotel lounge, as befitted his best suit, gold chain, and specially shampooed white moustache.

Elspeth's voice really was, as Angus had said, about as restful as a whistling kettle on the boil; and she could always be depended on to say what she had already said a dozen times before. 'Yes, Mary, I must say once more that I am very surprised at you, not finding out all you can about their antecedents. You have a right to know.'

Mary looked out of the window to see if the boat was coming. Her heart ached as she stared at the emptiness of the sea. She felt difficulty in breathing. Here was a different kind of birth, but she was going to feel it almost as sorely. That was downright foolish, of course, because, as Elspeth and Morag kept reminding her, the boys were not her flesh and blood; money was the cord that joined them to her.

'I don't think it's necessary, Elspeth,' she said. 'It's not as if it was for life.'

'But it could be, Mary. Remember that, it could be.'

'Well, if it turns out to be, wouldn't it be because they suited us, and we suited them?' She trembled as she spoke, because, despite all that Flora and Donald and everybody else

43

sensibly said, she couldn't help feeling ashamed that she should be taking money from strangers to give two little orphans a home.

Morag, grey-haired, with stooped back and sharp, busy face, chimed in: 'Don't forget, Mary, you'll be like the rest of us; you'll find you just can't do without the money. Even if you felt like it many's a time, it would not be so easy to hand them back.'

Morag had two girls boarded out on her. One's mother had died, the other's had signed her gladly away. Both were illegitimate, but bonnier, more biddable little lassies no one could look for. Though she scolded them often, as she had done her own family now dispersed, they were fond of her, and she of them; but it was an affection whose limits, on either side, could be too readily seen.

Elspeth kept two boys; they had come to her at different times, but a body would have expected that, sleeping in the same bed, eating at the same table, and sharing the same foster-mother, they would have become as close as brothers. The disconcerting thing was that they had remained strangers. Jessie Ogilvie of the school had said they seemed to blame each other for something, but what it was she couldn't tell. Jessie, though, was inclined to spy things in children's minds that nobody else could. Mary herself was sure that the reason simply was that Elspeth, convinced it was for their own ultimate good, kept reminding them almost daily that they were blood kin neither to each other nor to her. She carried her religion queerly, did Elspeth, and this belief about the boys was lodged in her mind like faith; nothing anyone could say would drive it out.

Both Elspeth and her sister Morag had insisted on coming to meet the boat. Being used to this business of foster-mothering, they had said that Mary would need their support and advice; besides, they knew she was not one to assert her rights. When she had pointed out that she had reared two children of her own, they had cried in unison that that was altogether different. Didn't Isa McGilvray of the hotel say that with human beings as well as with dogs and cats it was wiser to have them from birth, so as to be able to train them the way you wanted? But, as Mary thought, who was Isa to give advice, never having had child or pup or kitten, of whatever age, for love or money, and never, according to her, having wanted any? She didn't even approve of children as guests, although Ken, her husband, liked them well enough, if they were past the bed-wetting stage.

There were others waiting for the boat, some in the hotel bar, others outside, and some already down at the jetty. Most had no particular reason; they just couldn't keep away. You would think, as Donald often said, that the folk of Calisay were dying of loneliness. She had chided him for saying it, but there was some truth in it. When she had been a girl on the island, nearly fifty years ago, there had been three hundred inhabitants; now, with old Martha Galbraith's death last week, there were ninety-eight. It was surely a dying of some kind. In another fifty years, or much less, the island would be abandoned to the sea-birds, seals and midges. She often had a vision of her cottage with the roof broken and grass growing on the hearth.

Then someone outside shouted: 'Here she comes,' and when they looked out of the window, yonder, sure enough, very tiny against the vast bulk of Jura, twinkled the steamer's lights. Mary never saw them without a feeling of expectancy and gratitude; tonight, against all reason, she felt fear too.

Flora came dancing in, calm and smiling, in her black uniform dress and white apron. 'Well, she's coming at last,' she said.

'Are you sure, Flora, you can't manage down, just for the first minute or two?'

'I just can't, mother. But don't you fear. There's not a child on earth wouldn't be glad to have you welcome him.'

'It's not just as simple as that, Flora,' said Elspeth. 'We've been warning your mother that it's very important, right at the very beginning, to make them understand their position.'

'When I greet them,' said Flora, flushing a little, 'it's going to be as my brothers.'

'And that's just where you would be making a very grave

45

mistake,' said Morag. 'It's well seen you're young, Flora. That way, you'll store up trouble, as sure as you're alive.'

'But it's because I am alive, and so are they, and so is the whole island now that spring is here.'

'I'm thinking,' said Elspeth, with a grin, 'it's not these little boys you've got on your mind at all, but another bigger one, over in Islay.'

Flora flushed more deeply, but held her head up. 'I know this,' she said, 'it'd be a trouble to me, every day, to see these boys in my house and not think of them as my brothers.'

'We've been telling your mother, Flora,' said Morag, 'that she should get the big woman to tell her, in private of course, who their folks were.'

'Why? What difference does it make? They're young; one's nine just, and the other's six. Whoever their folks were, we're the ones responsible whether they grow up happy or miserable, kind or selfish, good or bad.'

'No, Flora. As Elspeth says, you're young. It does not do to go against the good book, whatever may seem to you in your youthful sufficiency to be right or wrong. It is written for our guidance, and we ignore it at our peril. What is bred in the bone cannot be got rid of; what is in the blood must speak.'

'Woman, with what blasphemous nonsense are you trying to poison my niece's sweet and generous mind?'

They turned at the rich, deep, self-important voice, with the contempt in it surging above the humour, and saw on the ruddy, white-moustached, blue-eyed face an expression to suit. Angus, Donald's elder brother, was very tall and always carried himself erect, even when, as now, he had enough whisky in him to have most other men sprawling on their knees. No one looking at him would have guessed that up to little more than a year ago he had been chief deckhand on one of the cargo boats plying between Glasgow and the Isles. Visitors mistook him for the laird, and were disappointed to learn he wasn't.

His sister-in-law was always a little uneasy in his presence. The truth was she could never believe he was genuine. All the years she had known him, during his infrequent and brief visits to the island, he had seemed to her, for all his grand manners, conceited and false. Then, more recently, he had not been forthcoming about the circumstances of his sudden retirement. A widow in Glasgow who had owned a shop had died and left him all her property, worth, it was thought, thousands of pounds; but whether he had been married to her, and if so for how long, not even his brother had been able to find out. It was thought the gold watch-chain had come from her too. He had retired to Calisay, where he had bought a cottage and a motor boat; the latter he used as a hobby only, which was just as well, for, according to Donald, himself an expert boatman, Angus was hardly fit to be trusted by himself in a dinghy on the loch, far less in a motor boat full of people on the open and dangerous sea. About once a month he paid a visit to Oban.

Neither Elspeth nor Morag liked or approved of him. They had known him as a boy; then, too, he had considered himself above the rest, though at lessons he had been little better than a dunce.

'No one was addressing you, Angus McArthur,' said Morag.

'I am sure of that, Morag. You would know better than to address such superstitious blethers to me. Mary, my dear, shall you and I go down together to welcome these small outcasts of a selfish and godless society?'

Elspeth and Morag turned away. 'Godless!' cried the former. 'Aye, indeed, Angus McArthur, wherever you are, godless it is; and that's a true and terrible thing. We will see you down there, Mary.'

Angus's smile as he stared after them made Mary shiver; he seemed to be despising not merely their work-bent bodies and narrow minds, but their very souls. She often had this feeling about him, despite his blue eyes which, so bright in his florid face, could go at times as innocent as an infant's.

'You shouldn't have hurt their feelings,' she said.

'Och, I don't know about that,' said Flora. 'Haven't they been trying to turn us all against the boys before we've even had a chance to see them?'

47

'You mustn't say that, Flora. They've got good hearts. They mean well. Didn't the big woman herself drop us a hint that it can be dangerous to become too attached?'

'Ah, this big woman!' Laughing, Angus stroked his moustache. 'As you know, I am interested in her.'

Flora laughed, and Mary too had to smile. Angus had been annoyed at missing Miss Mathieson. All his manhood, he had said, he had been searching for a woman big both in mind and body—not a Russian shot-putter or a lady wrestler from America, but one fit to be a model for a Rembrandt or a Rubens. Yet Mary had got the impression that his dead widow had been small.

'You have not to be thinking of two hippopotamuses,' he said. 'We would not be noticed, any more than jenny and jockie wren are noticed, because it would be our natures to be big, and what is natural is never out of place.'

'You've not to be saying anything out of place to Miss Mathieson,' said Mary. 'She's here on business.'

Flora glanced out of the window. 'She's getting awful near,' she said. 'Hadn't you better be going?' She went with them to the door. 'Mind now, you've not to be going straight home without letting me see them first.'

'But they'll be blind with sleep, Flora.'

'I'll not keep them a minute. Now off with you.'

Angus offered his sister-in-law his arm as they set off down the road. Moonlight glinted on the stones under their feet, and on the peaks of Jura.

'To look after a human soul, Mary, is a greater responsibility than keeping those stars in their courses. You will be seeing,' he added, without a pause, 'I have got on my skipper's cap, and you will be knowing I never was a skipper in my life; but you will be keeping quiet about that. It is not a matter of deception; it is a matter of courtesy. A woman as noble in size as this one—allowing a little off for playful exaggeration—should have a whole deputation of dignity to receive her.'

Her mind was only partly on what he was saying. The steamer was stopped now, so close to land she could hear the

48

voices of people aboard. Had the two boys been really hers, they might have, hands cupped to mouths, been trying to call to her, as Flora and Hector once had done.

'Calisay is a good place,' said Angus, 'a beautiful place, there is none fairer; but, apart from yourself and Flora, and one other, there is not one woman here that is a pleasure to look at, or converse with. Either they are old and tough in the hough, or they're middle-aged and dull in the brain. None of them has seen the world. Worst of all, they are undersized. Good God, a man would spend half the night looking for any of them in his bed; and when he found them what, in the name of conscience, could he do?'

That last sentence, murmured into his moustache, was meant for himself; he winked at the stars.

Mary could not help saying, thinking of him too: 'It's not easy to be yourself, supposing that's sufficient, which it often isn't, if you're thinking all the time you're a fraud.'

'Fraud? In what way, Mary, do you see yourself as a fraud?' There was a strange, quiet laughter in his voice as he asked the question, so that she wondered if he suspected that every woman on the island, including herself and Flora, thought he too was a fraud, though exactly how none of them would have been able to say.

'For taking the money.' She remembered that he, too, had taken money, and a great deal more than she ever would.

'You have not to be afraid of money, Mary. Besides, will you not be spending most of it on them?'

'That's what Flora says.'

'Flora is the best of us all, Mary. This young fellow over in Islay, he's going to be the luckiest man in all the Isles.'

Then they were on the jetty, among people, fish-boxes, and lobster creels. Donald was there, with Roy the dog. The big woman had written suggesting that it would be a good idea to bring the dog, as the younger of the two boys often spoke of it.

The motor boat was almost at the jetty, bringing the passengers. She saw Hector at the stern, the big woman looking cold, and then, with a pang at her heart, the two boys;

the older one had his arm round his brother's neck. Tears came into her eyes: not because they're coming to me, to my house, she told herself; if they were coming to anyone else on the island I would feel like this too. It is Calisay, my native island, which, dying or not, is going to give them the love they need.

Janet Lindsay of the shop pushed through to stand beside her. She was a childless woman, but unlike her friend Isa McGilvray she was not content to be. Sometimes, in her earnest, cautious way, like a cat in midstream, she spoke of adopting a child. Now she had brought her man Neil to admire the McArthurs' acquisitions; he could be heard somewhere, with his too ready shopman's laugh. Though incomers from Glasgow, they were a well-liked, obliging couple.

'You must be excited, Mary,' Janet whispered.

'I can't deny it, Janet.'

'Almost as much, maybe, as when you were expecting your own?'

Mary smiled.

'You see, if I was in your place, I would be awful excited, and I never had any of my own, as you know.'

She had her hands clasped, in a fervent way.

Just as Mary turned, in a small panic, to look for Donald, there he was at her side. The motor boat had reached the jetty. The first passengers, those for the hotel, were being helped up the narrow steps. With his hairy hat covering his bald head, Ken McGilvray came forward to welcome them. Then, forestalling Mary, Angus pushed to the forefront and gave a hand to Miss Mathieson; with his other he touched his skipper's cap. In Gaelic he said: 'Welcome back,' and then, in his mellowest English: 'Good evening, Miss Mathieson. My name is Angus McArthur.'

'I see. Couldn't—?' She looked about. 'Oh yes, there they are.' She waved to Mary and Donald.

They went forward shyly; Roy crept behind.

Up the steps came Hector, carrying the smaller boy. The other climbed up bravely by himself.

Others gathered round to look.

'Well, mother,' said Hector, 'here they are then.'

She knew he was eagerly offering them as replacements for himself.

They could never be that, she thought. 'So I see,' she said, and the moment it was out she realised it was what Morag and Elspeth, the canny time-taking ones, would have said. Far better at the beginning to err through excess and haste of affection, not through a slow rationing of it. So she bent and took the younger boy's cold hand in hers; but that too seemed a deliberately restricted gesture, so she did what she had not often done even to her own children, she kissed him. 'You'll be Tom?' she said.

Seated on Hector's knee, he was less than half awake. 'Is that our dog?' he asked.

Roy had sneaked under and was licking the child's leg.

'Roy!' she cried, and made to push him away.

'Roy? Is that his name? Good.' Then he fell sound asleep again.

'Give him to me, Hector,' said Donald. 'Andrew is waiting for you to go back to the boat.'

'Yes.' The hand-over was gently done. Hector hurried down the steps into the motor boat. As he passed he patted John's head.

It was not so easy with the older boy, though certainly no one could have said he tried to make it difficult for her. As if at bay, he stood smiling up at them all.

'And you'll be John?' she asked.

'Yes, Mrs McArthur.'

She had worried about that: what should she ask them to call her? Elspeth's called her Mrs McDonald, and Morag's Mrs Morrison. Others used the name 'aunt', while one or two of the younger ones were allowed to say 'mother'. But this wasn't the time to settle what would likely settle itself soon enough. She put her arm round him. 'You'll be tired, lad?'

'Just a wee bit. Tommy's tired.'

Donald laid his free hand on the boy's head. 'We'll have him in bed before Roy there can shake his tail a hundred times, and see how quick he's at it. I'm Mr McArthur.'

John bent and patted Roy, who was overjoyed.

'Well then, shall we be heading for home?' said Donald. He took John's hand.

Mary took the other, and so they made up the road. Folk murmured greetings as they passed.

Miss Mathieson, with Angus escorting her and carrying her bag, followed behind. She felt a little light-headed, as if she had been drinking champagne on an empty stomach. It must be tiredness, she thought, on top of emotional strain; but it couldn't be denied that meeting this tall, handsome man with the bearing and voice of an archbishop might have something to do with it. She knew she was being more affable to him than she should, but somehow she couldn't control herself. Once or twice she was on the point of taking his arm.

'Tell me, Miss Mathieson, are you one of those worldly people who believe that to live on a small island like Calisay is to bury yourself alive?'

'No, I wouldn't say that.'

'The television reception is so bad as to be worse than useless, because of the mountains of Jura. Would that distress you?'

'Why, no.' Yet she had a set at home, and looked at it often enough. In spite of the many people she met in the course of her work, was she really at heart lonely?

'I do believe that we have here an opportunity to acquire such qualities as courtesy, dignity, kindness—'

'There's plenty of kindness in the city, Mr McArthur.'

'I do not doubt it. But like everything else in the city its growth is distorted and forced, so that it inevitably lacks freshness. Do you not think so?'

'I'm not sure, you know, that I do.'

'Breathe in this pure air. Look at those stars. Listen. That is a curlew still not asleep. Is it not a more beautiful and consoling sound than the bellow and racket of traffic? Is it any wonder we on Calisay have peace in our souls?'

But had they? He sounded as if he might have himself, but there were others, she felt sure, whose souls were as restless and discontented as anyone's in the city. The city multitudes were luckier; they did not carry the burden of having to know everyone.

Janet Lindsay's shop and house were near the jetty. Before taking leave, she had whispered: 'They seem very nice little boys, Mary. I like the looks of the older one. He seems willing to be happy. Wherever he's been, his spirit's not been crushed. That's the important thing. He'll bring you happiness, Mary.'

'I'm sure he will, Janet; both of them will.'

As she went up the road towards the hotel she felt hopeful and proud.

Elspeth and Morag walked behind her, whispering to each other. They had murmured a word or two of welcome to the boys, and then withdrawn.

They all paused at the hotel. Flora came rushing out. Roy raced to meet her. 'Och, it's not you I want to see, Roy,' she cried. 'Wheesht too, or you'll be wakening old Mr Stockbridge who's fallen asleep on the lounge sofa again.' She crouched until her face was level with John's; she gripped his shoulders. 'I'm Flora,' she said, 'your big sister.'

He could not help grinning. Somehow she reminded him of Jean McDonnell.

'Oh, it's not a joke, so you needn't laugh. You'll have to be my new brother, whether you like it or not. Did you see Hector? He would be steering the boat, into all the big rocks. He's my brother, our brother I should say now. He's going away to Canada in three weeks. Did you know that?'

He shook his head, dismayed. Was this place the same as the Home, with people you liked going away and perhaps never coming back?

'Well then,' cried Flora, 'that's all settled.' She rose. 'And is this wee Tom?'

'Sound asleep,' said her father.

'And why not, and it past eleven o'clock? I'll be over some time tomorrow, mother, as soon as I can spare an hour or two here. Good evening, Miss Mathieson. Welcome back. Your room's ready. I see you've got the handsomest porter in Calisay carrying your bag. I'll take it now, Uncle Angus.'

'Not at all, Flora. It has been a pleasure to carry Miss

53

Mathieson's bag, and isn't the last part of a pleasure aye the best? Moreover, I have a little business in the hotel.'

Seven

From the hotel to the cottage was a little over a mile, first
along the road that ran diagonally across the island, and then
by a footpath that climbed up over grass and heather before
descending again by the side of a burn, past the birch wood,
and through the fields of their own croft. They walked slowly,
and every now and then other islanders, discreetly this night
either before or behind them on the road, kept turning off,
with good nights called in Gaelic, as indigenous as sea-birds'
cries. Her own heart so overflowingly at home, Mary felt
keenly the loneliness and strangeness of this child whose hand
she held; but to remove them would take time.

A little way along their own path they came to the cottage
of old Ewan and Kirstie McCuish, both over eighty, he
bedridden, and she unable to sleep or even to lie at rest.
Tonight, as usual, she was seated in her rocking-chair in front
of the house, in the lee of the peat stack. It was known for
her to sit there creaking and sighing all night, the island's
memory. As they approached they heard the creaking stop,
and there was a moment's starlit silence. Mary always thought
of it as the island's own heart ceasing to beat.

'It will be yourselves, Mary and Donald?' The voice, heard
first, always surprised strangers; they did not expect from it
to see so old and shrivelled a woman; and if they spoke to
her, the clarity of her mind surprised them further.

'It is us, Kirstie,' replied Mary, also in Gaelic.

'You have the two boys? They were on the boat?'

'Yes, Kirstie, they are here. They are very tired. The
younger one is asleep.'

'I shall not meet them tonight, Mary. They will be wanting
to go straight to their beds. But that is not it altogether. I do
not want them to think of me as an old witch that sits and
sings with the owls. Bring them to see me when the sun is

shining.'

Mary smiled in the darkness. Long ago Kirstie had been very bonny, and proud of it; now there were, so she said herself, folk across in Orsay brawer than she—though the only folk there now were the skeletons under the flat stones in the ruined priory.

'How was himself today?' asked Donald.

'Sailing round the Cape of Storms.'

In his youth her husband Ewan had sailed for years on a ship trading to San Francisco. Now he would lie in bed and talk about those old adventures; if there was no one to listen he talked just the same. The deeds were reckless and bold, the voice reciting them small and plaintive, like the squeaking of a gate pushed by a little breeze.

'I shall be stepping inside soon to have a chat with him.'

'Do that, Donald, and bring the bairns.'

'Surely. Good night, Kirstie.'

Mary stooped and whispered to John: 'Call good night to the old lady.'

'But I don't know the language.'

She was about to say English would do, but instead whispered the Gaelic to him. 'You can say it. Try.'

He tried and got it very well.

'Good for you. Now call it to the old lady.'

He did so, shyly but intelligibly.

'Ah, so he has learned the Gaelic already?' cried Kirstie. 'Blessings on you, lad, and on your brother, and on the hands that take care of you.'

As they went on he murmured: 'What did she say?'

'She was giving us her blessing.'

'Is she very old?'

'Yes, indeed.'

'Has she lived in this place all her life?'

'Yes, she has; and so have I.'

'If I'm here long enough, will I learn to speak Gaelic?'

'I do not see why not. And why should you not be here long?'

He took the question literally and answered it with an

earnestness that troubled her. 'Sometimes children went away from the Home just for a little while, and then came back. Jean McDonnell came back twice.'

'Was she a friend of yours?'

He was about to say no, she hadn't been, when he thought again, and realised, to his wonder, that she had been. Yes, he had always been glad to see and hear Jean; often when he had been feeling unhappy and uncertain Jean it was who had cheered him up and given him confidence, not by saying or doing anything in particular, but just by being herself. He shivered to think that he might never see her again.

They were now on the crest of the path. The stars seemed as near as the lights in the various crofts scattered about. Yonder, for instance, across the moonlit loch, shone the lights of the schoolhouse and the manse. In front, below, past the darkness of the birch wood, the moon glinted on the roof of their own cottage; and beyond it again, far out in the vast, tranquil Atlantic, the light of Dhu Heartach flashed. Emphasizing that tranquillity, rather than disturbing it, came the murmur of the waves breaking on the sands of Miloran Bay. The air was fragrant with peat-smoke, and many earth and sea scents. Even when she thought of Hector, soon to leave, perhaps for ever, Mary did not feel despondent as she gazed about her native island. Here life went on at the right pace for faith to keep up. Yet had it not been too slow for Hector, and those of his friends who had left before him?

'Yes,' admitted the child, in his quiet anguished voice, 'she was my friend.'

'What age is she?'

'I think she's a year younger than me.'

'And where is she now?'

'She's still in the Home.' Then he began to tell about Jean handing him the withered daffodils, and running away from them all to sit with her back to her tree, her face covered by her hands. 'She would have liked this place,' he said.

'I'm sure so will you.'

'I think so. Tommy will because of the dog.'

'But you'll like the dog too?'

'Oh aye; but I promised Tommy it would be his.'

'And so it will be then.'

As if to show he consented, Roy made that noise in his throat that Flora called his laughter.

As they crossed the fields in front of the cottage, a couple of peewits fluttered above their heads, complaining. John knew they were anxious about their nests. There had been peewits in the field next to the Home. Once, with some other boys, he had climbed over the fence and looked for nests. Finding one, he had picked up an egg. Now it seemed to him that in this strange place the birds had sought him out, to make him return it. He could not, because it had broken. He remembered its smell and its sliminess on his fingers; but most of all he remembered his peculiar feeling of guilt and uneasiness, that he, who had no home of his own, should be destroying the birds'.

*   *   *

As Mary turned up the lamp on the table she thought that at last they had reached the heart of the hospitable quietness. The light shone softly on the white cloth and twinkled on the dishes and cutlery. Quickly, with a feeling of removing a last doubt, she took off her coat.

'Well now,' she said, 'the first thing is to get this wee laddie into bed.'

John nodded; he could not help yawning.

'And you can follow him as soon as you've had a glass of milk and a scone.'

'No, please.' He was not afraid of these people, who were to be his parents, but he couldn't bear so soon to be parted from Tommy. 'I don't want anything to eat. I just want to go to bed too.'

'Are you sure?'

'Yes, thanks.'

Mary glanced at Donald, who nodded. 'Very well, then,' she said. 'We'll go right up.'

As he followed her up the stairs, with Tommy being carried

58

behind, the house, after the bigness of the Home, seemed very small; but he thought he preferred it, or that he would when he got used to it.

'We'll just be content with a quick wipe of your faces and hands for tonight,' said Mary. She whispered to Donald to go and bring up the kettle. Then she took Tom's clothes off, while John got their pyjamas out.

Five minutes later both boys were in bed in the little room with the sloping roof and the tiny window that looked out onto the Atlantic. As Mary tucked them in she was greatly moved to notice that trust had at last appeared in the older boy's smile; up to then it had been, so inoffensively, withheld.

Donald stood in the doorway, with the kettle in his hand. 'Good night, laddie,' he whispered.

'Good night. And thanks.'

Mary came over, pushed her husband out, and asked him to go down and put the kettle on the fire again. Hector would be in any time now.

For a few minutes more she herself lingered outside the door, on the small landing where there was room only for one person. She half expected to hear sobbing: children, when exhausted in body or mind, often sobbed themselves to sleep, and in the morning woke up refreshed and eager. But she heard nothing except the quiet movements of Donald below, and still farther below the surges of the sea. At last she opened the door and peeped in. Both boys were asleep. Moonlight lit their faces, and, outside the window, the sea. Turning from them to it she felt herself falling into a confusion; memories not only of her own childhood but also of her children's mingled in her mind. Among them was that of her brother Duncan who, forty years ago, on an expedition to Breac Point, for sea-gulls' eggs, had been drowned. He had been ten, she eight; and in private secret places, both on the island and in her mind, she had mourned him for years. There were times when she still did. He had not only been her brother, he had been her closest friend and companion too, as the little girl left at the Home in Glasgow had apparently been John Sneddon's.

59

When she went downstairs, Donald was seated by the fire, a hand spread out on each knee. She noticed how white his hair seemed against the sunburnt redness of his neck. When he turned to smile at her she saw that, though famous on the island for his drollness, he was still, as he had been all that evening, worried, thoughtful, and even a little afraid.

Going past him to the fireplace, she moved the kettle, not because there was any need to, but for the comfort and reassurance of doing it. So many thousands of times had she done this before that it represented more almost than any other act her being mother in this house. Her children had noticed it: her hand on the kettle handle, they had said, gave her the confidence their ancestors had got from the claymore's hilt.

'Well, woman, and what is this we have done?'

'A good thing, I think.'

After a meditative pause, he nodded; but there was doubt in it.

'And not just for them either,' she said. 'For ourselves, too.'

'Surely.' But he did not sound wholly sure.

'What is it, Donald?'

'Nothing really, Mary.' He laughed and put out a hand as if to clutch a tiller. Never was he happier and more confident than when in a boat, no matter how fierce the sea. Sometimes, though, the quiet hearth could frighten him.

'There is something, Donald. Are you disappointed with the boys?'

'No, no. They are fine boys, I am sure. It is a privilege for us to be given them to look after.'

'I think so, too. What is it then that's troubling you?'

'Well, Mary, to tell you the truth, I have been thinking that maybe we are trying to do what the good Lord never intended us to do.'

She frowned. 'I have been thinking the opposite, Donald. As soon as I saw them, I felt sure the Lord Himself had sent them to us. Do you not think He would approve?'

'In a way, yes.'

'In what way, no?'

60

'It is hard for me to explain, woman.' He held up his big, brave hands. 'As you know, I am not clever with my tongue. It is like this: are we not trying, in a way, to escape what is the lot of every man and woman who marry and have children? The children grow up and go out into the world; the old people stay at home and remember them. That is the way of it; that has always been the way of it. Are we trying to get a second chance?'

'And you think we should not?'

'I am not sure, Mary; but yes, it is blowing in and out of my mind.'

There had always been this streak of the timid old conventional wife in Donald. Mary spoke with rather more assurance than she felt. 'You are saying that loneliness, such as that of old Kirstie yonder, is what the Lord intends for us?'

'No, I am not saying it altogether, Mary.'

'Don't think only of our side of it. Think of the boys.'

'There, too. God help me, Mary, but there were times I felt, at the jetty, and coming across the hill, that I was little better than a thief. Was I not about to steal from them what should be their own parents'?'

'What are you talking about, man?' But she knew.

'Their affection, wife. If they stay here, they will learn to love you as their mother.'

'And you as their father.'

'Yes, yes.'

'And what would be wrong with that?'

He shook his head, and again reached out his hand. Here was a situation more difficult and more perilous than when, one day of sudden summer storm, he had been caught under the great cliffs, and the engine had failed. In the kettle's peaceful singing was again the roar and crash of the waves.

'I could understand,' said Mary, 'if it was taking the money that was troubling you.'

'No, it is not that.' His voice was firm. 'There is no shame in that. It is just that I cannot get the thought of their own parents out of my head.'

'That is true.'

61

'Are they both dead, Mary?'

'I do not know.'

'Elspeth was saying we should ask the big woman.'

'Elspeth says a lot more than her prayers. I do not think we should concern ourselves about their parents. Perhaps they are dead. Whether they are or not, they have given up all their rights.'

'That is so. I think I shall get used to it.'

For half a minute or so there was silence. Mary thought it would be more sensible to make the tea and have no more talk, but she could not resist mentioning something that Janet Lindsay had said at the jetty.

'Janet of the shop was saying that if she ever was to take a child into her home, it would be for life; she would adopt it properly, and so of course there would be no question of money.'

'She can afford it.'

There were times when Mary wondered if they too could have afforded it. Yet had not the big woman, when asked privately, given it as her professional opinion that the authorities would not consider the financial circumstances of the McArthurs good enough for outright adoption? Calisay was a fertile island, lucky in its situation; but it had to be worked, and most of the young, vigorous people left as soon as they could. No community could remain prosperous with such losses, and no family either.

'It would be Janet's first time,' said Donald.

'Yes.'

'But she will never do it.'

Mary agreed. Like a swimmer, Janet would put off until the sun had gone off the sea, and the water had become too cold, deep and dark. She would regret the putting off until she died.

Donald rose, found his spectacles on the dresser, put them on, and took down from the shelf the big Bible. She noticed, though no one else would, how he hurried; and she knew why.

He was afraid that Hector might come home and spoil the reading. It wasn't that Hector disbelieved or would be disrespectful; it was just that they had found a reading with him present was different from one with him absent. Perhaps he could not be blamed. He was of his age, and his views and values were not the same as theirs; otherwise why should he wish so strongly to leave the island where they had so contentedly spent all their lives? The change in him had happened before their eyes, and they had been helpless to prevent it, even if they had wished. He gave his approval to what the book said, but obviously its message did not sustain him—it saw things too simply, and there was so much it did not take into consideration. Useless to tell him that all those things he now desired would one by one become less and less important the older he became; he had to learn that for himself, many times with a sore heart.

From the first days of their marriage Donald had liked to show that he was head of the household by himself choosing the passages for family reading. Sometimes he did not choose, but opened and read at random; it had meant more than once a dry or awkward few minutes. Tonight, though, he chose, his big forefinger carefully turning the pages, reminding her a little of Roy herding the sheep down from the hill. But at last he found the passage he was looking for. He looked up, smiled at her, and was about to begin when they heard Roy barking outside and then Hector whistling.

'Go on,' she said quietly.

He considered, then shook his head, closed the book and replaced it. 'Another time. The lad will be hungry, and his tea not ready.'

But he could not hide his disappointment; this, she knew, involved not only Hector, but himself too, and perhaps even her. In him, along with so many better qualities, had always been a pinch of the McArthur conceit and ambition with which his brother Angus was stuffed; their father, old Neil, had been notorious from Oban to the Mull of Oa for his bragging. Apart from his service in the Navy during the war, Donald felt he had done nothing of note. This was not the first time the Bible had lost its savour.

63

Eight

Two or three times during that extraordinary supper in the tartan-papered dining-room, at the table under the stag's head, Margaret Mathieson almost found herself gabbling out the Sneddons' secret. It wasn't just the wine that Captain McArthur—plain 'Mr' was good enough for other people, he whispered—had insisted on ordering, nor was it the nudge of his knee against hers under the table; or rather it was those, of course, but above all it was the unaccustomed riot throughout all her feminine nerves. In her breasts, for instance, a great ache throbbed like the solemn beating of a gong; had they been overflowing with milk they could not have hurt more pleasurably. She found herself staring in fascination at his handsome pink face, reducing it, adding details from what she remembered of her own, and producing the image of the child she might have with him as its father. She was forty, a hard age for a first birth, but she had never been one to make a song about pain. He was about fifty, sufficiently virile for all his discreet movements and chiming voice. The alliance was not impossible. Already she had gathered from his modest murmurs that he was fairly well-off, and she had not only her own savings in the bank but those of her parents too. A woman must meet her lover somewhere. Where more auspiciously than on this beautiful Hebridean isle? On the stag's head above her she noticed moisture, like tears, frozen at the edges of the big amber eyes.

Stripped, Angus was thinking, she would make a magnificent sight, all the more so because she would hardly be aware of it. She wore brassiere and corsets, of course, but when they were removed the sagging would be slight, certainly far short of grotesque. Compared with Peggy, who had died, she was in manner brusquer and more cautious; compared with Nell, in Oban, she was, he was inclined to think, not so malleable.

64

But she was bigger than either, and once fed a little lovemaking her appetite for it would be even more ravenous than theirs. She seemed as well provided with the world's goods, too. This flat in Hillhead sounded as downy a nest as Nell's boarding-house in Oban still was, and as Peggy's house above the shop had been. If she insisted on marriage, why not? The fact that he had married Peggy had come in handy on her sudden death. Certainly the lawyer acting for her relatives might have resisted the will much more stubbornly had he not been. And if a woman was the highly-strung kind who could relax in bed only if married, was not a declaration worth hours, years of fat living and choice love-making, if he played the game with his usual skill? One thing was certain: she was as ripe for it as any of the—five, was it, or six? And who, if not a beneficent deity, had brought her by night into his arms?

As he pressed her to take a third glass of wine, he wondered if he should attempt her that very night, in her hotel bed. He knew the way up the back stairs. But he thought not: better let her boil a little longer. Tomorrow, when she went across to see Mary and the brats, he might entice her into his cottage, on to the striped divan with the grand view of the ocean, or, better still, offer to sail her back to the hotel. There would be time for a brief landing on Sanda, where the machair even in May was sweet and soft.

'What are you smiling at?' she asked.

'Thoughts that pass across the sky of the mind, like little white clouds.'

'What kind of thoughts?'

He reached forward and stroked her hand with his forefinger. Nail and finger were clean and finely shaped. She could imagine herself allowing it and its fellows liberties. She blushed.

'Flattering to you,' he murmured. 'You may be sure of that.'

'Tell me,' she said explosively, so that one of the English holiday-makers, also supping, but in a distant corner, burst afresh into giggles, 'tell me, truthfully, do you consider me attractive, in a womanly kind of way?'

Startled, his mind swerved, but he did not lose control.

'What a superfluous question!'

'All the same, answer it, please.'

'With the most exquisite pleasure. I find you remarkably attractive. Why else should I be here, enjoying myself so thoroughly?'

'Attractive in a womanly kind of way?' She knew she attracted men by her capability, her directness, and her impatience with pettifoggers; but those were hardly feminine qualities.

She was almost tiddly. God, one glass more, and she'd be pulling him upstairs. 'Most assuredly. In what other way, my dear?'

'I'm so big.'

'I would say—pardon the indelicacy—that in a bathing costume you would rival Venus herself.'

'As a matter of fact, I brought one with me; a bathing costume, I mean. It's May, after all; it should be warm enough for swimming.'

'Over on Sanda it's perfect. There are hollows in the sand where the sea grows as warm as a bath.'

'That's the tiny island to the west?'

'Yes. A bird sanctuary—and a sanctuary for lovers. Most peaceful spot on earth. Some prefer Orsay, but it has the ruins and the bones. Perhaps, if the weather's favourable, we might cross and have a look at it tomorrow. I have a little motor boat.'

She ogled her wine-glass aggressively. 'That might be a good idea.'

'I shall keep it in mind.'

*　　*　　*

Later, after she had gone upstairs to bed, and he was about to set off, on his moonlit chuckling, solitary walk home, Flora snatched a minute to come and scold him.

'You've been making her drunk,' she said.

'Nonsense, girl. She had three glasses of wine. Of course, if you are referring to some other kind of wine'—here he

66

stroked his moustache—'that I administered to the gracious lady, why, Flora, you and I know better than most that we handsome ones have no control over our powers of fascination.'

'I'd like to hear you say that to Jessie Ogilvie, of the school.'

'Flora, my dear, the great Achilles himself would quail before that particular Troy.'

She could not help laughing. Like her mother, she was sure he was a fraud, but what kind exactly she couldn't say. He pretended to visitors he had been a captain; well, there was little harm in that, and he had been a sailor for nearly thirty years; besides, she had seen pictures of admirals not half so suitable in appearance for the part as he. He pretended to be a scholar with his talk of Achilles and such like; but if he could get away with it, then good luck to him, for he had had to leave school at fourteen. But what struck her as less pardonable was his pretence of affection. His mouth was often ringing with claims of love for all humanity, but she often had the feeling that behind them he was laughing with contempt. Her mother felt it too, and so did Jessie Ogilvie, who detested him. It was thought he had once made Jessie an offer of marriage. If he had, well, whoever the great Achilles might have been, he certainly hadn't been any bolder than Uncle Angus.

'Well, just mind she's in a manner of speaking the responsibility of the family.'

'Hence my attentiveness. Of course my motives will be wrongly interpreted by the crude, coarse, suspicious folk we live among today. There was a time when the Gaels of these islands had in them a natural dignity and generosity of mind.'

'They still have.'

'No, girl, they have not. Against me, who try to keep those ancestral virtues alive, they conspire, behind my back. I am, you see, a living reminder of their own backsliding into primitive black-mindedness. I represent light, grace and joy. They hate me for it.'

'Nonsense, Uncle Angus. There's not a person on Calisay would hurt a fly.'

'Physically, no; spiritually, they would strip the wings off. They look out daily on God's abundant beauty, and yet their minds are narrow and brutish. Look at this cigar. Smell it. Is it not fragrant? Does it not in its simple way stand for the graciousness of civilized living? Yet as I pass tonight they'll thrust out their heads and sniff, and mutter to one another that the deil's gone by.'

'Don't be silly.' Yet she had to admit to herself that there was some truth in his remarks. After all, didn't she herself consider him rather wicked, in a way she couldn't quite understand?

*　　　*　　　*

Next morning, when she awoke, Miss Mathieson saw first, with anticipation that made her breasts throb, a patch of sunlight on the wall in the shape of a boat; and then next, with distaste that soured her stomach, her pyjamas. Of blue-striped flannelette, they were really a man's because those were the only kind she could buy ready made to fit her, and she had been too uninterested to have daintier ones specially made of cotton or silk. For some minutes she lay, thrilled and disgusted by turns.

When she got up she could scarcely bear to look at her body in those blue stripes, and dragged them off. Naked, she was about to tug open the wardrobe door and look at herself in the mirror on the other side, when the cries of children outside made her stiffen, and turn instead to the window. There were three of them, two little girls and a boy on their way to school. She thought she recognized them from her previous visit; like the Sneddons, they were boarded out. Hands on her breasts, she remembered how she, like Helen Montgomerie, was often guilty of the cowardice and sentimentality of believing that these abandoned children were in some mystical way hers. Sensing this, colleagues and disgruntled parents had sometimes suggested, more or less openly, that her vision would become clearer and more realistic if she were to have a child of her own, with the pain, blood and mess. In the office in

68

Glasgow were magazines and pamphlets from all over the world, dedicated to child care; from these she had learned that unwanted children were as numerous as shells on the seashore. Love squandered on these must inevitably be meaningless. Only one child ought to vex her heart, her own, the issue of this body which, as the mirror now revealed, would have been capable of producing a dozen. She thought of the Sneddons: filthily conceived, delivered in hate, and now brutally forsaken. Yet when she went this morning to visit them at the McArthurs' they would be running about in the sunshine, as carefree as the larks singing above, while her own child lay crouched and imprisoned in the darkness of her desires.

She spent at least twenty minutes longer than usual on her toilet, taking care to apply lipstick as if it had some other purpose than mere conformity. Her hair, too, she brushed more artistically, leaving it not quite so plain and repressed; in certain lights, she knew, it had golden gleams. She would not wear a hat or stockings. At the finish, in her tweed skirt and fresh white blouse, she thought she looked like a woman still with her own rights to claim and fight for.

At breakfast, intending to put on a mature charm appropriate to her appearance, she betrayed herself by suddenly being shaken with jealousy of Flora McArthur who attended to her. Without doubt the girl, despite the unglamorous waitress's uniform and the scarcely noticeable lipstick, mocked Margaret's own efforts at femininity. She did not intend to, which made it worse; it was not she, it was nature that mocked. Though careful not to overstep the line between guest and servant, she could not help conveying, as involuntarily as the larks kept singing, that she was a woman, young, pretty, and in love, who would as sure as the breath in her nostrils marry and have children. Do not forget, girl, Margaret kept thinking, as she crunched her toast, do not forget that your children, for all your gaiety and innocence, will inhabit the same world as the Sneddons. If you do not know yet just what kind of a world that is, you will after I have told you what I intend to this morning; and I have chosen you to be told because of your goodness.

69

'If you're going over to your parents' place this morning, Flora,' she said, 'I'd like to accompany you.'

'Of course, Miss Mathieson. Yes, I'm going to manage a couple of hours off. I'll be pleased to have you with me.'

'You see, there's something I want to tell you, Flora. Not here. Outside somewhere. In the clean air. In the sunshine.'

Flora looked surprised, but said nothing.

*   *   *

They stopped on the crest of the path, their cheeks pink, their hair stirred, and sat on sun-warmed lichened stones. A breeze, pleasant now but in ten minutes likely to be cool, blew from the sea. The tide was out, and the sun blazed on pools in the great white strand that separated Calisay from the much smaller island of Orsay. Sanda looked very green. Everywhere people, men and women, were busy on the land. Children could be seen and heard in the playground of the school.

'It's like paradise,' murmured Margaret.

Flora laughed. In her tartan skirt and blue cardigan she was in place there. 'It is beautiful,' she said. 'But it's not paradise, all the same. If it was, would the young ones leave? Hector, my brother, is the next to go. He'll be the eighth in the past year.'

'Why do they leave?'

'To tell you the truth, they find it hard to say. They say it's too quiet here, too slow, too much out of touch.'

'Out of touch with what?'

'That's what they can't tell. There's work enough. The farms are good. And the laird's very generous.'

'It can be dull enough in the world outside.'

'Yes, indeed. A lot of them admit that when they write home; but still they don't want to come back. What was it, Miss Mathieson, that you said you wanted to tell me? It's about the two boys, isn't it?'

'Yes.'

Flora scraped a piece of lichen off the stone. 'Shouldn't it be my father and mother you should tell?'

'Perhaps. I don't know. I'm using my own judgment. As a matter of fact, I am not supposed to tell anyone; but I feel I must, in the boys' own interest.' She paused, to consider if she still felt she was doing it in their interest; yes, she did, but she could not be sure she wasn't also using the revelation as an attack upon this young woman's happiness. 'What age are you, Flora? Twenty-five?'

'I will be in August.'

They heard a whistle. It was Jessie Ogilvie bringing in her scholars. With the children gone a great emptiness seemed to Margaret to descend on the island. It was a ludicrous feeling, but she could not easily shake it off.

'If it will help me to help the boys,' said Flora, 'I would like to hear it.'

'That's why I am going to tell you. They need help, especially John, the elder. But I must warn you that it will amount to taking on yourself a very heavy burden.'

'Is it about their people?'

'Yes.'

Flora was silent. She had plucked a sprig of green heather and was nibbling at it.

Margaret thought she could make out a ship far off on the sea.

'If I think I should,' asked Flora, 'can I tell my mother?'

'Once you know, the responsibility of speaking or of keeping quiet will be yours.'

'It sounds awful mysterious.'

'No, it isn't that. In a way it's pretty commonplace. To begin with, it's most likely that they are only half-brothers. Their mother, from all accounts, was little better than a prostitute. The younger boy's probably not her husband's. She was a worthless creature and made her husband's life a misery.' She paused then, remembering the conversation she had overheard between the boys at Rothesay Pier. 'In the end she drove him insane with jealousy. So he killed her, two days before Christmas.'

'Killed her?' In Flora's quiet voice were pity and horror.

'Yes. With the hatchet that he used to split the sticks for

71

kindling the fire in the morning. Everybody said he was a mild, hard-working, inoffensive little man. But he kept striking her until she wasn't only butchered, but was unrecognizable. Blood all over the place.'

'Where were the boys?'

'It was a room and kitchen. This happened in the kitchen. They were in the room.'

'When was it? I mean, how long ago?'

'Three years. The elder was six, the younger three. Not very pleasant, is it?' She shook her head in revulsion, as if a spider had been running across her face. 'Now, here is why I have told you. Nobody knows whether John saw or heard anything. When the neighbours broke in, he was in bed with his brother, but he was wide awake, and cold, and terrified; it seems he kept nodding all the time. It's more than likely that, hearing the shrieks, he crept through to see what it was all about; and saw it happen. The police were pretty sure he did. Of course no one's ever asked him directly. How could anyone? And he's never spoken about it, so far as we know, to a single soul. He's been told both his parents are dead, and, on the surface anyway, he's accepted it. His father isn't dead, though; he's in a criminal asylum, and is in pretty poor physical health too. So that's the situation, Flora. They have an aunt, their father's sister; but she's disowned them. No relatives of their mother came forward at the time, and aren't likely to, now. I believe she had an unfortunate childhood herself, being illegitimate. I don't need to stress that all this must be kept a secret from the other islanders. If it leaked out here John would have to be taken away.'

'Why?'

Margaret shook her head. Was the girl's goodness just naivety, after all? 'Because, Flora, people here are the same as people everywhere. They'd look on the boys as creatures of horror. Pity's the worst transformer of all.'

'But I know about it, and I don't think of them as creatures of horror.'

'I hope not.' But she hadn't seen them yet, in the light of the knowledge.

'And you've known all along, Miss Mathieson. Are they creatures of horror to you?'

'With me it's different. It's my job. I've got training and experience behind me.'

'Yes, but you're still a woman. I mean, they're just children and—'

'To me they're business; and not the worst I've had, either. So there you are, Flora. It seems incredible, sitting here, in the clean air, with so much space and beauty all round us; but it's here too, the horror, on Calisay, in young John Sneddon's mind. And in yours. You're rather young to have to carry such a burden.'

'The boy's a lot younger than me.'

'Yes, there's that. Perhaps if I had met your Uncle Angus during my previous visit I should have chosen him.'

'No.'

The word was spoken with a firmness that annoyed Margaret. She wondered if the girl in some dense way was trying to get a little of her own back.

'Why not?' she asked. 'He seems to me a mature, responsible person; and he knows the world.'

'You should have chosen my mother.'

'Don't you see why I could not? She's the one who will be in closest daily contact with him. The strain on her would have been too great.'

'My mother could bear it.'

'But ought she to be asked to? Which raises another question. It may be that you, and your parents, if you decide to tell them, won't care much to have the children of a murderer in your home. Few people would, after all. Well, if you wish to get rid of them, I shall personally see that it is done, as discreetly as possible.'

Now she had said everything, made the last attack, as it were, on the dark-haired girl's simple-minded happiness, and still, for all her trained percipience, she was not sure what effect she had had. Flora trembled a little, and scraped at the lichen with more agitation, but she smiled too. Nor was it the smile or snigger behind which insensitiveness frequently hid;

73

and it was by no means the grimace of crass incomprehension. No, it was, Margaret suddenly perceived, with a qualm that shook her bowels, the kind of smile which made a woman womanly, and so to her sweetheart or husband more beautiful and more desirable than anything else on earth. As she pondered she became aware that whereas Flora was crouched on her stone in a peculiarly feminine manner, she herself had her hands thrust into the pockets of her jacket, and was sitting with her legs wide apart.

She sprang up. 'Well, they're in your hands now, Flora. Shall we go down and meet them?'

She led the way, striding quickly, deliberately exaggerating her mannish gait, while Flora, hurrying behind, panting a little, was more womanly than ever in the way she pulled back a tendril of bramble, or held up her skirt to clamber over a drystane dyke.

Going through the birch wood, with the buds breaking into green stars above and the trunks hairy like crones' faces with grey crotle, Margaret paused. This anguish in her heart could not be hurried away from, but she did not know it was also in her face until Flora cried, in alarm: 'What's the matter, Miss Mathieson?'

'The matter?' She looked up through the green stars to where the larks sang. The matter was that she could not sing as joyously as that, nor listen like these buds of spring, nor make her eyes soft with the Mother of God compassion that came so naturally to this island girl, this semi-educated hotel waitress. 'There's nothing the matter. Why do you think there is?'

Flora shook her head. 'I thought you'd seen or heard something.'

'Why, is this the island's haunted wood?'

Flora smiled. 'No. The only place they say is haunted is the old priory over on Orsay.'

'Who haunts it?'

'St Orsay himself, they say, carrying a bell. But I've never met anyone who's seen him.'

'Girl,' said Margaret fiercely, holding out her hand, 'we

carry our ghosts about with us. Some of us have seen worse than what the Sneddon boy saw. Didn't you know that?' She turned and rushed on again.

Flora followed, unhappy and anxious. She remembered how, when she, Hector, and their father had been teasing Uncle Angus about the big woman, likening her to a lady wrestler from America or a shot-putter from Russia, her mother had made them stop. She had just said: 'The woman's more to be pitied than laughed at'; that was all, but she had left a mystery. Well, my goodness, Flora had thought, what was disgraceful or shameful about being an old maid, even one six feet tall and stalwart as a caber-tosser? Now she saw that Miss Mathieson hated to be so big and mannish. Like Flora herself, she had dreamed of love, children, a home, and a lad like Hugh. How horrible to be deprived of those not by oneself or anyone human, but by nature itself. It was easy enough to guess what were the ghosts she must carry round with her.

Was it possible to be sure of anyone, even of a person one loved? For Flora, trust had its home in her mother. Now for the first time in her life she doubted, and felt as a consequence parted from her mother, and also from Hugh; it was from love really, represented by those two. She was not completely sure that when her mother heard about the boys' parents, she would not send them away. The little boys themselves surely were innocent, but she would hate them if they caused her to lose faith in her mother.

These thoughts were still bewildering and frightening her when, coming out of the wood, she saw her home in front of her. Never had it looked so beautiful, so peaceful and so familiar; and what gave it its poignant familiarity that morning were the two strange boys. One, the smaller, was in the field beyond the whins with her father and Hector, who were spreading dung. The other was helping her mother to feed the hens in the corner by the house where the apple trees were in blossom. That they were apart from each other seemed to give the scene its air of security. Flora had somehow expected them to be close together, as they had been last night, and as they would always be in her imagination—they on one side, the whole world on the other. Now, astonishingly, they were apart, depending on others for company and happiness, and not on each other; and those others were her father and mother and brother.

She was so relieved and overjoyed that, leaving Miss Mathieson under the gean tree, she ran across the grass into the ploughed field that reeked and stank, right up to Tom, and hugged him. He suffered her politely for a few moments before wriggling his head clear enough to see who she was.

'I'm Tommy,' he said. 'I live here now.'

'And I'm Flora. And I live here too.'

He nodded, but he felt obliged to say: 'I never saw you before.'

Roy, a little jealous, was whimpering and sweeping the ground with his tail. She hugged him too.

'He knows you,' said Tom, as if it was the best proof in the world that she did after all live there.

'Come on, take me to meet your brother.'

Taking his hand, she went with him across the field. Her father and Hector called to her. She waved and called back.

Tom was anxious to assure her about something. 'Johnny never forgets anything,' he said. 'Sometimes when I don't know where I've left my tank he can tell me. Did you know I've got three now? I'm going to have battles.' He glanced up and thought she looked worried. 'It's just in fun. They're no' real tanks.'

Then they were amongst the hens that sidestepped indignantly, displeased at having their breakfast trespassed on. Flora loved them for being themselves, especially when she looked up and saw how her mother had changed.

'There you are, Flora,' said her mother, smiling. 'I see you've met Tom. This is John. He likes birds, so he's offered to look after the hens for me.'

Over the boy's head Flora saw Angus, splendid in his pale blue sweater and fawn twill trousers, meeting Miss Mathieson over by the big white gean tree. He went forward to greet her as if, thought Flora, confused by the blossom and by the imminency of meeting the boy's eyes, she were a bride. And

76

goodness, wasn't the big awkward soul letting herself be thus transformed? Angus, at his most gallant, reached up, broke off some of the flourish, and presented it. At that apocalyptic moment he seemed to his niece to represent a falseness, an evil, that, if not bravely confronted and repelled, would destroy the experiment in love and faith about to be attempted in this tiny green corner of the world where she had been born. Had not Jessie Ogilvie of the school said: 'Mary, he's your brother-in-law, and Flora here's his blood kin; but he's fond of one person only, and you know who that is: himself. Maybe he can't help it; maybe he was born like that; those who knew him as a boy say he was all for himself then too. We all are, of course, to some extent; it's just a matter of differing degrees. With him, though, it's a hundred per cent; it covers him like a fall of snow. I can't help but shiver when he comes near me.'

Nine

Jessie Ogilvie, Master of Arts of Glasgow University, was not
an islander, having been born and brought up in Dumbarton,
on the mainland; but she had been fifteen years on Calisay,
and would have been accepted by the folk there as one of
themselves had she not made it plain that, though at home
among them, she did not wish to belong to their or any
community. Not even the birds—pipits, twites, and even
cuckoos—that she enticed into her garden every summer were
able to claim her wholly, though some would eat from her
hand. As for her pupils, from them she kept a part of her mind
private and aloof. The result was that though they respected
her greatly and were no more afraid of her than the birds were,
still they did not love her. She knew it, for she had deliberately
brought it about; otherwise, she explained to any parent or
foster-parent rash enough to inquire, her pupils would not do
their best work for her. She had known teachers whose
children had loved them so much they hung on their arms in
the public street. In her opinion, any teacher who tried to win
that kind of love was dishonest; it must inevitably prevent her
from disciplining every child impartially and demanding from
it its utmost. The inspectors who came to visit the school
always went away impressed. More than one had hinted to
her that surely if she applied she must be given a post of
responsibility in a large mainland school. But she never
applied.

Some of the men in the hotel bar on a Saturday night were
inclined to connect her dourness with her physical unbrawness;
they liked her, respected her, and even held her in some kind
of fear, but her ugliness vexed them. It was known that she
kept the photograph of a young soldier in an Argyll and
Sutherland uniform on her dressing-table. Elspeth McDonald,
after months of hinting, had asked outright whether this was

the young man she had been going to marry if he had returned alive from the war, twenty years ago. She had got for an answer a silence like a fistful of snow over her face. However, Miss Ogilvie's prominent teeth, thick lips, and bleary eyes behind thick glasses had won for her an eminent friend: the laird's wife, no oil painting either, often visited her. It was known that they discussed birds, but what else was a mystery.

Jessie was going the rounds of her twelve pupils when the gate opened and she, like everyone else in the sunny classroom, down to Chrissie McFadyen, the youngest and smallest, looked up to see Mrs McArthur come into the playground with the two new boys.

'Mind your manners,' she said. 'Sit down and get on with your work.'

They obeyed at once, except Peggy Blair, who sought in anything new the thing she needed to love.

'You too, Peggy.'

Peggy, a girl of ten, sat down, took out her handkerchief, and began, very quietly and privately, to weep. Her classmates, as always, regarded her with wary sympathy. They were sorry for her, they understood what was the matter, but neither they nor anyone else could do anything to help her. Peggy wept like this three times a day at least. It did not last long; half a dozen quiet sniffs, a dab or two of her hankie, perhaps a stray tear, and then it was over; she wouldn't smile after it, but she would put her hankie away and get on with her work. Nellie McKenzie, with whom she was boarded out, quite often came conscientiously to consult the teacher about her. Peggy worried and told lies. She kept saying she had an auntie in Australia who was going to send for her; sometimes she forgot and said Canada instead, or New Zealand. The truth was, as everyone knew, she had no auntie at all. What her origins were none of them knew. They did not know their own; but she was the only one tormented by that ignorance, and so she invented. Her stories varied; but her favourite was that her father and mother had been sailing to Australia to visit her aunt when the ship had sunk in a storm and they had been drowned. When challenged as to why they had not taken

79

her with them she refused to answer; there was really no need to, because her lie impressed them all. It offered an explanation that their imaginations at least could accept for the terrible blank in their lives: their being without parents or relatives to look after them. That mythical liner, indeed, sailed and sank in all their memories.

Jessie was stationed at her desk in front of the class when Mary came in followed by the two boys. The children at once rose and wished the visitors good morning.

The teacher saw at a glance that the younger one was going to be no trouble. He was instantly interested in the other pupils, and even stepped aside to look at what Douglas Munro, who was his own age, was doing in his jotter. His brother was different; he might give trouble, but, like Peggy, only to himself. Jessie liked him on sight, though she felt sure he would not turn out to be much of a scholar. He looked honest, staunch, and slow-witted; if he suffered he would have no refuge. He would not be able to hide and smother his suffering in deep burrows of his mind; again, like Peggy, he would stand out in the sun and show his torment, like a poisoned rabbit.

'Here they are then, Jessie, two more to add to your burden.'

'I do my job, Mary. I carry no burden.' She turned to the boys. 'Well, and what are your names?'

'I'm John Sneddon, miss, and this is Tom, my brother.'

'You're from Glasgow?'

The children tittered. He spoke in such a Glasgow voice; they had too, once, but now theirs were softened with the West Highland lilt.

'Children,' said the teacher, 'meet John and Tom Sneddon, who have come to live with Mrs McArthur. You can tell them your names in the playground.'

'What's her name?' asked Tom, pointing to Chrissie McFadyen, who, with her yellow ringlets, sat in a front seat.

He was interested because she had already put her tongue out at him twice.

The teacher smiled. 'Stand up, Chrissie, and tell him your

name.'

Blushing but pert, Chrissie stotted up, with a clatter of her chair and a tossing of her curls. 'Christina McFadyen,' she said. 'He's *my* brother.' She turned and pointed to Alec, aged nine, who obviously wished she hadn't. He turned crimson.

'Have you got a mother?' asked Tom. It was meant to be a whisper for her alone, but everyone heard. 'A real mother?' He was sure she must have—she seemed to him so different from the girls he had known in the Home; even Jean McDonnell hadn't been so confident.

Chrissie looked at the teacher for permission to reply, but decided to do without it. ' 'Course I got a mother, and a daddy too. And my aunt Bella's over in Jura, and Uncle Archie's in Port Ellen in Islay, and Uncle Peter's in Glasgow.'

Frowning, he nodded. He would have liked to challenge these proud claims, but could not. Looking round, he picked out Peggy Blair as one like himself, without father or mother, uncles or aunts; and Nancy Dewar, too, though she had fair hair like Chrissie; and the thin, freckled girl, who was the biggest in the class.

'All right, Chrissie. Sit down and get on with your work.'

Miss Ogilvie turned to John. 'What are your ages?'

'I'm nine, miss, and Tom's six.'

'What classes were you in in your last school?'

'I was in primary three, miss; Tommy was just started.'

'I did drawing,' piped up Tom. 'Miss Ramage said I was to draw a picture of this place, and she would put it up on the wall. I'm going to draw Roy; that's my dog.'

Those boarded-out children older than he smiled. They were the experienced, the lurkers in cover, the wisely diffident; he was still at the stage of hopping out boldly into the open. Douglas Munro, just six too, watched with wary, sharp eyes; he had been on the island two years and, though happy with his foster-parents, had learned from the other children the advisability, if not the need, of caution and silence. He did not smile.

Nor did Miss Ogilvie. Not with her mouth anyway, and it was hard to see her eyes behind her thick glasses. Tom wasn't

81

sure about her. With his first glance he had thought she would be terrible, worse than the Matron; then he had hoped she mightn't be so bad after all; and now he just didn't know what to think about her. In his uncertainty he was about to take Mrs McArthur's hand, but the teacher didn't let him. She suddenly took hold of him and Johnny, and led them to empty desks, him to one at the front next to Chrissie, and Johnny to one at the back. The rest she ordered to get on with their work. To Tom's surprise and disquiet they all did, even Chrissie. Then she put in front of him a box of crayons and a sheet of black paper. 'Now go on and draw Roy,' said the teacher. He wanted to say he wasn't ready to do it yet, and in any case it was daft trying to draw a black dog on black paper; but he decided it was safer to pick up one of the crayons and look as if he was going to start drawing. He tried to squeeze out a tear of pity for himself, and to turn and look at Johnny. Chrissie across the passage saved him by putting out her tongue again. He forgot about his grief; smiling, he began to draw her; he would make her comic because of her cheek.

Meanwhile Miss Ogilvie was discovering that John was not as advanced in arithmetic as he ought to have been, considering his age. He did not seem to have heard of gills and gallons. She set him to do some sums involving the table of weight; this, he admitted rather vaguely, he knew.

She returned to Mary at the front.

'Maybe we could step outside a minute, Jessie,' the latter whispered, 'if there's anything you want to ask about them.'

'I don't think there's anything, Mary. Their school will send their report cards and medical cards, and of course I know their background already.'

'But there is something, Jessie.'

Jessie looked sharply at her friend. It wasn't like Mary McArthur to be so mysterious and anxious. Had Donald got cold feet already?

'Just as you wish, Mary.'

The class was quiet and busy, and would remain so. By the clock on the wall it was only ten minutes till the interval.

'There's no need for you to put on the kettle this morning, Jean,' she said to the tall, freckled girl with the serious smile whose job it was every morning to run across to the schoolhouse to put the kettle on for the teacher's eleven o'clock cup of tea. 'Roderick,'—This was to the biggest boy, with a fat keen face—'you'll see them out safely at eleven.'

'Yes, miss.'

'You've fairly got them under control, Jessie,' said Mary, as they crossed the grassy playground, slowly, in the warm sunshine.

'Maybe they're all terrified, Mary.'

'No, I'm sure it's not that. I used to be. In my day, as you know, there were three teachers, and the head one, Miss McIntosh, was a tyrant if ever there was one. She'd a great crown of hair that came down to her knees, they said, when she took the pins out. I still can't stand inside that room without shivering.' There was, of course, another reason for that. She was always reminded of Duncan, who had been drowned. Today his place had been occupied by little Nancy Dewar, one of Morag's charges, a sweet-natured little girl whom everyone liked. 'Not a scrap of brains,' was Jessie's grim verdict, but even she was fond of Nancy. Seeing the fair-haired little lass in Duncan's place had sweetened the instant and profound sense of loss.

The kettle was already heating on the hob. Jessie took it through to the kitchen to put it on the paraffin cooker.

'You'll join me in my eleven o'clock cup,' she said.

'Thanks, Jessie.'

Mary never felt quite at ease in the schoolmistress's home. She could never say why, for Jessie was hospitable enough, in her curt Scots way. Her taste, too, was very feminine and up-to-date, for a spinster. Her curtains and carpets, for instance, had the brightest colours of any on the island, except maybe for the big house and the public parts of the hotel. Perhaps it was the stuffed eagle in the little hall. One of the men had caught it in a snare and shot it, because—so he had claimed—it had killed one of his lambs. Jessie had appeared at his door, grim and angry, and had come away carrying the noble golden corpse. Now it stood on a stand in the hall, its wings arched, as if about to soar. It and Jessie, the men said, made a pair; and true enough, dumpy though she was, she did often give the impression of living in an eyrie, and of being impatient to fly off to it, away from the sparrow-like clishmaclavers of ordinary folk who lived on the ground.

'Do you think, Jessie, this is a wise thing Donald and I have done?'

Jessie was setting out the cups; dainty they were, pink and gold. 'It's not for me to offer an opinion on that, Mary.'

'But you've got such a lot of experience with children.'

'I can teach them if they're teachable; that's all.'

'No, there's a lot more to it than that.' But was it right for her to burden Jessie with the horrible thing that Flora had whispered last night, in the byre, when they were milking the cows? It lay in Mary's mind still, raw and bitter; it had kept her awake for hours, and would for weeks; it might leave a scar for life. She had not told Donald, and did not think she ever would. But Jessie, though single, was a woman; moreover, she was the cool, clear-minded expert.

'What is it that's on your mind, Mary?'

'Does it help you, Jessie, in your managing of your pupils, to know something about their backgrounds?'

'It's supposed to.'

'Does it, though?'

'Mary, I know that Chrissie and Alec McFadyen, to take two, live with the parents that gave them birth, and James Buchanan and Andrew Elliot don't. James's mother was a maid in a Glasgow hospital; who his father was, I doubt if she knew herself. Andrew's mother even was never known, for he was found by the police on their doorstep. Well, Chrissie's a sharp little minx, flirting already at the age of five; Alec is a shy numbskull. James is the best scholar in the school; he could easily, if he's given the chance, enter a profession; Andrew's a dreamer; I don't know what he dreams about, but it certainly isn't vulgar fractions and adjective clauses. If I didn't know the backgrounds of those four, Mary, and had been asked to guess, I would have guessed wrongly. And it's the same with the rest. Who would think Roderick McDiarmid and Jean Fairlie were castaways, with not a soul in the world of their own flesh and blood to care for them? So you see, Mary, I do know something of their backgrounds, but I can't say it has helped me much at all. As for these two of yours, if you tell me nothing about them, or if you tell me what is troubling your mind, it will make little difference. I shall take the children as I find them. If there are any discoveries to make, I shall make them myself. One or two of sugar?'

'Two, please. I see what you mean, Jessie, but this is different.'

'If it will ease your mind, Mary, out with it.'

'Yes, Jessie, I think I should.'

So, sipping her tea and nibbling her gingernut biscuit, Mary told. In the midst of it the children came out and began to play in the sunshine. Beyond Jessie's imperturbable grey head she watched them. A group gathered round John and Tom in the corner under the rhododendron that, as high as a tree, was aflame with red flowers. It was Jessie's pride.

When Mary finished there was silence.

'I haven't told Donald yet,' she said, 'and to tell you the truth I don't feel like telling him.'

Jessie still offered no comment.

'He's fond of them already, as we all are; but he can't see them as ordinary children. If they had come out of the sea itself, with a selchie for their mother, he couldn't be more nervous about them.'

'He'll get over it,' said Jessie drily. 'All the men on the island that have children boarded out on them felt it at first; some still do. It's just that a man feels he ought to have been the procreator of any child that sits at his table.'

Mary had to smile. 'You may be right, Jessie. But are not these two bairns rather special?'

'No, they are not. It would have fitted the big woman better to have kept her mouth shut. Is it true Angus had her out on Sanda?'

Mary was surprised by the sharpness with which Jessie had changed the subject.

85

'It seems so,' she answered, cautiously.

'With a spray of gean-flourish in her hand, I hear.'

Could it be, wondered Mary, as Donald sometimes joked, that Jessie really had a fondness for Angus?

'Didn't you warn her, Mary? They say there isn't a serpent on Calisay. They're wrong, while he's here.'

'Och, Jessie, he's maybe a bit insincere whiles, and thinks a wee bit too much of himself, but it doesn't do to exaggerate. He's not the devil you try to make him out to be. Forby, Miss Mathieson's a woman of forty. She's no fool, and physically is well able to protect herself.'

'What about that woman in Glasgow who left him all her money?'

'She was his wife, Jessie.'

'Did you know that? Did Donald? Did anyone? What do you make of a man that doesn't tell his own brother that he's married? I tell you, he's got no right here on Calisay.'

'He was born here.'

'And why does he sneak off to Oban so regularly? Are you sure he hasn't got another well-to-do bedmate hidden away there? Smile if you like, Mary. The man's wicked. He pollutes the air we breathe.'

Well now, Mary wondered, as she took a careful sip of tea, just what did happen in here, Jessie, that night he came to propose? You rejected him, but did you want to?

'What about the boys, Jessie? Do you think I should tell Mr McNeil?'

He was the new minister. He smoked a pipe and told jokes. His predecessor, old Mr McIndoe, had never worn anything but black and would have been as likely to dance a jig in the pulpit as smoke. Fashions changed in religion, as in everything else.

'You'll have to please yourself about that, Mary. I certainly wouldn't advise you to tell his wife.'

'No.' Mrs McNeil, to everyone's astonishment and shame, apparently disapproved of there being so many boarded-out children on the island. Had she known, she was reputed to have said (to Isa McGilvray of the hotel), she would never have agreed to come. What spite she had against the orphans no one quite knew; but everybody surmised that it must have to do with her recent miscarriage and the doctor's verdict that for her to become pregnant again would be dangerous. Yet she had only been married four years. It was rumoured that things at the manse were not as harmonious as they ought to have been; it wasn't expected they would get any better. Angus was quite a frequent visitor there; of course, he attended the church most faithfully, and was easily the best singer in it.

'The fewer who know the better, Mary.'

'I think you're right, Jessie.' She would not tell the minister. At the same time she wondered if Jessie, who had never slept with a man and hadn't even kissed one for nearly twenty years, was able to appreciate the extent and depth of the horror that might be festering in the child's mind.

'Excuse me.' Jessie got up and, going to the window, tapped on it. At once the children trooped back into the school, happily. John had his hand on his brother's shoulder; Roderick McDiarmid had his hand on John's.

As she gazed at the teacher's stocky body in the drab grey dress and cardigan, Mary was surprised to find a warm wave of relief flow into her heart. Jessie might say little, but she was a good ally to have.

'Well, Jessie, I'd better be getting home if there's going to be any lunch for the McArthur family.'

'First you'll go into the school and take your leave.'

'Do you think I should?'

'You're their mother now, Mary. They'll not expect you to walk away and leave them like cans of milk you've delivered.'

'No, that's right.'

As they crossed the playground, Mary could not help asking: 'Do you think it's possible the lad might have it stored in his mind?'

Jessie paused and listened to the birds singing. She could, Mary knew, distinguish each kind by its song. 'It's possible,' she said.

'Is there nothing we can do?'

'We can teach him to tell the difference between a meadow-

87

pipit and a willow-warbler.'

'I'm serious, Jessie.'

Jessie turned on her, quite fiercely. 'What makes you think I'm not, Mary? We have a good life on this island. Make it his life. I know there's Hector. But for all that, it is a good life. Don't be thinking that because we're far from Glasgow and London we don't count. It's us that do count. Remember that.' For a moment she saw the evil that life had placed like a bomb in the child's mind as symbolical of all the massed evil threatening to destroy mankind. She saw no reason why it should not be conquered.

'What have I to complain about?' asked Mary, smiling. 'Am I not getting two in exchange for one?'

'That's it, Mary; that's it exactly.'

When they entered the children all stood, John and Tom with them.

'Sit down,' said the teacher. 'Mrs McArthur is going home now to make your dinner; she has come in to say goodbye. Tom, would you like to show her your drawing of Roy before she goes?'

He scratched his cheek ruefully with chalky fingers. 'It's no' Roy,' he said. 'It's Chrissie.'

The other children smiled; evidently Tom's drawing had been admired by them all. Even Chrissie was amused.

'They warned me,' whispered Mary, 'that I might have trouble with him because he was such a cry-baby. But I haven't found him so.'

'Well, bring it here,' said Jessie.

Tom came out. 'I'll draw Roy later,' he said, 'but no' here; in the hoose.'

'Bless him,' murmured Mary, moved almost to tears. Then she was laughing at the picture of Chrissie, whose fair curls were portrayed as yellow corkscrews. 'It's very good, Tom,' she said.

'I'm no' very good at faces,' he conceded. 'But I can draw tanks.'

Jessie smiled up from the drawing to where John was still struggling with his arithmetic. She did not ask him to come out and show what he had done; it would be very little, she felt sure, and wrong into the bargain. But what was far more valuable than arithmetical accuracy was his utter lack of envy of his brother's triumph. He had glanced up once or twice while the class was laughing, and had smiled himself, in love. Why, though, should he be so watchful, almost like a dog? Well, hadn't he become his brother's guardian three years ago? Yes, but there was more to it than that. The big woman and the Matron had been right. This element of anxiety in his love couldn't altogether be explained by their having been cast together upon the mercies of society; it came from a source unknown to him now, but in time perhaps to be suddenly and disastrously revealed. Stay with us long enough, lad, she vowed, and we shall see to it that when the bandage at last falls away the wound beneath will be found to be healed.

Ten

Not even Todd with his ferret's leer could spoil it. 'Christ, Meg, since you came back from that trip to the wilderness a week ago, there's been a revolution in you. Look at those earrings: bloody chic. And the pearls. And the painted fingernails. Did you know the boss has been complaining about the noise you've been making, singing to yourself? What happened? Did you meet a handsome sailor on the boat?'

She hated Todd, so often had his lecher's eyes looked at her with disrelish, but she was grateful to him then. If she ever had any doubts about the worth and splendour of Angus McArthur, all she needed to do to remove them was to picture him beside her sniggering, grey-faced colleague.

Out visiting, or typing a report in the office, or sitting at home, she kept trying to remember what had happened on Sanda. She would halt in the middle of some tenement stairs, with puddle from a leaky lavatory under her feet, and the air would miraculously thrill with the cries of sea-birds and turn fragrant. Or striding along a crowded pavement she would suddenly find herself tingling all over, from the roots of her hair to the soles of her feet. It was a kind of madness. Her breasts would burn, and she wanted to pull the clothes away from them as he had done, but more violently than he, and see them reflected in these shop windows, gloriously blushing, exotic, like the wild rhododendrons on Calisay. Her nipples, which he had so tenderly caressed, comparing them to the sea-pinks round them in thousands, were in her own recollection like the butterfly that had hovered over them in the grassy hollow among the sand dunes; purple its wings had been, incredibly beautiful, but not any more so than his hand which remembrance broke into magnificent wild confusion like the kittiwakes and guillemots about the great cliffs—had fondled her where she had never dreamt any male hand could ever be.

She was not sure what had really happened: she on her back and he above her, white clouds in the blue sky beyond his white moustache and blue eyes; confusion then, and confusion now in recollection; and mingled with it all that experience of twenty years ago, in her parents' house, in the sitting-room in front of the gas fire on the white sheepskin rug, her partner the young soldier as inexpert as she. She was convinced now, though for years she had wondered, that there had been no consummation then. Had there been on Sanda? He had whispered, among so many other things, that there was no hurry. She had lain back, stricken. Afterwards she had found both fists full of sand and grass. But there had been ecstasy; not only her body and Angus's were ingredients, but the sea, the clouds, the flowers, the butterfly, and the blue sky; these were remembered with a clarity that made all the more wonderful this haze of rapture at the centre. Unlike Helen Montgomerie, she was now a woman who had attained the highest point of maturity. Even bearing a child could take her no higher.

What Helen had often hinted, and what Margaret herself had agreed with, about the universality and so the cheapness and degradation of the act, was now seen to be a jealous old maid's absurdity. That sluts achieved it, and drunken slobbering brutes, and hippopotami, and rats, could not take from it its grandeur and mystery. She would tell Helen, some day, that to be made love to by a man she loved was the only way for any woman to be able to gather all the many threads of her being into a glorious unity and fulfilment. Poor Helen! She was composed of many fine but irreconcilable strands.

Do I love Angus? Is it possible so soon? Does he love me? She threw these questions into the depth of her mind only to enjoy the ripples of delight and surmise that spread throughout her whole being. In a fortnight he was coming to Greenock, to see his nephew Hector on to the liner for Canada; then he would come to Glasgow. The date was already circled in all her calendars. 'I might ring you up,' he had said, with a smile. 'Please do,' she had replied, but her heart had been thumping then, and she knew that not this

Saturday but the next she would wait all day for the telephone to ring, her hands like gulls fluttering about it. She would invite him to her flat. Would she, though, ask him to stay the night? The following day being Sunday the place would be quiet, and he could be easily smuggled away without her neighbours being any the wiser. But what difference did it make if they, and all Glasgow, knew? They loved each other, and in time he would ask her to marry him and she would consent. Oh yes, she would, as it were, walk hand in hand with him to the edge of those dizzy cliffs and shout to the sunlit sea Yes! Yes! Yes! a hundred thousand times, so that her cries would be about her like the whirling birds.

After marriage, how happily they would live! On Calisay, during the summer; in her flat, during the winter. Their combined savings, with his pension, should keep them comfortably. They could afford a trip to some of the far-off countries he had so vividly described to her. They might have a child. Perhaps this unease in her was partly caused by conception. At forty-one she was not too old. Few wombs were riper. She hoped it would be a boy; but if it were a girl, let it be of ordinary size, all its life.

*   *   *

One morning, several days after her return from Calisay, she was in the office when the telephone rang. It was Helen again; this was the fifth time. Previously Margaret had cut her short, merely saying that the boys had been safely delivered, and she was sure they were going to be very happy once they had settled down. What else really was there to say about them? In her own excited state of expectancy she had not wanted to listen to Helen's rather barren inquiries. This time, however, she felt secure and fertile enough in her own hopes to risk prolonging the conversation. She felt, indeed, like a spiritualist medium, with Helen one of the bereaved seeking her intermediation with the dead.

'Yes, I know, Helen,' she said. 'I did promise, and I really must come out to see you one of these days. But you know how it is; work keeps piling up.'

'You can say that again, Meg,' muttered Bob Lawther, another colleague, who was working at a report in a corner. Margaret was glad he was there. She liked him, but he would also prevent her from saying anything indiscreet about Angus.

'What's happened to you, Margaret?' asked Helen plaintively. 'You seem to have changed. What have I done?'

'Nothing, Helen. Don't be silly.'

'It's not a laughing matter. You must come and tell me about him. For God's sake, don't you understand I loved that child as if he was my own? When I let him go—you must have noticed—it was as if I was standing at his graveside.'

No, Helen, on the contrary, you looked assured and cool, as you always do. Good God, though, is she actually weeping? Is it genuine, or part of some act I don't quite understand?

'You have lots of children left, Helen,' she said, gently.

'There always are when one dies. Does it console the mother? I've written to Calisay. It was like dropping a flower on his grave.'

'This is awfully morbid, you know, Helen. Let's keep our heads, shall we? He's a nice little chap, but nothing out of the ordinary, even taking into consideration his rather peculiar background.'

'Is that all the comfort you can give me?'

'Excuse me butting in, Meg,' said Lawther. 'Is that old Monty at the Home? Is she pestering you about some kid she's had to give up? Thought so. She's always at it. Bill McAry had a lot of trouble with her about two years ago. She damn near accused him of abducting the kid.'

Yet, thought Margaret, the fact that Helen has loved other children hardly discredits her love for this one.

Lawther got up, collected his papers, picked up his hat and left.

'Comfort, Helen?' she said, as tenderly as she could. 'I'm afraid there's precious little of that in our job. But I'm very sorry. What more can I say?'

'You can come out and talk to me about him. After all, you promised you would. There's no need to do it during working

93

hours if you're so hard pressed. You know I would be pleased to see you any evening.'

Margaret frowned. She could not look forward to such a conversation. Helen, she had to admit, was something of a hypocrite where her children were concerned, and now looked like becoming a bore as well. She was spiteful, too, and not above trying to use her influence with members of the Committee to spoil someone's chances of promotion if she didn't approve of him or her. Was it possible, thought Margaret, with flickers of hate, that I used to be afraid I was in danger of falling into a homosexual love for this soft-faced, splay-footed tyrant?

'Perhaps I ought to tell you, Helen,' she said, taking herself by surprise, 'that I may be getting married soon.'

She had no idea what Helen's reaction would be, but she certainly didn't expect this long hiss of disgust, and these contemptuous cackles. For an instant her own faith faltered; but then she pictured that butterfly again, and felt the gentle, strong, revivifying hand.

'Who is she, Margaret?'

Margaret turned cold. She felt no longer human. In the old superstitious days, Angus had said, people had believed that seal-women had frequented the caves at the foot of the great cliffs. She felt as if she had been changed to one of those.

'She?' she whispered.

'Don't be so coy. You know what I mean. They all say it about you, don't they? Ask Agnes, our kitchen-maid.'

Though within all was aslither, she tried to keep her voice reasonable: 'Am I to be insulted by your kitchen-maid, Helen? Do you allow your servants to insult me?'

'I didn't allow her. I just overheard her. You must have overheard such things yourself, Margaret, many a time.'

Yes, spoken by Glasgow voices like Agnes's, rough and good-humoured. She had been crucified by them.

'We are all victims of spite, Margaret. It only becomes unendurable when nature is the culprit. What reply can we possibly have?'

'Goodbye, Helen,' she whispered, and put down the

receiver.

For a minute or so she sat with eyes closed and mind arrested. Then, with trembling fingers, she took out her new compact. In its mirror she examined her face; it was, in its own way, intelligent, handsome, and even distinguished. But was that way womanly? Her skin was smooth and no hairier than Helen's. Her teeth were not large, though she remembered her father saying once: 'For goodness' sake, Margaret, don't chew like a navvy.' The ear-rings and pearls, too, were not ridiculous. Yet, even as she gathered these evidences of femininity, she felt threatened by unseen, impalpable, and impartial forces that were preparing to touch certain vital and secret places of her being, and so reduce her once more to the pathetic monster that Agnes the kitchen-maid, and Todd, and Helen, and so many others, thought her to be.

Then, shyly, she recalled the ecstasy on Sanda. Blushing and sweating, she felt it again.

The telephone rang. She wanted not to pick it up in case it might be Helen, with more disloyalty. But it was a police sergeant to tell her that Jean Gilmour, a girl of thirteen who was at present Margaret's responsibility, needed help again.

'What is it this time, sergeant?'

'Oh, nothing new. Her mother's been away for three days, with the latest fancy man. The girl's been living alone. She's not been going to school. The headmaster phoned us.'

'She's at the station?'

'Aye, she's here, making eyes at us all. If something isn't done soon, she'll be her mother all over again. But I don't see what can be done, except take her away altogether.'

'I'll be with you in ten minutes, sergeant.'

As she put down the telephone it occurred to her for the first time that what she had said to Helen about getting married had been a lie. Now, confronted by the reality of Jean Gilmour, who took sex like toffee, she had to admit that she had been romancing. Angus might not come to Glasgow as he had promised; or, worse, he might come but not bother to get in touch with her. What she had to give might have seemed to him not worth the patience and effort. So handsome and dignified a man could take his choice of women, and surely he would choose smaller, daintier, less equivocal ones than her? She must not, like Helen, start writing to the island. All she could do was wait and hope; but if he did come she must take every care that he enjoyed his visit. The transformation Todd had sneered at must be carried further. She must buy nightdresses. She could not walk on high heels, which in any case would make her taller than ever; but she could throw away her thick-soled, thick-tongued brogues and buy a pair of Italian shoes, the elegance of which would conceal the hugeness of her feet. If she was ever going to be a bride, she must at least look as if she thought it possible.

As she was about to leave the office the telephone rang. She decided to let one of the clerks in the other office answer it. But as she was going down the stairs Miss Simpson came crying after her: 'It's for you, Miss Mathieson. I thought I would just catch you.'

'Oh, all right. Thanks, Annie.'

'I think it's Miss Montgomerie, you know, from Gilbert held Home.' Then the clerk hurried to rejoin her companions in their own office. Margaret got on quite well with them, but she knew they giggled at her behind her back.

She snatched up the telephone. 'Miss Mathieson, Child Care, speaking,' she said. A moment later she frowned: this was her old, brusque, mannish manner, now renounced. 'Miss Mathieson,' she added, more softly.

'Is that you, Margaret?'

The voice was not only contrite, it was weary and hoarse with sobbing. More sobs were heard, harsh and sore. 'I want to say how sorry I am. I should never have said such cruel things. Please forgive me.'

Margaret's mouth tightened. Cruel things, yes; but, Helen, you still think them true. Why should I forgive what you so maliciously uttered, what you so obviously have been nursing for weeks, perhaps months or even years? Then, picturing Helen ugly with sobbing, she had a vision of all the many women like her, unloved, unmarried, and inescapably alone. Only a week or so ago she herself had been one of them;

perhaps in another week she would be one of them again.

'I can understand if you don't feel like forgiving me, Margaret. But it was my unhappiness that spoke. Unhappiness is never generous. You are right, too; I never really loved the boy. He represented something; God knows what, but it was, and still is, necessary to me.' She paused for almost half a minute, controlling herself. When she spoke again her voice was much calmer: 'I've no right to trouble you or anyone else with my obsessions. Let me, with sincerity, wish you and your betrothed every happiness. No doubt you will want the wedding to be quiet, but I should be pleased to know at least that it had taken place, so that I could send you some little reminder of our friendship.'

'I don't know when it will take place.'

'You are right to have kept it secret. Look what happens when one trusts.'

'All right, Helen. But I'm afraid I'll have to go. I was on my way out when you phoned. I had to be called back.'

'Good-bye, Margaret. You do forgive me?'

'Of course.'

But as she hurried downstairs and got into her car and drove through the traffic to the South Side police-station, she found that forgiveness smarting. Helen had pulled out the barb, but the laceration was still there. Only Angus now could heal it.

Eleven

Holiday-makers entering her shop, with its amusing variety of stock from fish-hooks to face powder, took Janet Lindsay to be one of the most interestingly primitive of the island women. Not only was she as brown-faced as an Italian peasant, with thin, muscular arms and hands that were seldom idle, but she was also as cautious with her words and smiles as with her scales and change. Even as a girl she must have been far from bonny, with her long face and the slight cast in her left eye. Now, flat-chested and skinny-hipped, she looked rather more than her barren forty-six years; but, being kind-hearted in her own peculiar, reticent way, she was well enough liked. Most folk, however, were now and then annoyed by her solemnity, and especially by her habit of listening to a joke or an amusing story about a neighbour with much patience but little appreciation. Only when the talk grew serious again could she take part in it, and even then she was canny with her words, trite though they were. It was thought her never having had a child had helped to make her so slow to laugh.

The odd thing was that Neil, her man, was a frequent and ready laugher. Big-bellied, with a large backside, he was much liked for his easy-oasy good nature; even his laziness was approved, as showing a more proper attitude towards the making of money. It was admitted that if he were left to manage the shop, it would fail in a couple of months; in his wife's firm hands it flourished. Yet, though it was obviously to the island's advantage to have a well-run, well-stocked shop, the indulgence shown towards Neil's incompetence was more spontaneous than the gratitude expressed for Janet's good management. He knew instinctively that the right way to live on Calisay was to be like a piece of sea-wrack that, in some shallow sunlit pool, was moved to and fro by the tide with infinite variations of slow grace. His wife, on the contrary, with her dour, pestering seriousness, was more like the Corryvreckan itself—the great whirlpool off Jura that could suck a fair-sized boat down into its depths. It was often wondered whether she blamed him for their having no family; that would of course be unfair, but if a woman was reckless enough to blame God Himself for so fundamental a deprivation, there was little wonder if she took it out on her man, as the Almighty's nearest male representative.

Two and a half years ago they had come from Glasgow. There Neil had been a joiner, but when an aunt of Janet's had left her a little money they had bought the shop on Calisay. That astonishing step, it appeared, had been a joint inspiration. Nobody doubted they were happy together, for all she laughed so seldom and he so often.

*   *   *

On the same Saturday morning that Hector McArthur was being seen on board the liner *Carinthia* at Greenock by his uncle Angus, Janet was discussing him with two women customers, Nelly McKenzie and Elspeth McDonald. He had left with the steamer very early on Friday morning, and the night before in the community hall a farewell party had been held. The two new boys had been present, and Hugh McEachern, Flora's young man over from Islay. To everyone's amazement Mary McArthur had broken down and wept. It had hardly been thought that she, respected for her resolution and intelligence, would shed tears even in private; that she would grieve and suffer was, of course, taken for granted, but not publicly, like yon, with her son's misery and guilt public too. If Mary had believed that taking in the two brothers would soften the pain of Hector's loss, she had been wrong; indeed, many got the idea that the sight of the two little laddies, looking so timid and somehow so out of place, had made her feel all the more desolate. Some had even whispered that she and Donald were minded to give them back. There was Flora, too, going to marry next spring, if not earlier. Still, those sorrows were customary for mothers; others on the island had

99

borne them in the past; it was disquieting that Mary, one of the staunchest, should have let herself be overcome by them so distressingly. Was it a sign, as many feared, that the old way of life on Calisay was coming to an end? That very soon the loved island would be like Orsay, given over to ruins and ghosts?

'I understand,' said Janet, 'that Mary's never forgotten her brother Duncan, who was drowned.'

'But that must have been over forty years ago,' said Nelly, a plump, conscientious woman who wore a smile all the time, in preparedness and propitiation. She, too, like Janet, had never had a child of her own. She doted on Peggy Blair, boarded out on her.

'Aye, Nelly,' said Elspeth, 'but the sea that took him is still there.'

'It always will be, Elspeth,' said Nelly, with a giggle.

'It will, Nelly, when there are none of us left to fear it.'

'How did it happen?' asked Janet. 'Did he fall off a cliff?'

'He was climbing for eggs on the Stacks. He shouldn't have been, for he was too young: just about the age of the older of the two Mary's got now. He was daring, climbed higher than he should, lost his grip, and dropped like a gannet into the sea. When they got him out he was dead. He had an egg in his fist. They say it wasn't broken.'

'Was he like Hector—in looks, I mean?' asked Janet.

'Nothing like him. Duncan was fair, like Mary herself. Hector and Flora are both dark, after Donald's side.'

'It's hard to believe,' said Nelly, 'that Angus was ever dark; now he's as silver as a duke.'

'As a shark, you mean, Nelly. During the war, he took to wearing a beard; it was as black as the deil's.'

'The right colour, some would say,' said Nelly, with another giggle.

Elspeth nodded grimly. 'You know my opinion. If he was to emigrate, not just to Canada but to the South Pole, I'm one would dance with joy.'

Nelly laughed at the idea of Elspeth dancing; even Janet smiled.

'You've always disliked him, Elspeth,' said the latter.

'Always. Even at school. Then too he was full of conceit. So was his father before him. So have all the McArthurs been, on the male side, anyway. Even Donald's not altogether clear of it.'

'What man is?' asked Janet.

'True enough. But it's not just Angus's conceit; it's his badness. When he looks at me I feel as if I'd stepped into icy water.'

'That's what Jessie Ogilvie says too,' said Janet.

'Don't you say it, Janet?'

'No. I often get holiday folk in here. He's the one they inquire about most. They take him for the laird. Whatever you say, you must agree he's a very handsome man.'

'His money won't last long,' said Nelly, cautiously, 'the way he spends it: drinks in the hotel lounge, and often dinner. They tell me he entertains some of the lady guests to dinner.'

'Like the big woman that brought the two boys,' said Janet. 'He got up at five o'clock to see her off.'

'And the day before he had her out at Sanda in his motor boat,' said Nelly. 'Well, as my Hamish said, she was one able to look after herself.'

'The man's vile,' said Elspeth, picking up her basket. 'It demeans us to speak about him. Well, Janet, that'll be all for now. Will we be seeing you at the hall tonight?'

At the hall that Saturday night, under the auspices of the Islands and Highlands Film Guild, was showing what the islanders liked best, a Western film. Everyone able would be there, including the laird and his wife.

'I'll be there, Elspeth. As you know, I miss the pictures.'

She saw her customers to the door. Coming up the path between the fuchsias were two small boys. They were Mary McArthur's charges; the black dog Roy was with them. The elder carried a basket. Before they realised that the three women were looking at them they were laughing eagerly together, and the dog, barking, was in the joke too.

'Poor wee lads,' said Nelly, softly.

Elspeth nodded, but she felt apprehensive, as she did in

101

Angus's presence. Unlike him, the boys were innocent; but they had been chosen—by whom was not for her to say—to represent what she knew to be a danger to her, to her family, and to every living soul on the island. Their source was not known. Everything about them therefore—their smallness, their dependence, their very sweetness—was shadowed with menace. She had tried to overcome this premonition before, and now she tried again.

'Jessie tells me better-mannered boys never entered her school,' she said.

'They came from a Home,' said Janet. 'They would have to have good manners there.'

'There's that, Janet; but I think it's in their natures too.'

The boys, now quiet and shy, approached. They were, Elspeth saw, much healthier-looking than they had been three weeks ago when they had arrived. The sunshine and the fresh air of the island had done them good already. Also, in spite of Mary's break-down on Thursday night, they looked more confident, as if, though lacking a known source, they nevertheless had found a sure resting-place. She could not think of it as a home; this, it seemed prophetically to her, they never could find.

'Well,' she said, 'and how do you like Calisay?'

'We like it very much,' replied John.

Tom merely nodded; he looked as if he thought he'd answered that question too often already.

'Better than where you came from?'

They noticed that he hesitated.

'You would have friends there,' said Nelly, kindly.

He nodded. 'But it's better here.'

'There was no dog there,' said Tom, his hand on Roy's head.

'And how are you liking the school?' asked Elspeth. She had been told by her own two foster-children that John Sneddon was quite a dunce.

'I like it.'

'Miss Ogilvie's a real terror, isn't she?'

He shook his head. He wasn't afraid of Miss Ogilvie. With

great patience she had shown him how to do sums that he had never understood before. That small revelation had given him faith that there would be more, and not only connected with lessons.

'Well, here's a sweetie for you, and one for your brother.'

They took them with thanks. Tom looked astonished; he hadn't expected her sharpness to be followed by this kindness. He resolved that, though it wasn't a very big sweetie, he would give Roy a share when she was out of sight.

Nelly patted them both on the head. 'Now Hector's gone, you'll have to take his place.'

At once Tom pouted; tears sprang into his eyes. 'We didna want him to go, did we, Roy?'

Roy licked his hand.

Elspeth looked over his head at the other two women, and grimly nodded. It was obvious that she saw in those tears confirmation, but of what neither of them could tell. Elspeth in her own way was as mysterious as Angus McArthur; indeed, in Nelly's opinion, far more so. But who could blame her for sniffing evil and misfortune in a wild-rose bush? Her two brothers had been killed in the war, and in times of peace her daughter, Elspeth, too, and her son, William, had died. Her other son, James, was in Australia, and never wrote.

When Elspeth and Nelly had gone, Janet turned to the two boys. Though she looked stern, she had a great desire to go down on her knees and hug them both. It had always been a girl she had wanted, but a boy would have done, especially if he had been like John, with the shy happy eyes and the ready smile.

'You'll have to keep the dog outside,' she said. 'No dogs allowed in the shop.'

'He'll sit quiet and touch nothing,' said Tom.

'No.'

'All right. I'll tell him.' He did so, ruefully. 'I don't need to tie him. He'll no' run away. If I tell him to wait, he'll wait. He does what I tell him, doesn't he, Johnny?'

The familiar, well-loved Glasgow accent had her digging her nails into the palms of her hands. There were times, as she told Neil, when she felt she was an exile in India or some such far-off country. To hide her emotion she turned to gaze down at the jetty. 'I didn't see you yesterday when Hector was leaving.'

'It was too early,' said Tom, but it was obvious he was communicating adult opinion, which he had to accept though he thought little of it. 'Look what he left me.' Proudly he brought a whistle out of his pocket. He blew it, and Roy yelped rather dismally, remembering Hector.

'Did old Dugald play the pipes?' asked John.

'He did.' There had been no keeping the old man away, though some thought that with his kilt full of holes and daubed with sharn he spoiled the sadness of those partings. But everybody agreed that he was still a good player. There had hardly been a dry eye on the jetty when the motor boat was taking Hector and Angus out to the steamer. Flora had cried as if to break her heart; her sweetheart Hugh had found that armful of grief precious, but awkward to console in public. Dugald had played his own tune, 'Farewell to Calisay.'

'He's teaching Johnny,' said Tom.

'To play the pipes?'

John nodded. She noticed that his fingers danced on the handle of the basket.

'He says Johnny will be a good player; better than Bobby McDiarmid.' He blew out his cheeks to imitate Bobby, and then laughed. 'Bobby's got a book about tanks. It's got lots of pictures. He's going to lend it to me if I keep it clean.'

Suddenly she felt strange. Her body ached. It was as if all the love accumulated in her for the children she should have had was straining to burst out. Again she had to look away, towards the sky this time, where larks sang.

'Well, I suppose you came for something, not just to blether to me?'

'A pound of sugar, a packet of tea, and some hairpins for Flora,' said Tom promptly.

They went into the cool shady shop with its various pleasant smells. Roy stayed outside, occasionally whimpering.

'In this Home you were in, in Glasgow,' she asked, 'there

would be lots of other boys?'

'About twenty,' said John.

'No' counting the babies,' added Tom.

'Were there babies?'

They both nodded.

'How old were they?'

'Different ages,' said John. 'Some were just days old. The police brought them. They were found.'

'I see. Found where?'

'Well, Agnes said—'

'Who was she?'

'The maid at the Home.'

'She had no right to be speaking to you children about such things; but what did she say?'

'She said one was left in a tramcar.'

'And one in Lewis's,' cried Tom. 'Do you know Lewis's? It's the biggest shop in Glasgow.'

'I know it well.' She paused, remembering the happy Saturday afternoons when she and Neil had gone shopping in the great store. She had liked being among the crowds, listening to their Glasgow talk. She had learned some Gaelic during her two years on Calisay, but she never used it; a customer would order in that language, she would answer in her Glasgow English. 'Sometimes I call this shop the Lewis's of Calisay.'

Tom looked round, with a polite frown. 'There's only one shop,' he said. 'In Glasgow there are millions.'

'I know. But, you see, there's a big variety of things in here. You can buy things here you couldn't in Lewis's. That peat-spade, for instance; and those tins of cow-medicine. Were there any girls in your Home?'

Before they could answer the door opened, and in came two of the hotel guests. They were English, and white-haired. The man wore khaki shorts and his wife a long tartan skirt. They made a fuss about pushing in before the boys, but Janet rather curtly told them it was all right, they were children of friends of hers and she wanted to speak to them. So the visitors bought tobacco, chocolate and biscuits. They were, they said,

105

about to walk across the strand to Orsay, to visit the priory.

'I hope you've inquired about the tide? It can be dangerous.'

'Oh yes. Mr McGilvray found out for us. We've got a clear hour and a half on Orsay. Gives an added zest, in a way, to feel it's a race with the tide.'

'We think,' said the woman at the door, 'that Calisay must be about the most heavenly spot in the whole world. Children brought up here are wonderfully lucky.'

Janet nodded. 'It's bonny enough.'

About to leave, the man glanced at the two boys. John was looking at the merchandise on the shelves, Tom was running his tank along the floor.

'I understand,' whispered the Englishman, 'most of the kids we see about the place are orphans from Glasgow.'

Janet said nothing, but stared as if she thought it was none of his business.

'It's a grand idea,' he said with enthusiasm. 'It helps to arrest the depopulation, and of course, as my wife has said, it's wonderful for the children themselves.'

'You may be right. I think they'd prefer the dirtiest back court in the Gorbals or Anderston, if they could have their own mothers to look after them.'

In instant but startled agreement, they took their leave. She watched them stride out. As they crossed the strand, splashing through the pools and squelching over the seaweed, they would perhaps consider what she had said to them. It was a truth that, like their race with the tide, should lend more interest to the ruins of the priory. When they looked at the slabs with the effigies of knights in armour, or through the cracks at the peaceful skeletons, they would remember the motherless children. In this sunlight they would hardly see St Orsay himself, but there was enough of a breeze for them to hear his bell.

She turned again to the brothers. 'Well, were there? Any girls, I mean.'

'Just the same as the boys,' said John. 'About twenty.'

'I thought it would be all boys.' She controlled her eagerness. 'What ages? Were there any your own age?'

That age, about nine, was, she had decided, the best for adoption, in her case anyway. She was too old to be very good at napkin-changing, bottle-feeding and pram-pushing. A child between two and eight was too young to understand the peculiar relationship between it and its parents-in-law. If, deceived into thinking they were its natural parents, it would have the blow of disillusionment in store for it for many years. But at nine a child could be made, without forcing its mind too much, to understand and accept. Moreover, at that age its future nature was surely conjecturable. What she dreaded most was to adopt and love a child, and then see it turn bad. Isa McGilvray was for ever warning her that this often happened. She had not been hard to convince, because she was always mindful that thieves, prostitutes and murderers had all at one time been children.

'Two or three,' said John.

'Tell me about them. Choose the one you liked best.'

'Jean McDonnell.'

'That's right,' added his brother, from the floor. 'Jean was the best.'

Janet felt her heart miss beats. She felt as if this unknown little girl was hers to take or reject. She put the last consideration first. 'Was she bonny? Like Nancy Dewar?'

John shook his head. 'No, but—'

'But what?' She saw that tears weren't far away. 'Maybe you think she had more spirit than Nancy?'

Again he nodded. Suddenly he hid his face with his hand.

Tom did not notice. 'Jean gave us some daffies,' he said, laughing, 'when we were leaving. She stole them. But they were all withered.'

'Stole them? Is she a thief, then?' She was too quick with the word. It told her something about herself: she could never get it out of her mind that the Home these children had come from wasn't the same as a reformatory. Being abandoned by their parents, in many cases from birth, was scarcely their fault, as stealing would have been; yet, in her mind as in Elspeth's, and, she was inclined to think, in everyone's, they seemed to lie under some kind of guilt. The truth was surely

107

that this guilt was universal; every human being shared it.

'She's not a thief,' cried John. 'She didn't steal them.'

Tom looked up in astonishment. 'She pu'd them, Johnny, and Matron said we hadn't to pu' them.'

'She was disobedient, then,' said Janet.

'They were withered,' muttered John.

'That's what I said,' cried Tom. 'But she took them.'

John went right up to the counter in his determination to explain. 'There were lots of daffodils all over the grounds, but especially among the trees. Jean had her ain tree. All the daffodils round it were hers. We all said it.'

'But Matron never said it, Johnny.'

'Everybody knew it. Everybody ca'd it Jean's place.'

'That's true, Johnny. But Matron never said it.'

'You see, Mrs Lindsay, when we were leaving Jean had nothing to gie us, so she pu'd some of her daffodils and gave them to us, just when we were going in the car. They all saw her. Matron was there. So was Miss Mathieson. Miss Mathieson said she must be a kind girl, and so she is.'

'But after she gave us them, Johnny, she ran away. She was frightened of Matron.'

'No, she wasn't. She wasn't frightened of anybody.'

Calmly, in contrast to his brother's agitation, Tom considered that tremendous claim. He himself at the Home had been afraid of so many things. He shuddered to remember them now. At last he said, in wonder: 'No, she wasn't frightened at a'. Remember, she fought the big boys outside.'

'Was she quarrelsome, too?' asked Janet.

'No, no,' cried John. 'Let me tell you. We were going back to the Home one day from the school. Some big boys stopped us. They called us names.'

She nodded; there was no need to ask what names. Yet those boys, those bullies, were to be pitied too; punished, aye, and sorely, but in the end pitied.

'Then they kicked Jim Murgatroyd and made him cry.'

'He was always crying,' added Tom.

'It was Jean stopped them.'

'But she got the worst of it, Johnny.'

'Her mouth was bleeding, and her ear was swollen.'

'But she didna cry.'

'I never saw her cry.'

'I did, Johnny. Once. It was the day before we left. She came up behind me and put her hands over my eyes. "Guess who?" she said. I knew it was her, and when she took her hands away I saw she was crying. Not much; just a wee bit. She ran away. Maybe she went to her tree and cried some more. I don't know. One of her laces was loose. She was the best in the Home at climbing trees. Wasn't she, Johnny?'

'She would have liked it here.'

'You think so?' asked Janet, her voice very dry.

He nodded. 'She liked adventures. She would go into all the caves.' It was Jean who had led the expedition over the wall into the field where the peewits' nests were; and she it was who had been so angry with him for breaking the egg.

Janet tried to remind herself they were talking about a little girl whom she had never seen and most likely never would see; but she continued to be agitated by a great hope. Her voice, though, was drier than ever when she said: 'Why was she in the Home?'

Tom at once looked guilty and miserable. He stuffed his tank into his pocket, and going over to the door pressed his nose against the glass. Outside Roy barked.

'She hadn't any people,' said John.

'I know that. That wasn't what I meant. I meant, why didn't anyone take her? Mr and Mrs McArthur have taken you two, and Mrs McDonald has taken James Buchanan and Andrew Elliot. Why wasn't she taken? Was it because she was always getting into trouble, disobedient and untidy? From what you've told me she was all those; and not very pretty into the bargain.'

'Somebody did take her, twice.'

'What happened? Was she sent back because she gave trouble?'

'No. The first time the people weren't kind to her; the second time her mother—the woman she was staying with—died. Jean ca'd her her mother.'

'Did she know who her real mother was?'

'No.'

'Ours is deid,' muttered Tom, still at the door.

'So she's been unlucky, this Jean?'

'That's what Agnes said. She said we were all unlucky, but Jean was the most unlucky.'

'I don't see that. If what you've said is true she's got a lot to be thankful for. She's got pluck, hasn't she? And she's got a good heart. Maybe she's not so unlucky after all. You'll not have a photograph of her?'

'No.'

'But you have,' muttered Tom. 'You've got the picture wi' us all in it.'

'That's right.' He smiled at being reminded of so cherished a possession. 'It's just the size of a postcard.'

'Is she in it, this Jean—whatever her name is?'

'McDonnell. Yes, she's in it.'

'She's at the front,' said Tom. 'Matron's in it as well. Agnes wanted to come in but Matron wouldn't let her.'

'I'd like to see it.'

'We're going in the motor boat this afternoon wi' Uncle Donald and Hugh,' said Tom.

'Any time will do. There's no hurry. Why do you think I would be in such a great hurry to see the picture of a girl I don't know, and whom I'm never likely to know? Next time you're here for messages will be soon enough. Or if you happen to be at the hall tonight to see the film, and if you happen to remember to bring it, then you could lend it to me. But there's no hurry.'

It would have to be thought about a great deal. Neil would have to be consulted, and made to think seriously about it. Too often he just laughed and said: 'Please yourself, Janet.' Isa's advice would have to be sought, and perhaps Mrs McNeil's, the minister's wife. The latter, Janet knew, was opposed to adoption, but for different reasons than Isa. A woman needed the children she cared for to be her husband's; she didn't just prefer it, it was a necessity. It had been a peculiarly embarrassing statement, uttered with a shrill

110

laughter close to hysterical weeping. Neither Isa nor Janet had commented on it, but afterwards, walking home, they had, without saying anything direct, let each other know that they knew very well what Sheila McNeil had meant. If there were never to be children, if the womb was irremediably barren, then to a certain kind of woman love-making, even in a lawful bed, must be without sanction, dignity or joy.

After the boys were gone, and she was waiting for Neil to return from his delivery round, she kept imagining the girl until soon she could almost see her, in the shop, outside, and in the house at the back. Once she even caught herself talking to her. Grim-mouthed, she said: 'Janet Lindsay, you're a fool. If you're not careful you'll become a silly auld wife greeting for the moon. Whatever faults Neil Lindsay may have, he doesn't deserve that.' Yet, as she set her mouth in a determination to allow only sanity into her mind, there came to her a vision of the Hangman's Rock, the famous strange projection with a hole in it through which in the old days the rope had been threaded to hang rebels, outlaws, and thieves, in sight of Orsay, which had been a sanctuary and where they would have been safe. She did not know why she should have recalled it then, so vividly. The only time she had climbed up to it it had been the view—of the strand, of green Orsay, and of mountainous Jura—that had attracted her; or so at least she had believed.

What I need, she realised, is someone with whom to communicate. I am too lonely. Neil, good man though he is, will not do; neither will Isa; nor anyone else. Only the child, or children, that she would never have, would have released the sunshine hidden behind the clouds of her nature. Would an adopted child be an adequate substitute? This little girl, Jean McDonnell, for instance, with her tree, daffodils, loose lace, and generous heart?

Twelve

By Saturday Angus had not written, and so Margaret did not know whether he was coming or not. She could not risk the disaster of missing him, and therefore that morning, neglecting her work and lying to her colleagues, she hurried to the Central Station shortly after eleven, where she waited for each train from Greenock. By one o'clock there had been four, but among their passengers no Angus. What terrified her as much as the fear of losing him was the revulsion against ordinary humanity that kept growing in her, until it seemed that her mind was as vast and clamorous with it as the great, sooty-ceilinged station. The girl who sold her the cup of tea and the cheese sandwich; the ticket-collectors who did not collect Angus's; the taxi-drivers who joked among themselves about her; the bow-legged, grey-haired porter who good-humouredly shouted 'Oot o' my wey, hen!' as he trundled his iron-wheeled trolley almost over her toes; and all those passengers from Greenock, Port-Glasgow and Paisley: every one of them was commonplace, so imprisoned in their ordinariness, that they seemed united in a conspiracy to make impossible, as utterly contrary to their own dreary nature, the appearance among them of a handsome and dignified man who, with his love and compassion, would save her. That was the extent of the miracle she prayed for: he could not make her smaller or daintier, but he could perhaps, if he loved her patiently and generously, remove all the innumerable gaucheries of body and spirit which caused her to be so conspicuous and vulnerable. The need for love had revealed to her imperfections that only love granted could cure. These three small women, for instance, with the child of three in their midst, might joke and laugh at her massiveness as they glanced aside; but she knew she was as much in need of protection as the infant they spoiled. If Angus McArthur did not give it her, who in the world would?

Several times it occurred to her that while she was waiting for him here in the station he might travel by bus; in that case she must certainly miss him. It was a prospect she could not bear to face. Then, when she saw he wasn't among the passengers off the 2.15 she remembered that there might be a special train from Prince's Pier, Greenock, bringing back the people who had been to see their friends off on the liner. Such a train would arrive at St Enoch Station.

She inquired from a ticket-collector at the Greenock platform. He must have noticed her hanging about for hours, and she supposed that he, more even than all the rest, was despising her and inventing all kinds of contemptuous reasons as to why and for whom she was waiting. It was, therefore, like approaching a vindictive enemy and begging a favour from him. No wonder she found it difficult not to bark and use her bulk in her 'lady bobby's way', as Todd had once put it.

To her amazement, the ticket-collector was affable and obliging in his tough Glasgow manner. 'Couldn't tell ye for sure, lady. Expect there will be, but you know these British Railways: if a service is wanted, take it off; if it isn't, double it. At least, so I'm told a dozen times a day. Your best plan would be to ask at the inquiry office. You know where it is?'

'Yes, thank you.' Gratefulness made her voice soft and sincere. 'When is the next train from Greenock?'

'In eight minutes, lady; at 2.35.'

'Will it be on time, do you think?'

'If the fitba' season hadnae been finished, I'd ha' said, definitely. Jock Findlay, wha usually drives it, makes a point o' gieing himself time to get oot to Cathkin, to see the Thirds.'

'Thank you.'

He gave her a grin that redeemed all his fellow human beings, and her too. Dazed with relief and joy, like one who has received wonderfully good news when bad had been prepared for, she withdrew, and, finding an empty space on a seat, sat down. On one side was a fat, sour-faced woman clutching a purse, and on the other a grey-faced man in a cap

113

who read a racing paper and every now and then added to the many spits at his feet.

Vividly she became aware of the grime, litter, and din of the great station, so sordid that not even the summer sunshine, had it been able to come leaping in, like tigers, could have lent it any glory. But the humanity around her, begrimed too, was now a comfort. Perhaps it was simply that, seated there between the fat woman muttering to herself and tightening her grip on her purse, and the spitter with his little Midas chuckles as he studied the horses' exotic names, she felt at last safely inconspicuous. Everyone had problems; if she was willing to accept those of others, and not find them contemptible, why should she think they would not be as tolerant towards hers?

If he does not come, and afterwards in the lonely flat the telephone does not ring, what do I do? I have been lonely before. What has altered that I cannot go on enduring my loneliness? Nothing, really. What I have been doing is taking hope and dressing it up, as a little girl does with the doll bought for her Christmas. Well then, do I not just strip it again and leave it as it was before, bare and grotesque? Even thus, it was still hope. If I think I am unfortunate, what of the two Sneddon children? And surely I am luckier than Helen Montgomerie? Afterwards I shall at least have illusions to weep over.

The train came snorting round the bend at the far end of the platform. The fat woman rose with a sigh and shuffled towards the barrier; she, too, was waiting for someone. The man in the cap spat, and chuckled on.

A woman announcer, unintelligible as usual, boomed through the loudspeakers. For Margaret, though, it could have been the voice of God, declaring that the promise given was now fulfilled. With an exaltation that had her feeling she was walking half a foot above the greasy paving, she saw Angus among the passengers who hurried towards the barrier, as if towards some promise of freedom. He did not hurry. He strolled calmly. He was no prisoner; about him was the spaciousness of his native island. She remembered that the feather in his tweed hat was from the wing of a Calisay eagle.

114

Seeing his moustache, so white though he was only fifty or so, she thought of the gannets that plunged so ecstatically from the blue sky into the blue sea.

She heard Helen's voice, quick and desperate: 'We could all get men, Margaret, if we were shamelessly to drag off our clothes and scruples, and offer them our bodies, souls and purses. We who have studied them so long know they are vain, lecherous and mercenary.' But she did not care. Yes, she would offer all those, and anything else of value that she possessed, to him. And why not, Helen? Love that isn't generous isn't genuine. You should have found that out long ago from your children.

As he came through the gate she stepped into his path. 'Hello,' she said.

Surprise, followed instantly by joy, turned the blueness of his eyes into that of the sky above Sanda; especially when, a moment after, he took off his hat, and there was his hair, soft and white as clouds.

'What a delightful surprise,' he said.

He took her hand and pressed it warmly. 'I never thought I could be so lucky as this.'

She could not help laughing, for joy; and she could scarcely keep from touching him all over, claiming him.

'I was just passing,' she said, 'and thought I'd take a look in to see if you might come off this train.'

Surely he had enough fondness for her already to know it was a lie, but enough, too, not to show it.

'How thoughtful of you, Margaret. This is just the sort of lovely gesture that the gods reward.'

She noticed the fat woman go past, with another, younger, evidently her daughter. Both looked anxious. The mother said: 'Did you remember aboot Geordie's suit?' Then they were gone, for ever.

Angus, though, thank God, was still with her. Again she had to restrain herself from clutching him to make sure that he, too, did not disappear into the crowd.

'I've got my car outside. Have you had lunch?'

'Thank you, yes. But I would not be averse to a cup of

coffee. Would you care to join me?'

'Here?'

'No, no. Somewhere more pleasant, more suitable for the celebration of such a delicious coincidence.'

Helen, she knew, would have condemned his way of talking, so unexpected in a sea-captain, as false; but Helen suffered from a deficiency of love, and so saw falseness everywhere.

'If you like, we could go to my flat.' There, she almost added, she had got in food in extravagant abundance, as well as a box of the most expensive cigars she could find.

'But of course I like. I should be charmed. Do they not say Glasgow folk are the most hospitable in the country? You are proof of it, conclusive proof.'

She laughed; to her dismay, a rather ridiculous note of coyness was in it, but he appeared not to find it incongruous. On the contrary, he gave her a wink to match. She blushed.

Side by side they walked across the station towards the exit. Thanks to her well-chosen shoes she was not quite so tall as he, and she took care to walk, not march.

'You're not to think,' she said, 'I make a point of meeting trains, accosting men, and inviting them to my flat.'

'Nothing could be further from my thoughts!'

'You'll have noticed I've taken your advice.' She showed the rings on her fingers, and shook her head to make her earrings tinkle.

'I hope I was never so impertinent as to offer you advice. An admirer's suggestion, perhaps. In any case, the result's exquisite.'

'Exquisite?' She laughed, but not in distrust. The word spoken in his Highland lilt, was like a caress. 'I'm afraid I'm much too big and clumsy ever to be that.'

'Not a bit of it.' He was very emphatic. 'Never for a moment think that. What other men say is their concern; for me, no small woman can ever be beautiful; pretty, yes; but only a large woman can be beautiful or magnificent.'

'Well.' It was all she could say. Her eyes sparkled.

'Was Venus de Milo small? Or Diana? Or Hippolyta?'

116

They reached the car. It was a green Morris Minor, only a year old.

'Diana's chariot!' cried Margaret.

'Very nice, too.'

They got in.

'Did you see your nephew off all right?'

'Ah yes. Poor lad.'

'Yes, I suppose so. Yet doesn't he think he's off to make his fortune?'

'Indeed, yes. But he will learn there is as much happiness here at home as anywhere.'

'Well, you should know, a great traveller like you. Did his parents come to Greenock too?'

'No. Mary and Donald took their farewells on Calisay jetty.'

'At half past five in the morning?' She laughed, for that was the time he had taken farewell of her on that same jetty. 'It was good of you to accompany the boy.'

He patted her knee. 'It would be a poor world if we didn't show some little kindness towards one another.'

She drove through the traffic with masculine decisiveness. 'His mother will miss him. He struck me as a very nice young man.'

'Like myself, in the days o' lang syne.' He sighed humorously.

She turned to study him. 'Yes, I think I can see a likeness. And how are the two newcomers settling in?'

'Like nestlings. They'll be out on the branches and up in the sky soon, singing.'

'I'm glad.' Some day, some day soon, she would be able to entrust him with the boys' secret. He would be a buttress to Flora.

Again he patted her knee, and again she tingled to the thighs. 'You're fond of children?'

'I'm afraid in my job I've got to keep my fondness under strict control.'

'Yes, I understand. There are different kinds of love, not all of them helpful. There's the kind that weeps and wrings

117

its hands and is useless. I don't think yours is that kind.'

'What kind do you think it is?'

'Deep, staunch, faithful, eternal.'

She felt a little disappointed. Though she had never yet displayed it—what opportunity had she had?—she knew she had in her a warmth, a fieriness even.

'Do you never wish you had children of your own?'

She blushed, though the question had come almost as a reading of her thoughts. If not a proposal, it was the beginning of one. 'Yes. Sometimes. Every woman does, I think.'

He nodded, as if in tenderest sympathy; but he was really thinking, with amusement, that that was probably why every woman, rubbed the right way, was willing to open not her legs only, but her bank-book too.

'It's too late now,' she said.

'Nonsense.' He was indignant. 'You are a woman in her prime.'

'I'm forty.'

And the rest, he thought; but it was fairer to wait until he saw her stripped. There were ways then of telling, not merely from the sag of the breasts, the paunchiness, and the varicosity of the thighs, but from the attitude itself to nakedness in front of a man.

'Many a woman's had a child at forty.'

'Yes, but the speedometer's registering all the time, isn't it? The wheels don't stop turning. I mean, one doesn't stop at forty.'

He had known what she had meant. Smiling, he looked out. There were the art galleries, and the university on its hill, above the green park. 'This is a pleasant part of the city,' he murmured, and sang a snatch of the song: 'Let us haste to Kelvingrove, bonny lassie-oh.'

'No so pleasant as Calisay, she said.

'Or Sanda.'

'Or Sanda. But they must seem very dull after places like Karachi, Bombay, Singapore.'

'Ah, you forget that on Calisay there's hardly a sprig of heather or a rock on the beach that hasn't its memory for me.'

'Well, here's where my memories lie,' she said, as she drove into the quiet, gardened square of solid, middle-class tenements where her flat was. 'Not so romantic as Calisay.'

She stopped the car opposite her close.

'What about my suitcase?' he asked. 'Do I take it up later, after dark?'

She began to tremble. This was his so tactful way of asking if she wished him to spend the night with her.

'You know what neighbours are, my dear. Just say the word, and I shall go to my hotel.'

Her mouth was dry. 'Have you got a room booked?'

'Well, to be candid, no.'

'I do have a spare room.'

'Yes, you said so, on Sanda.'

She almost hurled herself into his arms; in fact, the desire to do it was so fierce that for a moment or two she thought she had. Her whole body ached and yearned.

He reached back and tapped his suitcase. 'Now?' he whispered. 'Later? I think later. After all, we may have fallen out by then.'

'No. Don't say that, even in a joke.'

As they got out of the car a neighbour with a small girl of about four came along the pavement. 'Good afternoon, Miss Mathieson,' said the woman, her eyes on Angus. 'Good afternoon,' piped the child. 'We're going to Lewis's.'

Her mother frowned at thus having her business exposed, and as she walked on she could be heard giving her daughter a lecture on discreetness.

'Pretty child,' murmured Angus. 'A pity she has to be initiated into the suspicious and secretive ways of the world.'

Going up the tiled stairs, with the landing windows of stained glass, they passed Mr and Mrs Turnbull coming down. Good afternoons were exchanged: Margaret's was more defiant than she meant. Mr Turnbull was a bank cashier and an elder in her kirk; his wife was an official in the Women's Guild. They had four of a family all grown up.

'I could pass for your brother from Australia,' murmured Angus.

119

'They know I haven't one.'

'Your cousin then.'

She opened the door and hurried in. 'I'm glad you're not,' she said as she turned, almost at bay, her face wild in the hallstand mirror. Yet she recognized herself; this greed with which her face was twisted was familiar, if not in the looking-glass, then in her mind's eye. However modesty might be outraged, she would kiss him as vehemently as he did her—more even—and she would take the lead in the erotic, stumbling waltz into her bedroom. She would not merely submit willingly to all preliminaries; she would co-operate and incite. This time, too, she would take care that at the consummation she was not semi-conscious with shame and wonder; no, she would throughout remain the alert and responsive partner that, according to the books and to her own instinctive common sense, a lover required and deserved.

But as she stood ripe, all he did was hand her his hat to hang on one of the pegs. Then, with the chastest of pats on her hand, he waited until she showed him into the sittingroom. The curious result of his restraint was not to cool her desire, but rather to make it grow hotter than ever.

All afternoon she burned, and showed it by sudden cries, gestures and movements that were like sparks or flames. In offering him the box of cigars, taking one out and putting it in his mouth; in pouring out his tea; in pressing delicacies on him; in giggling; in uttering strange irrelevances; in lingering near him; in answering frankly his inquiries as to how her money was invested; in showing him, among her books, one that contained coloured reproductions of big nude women; in every act that afternoon she kept revealing the fire that raged in her. He, she felt sure, noticed it, though he himself stayed strangely cool. She did not think his intention was to damp her down. Often enough he would give her some little caress such as the nudge of his knuckle against her hip.

At the right time, his eyes seemed to be saying, he would lead her away to be appeased. Perhaps he intended to keep her waiting until they were married.

He did not help her clear away or wash up; she said he

hadn't to, and he didn't. He sat in the lounge and read the financial page of the *Glasgow Herald* as if, she thought—her cheeks as hot as the water in the sink—he was already her husband. She stuffed a dish-towel under her apron, and, thus pregnant, sang 'Kelvingrove' as she went on with her wifely tasks. She reflected that if Helen had heard him inquiring about the shares, she would have suspected him of some mercenary scheme; but as far as Margaret herself was concerned, there were things she was more than willing to buy from him: his name, for instance, his manhood and his seed. His love she could win with her own.

'Well then,' she said, as she returned to the sitting-room, apron removed, 'what do we do now? Go for a run in the car? Go to the pictures? Just stay in and talk?'

'I suppose you drive about a lot at your job?'

'Quite a bit.'

'So being my chauffeur wouldn't give you the rest you need and deserve. Let's go to the pictures.'

'Good. What's on?' She sat down on the arm of his chair, and, with her bare elbow touching his moustache, turned the pages until she reached the cinema advertisements. 'I don't know what your taste is in films; or in so many other things.'

'One thing you ought to know, my dear.'

She waited.

'I like your tea.'

'All I did was pour in boiling water.'

He put his arm round her; his hand rested on her thigh. 'No. A household is often centred round a quiet cup of tea. In the old days it would have been round the good book. In some cottages on Calisay it still is. But nowadays it is more often the quiet cup of tea; the Bible, you might say, is really still there, unopened, unread, but spreading its influence. What is needed is a good woman's hand on the teapot handle. There are not so many of them these days, alas. So that is what I meant, Margaret, by saying I like your tea.' His arm tightened.

She felt weak and foolish. 'Pouring it for you, Angus, is as great a pleasure for me—' She could not finish.

'As watching you do it is for me?'

Her heart singing, she scanned the list of films. 'This one?' she cried, laughing. It was called *Nights of Joy*. The advertisement showed a woman in panties, with her breasts almost bare. It had an X certificate.

He frowned and shook his head. 'In the name of truth,' he said, 'they have the effrontery to offer us dirt. It is the same with books. Every second one you pick up is full of disgusting descriptions of what ought to be private and sacred.'

She was still laughing.

'I beg your pardon, my dear,' he said, squeezing her thigh. 'I am old-fashioned; a sea-captain, brought up on the Bible, in God's clean air.'

'But, Angus, human love is a fact.'

'It is not only a fact,' he cried, squeezing harder. 'It is the most beautiful fact in existence; which is why we must not allow these people to pollute it. Also, it has to be enjoyed. But how can sensitive men and women, like you and me, enjoy it if it is portrayed in films, books, and on stages as ugly and bestial?'

So healthy his tanned skin, so fragrant his white moustache, she wanted to hurl herself upon him, and kiss and lick; but, so dignified was he, she could not be sure how he would react. Perhaps it was simply that, though the signs were clear, she, clumsy in intuition as in physical movement, was unable to read them.

He tapped the paper. 'Here's one that sounds wholesome. I expect it'll be rather stupid in many ways, but I can always forgive stupidity if it is accompanied by wholesomeness.'

She murmured agreement. Yet she was a little alarmed. It would be an honour and in keeping with his general gentlemanliness, but she did not really want him to make love to her wholesomely. She hoped for a passion to surmount and subdue her own; it seemed to her there must be some bestiality in it. After waiting so many years she did not think she could be compensated and consoled by what contented Mrs Turnbull of the Women's Guild. He had said big women could achieve magnificence; where best to show it than in the act of making

122

love? So much of life was little; here surely ought to be an attempt at least at greatness.

In the bathroom, preparing to go out, she again stood in front of the mirror, with her hands so tightly clenched that they hurt. She felt clenched like that all over; this torture, of never knowing whether opportunity was present or not, might leave her sexually exhausted, so that when the moment did arrive she would not be able. The right procedure might well be for her to wait until he was ready to pluck her like an apple off a tree, but what if he found her hard and bitter? Looking in the cabinet, with all its medicines, aspirins, disinfectant, pills and purges, she saw none that had this miraculous efficacy, to make soft, sweet, and desirable a body stiff and sour with twenty years' sexual humiliation.

She found the film tedious, and its love passages artificial, but during it she wondered if she had made a discovery. Beside her Angus laughed and chuckled so much at the rather naive situations that it occurred to her he was after all, intellectually, a simple sea-captain reared on a remote island. In the jungle of sexual love, she was herself no experienced or intrepid huntress; but it was probably just as true that he also was lost and timorous in those green shadows. She knew from her reading that many successful marriages would never have come about at all had not the women, throwing maidenliness aside, gone ruthlessly on the prowl; after the weddings they had become docile again, like sated tigresses. Tonight would be her chance to prey and pounce. Therefore she spent those hours in the cinema, and the two later at the night-club where Angus, to her surprise, was a known member, in provoking herself into the necessary ferocity. To help, she insisted on drinking far more than her stomach or head could comfortably manage, as she discovered driving back to the flat.

Luckily she met with no accident, for the streets were empty at that hour, one o'clock on the Glasgow Sabbath morning. To test the savagery stored up in her, she slammed the car door shut with a bang that re-echoed round the silent square.

'I don't give a damn what they all think,' she cried. 'Do you, darling?'

'It isn't a matter of caring what they think,' he replied, with a cautiousness that made her nails and teeth turn longer and sharper. 'It is a matter of not giving them a chance to think anything.'

Going up the stairs, she suddenly turned and caught him by the moustache. 'I didn't think a bold sea-captain like you would be afraid of bourgeois public opinion.'

'I am not afraid of it. I prefer not to give it anything of me to feed on.'

She growled, and playfully scratched his chin. 'My dear,' she whispered, 'on Calisay yonder, don't you know, all the ladies whisper about you behind your back.'

He was indignant. 'St Orsay himself, when he was alive and practising his sanctity, did not live a more God-fearing life than I do on Calisay.'

'You drink in the hotel, dear. Did the saint? You offer dinners in shadowy corners to spinsters like me. Did Orsay? Then what about your thoughts? He thought of God all the time. I think you think of other things, sometimes.'

Taking him by surprise, she embraced and kissed him, pressing her body hard against his. Burdened by his suitcase, he could not, with one hand, ward off so passionate and powerful a clutch.

'Remember where we are, for God's sake,' he whispered, when she drew back to breathe.

Disdainfully she looked round and saw they were on the stairs leading up to her flat. Half a dozen steps away was the landing on which lived the Moodies and the Stewarts. She could see their names inscribed in Gothic letters on the brass plates. She saw too in her imagination their respectable faces, sour with censoriousness. She wanted to roar defiance, hammer on the doors, and then lie down on the landing to mate gloriously with Angus.

He pushed her. 'Go on. Let's get into the house at least.'

When she reached it she could not open the door; somehow the key did not seem to fit the lock. He had to take it from her and do it himself.

Giggling, she embraced him again. 'You are my key,

124

Angus,' she murmured.

'Inside, please.' He had to shove her in. Then he closed and locked the door behind them. 'It's very late. Where is my bedroom?'

She wasn't having any of that. Breasts high and legs splayed out, she advanced on him, holding out her ringed claws.

'Aren't you going to share mine?' she asked.

'But, my dear, that was never discussed.'

'Is such a thing ever discussed?'

Then he spoke with great emotion. 'Margaret, you and I are not lust-crazy youngsters, tormented beyond control by our members. We are responsible, mature adults, who wish to be able to meet each other's eyes in the morning, with fondness and innocence.'

In one great shiver she found herself growing sober. Lust in retreat had her in a confusion of shrinkings and ashamed mumbles. Nor did it help when he stepped forward and, with sympathy but also with sexual dominance, put his arms round her and kissed first her mouth, then her eyes and her ears. Lust's retreat was arrested; she thought he was fondling her as a lover, not as a mere consoler. So she blazed once more, and, seizing him by the breast, tugged him desperately towards her bedroom. She whispered all kinds of entreaty and promise.

He let himself be pulled through the door and into the room, but not down on to the bed on top of her. At that point he exerted all his male strength and became as rigid as a rock in the sea. In her, desire surged and beat like waves, in vain. She clung to him, her arms round his waist. Losing him now, she must surely drown in these tremendous black depths of love unfulfilled.

'You must, you must, you must,' she kept whimpering.

He stroked her head, gently, but it was like a wind agitating the waves still more.

'I must not, dear. Do you think the temptation is not strong for me too. We must help each other to resist. For our future happiness's sake. We are not old. We are not going to be decrepit and dried up tomorrow, or the next day, either. There will come a time. Soon. Tonight you are over-excited. Perhaps

125

you have had too much to drink. It would be quite unforgivable of me to take advantage. In the morning, you will see, you will be grateful.'

'No, no, no. You must. Not tomorrow. There have been too many tomorrows. Now. You did, on Sanda.'

'My dear, this is your home. Your parents lived and died here. Here are your familiar and cherished possessions. I am your guest. There must be no intrigue. Take a glass of milk and go to sleep.'

He struggled free and left her sobbing and stricken, as if idiotically drunk. Quickly he found the other bedroom, and smiled to see that it was prepared for him, with the sheets turned down. Within five minutes he was undressed and in his silk pyjamas. On his way back from the bathroom he peeped in and saw her, still huddled where he had left her. He said nothing, but quietly withdrew and slipped into bed, not to sleep, to wait rather, and smoke, with patience that would not soon grow weary.

About an hour later, his patience still fresh, the knock he had been sure of was heard on the door—like a small dog's tail thumping, he thought. He got ready to pretend he had been roused from sleep.

'Angus, please,' she called, in a piteous voice, not unlike that same whipped dog's subservient whine.

After a long pause he said, sleepily: 'Who is it?'

The door opened, and there she stood, in, as he'd bet himself, a white flimsy nightgown.

'Is it you, Margaret?'

With sad sighs like hiccups she crept towards him. Her feet were bare. She reeked with scent. Under the carpet the floorboards groaned. The bed, he hoped, was a strong one; she and he together must weigh two dozen stone, at least; quiescent, a burden for any wooden-legged bed; frolicking, likely to prove too much. Should he, though, consent to frolic? Was she ready for the next stage? Would it not be advisable to put it off until tomorrow morning, about eleven, say, when the kirk bells were ringing? But there was no need. Given it now, she would beg for it every day after. On the other hand, refused it, she might decide to do without it for the rest of her life. There was no telling what the kirk bells might say to her.

'Is there anything wrong?' he asked, his voice mellow and loving.

'I can't sleep.' A long sigh disrupted her words.

'Did you take that glass of milk?'

'All the milk in paradise wouldn't give me sleep tonight.' She stumbled down on to her knees and crawled towards the bed. 'I love you, Angus. Please don't shame me. Every moment since I waved goodbye to you on Calisay I've thought of you. If I'm being shameless, please don't despise me.'

He put out his hand. She clutched and kissed it.

'I'm not asking you to take me only. I've got more than six thousand pounds; and this flat's mine.'

He tried, but not too hard, to withdraw his hand. She was already, much earlier than he'd planned for, singing the tune he wanted to hear. But would she still be singing it next week, next year?

'This isn't the time or place to speak about money, my dear,' he murmured, as if shocked.

'Why not? You said yourself, we're mature and responsible adults. We know it's an ingredient.'

He had difficulty in making out her words, so distorted were they by sobs. 'An ingredient of what, my dear?'

'Marriage.'

Moving over and pulling at the same time, he had her in bed beside him. It certainly creaked and sagged; but he suppressed his chuckle. She was cold as a dead seal. As she clung to him she kept shuddering, and when she spoke her teeth chattered: 'Love me, love me, oh love me always.'

'I'll love you, dear,' he whispered, and he did, making, he thought, a good job of it, all things considered. One of those things was the rather disconcerting and distasteful sweat into which she broke, and another was her insistence, at the climax almost, on trying to gabble to him something about the two boys Mary and Donald had boarded out on them. He made out the words 'blood' and 'hatchet', but, though startled, he

127

discounted them at the time. Women, he was well aware, were liable at such moments to blurt out the most astonishing disclosures, by no means all of them true. Hadn't Peggy, now dead, told him at the very topmost gasp that she had decided to leave everything to him in her will? Afterwards it had taken skill and infinite endurance to keep that decision of hers in being during the much cooler, rather less ecstatic and far more numerous moments of everyday dourness; but he had managed it.

She lay close beside him, quite naked; the drenched nightgown had been thrown off. His hand caressed her. She kept moaning. In gratitude? Regret? Joy? He could not be quite sure.

'What was it you said about Mary's two boys?' he asked.

'No, no. Don't let us talk about them, darling.'

'You said something about a hatchet.'

She shuddered.

'What was it?'

'It's hateful. It has nothing to do with us. Don't let it come between us.'

'Nothing is ever going to come between us, my precious. How could it? Look how close we are. I don't expect you to tell me all your secrets, dear. Every human soul is entitled to privacy; even love itself should not intrude. But if you begin to tell me, and then change your mind, what am I to think? That you thought you could trust me but now have decided you cannot?'

She wondered at what he was saying; she thought she had put herself in relation to him where even trust was as of little consequence as money.

'It's just that it's so horrible, darling; and I'm so happy now.'

You don't sound it, he thought, and these shudders hardly indicate it, either. But did not the most beautiful fish continue to struggle in the net?

'Horrible, love?' he murmured. 'How can it be horrible? Everybody on Calisay's fond of the children already. I rather like them myself. The smaller one comes visiting me to show

128

me his tanks.'

He did not add that the dog accompanied Tom but would never come into the house with him. Roy always slunk away from Angus; yet the latter had never once so much as stooped to lift a stone.

'Are you fond of children, Angus?'

'Fond enough.'

She turned and heaved up to whisper into his ear that he would have to be, because perhaps after tonight she would be going to have one.

'This horrible thing, what is it?'

Still with her mouth close to his ear, and her breasts crushed against him, she told him about the Sneddons' parents.

Numbed though his shoulder was with her urgent weight, he was keenly interested, and asked several questions. Between kisses that grew more and more demanding, she answered. It was going to be, he saw, an arduous night. How much had she said: six thousand? And of course the flat was worth another three or four. But it was what she had told him about the murder that came most into his mind during the subsequent love-makings. Before he got to sleep he had decided to visit the Mitchell Library on Monday morning to look up the newspapers dated about Christmas three years ago. If the attendant wasn't looking he might be able to tear out any pictures there happened to be. It would be interesting to see what the blonde adulteress and her puny obliterator had looked like before the hatchet struck.

129

Thirteen

Hugh wasn't waiting in the porch as he had promised, but before Flora could complain to the Colonel, as the biggest of the trout in the glass cases was called, round the corner from the bar he came running, the hair at the back of his head sticking up as usual like a fin.

She seized hold of his jacket to pull herself up to smell his breath. 'I knew it,' she cried. 'Stinking of beer. Very well, Hugh McEachern, if that's what you think of me.'

As if affronted, humiliated, and cast into despair, she raced sobbing out into the moonlit road and along it, towards the village hall.

He went panting after. 'One pint, I swear to God.'

'Now, it's profanity too.'

'It was your own fault, woman. You were five minutes late. I was ten minutes early, and John Galbraith and Donald McDonald assured me a man waiting for a woman's the most pathetic sight in the world, so they took hold of me and carried me with them into the bar.'

'The bar, indeed. If you have to booze, why don't you do it in the lounge, like a gentleman?'

'Here, do you think I'm your Uncle Angus?'

She chose to spin round then, as if in fierce defence. 'It would fit you and the rest of your heather-louping beer-swillers better if you were like him. You're all jealous of him because he's got decent manners.'

'Jealous, good God! Are you saying I'm jealous of yon old faker?'

'He's not old. Yes, you are jealous, and so are the rest. And what's this you're hiding so foolishly behind your back? Is it a stick? Has it come to that?'

'I can see it might have to. This,' he added, producing it, 'happens to be a box of chocolates. They're for taking the

130

smell of beer off my breath.'

They looked at each other, and, suddenly bursting into laughter, embraced and went waltzing along the road, Hugh making Gaelic mouth-music.

'Wait! Stop! There's folk ahead.'

He gave her a long beery kiss with her two feet off the ground.

'So you are a bully,' she gasped, as soon as she could.

He gave her bottom a skelp. 'If I am, I'd better act up to it.'

'If you were sober you wouldn't dare. Heaven knows what kind of life I'd have led if I had married you.'

'When you marry me, you mean.'

'In October.'

'August.'

She nestled close, suddenly serious, but still playful too: an attitude common to her that he found always delicious.

'You promised to wait,' she whispered.

'Haven't I been waiting for months? And this is just the beginning of June. Waiting till August is waiting, isn't it?'

'But you've got to learn to think of other folk besides yourself.'

'If you mean Ken McGilvray and his damned hotel, no thanks.'

'But it's really not easy for him to find a maid in the middle of the season. Besides, he's been a good friend to me.'

'From what I've heard it's thanks to Isa he's not been too good a friend.'

'Hugh, you've got a filthy mind.'

'Flora, I admit it, gladly; and I'm hoping yours isn't all that clean.'

'We'll never get to the hall at this rate.' She took his arm and walked him smartly along. 'And there's folk behind us.'

'What are we going to the pictures for, anyway? It's far too good a night. Let's go for a stroll through the policies, or take a boat out.'

'No. I like us to be with the rest of the folk.'

He squeezed her arm. He liked it too, and he would like

it even more when she was his wife and the folk were his own, over in Islay.

'And it's all right for you to talk,' she said. 'In Port Ellen you see the pictures every single week.'

'Well, after August you'll be there yourself.'

She groaned.

'What's wrong now?'

'I've just remembered it's got four bars, and three distilleries.'

'And a public lavatory.'

She gave him a push. 'And a pier.'

'Don't say a word against that pier.'

She smiled. It was her turn to squeeze. Port Ellen pier had been where they had first met, two years ago. She had been working in a Tarbert hotel on Loch Fyne then, and was on her way home. It had been October, and the crossing had been very rough, with gales and heavy rain. She had had to come off at Port Ellen to spend a night with her aunt at Bowmore, for the steamer that evening did not go on to Calisay. Hugh had seen her, green in the face, struggling with her suitcase down the gangway. He had gone racing up, taken it from her, and seen her safely into the Bowmore bus. Since then they had strolled arm-in-arm on that pier several times.

'But seriously, Hugh, wouldn't it be fairer to wait a while longer, now Hector's gone?'

'No, it wouldn't; not fairer to us, anyway. Hector pleased himself. You know what I think about him. He shouldn't have gone. You've got a good croft here, and now there's no one to help your father work it, and the boat too, except the two boys, and they're as yet far too wee.'

'Angus has promised to lend a hand; and old Dugald too.'

He laughed scornfully. 'Angus! Have you looked at his hands lately? They tell me he rubs oil and scent into them. He spends half his time smelling them. Can you see him forking dung?'

'Was it in the bar you heard that?'

'There's a lot of truth spoken in the bar.'

'And a lot of ill-minded blethers, too.'

'Och, that's a silly ill-minded woman's blether itself.'

'Is that so?' She pretended to go into a huff, but she was thinking, with love, and yet with something else hostile to love, of her intention to share with him soon what the big woman, Miss Mathieson, had told her. She would not tell him to test his love: that did not need testing. Nor would she tell him to test him himself; whatever faults she might find in him, before or after marriage, could make no difference. Without him the sun would shine in vain for her, bird-song and laughter would be meaningless, and marriage a bitter dream. Nevertheless, there was this something else.

'To get back to Port Ellen,' he said, 'did I tell you the cottage is almost ready?'

'Twenty times at least.'

'And that the two interior grates are put in?'

'Considering it was I chose them out of the catalogue, was there any need to tell me?'

'And the ceilings have been taken down and done again, better than new?'

'They used to have more ripples in them than the sand has on the strand between here and Orsay.'

'And the whole roof's been reslated?'

'What an awful dilapidated wreck this cottage must have been to need all that attention!'

He laughed. All his life he would remember her cries and gasps of joyous discovery when he had first taken her to see the cottage. He as a builder had seen its potentialities, she as a wife and mother. Close to the sea, yet sheltered, with a garden of trees, azaleas, and flowers, it had at the same time a magnificent open view. They had wandered about it, looked out of every window, paused in every corner of the garden, and seen their future ahead of them as lovely and illimitable as sea and sky. Most important of all, three minutes' walk away, like a promise sure to be kept, was the main street of the village, with its shops and people.

'By August,' he said, 'it will be ready by August.'

She shivered with gratitude. There seemed to be nothing on earth able to spoil or even threaten their happiness, not even what lay buried in John Sneddon's mind. It was in hers too, not inert, but active, out of sympathy for the child; but it had not in any way festered there. On the contrary, it seemed to her miraculous that out of so much human misery and sordid violence two such delightful little boys should have emerged, not only innocent in themselves, but inspiring innocence in everyone who met them. Thinking of them, she thought of her own and Hugh's children, who would be related to John and Tom, and to the children of everyone else.

'Flora McArthur,' he said fondly, 'did nobody ever tell you you're a creature of queer silences? Walking with you's like being dropped by parachute into the middle of the Mull of Oa. What are you thinking about now?'

'Us.'

'Well, what's so sad about us?'

'I'm not sad. Goodness, I'm not feeling sad at all. In spite of Hector.' Yet she began to cry. 'I'm happy. That's all. Isn't that worth crying about?'

Below, not far away now, outside the hall, people could be heard laughing and talking, and beyond them, away towards the sea, sea-birds called; both laughter and thrilling calls seemed to happen not outside of him at all, but within, as if he, for that moment as Flora sobbed, was not just plain Hugh McEachern with the big ears and the wiry hair, over from Port Ellen where he was a building contractor like his father, not a man merely, but a presence that embraced this whole island and all its living creatures and the things that grew on it. Thus he felt as he stood there, his arm about Flora. There was no other way of containing his joy, pride, and love.

'For goodness' sake,' she said, 'lend me your hankie. I can't go down there, looking as if you'd been brutal to me.'

'Now who would think that?' he asked, as he handed her his handkerchief. 'Do you know a certain body took me aside today and gave me some advice?'

'About me?'

'About you.'

'What did she say?'

'I haven't said it was a she.'

134

'But it was; and it was Elspeth, too.'

He laughed. 'Elspeth it was. She said: "Hugh lad, you're getting one of the finest lasses this island has ever produced."'

'Good for Elspeth.'

'Ah, but she had something else to say. She said: "But you'll find you'll have to be firm with her. She's the kind that likes to manage. When she was at school, she was the one who showed the rest what to do. If one fell and got hurt, Flora it was they'd to run to. She saw to that. She's still the same, Hugh."'

Flora sniffed. 'And what did you reply?'

'Och, I said I couldn't understand what she meant, because I always found you ready to agree to everything I said.'

'Pity for you, if I was. But we'd better hurry, if we want to be there before the picture starts.'

The hall was already crowded, with most of the natives seated in their favourite places, and a few hotel guests come for the experience rather than for the film itself. As soon as Flora and Hugh entered, a voice shrieked: 'Flora, Hugh, here! We've kept seats for you.' It was Tom Sneddon, standing and waving.

People turned to look at him, and laughed; whereupon, increasing their amusement by adding tenderness to it, he sank down and hid his red face behind his hands. Beside him her mother smiled, whispered and patted his knee. On the other side his brother John also smiled and kept his head up, as if he was aware the laughter was kindly and, indeed, was a recognition that he and his brother were now members of the community.

Flora felt very grateful, but also surprised, for it had been he who had been causing her some worry. No child could have been easier to like, with his keenness to help and his utter lack of deceit. Yet she hadn't been able to get rid of the suspicion that always a part of him was kept resolutely private. Accepting everyone, he did not expect in return ever to be wholly accepted himself. So she had thought; but now she wondered if knowing what she did had made her see in him a loneliness that didn't really exist. Most likely what Jessie Ogilvie had

135

said was true: he was just a shade slow on the uptake. All the same, Jessie was maybe too ready to attribute folks' shortcomings to the degrees of stupidity in them.

Tom, on the other hand, was already as kenspeckle as Roy, his companion. People said of him, meaning no disrespect, that he had settled down like a pup in its new home after its first separation from its mother. Because of that affection which he had so quickly won, there had been canny inquiries about his mother; and the answer that nothing was known of her, or of his father, save that they were both dead, had been received with quiet remarks that it was surely up to all of them on the island to make up to the two lads a particle at least of what they had missed.

Now, as she watched him cover his face in the packed hall, she realised that he too, young though he was, was still at the world's mercy. Her heart sank as she remembered how vulnerable and unpredictable children were. In the midst of laughter and kindliness life was often as cruel as thorns; no one could prevent it.

Before going up the aisle to join her family, she was beckoned over by Mrs Morton-Home who, with two friends, sat near the front in ordinary seats.

'Good evening, Flora. I wanted to ask you if your mother's all right again, I mean, after that heart-wrench of Hector's going? I haven't had a chance to speak to her since.'

As Flora listened and answered, she looked towards the back where Tom Galbraith, Archie Campbell and Ian Robertson sat. They were Hector's friends, and the only young people now left on the island over school age, except for Margaret McIntyre and Sheila Donaldson beside them. She noticed how, in spite of their loud guffaws and ostentatious loungings, they really felt cut off and lonely. She had seen it in Hector too, and because of it had regarded his going as necessary. There were old men on the island, such as Ewan McCuish, helpless in bed, or Isaac McKenzie, there in the hall, white-haired and eighty, waiting as eagerly as any child for the picture to begin, whose minds were still active and more interesting than ever with a store of island memories. There were mature men like her father, for whom life here, crofting and fishing, with the comradeship of hill and sea, was satisfying and good. But for these youths Calisay, despite its wide horizons and lofty bright skies, was a prison, as it had become for Hector; they would soon have to be released, or they would escape. She understood, because not so long ago, before she had met Hugh, that desperate dissatisfaction with living at a slower pace than the rest of the world, and with being shut off from all that seemed vital, had tormented her too. One's blood went racing through one like the tide between the islands, while the land slept and even the sky was stagnant.

'But I see the little fellows are settling in nicely,' said the laird's wife. 'They'll help to take her mind off Hector.'

On her way to join her family it occurred to Flora that this hall and all its equipment had been supplied by Mrs Morton-Home and her husband; that every crofter on the island was their grateful tenant; that every tree and flower in the beautiful policies, and every salmon in Loch Miloran, was theirs. She felt therefore a kind of guilt, foolish but persistent, at keeping from them this secret about Tom and John. A part of her mind, the modern part she was proud of, told her not to be daft; but another part, where irrational fears and superstitions lurked, whispered that if the landlord's permission had to be obtained for importing a car, then why ought he not to be consulted about what, if it ever became generally known, might be a far worse disturber of the island's peace?

She made a great effort to be cheerful in greeting the boys and her parents.

'Move over, fatty,' she said to Tom. 'I want to sit between you.'

He moved with alacrity. 'Where's Hugh going to sit?' he whispered.

'On my thumb,' said Hugh.

'He's jealous,' said Flora. 'Don't heed him. He wants to sit beside me, but I prefer you.'

Tom chuckled.

Hugh leaned across and shook his fist. 'Don't you be kissing her when the lights go out. She's my girl.'

137

'She's my sister,' whispered Tom, his face red again, but this time he did not hide it.

'Don't tease the laddie,' said her mother.

'Yes, yes, leave them alone,' murmured her father. 'They're doing fine.'

Elspeth appeared, and spoke to Hugh, who had the outside seat. 'Did you see my Donald at the hotel?'

Hugh nodded.

'Cosy in the bar, I suppose? Showing no sign of leaving it?'

Hugh grinned as he remembered with what dignified wisdom her husband Donald and his cronies had preferred their own blethers in the bar to attendance at a cowboy picture.

'He looked quite comfortable, Mrs McDonald,' he said.

'I'll comfortable him.' Then she went back grimly to where her sister Morag sat smugly beside her man Alec who, plump and bald, liked a pint as well as any man, but recoiled from its price.

Near the front most of the children sat and clamoured, boarded out and parented together. Alec McFadyen stood up to wave and shout to John to go and join them. John shook his head.

'Go if you want to,' said Flora.

'I'd rather stay here, please.'

'Quite right,' said Hugh. 'They all make so much noise chewing sweeties you can't hear the guns banging.'

'It's no' that,' Tom assured them.

'Well, what is it?' asked Hugh, with a grin.

'Whatever it is, it's none of your business, Hugh McEachern,' said Flora. 'Tom's talking just to me.'

'It's because Nancy Dewar's there.'

Flora looked and saw the pretty little fair-haired girl seated next to Peggy Blair.

'She's Johnny's girl-friend,' confided Tom, with a chuckle. John smiled and shook his head.

'Well, isn't Chrissie McFadyen yours?' asked Flora.

Tom's eyes bulged. 'Her? She pushes me, and yesterday she wouldna gie me share o' her toffee.'

138

'I would say that's as sure a sign as any,' said Hugh.

Then the Lindsays arrived, with Isa McGilvray. On her way past Janet paused to speak to John. At the same time she stared with challenging pride at Hugh and Flora.

'Did you remember the photograph?' she asked.

His mouth fell open in dismay and shame. 'I forgot.'

'Never mind. There's no hurry. Next time you're in the shop.'

'What photograph's this, Janet?' asked Flora.

'That's a secret between us, Flora.' With a strange smile Janet nodded and went to join her friend and husband.

Flora thought she had never before seen her so relaxed in body and mind; she was like a woman who has just found out for certain that she was pregnant. But in Janet's case that was scarcely possible.

'I'll tell you,' whispered Tom.

'But if it's a secret maybe you shouldn't.'

'She didn't tell us it was a secret. Did she, Johnny?'

His brother frowned and shook his head.

Flora whispered: 'I don't think Johnny wants you to talk about it. Maybe it's a secret between him and Mrs Lindsay.'

'I was there too. It's because of Jean McDonnell, you see. She used to be Johnny's lass.'

'She didna,' said John, not angry, but very intense.

'Well, you liked her, Johnny; and she liked you. It was you she pu'd the daffies for.'

'Is this the little girl you used to know?' asked Flora.

'Aye. She was at the Home.'

Flora thought she was beginning to see Janet's interest in the matter. 'How old is she?'

'About nine.'

'She's in this photograph Mrs Lindsay wants to see?'

'Aye. Everybody is. So's Matron.'

She had to smile at the grimness with which he added that.

'Mrs Lindsay asked us lots of things about Jean.'

Flora's mother looked at her and shook her head. 'This is Janet's business,' she murmured.

'And theirs too, mother.'

139

'Maybe so. But that doesn't make it ours.'

Flora thought it did. She, too, wanted to know more about this little girl who had been their friend.

'Your mother's right, Flora,' said her father. 'What happened before is not our concern.'

She met her mother's gaze.

Then the lights went out and on again. It was the signal the picture was going to start. Those outside came hurrying in. A boy fired off a gun with a cap in it. People laughed. Some cried, 'Wheesht now!' There was a smell of oranges. A minute later they were all watching the mysterious unshaven horseman ride down the street of the Arizonan town eighty years and five thousand miles away. Flora found her hand gripped: it was Tom; his other hand was clenched at his mouth. When offered a chocolate out of Hugh's box he took it mechanically; it must have tasted like the whisky the gunman was at that moment drinking in the saloon.

Flora could not forget what her father had said. Contrast with the violence on the screen made the quiet decency of the folk round her all the more evident; nor were they the dull-eyed heather-chewers a casual stranger might assume. Most of them she had known all her life. Still, she would marry Hugh in August, and though Port Ellen was only two hours away by steamer and another hour by bus, she would not be present from day to day, on guard. Supposing, for example, that the secret leaked out. Only three persons knew it—herself, her mother and Jessie Ogilvie; none of these was a heedless or malicious gossip. But others on the mainland knew it. Their father, now in the asylum, might die, if not soon then in one, two, or ten years; and in some way that she could not now foresee, his death might drag his sons out into the open, with the murder round their necks. Moreover, as Miss Mathieson had warned, there was always the danger that John himself might one day shout it out, under some stress that no power on earth could preserve him from. It might therefore leak out. Some would hear of it with horror and distaste, Elspeth and her own father perhaps among them; but even these, who in her opinion misinterpreted the Bible and read into God's mind a vengefulness they would have been ashamed of in their own, would with terrible but endurable reticence spare the boys; they would be content to leave the retribution to God. Most people, however, would react with sturdy common sense and compassion: whoever was at fault, they would declare, no one in his Christian senses could say the boys were. But, as she well remembered from her own childhood, worse even than being called names, was the imagining of the names that might be called. In the first case, the names were known, they could be related to the persons calling them, they could be despised and rejected; in the second case, on the other hand, what it amounted to was that one was put at one's own mercy, which was a situation where even love could become feared and hated.

Better, she thought, with a shiver, better for them to go if it became known: not to Port Ellen, where Hugh might be willing to take them for a little while for her sake, but back to the Home in Glasgow, to the Matron and to the little girl who had been their friend. Better, therefore, if no one else, not even Hugh, was let into the secret.

Fourteen

As he got off the tram-car at Charing Cross to walk down North Street to the Mitchell Library, Angus noticed that the drizzle, mentioned in the eight o'clock news that morning as already covering the Western Isles, had moistened the pavements and caused women's coloured umbrellas to be raised, though when he put out his hand he felt only a silky dampness. As he passed shops and office buildings and crossed busy, noisy, intersecting streets, he remembered how once, on Calisay, in such a Scotch mist creeping in from the Atlantic, he had stood watching the tiny silvery beads of moisture on the gossamer shiver and gleam with the vibration of the foghorn in the lighthouse miles out at sea. The vision he often had, of himself a lord or god among ordinary people shaken by scruples, had been particularly powerful then, beside the webs whose threads irradiated like a great city's streets. So it was again, this mild, moist, Monday morning, as, calm and dignified among the scurrying wage-slaves, he reached the library and entered.

In Jehovah's many-mansioned castle, he thought, there would be immense archives to consult; and as he glanced in for a moment at the great hall, where already dozens of people, mostly students, were reading and writing, it was easy to pretend they were his minions, for ever collecting the information which he might or might not use when arranging the future.

Upstairs, where the newspaper files were kept, was the past. It amused him that the room, panelled in dark wood, was as quiet as a mortuary. Here was no green heaven or smoky hell, only a dim, damp room and bundles of old newspapers, yellowish and dusty.

He asked for the issues of December 23rd, 1957, of all the Glasgow newspapers, both morning and evening.

'Sorry to trouble you,' he said to the attendant. 'Some necessary research.'

'No trouble. That's what they're here for.'

As he waited, tapping index and middle fingers on the counter, he suddenly saw them as himself and Margaret, making love. He could hardly keep from laughing as he noticed how ravenous for it she still was after two nights and a Sabbath, and yet how gratefully submissive too. But as he compared his knuckle wrinkles with those on her belly, he found the joke losing its savour. To say he had become fond of her, or even felt pity, would be ridiculous, but still there had been that look of fidelity and appeal that had reminded him at the time, and now here also in this storehouse of the dead, of Roy, Donald's dog. Yet did it not distrust him and sneak away, refusing to enter his house? If he asked her to, she would for the sake of receiving his love go down on all fours. In such ludicrous acquiescence there was also an element of pathos, perhaps. Well, as he had often enough warned himself, there were bound to be discrepancies when a god mated with a mortal. Was not mythology full of instances?

Such reflections were dangerous: he made his fingers become fingers again. Then, almost as if he were a mortal himself, he remembered Nell in Oban, so stupid and faithful that for a year she had continued to believe he was still a sailor, and had even written to him care of the Shipping Company here in Glasgow; but—he almost leapt with shock to recall it—*she* was the indolent receiver in their love-making, the smeller of the Elysian flowers, he the industrious purveyor. As shapeless as a snow-woman, with fat on her belly that she loved to grab by handfuls as if it was her money in the bank, and low-hung breasts that she urged him to suck, she had been making him labour at that degradation on the strength of a promise which, remembering her soft cackles of gratification, he now not merely strongly suspected but felt in his very bowels would never be kept. He wondered if she was aware that his marriage to her was bigamous; it could be that that secret, which he had so resourcefully been keeping from her,

143

had long ago been reached by her ant-eater's curiosity. Would he, when in jail, put there by her treachery, hear her cackles of triumph? Why had she so frequently, at intimate moments, praised her niece, the strait-laced teacher from Dingwall, whose portrait in graduation robes sat on the table beside the bed? The last of his duties, before climbing in, was to turn the picture to the wall. Grotesque modesty had been the reason, so he had thought; now he suspected another, hard to conjecture. There could be no doubt, however, that he had been the one exploited. Human depravity being what it was, he ought to have realised long ago that a promise so often and so readily given was not meant to be kept: she would never put his name beside hers on her bank book. It had been a bit of stinking fish she had dangled, and he, like a mewing tom, had leapt for it—how many times? Sixty at least. No wonder his hams ached now at the recollection.

With Margaret, the huge crawler and whiner, it was altogether different; with her he was gloriously the god. Yes, now; but in a month or two's time would she not be displaying that female arrogance of the bed with which all women, whatever their size, were born? And by Jupiter, with her bulk and strength she could be really formidable. What, too, in the name of God Almighty, if she fell pregnant, as she was so obviously set on? There was always Australia, of course, and it would be but just if his flight were to be financed with her money.

The attendant returned with the newspapers.

'Ah, thank you,' said Angus. 'Oh, I'm terribly sorry, but it has just occurred to me that what I'm looking for may not be in these at all, but rather in the issues of December 24th.'

'Well, sir, I'll look them out once you've seen through that lot.'

'Thank you. You are most obliging.'

The attendant felt flattered as he watched his unusual customer walk to a table with the newspapers. He wondered who he was: a gentleman, obviously; not everyone was as appreciative. An author, maybe? More likely a retired army officer, a colonel who had seen service in the East. Though

144

his eyes were as blue as a baby's, he had the look of a man smart at his own job and good at making others smart at theirs.

Angus sat down where the attendant could see him. If there was a picture he intended to tear it out, but it would be easier if first he established confidence in his integrity.

On the front page of the newspaper on top of the pile was a picture of Santa Claus in a city store, handing out gifts to apprehensive children. Inside, too, were Christmas advertisements. No wonder old McIndoe, the minister on the island before this present fellow McNeil, had made a point of eating only dry bread and drinking only cold water on Christmas Day. Angus himself preferred turkey and whisky, but had he been a minister it would have been different.

Then he saw the first sign of what he was searching for.

*   *   *

When the door bell rang Janet turned from arranging the pea and bean tins on the shelves. Gleaming like small seals in their oilskins and sou'westers, the two new McArthur boys slunk in. Their faces were pink from walking in the rain. The elder carried a tattered shopping bag belonging to old Mrs McCuish, while the younger had a long hazel stick with rings of bark cut from it.

As she prepared to serve them her face was grimmer than usual, so that Neil, her husband, calculating at the post office counter, knew at once she was thinking about that photograph she had mentioned to him. He wondered whether she would speak about it if the boys didn't. Half of her nature would be crying out to hurry, there wasn't a minute to lose; the other half would be saying dourly it didn't matter, she had been waiting without hope for twenty years, another minute or two made little difference. So it had always been with this wish of hers to adopt a child. Adoption was, he agreed, important; it needed careful consideration. But Janet had made of it a long walk over fiery coals with her feet and soul bare. He had read of men in the East who could do that

145

without so much as a blister. Lost in the middle somewhere, poor Janet, not having the knack, would burn through to the bone.

'That's the fog-horn,' remarked Tom, breaking the silence that irked him. 'It's like a big bull out on the sea.'

'Yes,' she said. 'Well, what is it you want?'

'It's no' for us, it's for Mrs McCuish. An ounce of tobacco, a packet o' Abernethy biscuits, and a quarter-pound packet o' margarine.'

'So you're Mrs McCuish's message-boys now?' asked Neil cheerfully. 'It used to be Andra Elliot.'

'We're nearer,' explained Tom. He stepped closer to Neil, keeping a wary eye on Janet at the same time. 'Is it true she sits oot all night on her rocking-chair?'

'I believe so.'

'When the moon's shining?'

'I expect she'll like it better then.'

'Is she a witch?'

'She's a nice kind old body.'

'Who's been putting such silly notions into his head?' snapped Janet to John. 'Not you, I hope?'

He shook his head.

'Somebody said,' muttered Tom, 'owls came and sat on her heid.'

'Rubbish,' said Janet. 'She's over eighty. She's got a lot to remember, so she finds it hard to sleep. There's nothing strange about it. We all get old some day.'

'Janet, they're just bairns.'

'That's why they've got to learn.'

Tom scraped at the floor with his stick, in a huff. 'Johnny's brought the photo,' he muttered, as if he felt she shouldn't be shown it for her cheek.

'What photo's that now? The one of you in the Home?'

Neil wondered if she was deceiving the boys; not the older one, he thought.

'The one wi' Jean McDonnell in it,' said Tom, impatient with such shortness of memory.

'Sometimes I think,' she said, 'you must have cut off your

146

brother's tongue and flung it into the sea where the sea-gulls have eaten it.'

John blushed. 'I've brought the photo,' he said, feeling under his oilskin.

It was in an envelope.

Janet glanced out of the window. Coming up the path towards the shop were old Maggie McBirnie in her black shawl and buttoned boots, and her daughter-in-law big Annie, who had a voice, it was said, to scare the shepherds over on Jura. She had a mind, too, about as delicate in its attitude to other minds as a cow's itchy rump to a stob post. She was Robert McDiarmid's foster-mother; it was said she was lucky to have so fat and easy-natured a boy to look after, any other would have been terrified by her roaring kindness.

'Quick,' cried Janet, pushing the two boys in front of her. 'We'll go the back way into the house. Neil, here's Maggie and Annie McBirnie coming. You attend to them.'

'Mind, Janet,' said her husband, 'it's just a photograph.'

'My goodness, what else would I think it was?'

At the door Tom resisted: 'What about Roy?'

'Don't tell me that dog's with you?'

'He goes everywhere with me.'

'You explain to them, Neil,' she said, and pushed Tom out.

'But what explanation, woman,' asked Neil, with a sigh, 'is big Annie not going to crush like a dog a bone, with old Maggie picking up the fragments to gie them a bit sook with her auld gums?'

The house was about twenty yards from the shop. A breeze blew the soft rain against their faces. On the other side of the wild-rose and fuchsia hedge Roy could be heard whimpering. He knew they had come out of the shop.

'If you had a bone or something,' said Tom boldly, 'it'd keep him quiet.'

'We'll see.'

'He'll eat crusts if that's all you've got.'

In the living-room, where a fire was burning, she dried her hands nervously on her apron. John brought the envelope from under his oilskin.

147

They heard the dog whining.

'I think it would be better to gie him what you've got to gie him,' suggested Tom.

She found herself hurrying into the kitchen, lifting down a bone with which she had meant to make stock for soup, and returning with it to hand it to Tom.

He dashed out, bare-headed, gleefully shouting: 'Roy, look what I've got for you.'

Again she wiped her hands. 'Don't you think you should take off your oilskin?'

He had already removed his sou'wester and made Tom remove his.

Her fingers had hardly enough strength to slip the photograph out of the envelope. For God's sake, she told herself, what do you expect? Neil is right: it's only a photograph, and not a single soul in it is anything to me or ever likely to be.

At last she had it out. There were rows of children. Her eyes blurred.

'Do you see my specs anywhere?' she asked. She could not look for them herself. Blind and weak, she had to sit down, the photograph shaking in her hand.

He found the spectacle case on the sideboard beside the framed portrait of a woman with two girls. He wondered if one of them was Mrs Lindsay when she was a child.

She took her glasses out and put them on. 'Sit down,' she said. 'So this is the famous photograph?' She stared first at the woman about her own age, evidently the Matron, short and stout in a dark dress with a white collar. But for the strictness of her expression she could almost have been taken for Mary McArthur. For some reason that resemblance struck Janet as unlucky.

John rose and came forward. 'Jean's the one—'

'No, no, no, don't tell me!' she cried, pushing him away. 'I'm sorry, boy. Let me pick her out for myself.'

He nodded, but he didn't see how she could, since she had never seen Jean; and even if she had it wasn't really very like Jean.

Janet's eyes devoured the photograph. There were at least

a dozen little girls she could have chosen; but she wanted one only, and that was the child who had been with her ever since the boys had first mentioned her. She knew her, had spoken to her, had even washed and combed her red hair; so it should have been easy and delightful to pick her out. But it was not: her finger, creeping along the row, hesitated at one after another, not because every one represented a disappointment, nor because her finger, with instinct like an animal's, recognised that in their faces did not flow the same blood as in it; no, no, it was simply because they were all dressed alike, and the photograph besides, wasn't clear.

She found respite in picking out the two brothers. There was John, standing peculiarly straight; no other boy held himself so stiffly. Why did he? Somehow she was reminded of the Celtic cross in the field in front of the mined priory on Orsay; perhaps because it was so erect in contrast with so many other stones there flat or leaning, and perhaps, too, because on it was sculptured the crucified Christ.

His hand was on his brother's shoulder in front. Tom was pouting, as if either he was about to cry or had just been crying.

'This is you all right,' she said, 'and your brother.'

He nodded and smiled.

'What was the matter with him?'

He hesitated: 'Sometimes he was frightened.'

'Of what? They weren't bad to you there?'

'No.'

'The Matron looks as if she would be fair enough. A bit severe, maybe, but she would need to be in such a job.'

Again he nodded. He couldn't explain to her that Tommy needed the sort of kindness that no one in the Home had been able to give him: Matron's had been too stern, Agnes's and the other servants' too brief and sentimental. Mrs McArthur and Flora treated Tommy in the right way; that was why he had become so happy and confident and seldom cried.

'And this—' Janet was really choosing at random—'is your friend, Jean—what's her name?'

'McDonnell. No, that's not her. That's Peggy Morrison.'

149

'This one then?'

'No. That's Molly Jamieson.'

'This?'

'No.'

'You show me then. How do you expect me to know? I've never seen her, and I'm never likely to. Goodness, I can't even remember her name.'

'It's Jean McDonnell. That's her.' He put his finger, accurate with pride and affection, on the little, rather glum-faced girl next to the Matron.

'Her? But I thought you said she was always laughing?'

As he gazed at Jean, he remembered how she had not been feeling well and so looked sad. But he could hear her laughter now, in this quiet room, and all over the island.

'So this is her?' Janet, though, was not looking at the photograph as she spoke; she was seeing in his eyes the fulfilment of the promises with which she had been sustaining herself. Any child that could inspire such joyful memories in another, both of them orphans, must be a treasure.

'And her hair's red?'

'Yes.'

'You mentioned freckles?'

He touched his own nose.

'One thing I'll say about her: she does look as if she's got pluck. She's the one faced up to the bullies?'

'Aye.' She had, indeed. She had more courage than he would ever have. She could have climbed higher on the cliffs than even Andrew Elliot.

'I think you miss her?'

He turned away, almost in tears.

'I'm sorry, lad. Do you think a girl like her would do well here? On Calisay, I mean? Would a place like this suit her? I think you said it would.'

Oh yes, it would. She would climb higher than Andrew, run as fast as Angus McFadyen across the sands, plunge into the sea to shout back at the seals, and lead the expedition across the strand to Orsay that even Robert McDiarmid and Jean Fairlie only talked about.

'You don't want this photograph?' asked Janet.

He turned pale.

'I mean, not now? Can I keep it, for a day or two? You'll get it back.'

Though he nodded, his eyes were on the photograph like a cat's on a mouse. She felt if she gave way to her desire to slip it into her apron pocket, his hand would pounce and snatch it. 'There's no need, is there, to mention to Mrs McArthur or Flora that I've borrowed it?' Perhaps he, being a child, did not need an explanation, but the world would: 'You can understand, I'm sometimes lonely here. I've got no children.' She saw him glance towards the portrait on the sideboard. 'Those are my sister's. They're in New Zealand. I'll just look at this for a day or so, and then you can have it back. That won't do it any harm, will it? These children, you see, they haven't got mothers; that makes them in a way like me.' Then she was forced to a stop, faced with a blankness that might have panicked her into weeping had not Tom come marching in, grinning as if it had been he who'd just enjoyed the bone.

'I clapped him on the heid while he was eating it,' he said, 'and he didna growl.'

*   *   *

Under the heading HORRIBLE SOUTH SIDE TRAGEDY it said:

Last night the police were summoned to 215 Findlorn Street, Govanhill, where they found the body of a woman who had apparently been savagely beaten to death with a hatchet in the decorated kitchen of her house. She is understood to be Mrs Olive Sneddon, twenty-six years of age, mother of two children, aged six and three respectively. Her husband, John Sneddon, has been taken into custody.

There followed some cautiously edited comments by neighbours. These were to the effect that Sneddon, a cobbler, had been well liked, though very quiet. He had doted on his sons.

The silence on Mrs Sneddon was significant enough. Yet it was of her that this particular newspaper had unearthed a photograph. In it, with hair straggling down to her neck—probably lousy too, in spite of the scented shampoos lavished on it—she sniggered in a crass, brazen way, almost skelly-eyed with amorous appeal. From the glimpses given it looked as if she had been well enough papped, unless, of course—which was more than likely—she used foam-rubber aids. Her own tits would have been as abortive as her mind.

Alive, she would have disgusted Angus—he would not have touched any part of her with the point of his walking stick; dead, though, her face a more brilliant jumble of decorations than any Christmas tree, she was quite fascinating. He had read once in a book on psychology that such murders, provoked by sexual jealousy, were like orgasms: the hatchet the member, fate the womb, death the offspring. Afterwards, however, what of that little shudder of dissatisfaction, followed by the spasm of zeal to try again in the hope that next time would bring one nearer to the anticipated glory? And what had the poor bastard her husband done, after the last climactic stroke? With the hatchet wilted in his hand, had he sunk down on his knees to pray beside her? So, according to Margaret, the neighbours had found him; and so, according to those neighbours, his son, the elder boy John, must have peeped in and seen him.

In another of the newspapers was a photograph of the family walking along the promenade at Rothesay. He recognized the place from the Pavilion gardens in the background. The man was pushing a go-cart with a baby in it; the woman had the other child by the hand. She had her hair cut with a fringe across the brow; her dress was very tight, no doubt to display her buttocks tastily, and she was shambling along on very high-heeled shoes—a prostitute on holiday. Her husband, looking at least fifteen years older, in cheap flannels and sports jacket, was commonplace and plebeian, with not a ha'pennyworth of distinction about him. The baby could not be seen, but the older child could, and there seemed no reason

152

at all to be surprised at his parentage.

Angus found it easy to imagine her slipping off in the evenings, missing never a dance, and afterwards sneaking away with pick-ups to drink and be adulterous. At home, in the single-end for which he would be paying at least fifteen pounds for the Fair Fortnight, her husband would be waiting, not only for her to come clip-clopping sated back, but also for the moment when the hatchet would be raised.

In the last newspaper was a photograph of the boy, John. Though it had been taken three years or so before, it was very like what he was today. He had an eager, cadging sort of smile, thrusting himself up to destiny as if to an indulgent grandfather. Well, look what destiny had put into his pocket.

The whole affair, like every other like it, indeed like every human activity, no matter on what level or of what nature, was further proof of mankind's irredeemable primitiveness. The fools who laughed on Sunday afternoons at the antics of chimpanzees and blue-arsed apes in zoos never seemed to be aware they themselves were being similarly laughed at by the Superior Being through his few chosen representatives.

It would not have been easy to tear out the pictures if distrust had caused the attendant to keep watching. Two of them were in the centre of the page, and a penknife had to be used. But they were got out neatly and successfully, including the account of the murder. Then, folding the newspapers, Angus returned them with such courteous thanks that it never occurred to the attendant to inspect them.

Fifteen

Herself neurotic, with her constitutional timidity and fatalism never quite kept out of her protrusive pale-blue eyes, Sheila McNeil, the minister's wife, nevertheless felt it her duty to support and defend her husband, somewhat to the surprise and sometimes to the indignation of those against whom she considered he needed defending. He was as robust physically as she was delicate, and spiritually was embedded deep and immovable in a form of Christianity so old-fashioned and yet to him so satisfying that more subtle-minded, modern, and rather less confident colleagues were often exasperated into thinking him stupider than he really was. He could not see his Christ as a hangman; therefore he was opposed to capital punishment. He could not see Him approving, for whatever reason, weapons intended to incinerate or poison millions of His creatures; therefore he belonged, quietly, with no platform or procession appearances, to an association of Presbyterian clergymen devoted to nuclear disarmament.

Parishioners began by distrusting him because he had not been bred for the ministry. Before and during the war he had been a sea-going engineer. His experiences then had encouraged him in his hitherto vague ambition to enter the church. For years he had studied and saved, until he was able to go to the university, take a degree and be ordained. Slow, patient and tolerant, he could also be very stubborn. Most people grew to like and respect him, but only after knowing him for some time; at first they were put off by his apparent self-sufficiency and muscular certainties.

In Munnock, the village in Dumfriesshire where he had been minister before coming to Calisay, everyone had been taken aback when he had married Sheila Broderick, only daughter of the old widowed doctor there. With her beautiful fair hair coiled heavily on her fragile head, her bulging anxious

154

eyes, and her thin, poorly developed body, she had not seemed to the dour farmers and their practical wives the kind to find much comfort or delight in any man's arms, and especially in arms that, though clad in black, were brawny and perhaps no more tender than a ploughman's. Moreover, with her frequent illnesses, she had hardly seemed suitable for the responsibilities of a manse's mistress. At heart she agreed, and probably never would have married him if her old father hadn't died, leaving her alone and bewildered. That Archie was not at ease among the green fields and hills of Munnock helped her to make up her mind to accept him.

After marriage she had with remarkable and commendable earliness become pregnant. Joy had given her beauty and assurance. People who had been sure she'd pass straight through immaturity into empty middle age, were delighted to find her looking young, and talking at last as if she had a long, happy life ahead of her as wife and mother, and not only a dutiful one as a minister's helpmate. Then, through miscarriage, the child had been lost, and with it all her gains. For weeks she had been very ill, and hadn't wanted to recover. When therefore her husband had got the call to Calisay, the folk of Munnock had decided it was for the best, the change might do her good, although, like parishioners everywhere, they were secretly convinced he would have done better to stay where he was, Christian souls being Christian souls, whether they manured their fields with dung or with seaweed. Besides, his stipend on Calisay would be fifty pounds per annum less. As against that, he would have there all the sea he wanted, storms and gales of it. She, though, might well find more of it than her delicate health and depression could abide.

They had come to the island in March, and so that afternoon in June when Janet Lindsay and Isa McGilvray walked up to the manse on their weekly visit, they had been there only three months. His tolerance was still regarded with disquiet and suspicion: he smoked a pipe, even on Sundays; worked at his boat like a joiner; laughed at remarks which old Mr McIndoe would have condemned as containing the seeds at least of sin; was suspected of not being rigorously opposed

155

to drink; occasionally went to the pictures and laughed as heartily as any; danced at parties; and was thought to have the notion of visiting the hotel bar some Saturday night to discuss beer and other secular topics with the men. His sermons were thought passable; he could give one, too, in intelligible Gaelic; and it was openly admitted to be in his favour that he never accused anyone personally from the pulpit, as his white-haired predecessor had done, or burst into senile railings against the wickedness of the world. Among the men it was considered very much to his credit that he loved the sea, and had served on it for years—bravely, too, as was accidentally discovered. The women really had only one thing against him: he was inclined to make himself too common, as if he was an ordinary person. As Elspeth put it, what was the good of a minister if he couldn't give the impression that he had some influence with the Almighty, to use if necessary on his flock's behalf?

As for his wife, though all felt sorry for her, she wasn't popular. There was, for instance, her unchristian prejudice against boarded-out children. Then she was always complaining. True enough, the loss of her child and the unlikeliness of her having another were something to complain about. Still, hadn't she knees, and faith, and a God to pray to? But these were preliminary opinions; if she deserved better she would get them.

She was waiting for her visitors in the corner of the little walled garden, among the rose bushes and apple trees that old Mr McIndoe, whose memory she hated, had let go to ruin. His most unforgivable neglect, however, had been to die in the manse. With a superstitiousness thought strange in a minister's wife, she saw death as obscene. She would have explained that it was because she desired life so much, in the shape of children sprung from her own and her husband's bodies.

Indeed, coming along the road, Isa had remarked to Janet that she would have to stop these visits if Sheila kept on spoiling them by talking about those children she was determined to have, no matter what the doctors advised.

Janet understood both her friends. Didn't Isa herself keep saying, with an almost equal obsession, that she had never wanted any children? Yes, but it wasn't true, it was only Isa's way of trying to disguise what wasn't only an incurable regret but also a shame. For all her hard voice and insulated face Isa was really a sensitive woman, in whom Janet could read her own saga of childlessness, beginning with the courtship when every flower, bird, cloud, and baby had been lovely and one's own, and ending now with the onset of the menopause, and grief the only yield of all those long years of waiting. Those love-makings, with one's husband shamed and guilty; the many false promises, as if nature was considering, only to decide still once more this seed wasn't necessary in its plans for perpetuating the race; and in Isa's case the promise at last kept, the pregnancy known, seen, felt, and come in agony to fruition; the unripe fruit loved for a week and watched withering into death. Only once had Isa spoken of her child, and then with a flippant toughness that had moved Janet more than passionate tears would have; it had frightened her too.

Sheila was dressed in a blue frock, with a pink long-sleeved cardigan. Her face was blotched, as if with midge-bites, and her eyes stared. But her hair gleamed in the sun like a crown. As Isa had said, it was worth visiting Sheila just to see her hair. Isa's own, like Janet's, was dark, lustre-less and streaked with grey.

'Archie's gone with Donald McArthur across to Sanda,' said Sheila, 'with those two orphan children.'

Isa, seated on one gilt basket chair, glanced at Janet on another: her look meant, here we are not a minute arrived, and she's on to the orphans already. Janet did not nod; instead, she frowned and trembled. She too that afternoon intended to talk about them. In her bag she had brought the photograph.

'Yes,' said Isa. 'I'm surprised they haven't got more than the two with them. It was James McFarlane, the journalist from Glasgow, who hired the boat. He's with us this week, writing an article for *Scottish Field*. More free publicity.'

'I believe you're full up,' said Sheila.

157

'If we were six times as big we'd still be full up. As a matter of fact we're having Hugh McEachern and his father over from Islay to see about an extension.'

Sheila leant forward, and whispered: 'Apparently Donald's not at ease in his mind about them.'

'Did he say so, Sheila?'

'Not to me. He was speaking to Archie about it.'

'It would be private then.'

Sheila, aware that she was being gently reproved, pouted and sniffed. 'Not very, Isa,' she said. 'I believe he's mentioned it to others.'

'It's true,' said Janet. 'There's a change in Donald McArthur.'

'Well, hasn't he lost Hector?' asked Isa.

'Yes, there's that, of course. But he was always such a humorous man. You mightn't think it to look at him. Mind last Hallowe'en, Isa? He came to the party dressed as an old woman. You never saw anything funnier.'

And I never heard anything funny described more seriously, thought Isa. But her heart warmed towards her solemn, hard-working, fair-minded friend.

'I understand Donald's feelings,' said Sheila, with a shudder not quite involuntary. 'It's how I would feel myself.'

'So you've told us before, Sheila,' said Isa. 'Well, there's one happy girl on the island, now we've decided to have the builders in.'

'Flora?' asked Janet.

'Yes.'

'Well, she deserves to be happy.'

Isa nodded: at forty-nine, she could have had a daughter like Flora; the child she had lost had been a girl. 'I've told Hugh he's a lucky man.'

'And she's a lucky girl, Isa. He's a fine young fellow, and he dotes on her.' Janet had to restrain herself from picking up her bag and taking out the photograph.

Sheila clapped her pale, thin hands. 'They'll have half a dozen beautiful babies and live happily ever after,' she said. There were tears in her eyes.

Isa changed the subject. 'Just another month or so to the

158

Islay Fair,' she said. 'Last year was a triumph for Calisay. Mr Morton-Home was so pleased. A first, two seconds, and at least one third.'

'For what?' asked Sheila.

'Oh, all kinds of things: cattle and jam-making, for two. Donald McDonald, Elspeth's man, got the first for his Ayrshire cow, Aileen of Calisay.'

'I think it's shocking how cattle are named as if they were human,' said Sheila.

'I'm sure if you were to ask Donald he'd tell you his Aileen's more human than his Elspeth. Certainly the cow gives him more peace.'

'Why shouldn't she nag him? He drinks. But there's one thing I've noticed.' Her face turned pinker than her cardigan. 'I hate to talk about it.'

'Don't, then,' said Isa, smiling.

'I've got to. It's the horrible way they have here of mating their animals.'

'You mean, taking the cow to the bull?'

'Yes, in public. You could be in Munnock twenty years and never see it. I've seen it twice already. At the side of the road, if you please. And who, on one occasion, was holding the halter? A child, a small boy. I've spoken to Archie about it.'

'And what did he say?' asked Isa. She liked the minister, well enough to tell him she didn't believe in his or anybody's God.

Again Sheila blushed. 'He's silly in some ways. He thinks as a minister he's got to see good in everybody and everything.'

'Well, hasn't he?' asked Isa, laughing.

'What's good in that? I think it's filthy. Don't you agree, Janet?'

Janet did. Coming from Glasgow, she had never been able to accept this public mating of cow and bull. Even her cockerel had to wait till her back was turned. 'I think a place could be arranged for it in private. But here's something I brought to show you.'

She opened her bag and took out the photograph. It was

159

in its own envelope, and also in another, larger and stronger.

Trying to keep calm, she couldn't prevent her fingers from suddenly becoming awkward, as if attacked by the arthritis that troubled her every winter.

Her friends watched, Isa amused and affectionate, Sheila superior and a little irritable; at times she found Janet rather stupid and common.

'I got this from Mary McArthur's two boys,' said Janet. 'They were in the shop, and showed it to me. I thought you might be interested. It's all the children in the Home.'

She held it out first to her hostess, who wanted to take it as if it didn't interest her, but her nostrils, thin and almost transparent, quivered like a bird's breast.

'It seems there are babies too,' said Janet, 'but of course you wouldn't expect to see them in the photograph. When they're picked up off the streets, abandoned, they're taken to the Home.'

'Is that what happened to the McArthur boys?' asked Sheila, seeking them out.

'Nobody knows that,' said Isa. 'Not even Mary. I think it's a bad mistake. There's such a thing as heredity. Look at it in horses and cattle; it's bound to be the same with human beings. These children could be sprung from thieves or worse.'

Janet knew this was Isa's opinion; she had combated it before, and she did so again, but this time with greater determination.

'I don't see what difference it makes, Isa,' she said. 'Because a wean's father was a thief it doesn't mean he will turn out to be one too. That's to say if honest folk have the rearing of him. Same with a lassie: even if her mother was a prostitute off the streets, the girl could grow up to be as good a woman as any of us. I'm sure the minister believes that.'

'Yes, Janet,' said the minister's wife, 'but as I said, Archie's got too simple a view of things. I agree with Isa. If it's in the blood not all the best upbringing in the world is going to get rid of it.'

'That's Elspeth's opinion,' said Janet. 'I'm surprised you agree with her. In other things you don't. Her head's full of

160

the superstitions of these islands. There's little difference between her and the women who lived here three hundred years ago.'

'There was heredity then, too, Janet,' said Isa.

'I think it's a terrible belief.'

'So it is, Janet. But that doesn't mean it isn't true.'

'I'll tell you both one thing: I don't see how anyone could believe in Christ Jesus who believed such a thing about children. Are you trying to make me believe every thief is descended from a thief and every prostitute from a prostitute?'

'No, Janet. I'm just saying that a child that's descended from a thief is much more likely to be a thief than a child descended from honest people.'

'Even if he's not brought up among thieves? Wouldn't that lessen the chances?'

'It might, Janet. I'll be fair, and say it might.'

'And supposing he, or she, if it's a girl, is shown right from the start a good example, and is given affection, and is made to feel happy and at home? Wouldn't that lessen the chances still more?'

'I think it would, Janet.'

'I know you can't get rid of the possibility altogether. But can you do that with any child, whoever its parents are? Every child's a risk, surely; if I had one born to me tomorrow, how could I know how it would turn out? No mother when she sees her bairn in her arms for the first time ever thinks it's going to be reared to be a murderer. Yet murderers exist.'

Isa tried to make her voice gentle; at the same time she refused to acknowledge Sheila's smile of triumph. 'Are you still thinking of adopting one, Janet?' she asked.

'I haven't said so.'

'But you are?'

'It's no secret.'

'One of these?'

Janet reached forward and took the photograph from her friend's hand. She looked at Jean and felt bold. 'Maybe,' she said. 'What do you think of the Matron? Does she remind you of somebody?'

They took the photograph again.

'She seems an intelligent kind of woman,' said Sheila.

'Good at her job, I would say,' remarked Isa.

'She doesn't remind you of somebody?'

Both shook their heads.

'Well, it doesn't matter.' She held out her hand again for the photograph.

Sheila was unwilling to give it up. 'Which one were you thinking of, Janet?'

Janet with a proud smile shook her head.

'There are one or two nice little girls,' said Isa.

'Thieves and prostitutes, no doubt.'

Isa smiled. She loved her friend for feeling offended. 'I'm sorry I've upset you, Janet. You do what you think is best for you. It'll turn out well.'

Janet at last got the photograph back from Sheila. 'You haven't upset me, Isa,' she said. 'I've got my own beliefs.'

'But couldn't you apply for one to board out first? Then, if you liked her, you could have it changed to full adoption.'

'How long do I wait, Isa? At eight she could be as nice a wee lassie as you could find, at fifteen a thief, at twenty a prostitute.'

'Which one are you thinking of, Janet?' asked Sheila again.

Janet shook her head and returned the photograph safe in its two envelopes to her bag, which she snapped shut.

'The boys spoke of a little girl they knew at the Home,' she said, unexpectedly, joy in her voice. 'You should have heard them. You should have seen the liking for her in their eyes. According to them—and what better judges could you get?— she's as brave, generous, and cheery a little lass as you'd find in a lifetime's search. Bonny enough too, with red hair. Do you think it matters to me if her father was a thief or her mother a prostitute?'

They saw tears streaming down her cheeks, but to have tried to console her would have been an impertinence. She was experiencing a joy each of them had known once and in all likelihood never would again. They were the ones to be pitied, not she. So they sat in silence, watching her wipe away her

162

tears, listening to her mutters of apology, hearing too the larks above, and finding in their souls for those few moments a tranquillity as spacious as that of the blue sky.

Sixteen

Joy enabled Margaret to forgive, especially one like Helen who was for ever deprived of that same forgiving joy. To communicate it, true, was not easy: Helen might understandably receive it as condescension; therefore Margaret continued to carry it banked, as it were, in her own heart, or rather throughout her whole awakened body, during those jubilant days between that first visit of Angus's and his promised next.

Helen, too, preserved silence; but whether hers was imposed by jealousy chained but still savage, or by penitence for her display of viciousness, Margaret could not tell. Then, less than a week before Angus was to come again, a letter appeared on Margaret's desk, with the Calisay postmark. Trembling, she thanked God it was not in his handwriting, for if it had been she felt sure he would be, for some no doubt valid reason, putting off his visit. However, this letter was not even addressed to her, but to the Department. Her chief, George Gilliespie, had scribbled in pencil on the envelope: 'Will you deal with this, Meg? You know these wild Hielanders better than any of us.' At first she wondered if that was a reference to her friendship with Angus, but she thought not, for how was George, or even Todd with his hairy, lecherous ears, to know? The evidence of her jewellery and gleaming eyes was hardly enough. But even if they had been laughing at her, what woman in the world was better protected against them?

The letter was from Mrs Lindsay, who kept the shop on Calisay. She wanted to know, in sentences as stark and stiff as her writing, whether it was permitted to take a child for boarding out and then later, 'if it was so desired', adopt it for good. Her financial circumstances were satisfactory; she had her husband's approval. She hoped for a favourable answer as soon as possible. Her last, proud, stalwart sentence was as

164

poignant as a cry of grief: 'I have never had any children of my own.'

To reply, as an official, was simple: yes, madam, it is permitted, even encouraged. As a woman, however, also with no children of one's own, replying was more difficult; the cold sentences were then as much a hurt to oneself as to the lonely unhappy woman in the house by the jetty. Still, it had to be written, officially, and sent in to George for his approval and signature.

Later he joked to her about it: 'Looks like another order from Calisay, Meg. You make a good commercial traveller.' Then he added, misinterpreting the glitter in her eyes: 'Sorry.'

'No need to apologize to me, George,' she said. 'I'm all right.'

That afternoon Todd stopped by her desk, bent over, and whispered, his breath foul: 'I hear you're all right, Meg. Care to let me find out for myself? A couple of weeks ago I'd have said there was no need for experimentation. Now I'm not so sure. What about it?'

The proposal, viler than his stink of rotten teeth, had her smiling, where formerly she would have been outraged. If Todd was compelled to compliment her, she must indeed have blossomed miraculously: this joy within her was really transfiguring her whole appearance. She felt softer, sweeter, more relaxed, truly feminine. Even her feet moved quietly and with some grace; glimpsed under the desk, in their green kid shoes, they had about them a stillness that conjured up, strangely, those mossy stones that lay in the grass about Angus's cottage. She pictured herself some day soon walking among them up to the red-painted door. Blue as the lupins, as the sky, as the sea, his eyes watched her coming.

'How is Chrissie?' she asked, with sincere concern.

He groaned. She saw the hairs sprouting from his chin, a bit of food or dried spit at the corner of his mouth, his blackish teeth, and the boozer's veins in his swollen nose; and beyond all those she saw his little, shrewish, invalid wife.

'For Christ's sake,' he muttered, with a sour grin. 'She's all right too.' Then he slunk off.

165

So joy brought power also. Her whole body yearned for Angus to prove to him its gratitude.

Next morning Helen telephoned. Luckily the office was empty. Her voice was a little sharper than before, but cordial enough.

Poor Helen, thought Margaret. She is trying to show she has forgiven me for provoking her into that display of her naked, unhappy soul. She learns and unlearns; a multitude of little repetitive experiences will in the end have taught her nothing. Only the glory of love can bring joy, knowledge, and wisdom; she knows it can never descend upon her.

'Good morning, Margaret. I thought you would have paid me a visit by this time. However, I've received a letter this morning which I would like your advice about. It's from a woman in Calisay. Lindsay's her name. What's the matter?'

'Nothing. It's just that she wrote to us yesterday.'

'About the girl?'

'What girl?'

'I see. Never mind. What did she want from you?'

'Some information. She wanted to know if a boarded-out child could later be adopted by the foster-parents. But she mentioned no girl.'

'These people appear to think it's a shop I keep. They want the goods on approval. They even order by post.'

Was this another of Helen's favourites in danger of being snatched away? Had Mrs Lindsay been asking the Sneddon boys about the other children in the Home? She had, Margaret now recalled, inquired of her, but very vaguely, as indeed so many others had done from whom nothing further had been heard.

'As a matter of fact, Helen, she keeps the shop on Calisay. Not the bonniest or cheerfullest of women, but I believe she's well respected.'

'Well, am I to have the pleasure of discussing the matter with you personally?'

Aren't we discussing it now? murmured Margaret, but to herself. To Helen she said, trying to keep pity out of her voice: 'Of course. I'll try to take a run out tomorrow morning.'

'Thank you. By the way, Margaret—' she paused, and seemed to be chuckling.

'Yes?'

'You sound quite rejuvenated.'

Better to say nothing, to remain safe and content, risking no bite from the serpent that might lurk within this compliment. Yet how delightful, and how irresistible to cry: 'But of course, Helen. How else did you think I would sound? I am rejuvenated. I think you'll see a difference.'

Again that chuckle.

'Do you know, I've even taken to wearing ear-rings.'

'Have you taken advice? I mean, my dear, women like you and me, who for years have lagged behind fashion, out of contempt for it to some extent, must surely find ourselves somewhat at a loss when we decide to conform.'

Then she hung up.

Next morning, before going out to the Home, Margaret drove to her flat and stole an hour of the department's time to pamper and embellish the femininity that love had released in her. Her hair, newly permed, needed only a luxurious combing; it was, as the girl in the hairdresser's had said, very attractive, with its gloss, its reddish tints, and its natural curliness. Remembrance of Angus was enough in itself to make her eyes sparkle, and where more likely to remember him than in Helen's so barrenly chaste parlour? Lipstick, coral in shade to suit her smart new costume of green jersey wool, was applied with a deftness that had her giggling. How wrong Helen was, to think that any woman in love could ever be at a loss in devising ways to make herself beautiful! To her ears then were clipped, with fingers as sure in their movements as a spider weaving its web, the ear-rings of real pearl that the jeweller, representing his sex rather than his occupation, had said became her magnificently, made her queen-like. Stockings of dearest nylon, and shoes of green glacé kid, turned her legs and feet, hitherto her gauchest parts, almost into elegances. A few dabs here and there of Chanel Number Five completed, not the transformation, for that had been achieved weeks ago, but this present climax of it. As she stared at herself in the

167

long wardrobe mirror, she felt a little of the excitement that Todd, for instance, must have felt. The new foundation garment had been very expensive, but as the corsetière had declared, and as the looking-glass once more confirmed, it was well worth the extra money, for it did what a cheap one couldn't—it collected unobtrusively and comfortably all the makings of a good figure about which she had been so careless for years, and moulded them into this tall shapeliness that had her now putting her fingers to her upper lip to tweak the moustache Angus had there.

Tripping down the stairs she passed Mrs Turnbull puffing up. That stout, unglamorous lady in astonishment moved her shopping bag stuffed with cabbages from one hand to the other, gaped as if a plum was stuck in her mouth, and gasped 'Good morning'. Stricken by a realization of her own comparative dowdiness, she stood still, while Margaret, with a gay greeting, raced blithely downstairs. Mrs Turnbull, she knew, had always agreed with the rest of the neighbours that Miss Mathieson, though on the big side, could have been quite a handsome woman had she paid a little more attention to her appearance. Well, now she had supplied herself with more than they had ever bargained for: not lipstick only, nor earrings, nor a good corset, nor thinner-soled shoes, nor an escort merely, but a lover, privileged, potent and magical.

Driving through the Home gates she felt the bump in the road there, and remembered when she had taken the Sneddon boys to Calisay, or, more memorably, herself to Angus. She was not now the same woman. Nothing, indeed, was the same. Everything was touched with glory. These daisies and buttercups at the side of the drive were as strange and as evocative of joy as the rings glinting on her fingers that clutched the steering-wheel. The Home itself, with its ivy and its background of tall ash trees, was not an institution of charity, but a turreted castle of romance and hope.

Loudly and happily she sang Angus's song: 'Kelvingrove'.

In the hall she met young Nurse Greer, who gaped as if at a marvel, and was still gaping when, at the turn of the stairs, beside the blind, noble head of Walter Scott, Margaret glanced round to smile like a queen and wave. Well then, if ambitious seventeen thus admired and envied, what would resigned forty-eight do, in the person of Helen? So exultant did she feel that, as she paused to stroke the white plaster curls of the Emperor Augustus, she reflected boldly that his had been the reign of Christ's miracles, none of which had been any more wonderful than this metamorphosis which love had wrought in her. Knowing that Helen would have been shocked by such a blasphemy, or at least would have pretended to be, made it all the more exciting. She wanted to stand there at the top of the stairs and shout it throughout the great house, making the babies in the nursery below wail still louder, and causing ex-Lord Provost Macrae's small benign eyes to creep still closer, as if the one needed the other to reassure it, confronted by this tall woman so splendid and puissant in her love. Yes, she wanted to shout to all the world: thank God for babies, for philanthropists, for islands, for rings, for daisies, for emperors, for saviours, for men and women in love.

Helen was standing with her door open. She was like the Mother Superior of a convent: face calmer than the white collar, hands plump but ringless, hair tied in a tight bun, broad brow glistening as if the white bone was too close to the surface, ears small and unadorned, feet in old black shoes because of bunions, and short, thick legs in black lisle.

In comparison I, thought Margaret, her heart thrilling, am really like a queen, even if these grey, sexless eyes are trying to suggest I am instead some kind of harlot.

'Good morning, Margaret,' said Helen, smiling. 'Please come in. It's good to see you again. It's a beautiful morning.'

'Ah yes, but wasted on old smoky Glasgow.'

'Please sit down.'

'On Calisay, for instance, this sun would be like the beginning of time.'

Margaret had a vision of primeval innocence: Angus was foremost in it, and Flora, and the two boys, and she herself.

'I have never been an admirer of primitive communities,' murmured Helen. 'Agnes will bring coffee and biscuits in a few minutes, but before she does I must, now that we are face

169

to face, apologize again.'

Disenchantment threatening, Margaret cried: 'No, don't.'

'But I must.' Helen's voice was gentle but inexorable. Her role was that of the witch who had to restore the victim to the old detested shape.

'No, no, no.' But the restoration had begun. Margaret was slapping her nyloned knees in protest. With an effort she stopped, and said, with gasps: 'I'd really rather you didn't, Helen.'

'For my own sake, Margaret. I should not be able to find rest in my mind again if I did not.'

'It's unnecessary. You've apologized once. That's enough. I accepted it. So it's finished and done with. I didn't come here to talk about myself; I came to talk about Mrs Lindsay.'

Into Helen's voice now crept an artful whine: 'Would you be so cruel as to leave me nailed to my own remorse? I have suffered a great deal, Margaret. I am still suffering.'

Margaret's voice was again the police-woman's; she could have wept at being unable to prevent that gruffness. 'I'm sorry, Helen. But I just won't have it, do you hear? If I'm the one who was insulted, then I'm the one surely who ought to say whether it's finished or not. I want to forget it. I've accepted your apology as sincere. If you go on about it I'll start thinking perhaps it couldn't have been sincere at all. I don't want to think that. Don't force it on me, Helen. On us both, I should say.'

'But to repeat, as I did, the filthy, vulgar, obscene, malicious gossip of kitchenmaids!'

'Drop it, Helen. I'm warning you, drop it.'

'Why are we so cruel about other people's peculiarities? If a man has a large nose, he is laughed at. Yet is he to blame? We all require one another's charity.'

Margaret jumped up. 'I'll have to go, Helen. I'm sorry, but you leave me no alternative.'

'Very well.'

After a long pause, during which she sat with her hands clasped and her eyes closed, Helen said: 'This woman, Lindsay, judging from her letter, seems a crude, selfish person, hardly to be trusted with a dog, far less an orphan child.'

Margaret sat down. 'I wouldn't say that, Helen. I've spoken to her. Of course, she isn't very intelligent, and it's true she's got little humour; but she's well liked yonder, though she's an incomer, and in her own way she's kind and decent. As a matter of fact, she did mention something to me about the possibility of her adopting a child. But you know how it is, thousands of lonely, disappointed women all over the place have the same idea. Any number of them have spoken to me, as if I was some kind of traveller in children.' She laughed a little grimly, at old George's joke. 'Ninety-nine times out of a hundred it comes to nothing. They nurse the idea into their old age.'

'In her case I shall certainly do all I can to make sure it comes to exactly that: nothing.'

'But that's unfair, Helen. May I see her letter?'

'Certainly.' Surprisingly she took it out of her pocket. As she handed it over her fingers seemed to caress it, curiously. It looked as if it had been read several times, and once perhaps crushed in a sudden anguish.

Seeing that postmark Margaret almost lifted the envelope to her lips to kiss it. In her imagination again were the sunlit island, the red-doored cottage, the divan upholstered in orange and black stripes, and the sea with sparkles on it like birds of glory. As she took out the single sheet of notepaper there was a knock at the door, and in clattered Agnes carrying a tray with coffee things on it. Evidently she must have been prepared by Nurse Greer, for her eyes instantly looked to see if this incredible transformation had really taken place. Her eyes, mouth, and the hands that banged down the tray acknowledged that it had. The ear-rings especially fascinated her, so that Margaret, her heart singing, felt like crying to the rough, frank, good-natured servant as if to an admiring child, yes, they were real, these pearls, would she like to touch them, would she even like to try them on?

'Thank you, Agnes,' said Matron. 'That will do.'

But at the door Agnes turned and addressed Margaret: 'Johnny and Tommy Sneddon, miss, are they all right? We've never heard so far. Johnny said he'd write, but you know what bairns are, they forget, thank God.'

'Yes, Agnes, they're all right. They're very happy.'

'Wee Tommy?'

'Especially wee Tommy.'

'Has he got his dog?'

'It was at the jetty to meet him.'

'Are they the kind of folk who'll let him play wi' his tanks?'

'Yes. Mrs McArthur understands children.'

'Aye, but it's possible to understand them, miss, and no' make the right use of it.'

'Mrs McArthur makes the right use of it, I assure you.'

'I'm very pleased to hear it, miss. Will you ever see them again?'

'I think so. Yes, I'm almost sure I shall.'

'Then will you tell them that Agnes was asking for them? And Nellie and Cookie?'

'I'll be sure to.'

'Thanks, miss.' Then with a jerk of her head at Matron, which seemed a gesture of dislike and defiance, she swaggered out.

'Insolent creature,' murmured Helen, smiling. 'She is under notice.'

Another knock on the door, and in again was thrust that coarse, dour, unabashed face. 'If you hae a minute to spare, miss, would you hae the kindness to go and see wee Jean? She's the one gied them the withered daffies, if you mind.' A scowl at Matron accompanied those words.

'Isn't she at school?'

'No. She's just had her tonsils out. She's in bed. There's none braver, but we've no' to think that because a wean doesna greet as much as others she's got no feelings. There's no' a more feeling-hearted wean than Jean McDonnell in the whole world.'

The aggressive praise was really a challenge to Matron, who merely smiled.

'I'll try to take a look in before I go,' said Margaret.

'Thanks, miss. You'll get your reward.'

172

With another glower at Matron, Agnes withdrew.

'From heaven, I think she meant, Margaret. Hardly my own idea, however, of God's messenger.'

'You didn't punish that child for pulling the daffodils, Helen?'

'No. After all, it is true they were withered. But I had to punish her for disobedience. She knew, as every child here knows, that flowers in the grounds are for pleasure, not for pulling.'

'But she had no other present to give them.'

'Children have as many excuses for disobedience as there are daisies on a lawn. You were about to read the letter.'

'You've changed, Helen.'

'No doubt. Nothing is ever quite the same as it was a minute ago.'

'But this is such a noticeable change.'

It was also a terrible one. In those few weeks Helen seemed to have acquired wisdom and courage, but was determined to use them evilly. She was going to have mercy on no one, especially not on herself. Had she really loved the Sneddon boy, and the others before him, with the force of a mother, so that the partings from them—over a hundred in the past fifteen years—must have been like the tearing-up of trees whose roots were deep and wide? Was her heart therefore ravaged and bare? Poised between pity and denunciation, Margaret glanced down and saw, at first, the abyss; then she saw her green shoes, felt the pinch of the ear-rings, remembered the cottage with the red door, and was aware of the letter in her hand.

The writing was the same as in the one she had already read and answered, but here it was even more painstakingly done, as if for an examination. The reason was plain enough: the poor woman, though she did not seem to know it yet, was applying for a child. If she came in person she would have on her best clothes; the result would be no more elegant or fashionable, but just as moving.

173

Dear Madam,

I take the liberty of troubling you. The two little Sneddon boys, Tom and John, who are boarded with my friend Mary McArthur, often come into my shop. I know you will be happy to know they are settling in very well. Mary McArthur is a good woman respected by everyone. The boys showed me a photograph of all the children in your Home. They showed me a girl who they said was their special friend. Her name is Jean McDonnell. If what they say about her is true she is the kind of girl any mother would be proud of. I have no children of my own. But if you have any time to spare to write about her and the other children I would be only too pleased to pass it on to the two boys.

It was heart-warming to picture the serious, grey-haired woman concentrating, keeping the pen at its task on the paper, like a stream of ants, with many journeys to the ink-bottle. Afterwards had she risked letting her lazy, fat, easy-going husband read it, or had she at once slipped it inside the envelope? A woman might not tell a man everything, even though he shared her bed every night.

'I can't see what harm's in this, Helen,' she said. 'I feel sorry for her.'

'Take care you don't cheapen your pity, Margaret. Is the woman merely simple? Does she really think that if I had anything I wished to tell the boys I would choose to do it through her?'

'She just wants to be in the picture, Helen. It's like a little fire she's discovered, to warm herself at. Why drive her away from it?'

'Because she did nothing to kindle it, Margaret, and does nothing to keep it lit. Women like her, with a man in their bed every night, can never bring themselves to accept and cherish the fruit of some other woman's more fruitful love-making. Especially if, as in the present case, the other woman was a prostitute.'

'Is that true, Helen? This little girl's mother really was a prostitute?'

174

'Yes. I am of course telling you in confidence.'

'I didn't know.' Margaret shivered and sighed. She saw herself once more under the gean tree. Angus had broken off a spray of the white blossom for her. She had cried out at its beauty, and he had then, breaking off a tiny piece, asked her to taste it. It had been nasty and bitter. But, he had murmured, the loveliness of the blossom was in no way invalidated: wasn't this the pattern of life, beauty and hideousness, joy and grief, purity and slime, not only side by side, but inextricably involved? Consider the fields where dung brought forth sustenance, consider the human body itself, where the shrine of love and the fount of being were situated in the place of excrement.

Suddenly she became aware again of the limpid beauty of Helen's large grey eyes, and she remembered what she ought never to forget, that for years Helen had run this Home so well that it had become an example in the city and throughout the whole country. No orphan children anywhere were better fed, more warmly clad, or more justly treated. If love had not been given them, perhaps Helen in her stern conscientiousness had thought it was not hers to give.

'But you'll reply to her, Helen?' she asked gently. 'She may be married, but she's still a woman without children, as we are ourselves.'

'I never regard myself as childless.'

'I'm afraid I do.'

'But it is not yet too late, Margaret?'

'I hope not. You will reply to her?'

'No. You see, I have been thinking of paying a visit to Calisay myself next month.'

For one foolish moment Margaret thought Helen, having heard about Angus, was going there to try and entice him away from her. Next moment only the anger remained. What right had Helen to intrude? She herself had been contemplating spending her holiday on Calisay. By that time she and Angus would be recognized as engaged. She would not, of course, amid so strict a community, be able to live in his cottage, but with his motor boat and so many desolate but

175

beautiful seanooks there would be opportunities in plenty. Butterflies, flowers, guillemots and seals were not hostile to lovers.

She would have to make sure her visit and Helen's did not coincide.

'A good idea,' she said, with a smile. 'When are you taking your holidays this year, Helen?'

'I have still to decide. I was thinking of taking one of my children with me.'

'That would be a grand idea. This little girl, Jean McDonnell?'

'Hardly. I wish to enjoy my holiday. She is incorrigibly disobedient. If there is trouble you may be sure she is at the heart of it. You would notice how Agnes admires her. So do the other children, or at least they would if they were allowed. The rebellious and the inexperienced alike often confuse defiance for spirit. But I don't want to be unfair to the child. Considering her origin, she has some fine qualities.'

'Considering her origin! I thought it was a point of honour in you, Helen, never to do that.'

'If I have to punish her, don't think I enjoy doing it. Why are you shaking your head, Margaret? Are you suggesting I do enjoy it?'

'No, Helen. But I'm wondering if you don't rather enjoy punishing yourself. Everyone in the department knows how staunchly you fight on behalf of your children. You see they get every possible advantage. Why then pretend that your attitude is merely correct? It's far, far more than that. I think you really loved the Sneddon boy.'

'Why the past tense, Margaret? Did you see him buried on your delectable island?'

'You know what I meant. And the island is delectable. If you do go, please take Jean with you. The boys will be delighted to see her.'

'And no doubt so would Mrs Lindsay. Am I to be a traveller in children too, carrying my samples with me?'

'I'm sorry. Yes, it might look like that. Well, Helen, is there anything you want to ask me about the boys or the McArthurs?'

'Thank you, Margaret, but there's no need, now that I

intend to visit them myself.'

Don't be so sure, Helen. The hotel happens to be booked up for the whole summer.

Margaret smiled, with love. It had been Angus who had suggested she should book.

'Very well, Helen. I suppose I must go now. Thank you for the coffee. You must come out some evening and pay me a visit.' She stood up. 'By the way, can I see the little girl, for a minute or two?'

'Why do you wish to see her?'

'My goodness, need you ask that? She's just had her tonsils out, she's lonely, and she's recently lost two friends whom I can tell her a little about.'

'Are you sure you wish to see her? Isn't it rather that you wish her to see you?'

Margaret blushed. 'I resent that, Helen.'

Helen laughed. 'I don't think you do, really. You should have seen yourself when Agnes was staring at you. However, if you think you can make the child any happier by talking to her for a minute or two, I have no objection. I shall go with you.'

As they walked along the passages, Margaret said: 'If I'd known I'd have brought her some comics to read.'

'She has enough. Besides, she has her school work to do.'

There were eight black iron beds on the waxed floor. Everything was clean and tidy as in a hospital; even the school books on the chair by the girl's bed were neatly arranged. Yet that bed had obviously been placed to get most light from the window and also the best view of the grounds with its great green trees. Jean was propped up on pillows. Her face was pale; her very freckles seemed faded. Round her neck was a pink scarf. She was reading a comic.

'Someone to see you, Jean,' said Matron.

By the child's side lay a doll dressed, touchingly, in pyjamas of the same blue-and-white striped material as her own. Though she smiled up at the two women, she put her hand on the doll's thin, patchy hair as if to reassure both herself and it.

177

'Good morning, Jean,' said Margaret. 'I thought you would like to hear about John and Tom Sneddon.'

Jean nodded eagerly. 'My froat's still a wee bit sore,' she said huskily. 'Are Johnny and Tommy all right?'

'Throat, Jean. Miss Mathieson knows you have just had your tonsils out. She was always having sore throats, Miss Mathieson. I think it must have been because she was always shouting louder than anyone else. Do you see those trees? The highest ones? Well, this little monkey climbed to the very top; last week, too, when her throat was bad.'

It surprised and moved Margaret to see the relationship between the two: the child of eight and the woman of almost fifty, each as resolute in her own way as the other; whatever else was between them, respect certainly was.

'I was just pretending I was Robinson Crusoe,' murmured Jean. 'If I climbed to the very top maybe I could see—It was daft.'

'Foolish,' said Matron. 'And of course it was very dangerous too.'

What, wondered Margaret, had the child pretended she might see? Rescue coming? Or the far-off island where her friends had been taken?

'Yes, Jean,' she said, 'they're all right. They send you their love.'

She grinned, pleased. 'They'll have forgotten me already.'

'No, I don't think so.'

'Could you please tell me about the place, miss?'

'Miss Mathieson's a busy woman, Jean. She hasn't time to stand blethering to you.'

'Just for a minute, Matron.'

'Yes, I think I can spare a minute.' Margaret sat down on the edge of the bed and, not curbing her own enthusiasm, described Calisay, its sands, caves, cliffs, sea-birds, flowers and ubiquitous sea.

Jean listened with eyes closed. Her fist was clenched on her doll's head.

'I'd like it,' she said. 'Is there a school?'

'Yes. It's only got a dozen pupils.'

178

'I hope the teacher's good. Wee Tommy used to get worried about his lessons. Has Johnny got a pal yet?'

'Friend, Jean.'

'I don't know,' said Margaret. 'But I'm sure he will have.' 'Are there boats?'

'It's an island, you see; there are lots of boats.'

'Will Johnny and Tommy get sailing in them?'

'Of course.'

'Tommy said he was to get a dog. Did he get it?'

'Yes. It's black and white.'

'What's its name?'

'Roy.'

'Is it for the sheep?'

'Yes, and for the cattle too.'

'Does Tommy go wi' it to bring in the sheep?'

'I'm sure he does.'

Jean picked up one of her school books, and took out of it a sheet of paper. 'This is a letter I've just wrote to them. Do you think I could send it?'

'That's for Matron to say, dear.'

She was reluctant to let Matron have it, but had to. She watched anxiously as it was censored.

'I don't see why not,' said Matron, and handed it back.

Delighted, Jean gave it to Margaret. 'Could you send it for me, miss?'

'Miss Mathieson is not a postman, Jean,' murmured Matron. 'We have envelopes and stamps of our own, you know.'

'It's all right, Matron,' said Margaret, quickly. 'I'll send it. I would like to. As a matter of fact, I'm writing one myself to Calisay.'

She noticed Helen smiling.

'Is your letter to Tommy and Johnny, miss?' asked Jean.

'No.'

'Is it to the folk they're staying with?'

'No. Well, not really.'

'Don't ask impertinent questions, Jean. Miss Mathieson needn't tell you to whom she is writing.'

'No, but I wouldna like my letter to go amissing.'

179

Margaret smiled. 'Don't worry. It won't.'

'You've no' read it yet.'

Margaret had been a little nervous about reading it. She might want to shed a tear or two, but could not with Helen there.

Deer Tomy and Jonny this is me your pal Jean im in bed my tonsuls are out are ther roses wheer yous are heer ther butiful wif a lovelly smell Jim murgytroyyd got a toof out wif the dintest sombuddy asked for wee jim cameron so hes gon everybuddy is asking for you hop youve got a dog tomy oh and nancy broons gon as well she was reely glad rite soon.

'It's got lots of mistakes,' admitted Jean. 'I'm no' very good at spelling, and I always leave out commas.'

'You must write it out again with all the mistakes put right,' said Matron.

Jean made a face. 'But that would be cheating,' she said.

Margaret rose. 'No, Helen,' she whispered, her own voice husky. 'It's much better as it is. I'll be sure to send it, Jean.'

'Thanks, miss.'

'There is only one thing,' said Matron. 'What do you mean by saying that Nancy Brown was 'really glad'? Were we all so cruel to her here?'

Jean shook her head, and scowled.

'Nancy was really very sorry to leave us. Why do you tell such a lie?'

'She said to me she was glad.'

'You think, Jean, because you would be glad to go yourself that everyone else must be.'

Again the child shook her head. In spite of her effort to restrain them tears came into her eyes and trickled down her cheeks.

Suddenly Margaret bent and kissed her on the brow. All three were surprised. Matron was amused also.

'Goodbye, Jean,' said Margaret.

'Goodbye, miss. You're looking awful nice.'

Outside Margaret had to dab her eyes with her handkerchief. 'Sorry,' she muttered.

'Am I to admire your tears, Margaret, like your ear-rings?' Then before Margaret could find anything to say, Helen had turned and waddled away, with apparent serenity.

As Margaret slowly followed she wanted to cry not only to Helen but to the whole world: 'My tears are a thousand times more precious than my pearls.' But she said nothing, and when a minute or two later she took her leave she had made up her mind to write to Mrs Lindsay and urge her, if she really wanted to adopt a child, to take Jean McDonnell before it was too late.

As she was crossing the hall downstairs she was accosted by Agnes, who had been lying in wait.

'I just wanted to tell you, Miss Mathieson,' she said. 'You're looking a treat.'

Then with a wink and a jerk upwards of her thumb she rushed away again.

Driving back into the city Margaret again sang 'Kelvingrove' and felt herself to be at last where she had always wanted to be: at the heart of a rich muddle of human life. She knew she would never understand half of it, and would find sorrow and anguish such as could be avoided if one remained on the outskirts, as Helen always would; but she would find moments of perfect love and joy too. She remembered how, walking with Angus across the sands of Sanda, where only the footprints of birds mingled with their own, she had seen hundreds of shells, all broken, and then had come upon one altogether perfect in shape and colouring. She had stood holding it, while Angus laughed at her child-like pleasure.

All her life now she would hold that shell in her hand.

Seventeen

From his second visit to Margaret Angus brought back three letters and two problems; the latter, he hoped, might with luck be made to cancel each other out, but in the process he could not be sure where he himself would end up: in Margaret's bed and bank-book, perhaps, or in Barlinnie, or on Calisay, slaving like Cain in his brother's fields.

As for the letters, two of these he had at first flung aside in indignation. In the grip of so pythonic a personal crisis, he had neither time nor breath to waste on such incidentals. One was from some girl in the orphanage, a prostitute's mistake, it seemed, to Donald's charges, the murderer's gets. The second was from Margaret herself to dreich-faced Lindsay of the shop, comforting her and urging her to make up her mind soon about this same little girl, whom it appeared Lindsay was trying to delude herself into believing she wanted to adopt. He had noticed that Margaret, unfairly in his opinion, had kept quiet about the girl's origin.

'Why not send them?' he had asked. 'A stamp only costs threepence.'

'Because, darling, I want them all to know what exists between us.'

'And what, my dear, is that?'

For answer she had kissed him—the conversation had taken place in bed—and though he had winked in the midst of it, hard enough to inconvenience his eye, there had somehow been no sanctioning wink in return from God the Joker.

The temporary withdrawal of sympathy and approval was the chief of his problems. He would have shaved off his moustache rather than admit he loved or even was fond of her. Yet there were times when the contrast between her gazelle-like trust and her lioness-like bodily strength had roused in him not pity, nor tenderness, nor solicitude, but something tinged with all these. Moreover, she had got it into her head that she was already pregnant; apparently she had been having dreams and visions, as well as physical disturbances. Well, it was possible enough, for he had taken no precautions, nor had she, although he had hoped that so prolonged a virginity would, like a drought, have withered in her all the delicate processes of conception. To marry her and father the brat would, of course, mean the end of his defiant aloofness from the despicable squabble of human existence. The Joker would never again wink back; the stars, though, would.

The third letter contained the second problem. Collected from the Shipping Company in Glasgow, it had dragged him down to human level. It was from Nell, in Oban, and surely she must have got her prim niece from Dingwall help her write it, for only educated, crass innocence in alliance with sexual revengefulness could have concocted such astute vindictiveness. Apparently others besides himself had been carrying out researches recently. It had come to her notice through a well-wisher, wrote Nell, that Angus at the time of his marriage to her was already married to a woman in Glasgow, who had since died and left him money. Therefore he was now well off and a bigamist. Let him estimate himself the damage done to her reputation and nerves. She had lost more than a stone since learning of his treachery; but she did not seem to count that in his favour. If he did not see fit very soon to compensate her for the love, food, and lodging lavished on him for years, she would have to take steps. It was for him to see to it that their association ended on a friendly basis, with both of them satisfied. She was thinking of retiring, and would be grateful for any help he could give. He knew her opinion of meanness. If a man committed murder, she might in certain circumstances find it in her heart to forgive and even shelter him; but if he were ever to insult her personally with a display of meanness, she would do everything she could to see him flung behind bars. And was there, in the world, more shocking meanness than for four years to eat at a woman's table, sleep in her bed, make use of her body, often borrow her money without paying it back, and all the time pretend he was her

183

lawful husband? She left it to him to do what was decent. Otherwise there were those who would scour the seas and sweep the skies and delve in the earth until they found and punished him.

He had to admit that she showed more character and originality in her letter than he could remember her doing in any other activity. But he was not surprised. She was bound to have benefited from her association with him. He had taught her little about the art of love-making, but had obviously inspired her fat wits. It looked as if he had escaped from her just in time. In another year or so he would have been the one exploited; his money in her purse, she would have had him trimming hedges, fixing fuses and emptying slops. All the same, to pay her blackmail as the price of getting rid of her would be not only disastrous to his bank account, but also paralysing to his male pride. Remembering her at table and in bed, he could not help shuddering: so sly a slobberer, so voracious a gobbler would never be satisfied with less than a thousand, or even two. Rather than give her a penny he would throw himself over the cliffs.

Nor was it a solution for him to marry Margaret and pay the ignoble tribute out of her money; because in that case it would have become his.

He saw himself entangled in the thorns of an absurd human predicament: married to an Amazon daily learning to use her strength; pursued by a hideous, sticky-fingered, infantile parody of himself; menaced by a jealous, fat-bellied, mercenary Medea; related to a murderer's spawn; jeered at by triumphant virgins like Jessie Ogilvie; inflamed with silly lust for the minister's golden-haired, insipid wife; and forced perhaps as breadwinner to dung fields and catch fish.

There was one way of escape left: emigration. But if he went to Australia, he might have to run the risk first of marrying Margaret in order to get his hands on her money. Yes, that was it, surely: marry her, give her in compensation a child if he hadn't already done so, take her money, and slip off. She could have his cottage, and her child could have the murderer's boys and the prostitute's girl to push its pram or take its

184

hand when it tottered across the machair to pick flowers.

But did he really want to slip off? A man of his charm and resourcefulness would prosper in the new world: the widows and middle-aged virgins there were more gullible and much richer. Why then be reluctant to seek his fortune, like Columbus or Jason? The reason was—he held it close to him and examined every facet of it through the magnifying glass of his incredulity—yes, it must be that he was far more attached to his native island than he had ever admitted, especially to himself.

He went and stood outside his cottage, at the back, among the tall nettles and brine-rusted briers, and gazed towards the sea. If he closed his eyes, he could picture every lichened rock, every bush, every cluster of flags and every sea-weeded boulder. Exiled to Australia or Canada his heart would yearn for these. Yet were they not unnegotiable, bringing no return but themselves?

'I am on a threshold,' he murmured aloud to a bee buzzing in the clover. 'My hand is raised to knock. But what is the house? Who are within?'

Far away he heard a sea-mew crying; it was too like a baby.

'If this is so, then for God's sake let me retreat, before I find it's too late.'

*   *   *

Retreat took him, half an hour later, to Mary's house, the letter for the boys in his pocket, and beside it, also in an envelope, the newspaper cuttings.

Donald, he knew, was out in the boat looking at his lobster creels. The boys were at school. It was an undisturbed hour. Over a hospitable cup of tea he could discuss it quietly with Mary.

As usual in summer the door was open. Fragrances hung about it, of peat burning, of roses, of tangle and of kindness. Roy dozed in front of the house, now and then opening an eye to warn a white hen that seemed to be pecking around for an opportunity to dart inside. Compared with Angus's own, the cottage, outside and in, was bonny and snug. He liked the flowers, though he despised the menial assiduity necessary to make them bloom so well. He liked too the air of homeliness that was itself a welcome without a word having to be spoken. Again, stronger than ever, he had that feeling of being on a threshold. Yet, though he smiled, he felt regret when the dog got up and slunk away as he approached. It might not always be possible, he realised, to make use of fidelity, trust and generosity, and at the same time preserve one's contempt for the creatures so prodigal of them. There was a danger, soon or late, of a door banging shut behind him; but in what house he might be then he had no idea.

In the kitchen Mary was working and singing. Why not, it suddenly occurred to him, for all creation was singing, from the thrush in the apple tree to the selchies under the sea. She sang a Gaelic song of youthful happiness in the summer sheilings of the past, and in it was just enough sadness to cause a Gael's bones to soften with longing. Eagles and gulls, wings over hill and cliff, salmon in the river, peat reek from the chimney, friends at the fireside, the cattle lowing and the curlew calling: they were all in the song, as they were all in an islander's blood.

Those tatties that Mary was peeling would have a grace said over them, and would taste like manna. He remembered his mother, tall and pale, handing him his portion so many times. Was it true that he always glanced to see if Donald's was bigger?

'It's me, Mary,' he called, as he waited in the doorway.

She came to the narrow scullery door; in one hand was the knife, on the other a piece of potato peel. He saw in her the eager little girl Mary McIntyre who had sat at the next desk to his brother's, and whose brother had fallen from the cliff and been drowned. He had gone down alone into the grave-yard by the sea after the burial, and wept in sympathy for her. No one had ever known. For the rest of his life he would not be able to see purple orchises without experiencing those tears again. In the graveyard they still grew in beautiful profusion.

'I thought it was you I heard singing,' she said. 'Come on

186

in.'

He was astonished. 'Me, Mary? Every bird on the island, yes; and yourself. But not me.'

'Oh yes, it was you. Now isn't it a happy man that doesn't know he's singing?'

'Happy? Well, maybe. You are, though, as usual. Some day, Mary, you'll tell me the secret.'

'That's easily told, Angus. Sit down. The kettle's on. You're just in time for a cup of tea.'

He sat down. 'Thank you, Mary. Donald will be out at his creels?'

'Aye. Dugald's with him.'

'Well, that's a good thing to have company, though if there's a sillier man in a boat than Dugald, I don't know who he can be.'

She laughed, and though he could not see her face he guessed she was thinking that the sillier man was himself. A week or so back he had cast his anchor without first making sure it was fixed; it hadn't been, and had gone down to the bottom. Donald had been there, and with a touch of his old drollness had asked: 'Is a thing lost if you know where it is?'

She began to put cups and saucers on the table. Her face was straight enough, and even kindly; but there was on it a certain human quality of complicity that he found provoking.

'I've brought a letter for the boys,' he said, taking it out. Voice and fingers were at their smoothest. 'From some child in the orphanage, I understand.' It was in an envelope on which Margaret had written: To John and Tom Sneddon from Jean McDonnell.

Pleased, Mary picked it up. 'And where did you get it?'

'Well now, does that matter?' To his annoyance, though his voice was as mellow and steady as always, a blush warmed his cheeks. It had happened before; against the shampooed, silky whiteness of his moustache the faintest pink of embarrassment glowed like the crimson of shame or discomfiture. He felt a spasm of general vindictiveness. It affected him like sexual desire. But as far as Mary was concerned he might have been a eunuch, not because she was his brother's wife, and

187

not because, either, she suspected the hollowness at his core; no, what made her repellent to him in that sense was her pity for him. Jessie Ogilvie, who hated and condemned him, he had once humiliated in bed, and hoped to do it again. Yet in every womanly way Mary was far bonnier. There was Margaret, too. His blush returned, warmer than ever, as he recalled how last time he made love with her he had treated her with a tenderness not wholly satirical. His hand on her great soft hough had, almost in spite of him, patted with husbandly indulgence.

'Jean McDonnell,' said Mary, still as pleased as a child, and unwilling to put the envelope down to get on with setting the table and making the tea. In the scullery the kettle boiled. 'Well now, isn't that nice of the wee girl? They'll be delighted. I hear them talk a lot about her.'

'I believe Janet Lindsay of the shop's been showing an interest in her.'

In Mary's laughter was affection for Janet, for the little girl, and perhaps even for Angus himself. 'Aye. She's got a photograph of theirs with the girl in it. I haven't seen it myself. This was weeks ago. They're getting worried about it. Flora's going to ask her to let them have it back. I hope Janet decides to take the girl. It would do her good. It would do them both good.'

'Not this one, Mary.'

She glanced at him in surprise. 'Why not?'

'Her mother was, probably still is, a prostitute. The father? Any one of a thousand customers.'

She smiled. 'I sometimes think, Angus, every woman's little better than a prostitute in your estimation.'

'I don't know what you mean by that, Mary.'

'You've never thought very highly of us. When you were a boy it was the same.'

'That isn't so, Mary.'

'Now you've got hold of some filth, and you're going to rub our noses in it. If this woman was a prostitute, in what way does it defile the child?'

Just then the white hen, which had been clucking peevishly

in the doorway for the past minute or two, stalked boldly in, and looked up at Mary with an amber eye cocked demandingly.

'Well, cheeky,' said Mary, dropping some fragments of biscuit, which it instantly gobbled up. 'She comes in every morning. When I've got a visitor, though, she sometimes keeps out.'

'So I'm favoured?'

'It looks like it.'

'And she's female enough.'

Mary shooed the hen out. It went cackling proudly. Then she went into the scullery to make the tea.

'You're not thinking of telling Janet, are you?' she called.

'I don't know, Mary. What do you think?'

'I think it's none of our business.'

'But if Janet knew would she still think of adopting her?'

'I don't see why not. I'll tell you this, if Janet doesn't take her, she'll rue it to the end of her days.'

'Janet always looks as if she's rueing something.'

Mary came in with the teapot. 'According to Neil, she already talks as if the girl was hers. She's full of plans. She even talks as if the child was in the house. Neil's worried.'

'He'd be worried a lot more if he was asked to father a prostitute's brat.'

'He's not a bitter man, and he's fond of his wife.'

She poured out the tea. Smiling, he watched. All his life this pouring out of tea had been for him the symbol of home. When he had praised Margaret for it he had been sincere. With the sea stormy and his father out on it, or with death in some croft near by, that steady pouring had always reassured him as a child. Now in Mary's hand it could not have been steadier. He felt very grateful.

'But it wasn't Janet I came to talk to you about, Mary.' As he spoke he put the other envelope, containing the cuttings, on the table. 'Has Flora told you?'

'Told me what?'

'About the boys. Miss Mathieson said she'd told Flora, but she didn't know if Flora had told you.'

189

Mary was silent. He could not read her thoughts. Suddenly she picked up the envelope and took out the cuttings. For almost a minute she looked at them, while outside in the sunshine the thrush in the apple tree sang as if in passionate warning.

'Does Donald know?' he asked. 'Have you told him?'

Still calm, her voice was deeper with emotion. 'Donald and I are man and wife. You are not to interfere between us.'

'He's my brother.'

'You remember that only when it suits you. So it suits you now to try to bring ruin upon him?'

'He doesn't know, then?'

Pale and tight-lipped, more womanly than ever, she had become strangely dear to him. He wanted to stroke her grey hair, kiss her soft cheek, and press her plump hand, to comfort her and protect her against this evil that he, like Iscariot, had been chosen to represent.

'He has a right to know, Mary. It was he who signed the forms, remember. And he wants to know. He told me himself that it wouldn't matter where they had come from, if only he knew.'

Almost at the same instant tea splashed from the cup she was holding, and tears from her eyes. He was amazed. Why should she weep? Didn't she have the secret of happiness? Was the love between her and Donald diseased in some way?

But if so, why be amazed? No love was ever altogether healthy in its infancy, and its deterioration was inevitable. No one was much to blame. The little, shy, mad murderer in his prison cell was perhaps the happiest of all. Yet on whose behalf did the birds sing and the flowers smell sweet?

'The boys are mine, not yours,' said Mary. 'Donald is mine, not yours. If he has to be told I shall tell him myself.'

'That would be best, Mary.'

'If you think he will have them sent away, you are mistaken. He loves them.'

'I think we all do.'

'No, Angus; you've never loved a single soul in all your life. Only yourself.'

190

He remembered the boy weeping for her sake in the graveyard among the orchises. 'If that is so, Mary, am I not to be pitied, rather than blamed?'

He pitied himself then, almost to tears. The thrush, too, was suddenly silent.

'No,' she said. 'You've enjoyed loving only yourself.'

The truth was, of course, that everybody fundamentally could love only himself; selfless love was beyond the capabilities of human beings; where it appeared to exist it was really self-love in some pathetically ineffectual disguise. So he had always believed, not because he was by nature misanthropic or pessimistic, but because he honoured the truth. He had studied minutely his own reactions, and he did not think he was so different from other men as to invalidate his conclusion. As for women, surely there could be no argument: loving their husbands or sweethearts they were loving the fathers of their children, loving their children they were loving extensions of themselves. Men, he would admit, made the effort to carry their love outside their narrow selves; women contemptuously saw the absurdity of that and were therefore never surprised by its failure.

'After all,' he murmured with a smile, 'Donald's got his faith to guide him.'

'Don't mock.'

'I am far from mocking, Mary. No doubt it is a comfort to have a sure belief in God. Still, in this case, he might think it his Christian duty to have the boys sent away. It does state, I believe, categorically, that the children must suffer for the sins of their fathers; and of their mothers, too, I suppose. Does it not say so?'

'Yes, it does; and it's true. But it's for God to make them suffer, not for us.'

'Ah, Mary, He's got to choose His executioners. He can't do it Himself. It's likely enough He might choose us.'

She stared at him in hatred; not only of him, but of herself too, and of all humanity. He understood and sympathized: it was a position he had reached himself, by revelations as bitter as this she was now experiencing. They laughed at him for

191

claiming that his knowledge of the world had given him an insight into the human mind unobtainable by them on their remote island. But his claim had not been without justification. Had his sailings taken him not merely to Stornoway, Lochinver and Oban, but as far away as Bangkok and Hong Kong, as he had pretended to Margaret, he could not have reached a profounder understanding of his fellow-men. Sometimes, indeed, he had wondered if that inspired understanding was not itself the one contradiction to his belief that selfless love was not possible. How, he had once realised, sitting in a Tobermory bar, can I understand them so well, almost as well as their Maker, if I don't love them as He is reputed to do? But does He? That was still the question. Here it had arisen again. Was it a sign of God's love to be chosen as His executioner?

'Let's accept it, Mary,' he said earnestly, 'if for no other reason than that we must. Not only Donald, but everybody on this island, is bound to know sooner or later; that's to say, if the boys stay among us. If they go away, then it's somewhere else the whole thing's got to be suffered. Better here, surely.'

'No. It would be a kindness in comparison to throw them off the cliffs on to the rocks below.'

He was impressed, and even a little alarmed, by her bitterness. She was a grey-haired, middle-aged woman, drinking tea in her own parlour, but within she was at the same moment a huntress, all claws and teeth and savagery. He was reminded of her and his own ancestry.

'That's been done before,' he murmured. He was referring to an episode in the seventeenth century when some children had been abducted from Mull, brought to Calisay and flung from the cliffs, as a reprisal: a few months before, men from Mull had raided Calisay and had thrown children over. Cliff and rocks were known and named.

'Isn't the world today full of children, refugees, who never knew who their people were?'

She was of course right, and as he sat staring into the sunshine, where the thrush had begun again to sing more rapturously than ever after its pause, he thought of countries like Hungary, Germany, China and Palestine, where recently, because of the brutality of men, hundreds of thousands of children had been orphaned and forsaken. As he waited, smiling, the bird singing, the sun shining, the roses smelling sweet, the woman breathing passionately, he felt, God help him, that on his way to the shop to deliver Lindsay's letter he would have to go by some lonely path, along the cliffs or over the mountain, to avoid those abandoned and revengeful hordes. But of course, even if he went under the sea itself they could not be avoided; their eyes would be the glitter on lobsters' claws.

Mary was speaking, with a strange harshness: 'You're right. He would send them away. He loves them, but he would send them away.'

He nodded. 'Don't blame him, Mary. We must do what's in us to do. All of us, you, me, Donald, the boys themselves, we've all got to abide the consequences.'

'What consequences will you abide? If your cigar falls into the sea, it's a worse consequence to you than if the rest of us were to break our hearts.'

He smiled: the incident had occurred. On the jetty once someone had slapped his back and caused his cigar to jump out of his mouth, down through a crack between the boards into the sea. They had laughed, and it had been their laughter rather than the loss of a good cigar that had angered him. Had it been malicious he might have respected it, but no, it had merely been cloddish, neanderthal. He had felt profoundly betrayed.

But now he smiled, without rancour. Mary, he realised, to his astonishment and gratitude, did not blame him, or rather she merely included him in a universal condemnation. Though not particularly intelligent, she was also not a stupid, impercipient woman. Could it be that she, and the others like her, despite their limited experience, also knew about the impossibility of selfless love and the inevitability of acting as God's executioners?

He watched her then, as if he expected her to become transfigured, as Margaret indeed, though in rather a commonplace way, had done; and surely Mary now did, shedding all her ordinariness, as she lifted her eyes with, of all things, that human complicity in them and in every tear that slid down her cheeks.

'Whatever the risk,' she said, 'I'll have to tell him.'

His nod was as circumspect as a mouse's sniffing of cheese in a trap. He was pleased, but he was also far from sure that she did not in some hidden way intend him harm.

Eighteen

Calisay Manse, built of the grey native stone with walls three feet thick, crouched at the top of a hill, its back towards the Atlantic gales and sunsets, and its dour front peering down on the green strath that ran diagonally through the centre of the island. It had been set there, with much inconvenience, because the minister at the time, the Reverend Isaac McDougall, had wanted to be not merely apart from his flock but also above it, just as in the sky overhead, especially when it was dark purple with impending storms, he in his turn had been transcended by Jehovah. There was a photograph of him, mildewed and spotty, on the vestry wall. Gazing up at it during her first visit to the church, with the wind howling outside and the sea roaring, Sheila had felt a strange, tender exasperation against her husband. In the cold, damp church Archie had been going about, whistling like a linnet in his pride and joy. So ordinary, human and fallible, he was confident of undoing what this bearded, fierce-eyed predecessor had so capably done; which was to stiffen and darken the islanders' respect for God with fear.

At the very outset of his ministry Archie had thrown fear overboard. She hadn't said what she privately had thought, that some of it at least ought to have been kept as a kind of necessary ballast. Love as a replacement did not seem to her altogether adequate. Though she felt embarrassed sometimes by his enthusiasm, expressed too in his roughest, most plebeian voice, and often enough impatient with his blitheness in tackling, with no more than ordinary human qualities, a task calling for miracles, yet she staunchly supported and protected him wherever she could.

In one respect God had certainly appeared to favour the Reverend Isaac and his ways, for he had had eleven children, only four of whom had died in infancy. Archie, on the other hand, was likely to have none at all, especially if he had been given his way about her never again risking a pregnancy. He had not, though.

Therefore that evening, when she caught sight of Mary McArthur coming across the hill path towards the manse road, she knew she might already have conceived and so felt happier than she had done since her miscarriage. Archie, dressed in old grey flannels and a shirt torn at the elbow, was busy with shears and a bill-hook getting rid of brambles and briers, as dense and thorny, he had said, as old Isaac's sermons. Often she glanced towards him and laughed; in spite of his rags and of the anchor tattooed on his forearm, he wore his clerical collar. Some of them on the island, he had grumbled, seemed to think he ought to go to bed with it on.

So she felt renewed and very happy that calm, grey evening as she stared over the wall down into Glen Massan where the loch gleamed like silver, and the school, hall and kirk stood together on its shore, under larch and beech trees. If she raised her eyes to the left, yonder, past the green headland and the sandy bay, under an immense canopy of pearly cloud, slept the sea. To the right, between the hills, she could just catch a glimpse of the Sound and the Paps of Jura.

Pleased with all creation, she imagined it an evening of conception, quiet, still, clear, haunted with expectancy. After it would come the long excitement of formation, followed by the short stress and violence of birth, with in the end the sunlight and blue skies of motherhood. Laughing at her own foolishness, in tears a little, she nibbled at her knuckles on the mossy wall. A glance, shy and secret, showed three swans on the loch, another a croft in a nook of the hill, and still another tiny figures running so fast along the wide yellow sands, they must be children. She listened, but could not hear their happy cries: they were too far away. But as she listened she heard a curlew calling, the same cry that she had heard so often in her garden at Munnock, and indeed this inspired evening it seemed to be speaking to her across her whole lifetime; her dead mother's and father's voices were in it, confirming the hope in her heart.

196

There were midges. Already, a fair-skinned, sweet-blooded victim, she had itchy lumps all over her brow; but she refused to let them drive her indoors. The secret of this evening was hers, and she wanted to enjoy it as long as possible. Often, as she turned to look at Archie, she felt like running over and just touching him. He seemed to know it, for every time she looked she found him looking too, and waving. His pipe was clenched tightly between his teeth, and he tried, with frantic puffs of smoke, to repel the midges that swarmed up in thousands out of the ravaged bushes. His exertions and his scratchings had pulled out the tail of his shirt.

Before catching sight of Mary McArthur, she had been gazing at the school, thinking of her and Archie's son, already conceived if her prayer last night had been granted. He would be fair-haired and delicately featured like her, but strong in body like Archie. He would have his father's honesty of mind and her own sensitiveness. He would be bright, cheerful, and manly. She prayed that she be spared to enjoy the wonderful felicity of helping to bring him up; but even if she were not, and died in giving him birth, she thought that, wherever she might be, she would not regret it: her child and her husband together, remembering her with love and sorrow, would make heaven itself tolerable.

Tears in her eyes at first kept her from being sure who the woman was, walking so steadfastly across the immense hillside of heather, bracken and boulders. When she saw it was Mary McArthur, she at once frowned, and had consciously to change it to a smile. She did not dislike Mary, but she could never help resenting what struck her as the older woman's too infrequently examined reputation of wise and motherly compassion. Sheila was inclined to think of her as quite arrogant and relentless in her own placid way. Archie, though, thought that in her the simplicity and dignity of island life were seen at their best. It was true she had a smile for everyone, and a harsh word for none; but Sheila had noticed, or thought she had, that on every occasion Mrs McArthur took care she got her way: what she so quietly said was always the last word, and what she did was always the right thing to do. For instance, look how too gullible Archie was in praising her for having in a few short weeks transformed the children in her care from pale-faced, timid orphans into pink-cheeked, robust, happy youngsters. Sheila, silent, had not agreed. Apart altogether from her prejudice against the inhuman system of boarding children out and making motherhood a paid service, she felt that Mrs McArthur was getting the credit that really belonged to Flora, her daughter, Roy the collie, the island itself, and her husband Donald who, beneath his rather lugubrious exterior, was a man giving and taking laughter. As far as Sheila had seen, he had tried harder than any to make the boys feel at home. Often he had them out with him in his boat or on the hill. Mrs McArthur just sat back and exerted her influence; that seemed to Sheila the limit of her contribution.

She called to Archie: 'Well, we're having a visitor after all.'

'Not Dugald again?'

She laughed at his more than mock alarm. Dugald, the island piper and worthy, came almost every night, up from his thatched house that was more like a hollowed rock, and paid for his cup of tea and cheese sandwich by insisting on teaching Archie how to play the pipes. He had taken a great fancy to Archie. Unfortunately, from Sheila's point of view, he stank, and was regally heedless in such matters as belching or fastening his fly buttons. He was over seventy.

'No, it isn't him,' she cried. 'I think it's Mary McArthur.'

Pleased, he came over, carrying his bill-hook. She loved the scratches on his hands and the sweat patches under his arms. The contrast between his collar and the rest of his dress struck her as funnier and more endearing than ever, because Mary McArthur was always so neat in her person and dress. There were fragments of withered bramble leaves on his hair. Somehow they made him look worn and tired, despite his laughter. She remembered his agonies of conscience, strange and terrifying in a man so sure of Christ's example. When she had married him she had discovered that he contributed fifty pounds every year to organisations for the relief of famine and similar distress throughout the world. He still paid it.

198

'You'll have to get changed,' she said, fondly.

He patted her bottom, and then stood beside her to gaze over the wall. 'You think so?'

'My goodness yes. Surely you've noticed Mary in church. There's none straighter, none more precise.'

'And none more appreciative.'

'I wouldn't say that, Archie. I think you're on the lenient side for her. In her own way she's all for hell-fire, like the rest of them.'

'I don't think so. It is her, though.'

They watched as the small, grey-haired woman, wearing a dark, visit-the-manse dress, approached where the path joined the private road up to the manse. She sat on a stone there for a minute or so, resting, and keeping the midges off with a frond of bracken.

'Perhaps she's not coming here at all,' said Sheila. 'She could be going across the hill to the hotel to see her daughter.'

Past the manse was a path that led across the hill to the main road about half a mile or so from the hotel. It was a short cut for vigorous walkers only.

Mrs McArthur came on again, not slowly, but not hurrying, either: a crafty, self-satisfied sort of pace, Sheila thought, such as a woman would adopt thinking things out to her own advantage. That's unfair, she told herself. Am I jealous of the woman because the influence she exerts is really the magic of motherliness, which I am afraid I shall always lack?

'She's coming here,' said Archie. 'I'd better go in and make myself more respectable.'

'Hide that tattoo anyway.'

He hurried away, laughing.

Head high, Sheila went to the gate to welcome her visitor, or rather to meet the latter's challenge, and was taken aback by the look of sadness that she surprised on the older woman's face. For the past half-hour or so Mrs McArthur had been alone, with no need for the smile behind which a human being hides from another. It now appeared, rather wearily, obscured by the bracken.

Sheila's greeting was more than hospitable, it was involuntarily cordial. 'Good evening, Mrs McArthur. This is a very pleasant surprise.'

'Thank you, Mrs McNeil. I am afraid I am disturbing you.'

'Not a bit of it. Aren't the midges wicked this evening?'

'Indeed they are so. Is the minister in?'

'Yes.' Her own happiness then as his wife rather than any desire to confide, caused her to cry: 'To tell the truth, he was cutting those brambles, and when he heard you were coming he ran in to change.'

Mary smiled. 'There was no need.'

'You'd be surprised, Mrs McArthur, to know how upset some people can be when they find the minister not in his black.'

'No, I'm not surprised. Folk are foolish. But perhaps it's a disappointment to them to think he's just a being like themselves. We all like to think the minister's different.'

'My goodness, Mrs McArthur, as a minister's wife, I don't like to think that at all.'

Mary nodded. 'But a minister's bound to be different,' she said, quietly. 'He has had God's hand laid on him.'

Sheila shivered, and ushered her in. In the little hall Archie at once appeared, dressed in his black suit; he hadn't had time, though, to remove his old sandshoes. He looked so eager and welcoming that he couldn't have been more human had he tried. If Mrs McArthur was disappointed, Sheila was relieved, and showed it by going up to him and removing, with love, a leaf from his hair.

'Mrs McArthur has come to see you, dear,' she murmured.

'I won't be keeping you long, Mr McNeil.'

The restraint between the two women saddened Archie a little, especially as Mary McArthur seemed to him the kind of woman that Sheila, granted happiness—which in her case meant a family—would develop into: mature, responsible, wise, and not only happy in herself but able to bring happiness to others. Otherwise, as he well knew, there was a danger that she might develop in a different direction altogether, becoming peevish, embittered, hypochrondriacal and envious. He wanted her to be friendly with Mary, and he could see no reason why

200

she should not be; yet here again was this restraint which always appeared between them, owing to Sheila's fault, he had to admit.

'You'll join us in a cup of tea afterwards?' asked Sheila, making the effort he was appealing to her to make.

'No, no. I'm here self-invited.'

'That you aren't, Mrs McArthur,' said Archie heartily. You're welcome here any time.'

'Thank you. But you should think of your wife, Mr McNeil.'

'He is thinking of me, Mrs McArthur. Of course you'll be welcome here any time you wish to come.'

'I just meant that no woman, not even if she's a minister's wife, likes to think her home is never her own.'

'But I thought,' said Sheila, 'that the Calisay folk are proud of the fact that everyone's house is always open to everyone else.'

'So we are, Mrs McNeil.'

'Well then, aren't Mr McNeil and I Calisay folk now?'

'Yes, indeed.'

'You say so, but you don't really think so. We were warned before we came that we'd still be regarded as outsiders after twenty years. If that's true, and sometimes it looks like it, then surely it isn't fair, Mrs McArthur? Why invite us to come among you and then treat us as strangers? Look at Mrs McGilvray and Mrs Lindsay: they've been here for years, and yet they're still made to feel that they've not been accepted.'

'With some folk trust's like a tree growing, Mrs McNeil. It can't be forced, it must take its long time.'

'We're not trees.'

Archie intervened. 'No, but we're prepared to wait, dear. Well, Mrs McArthur, if you'd like to step into what I call my study—'

'Thank you.' With a smile at Sheila, who was trembling, he went into the little room that smelled of tobacco smoke.

Archie gave his wife a rueful kiss.

'I'm sorry, Archie,' she whispered, gripping him tightly. 'But if we have a child, how could we possibly bring him up

201

among such people?'

'They're fine people, really. They take a little time to get to know, that's all. But she's waiting. You go and get the tea ready.'

'But she refused it.'

'Get it ready just the same. After all, Dugald might come.'

In the study Mrs McArthur was still standing. He had to admit that the glance she gave him was peculiar. Was there pity in it for him, and contempt for his wife? Or was it the other way round?

'Please sit down,' he said.

She did so, and sat as if in church. 'I am very pleased to see Mrs McNeil looking so much better.'

'Thank you. Yes, I'm glad to say she's feeling a lot better.'

'So the air of Calisay suits her?'

He wondered if there was irony in her smile. 'It would suit anyone. Your two little chaps, for instance. What a difference there is in them, in a few weeks too. You and your husband should be very proud.'

He noticed her lips go curiously tight for a moment.

'It's about them I've come,' she said.

He waited, uneasily. Somehow Sheila had affected him. Mrs McArthur seemed to him deep and not quite candid.

'I have found out who their parents were.'

'I see.' He put out his hand towards the drawer where he had put his pipe, but withdrew it quickly.

'Donald doesn't know yet. I have not told him.'

He smiled. 'Why not? Is there any special reason?'

'Special enough. Their father took a hatchet and killed their mother in their house in Glasgow three years ago. She was going about with other men.'

Her voice was so calm, her hands clasped on her dark lap so still, that at first he didn't grasp the horror of what she had said.

'He is now in the prison for criminal lunatics.'

'Good God. How did you learn this?'

'The woman who brought them told Flora. Flora told me.'

'But why did she tell Flora? Flora's a young girl.'

'Like the boys themselves, she's young and looks ahead at what's still to be done; she wastes little time in worrying about what's already done. Forby, she's got a good heart.'

'There's none better.'

'It's possible that John—he's the elder of the two—saw the thing being done. The police think he must have. But he has never spoken about it to anyone; not even to Flora, so far. The woman thought somebody here should know, in case it rose up out of the darkness of his mind.'

Her hands on her lap were no longer still. His own, though, were far more agitated; he rubbed his chin, struck his knuckles together, fingered his collar, and tugged at his lapels.

'What I am here for tonight, Mr McNeil, is for your opinion as a minister. If I keep this thing from my husband, am I doing wrong?'

'But is there any reason why you should?'

'He would send them away.'

Though he got ready to argue, he knew she was right: Donald would see it as his Christian duty. 'Surely not,' he said sternly. 'I thought he was fond of them.'

'He is. But like the rest of us he knows that the Almighty, having no one else, has to choose us to carry out what punishments He thinks fit.'

Here it was again, the stench and murk of hell-fire. Archie tried to keep his voice down. When he shouted, Sheila had said once, he sounded like a coalman accused of giving short weight. 'But that's nonsense, Mrs McArthur.'

'Is it? It may be. Things happen that I can see no reason for, but still there must be one, in the Almighty's mind. I can't see far enough, that is all.'

And you think I can't either, he wanted to shout. Instead he whispered: 'I would rather see it like this: God chooses us to express his love and compassion.'

'That's true too.'

He found himself stammering in his earnestness. 'There's a simple test, Mrs McArthur, for us who believe in Christ. What would He have done? Think of Him on the island at this moment, as He is. Think of Him in this room, as He is.

203

Ask Him what he would do about these little boys. Send them back to the orphanage, rejected, humiliated, despised? Or keep them here, protected, cherished, made to feel at home, given a chance? What do you honestly think He would answer?'

'I don't know.' And she looked at him as if she was sure he didn't know either.

But she was wrong. He did know; he must know. Not knowing would be a thousand times worse than when, during the war, the ship he was on had been torpedoed, and they hadn't known whether it was going to sink or blow up. It had sunk, but only after it had been torpedoed again. Men had been burnt alive.

He clasped and unclasped his great, hard, engineer's hands. 'We're all responsible for one another. If one of us sins, we all do. We are one family.'

'You've not to be thinking I want the boys to be sent away,' she said. 'And don't think Donald does either. But he will see it as his duty.'

'But surely his duty is the very opposite, to protect the children from the consequences of their parents' wickedness?'

She was silent for a few seconds. 'You and I may think so, Mr McNeil,' she said. 'Donald will not.'

'Don't tell him then.'

'He is my husband, it is my duty to tell him.'

'Then wait for another few weeks. He'll have become so attached to them he won't let them go.'

'I think the more attached he is the more he'll consider it his duty to send them away.'

He ran his hand through his hair. 'I don't understand,' he muttered. 'In a boat he's a man you'd trust in the fiercest storm.'

'Ah, if there was never any need to come ashore,' she said, rising.

He rose too. 'What does Flora say?'

'I've not spoken to her about it yet.'

'What will she say?'

'Donald is her father. In any case, will she not soon be

married and over on Islay?'

In the hall Sheila came out of the sitting-room. 'Well, have you had your little chat?' she cried. 'Now it's time for tea.'

'No, no, thank you just the same. I must be going. It'll be dark soon, and it's a long walk round by the road. And to tell you the truth, I'm not feeling like tea. Good night.'

She hurried out, and Archie ran after her.

'You don't mind if I speak to Donald myself about this?' he asked.

'You have your duty to do, minister, just as we have ours.' She turned at the gate. 'I'll tell you this, if the bairns go, I'll not be long here myself. There's Hector in Canada sending for me already. I laughed at the lad, but maybe I'll not be laughing much longer.'

He watched her as she went, stumbling, in grief he thought, down the road and on to the path. For a few moments she was silhouetted against the darkening sky.

At least he could pray for her, and he did so, while Sheila rather impatiently called from the house. Midges crawled over his face, making it itch unbearably.

A minute or so later he walked slowly back to the house.

'Well,' said Sheila, 'that, I suppose, was island courtesy?'

He took her hand. 'Don't misjudge her, Sheila. She's greatly distressed. And, God help me, I could do nothing to help her.'

'What's she distressed about?'

Her tone was sharp as nails. She had used it before to puncture what she considered his sentimentalities. A moment ago eager to seek her support, he was now afraid she would refuse to give it. Yet last night, sobbing in his arms, she would have given him the whole world.

'Well, what's the mystery, Archie? Am I not to be told?'

'I'm not sure I'm at liberty to tell, dear.'

'I happen to be your wife.'

In spite of her huffy, haughty face he embraced her. 'Of course you are,' he whispered. 'It's just that she's discovered who the parents of the two boys were.'

She pushed him off so that she could see his face, or perhaps so that he could see hers, hardened by a kind of triumph.

205

'I should think so,' she said, embracing him again. 'She should never have taken them in the first place without knowing. So it has been a shock? What did she expect? Women who abandon their children are bound to be the scum of the earth.'

'Some do it, Sheila, because they are very unhappy.'

'No doubt. But unhappiness can be deserved. Who was she?'

He was reluctant to say; it would be like handing the dead woman over to the virtuous, to be ripped to pieces.

'Some horrible creature, I suppose? Is she still alive? Archie, you don't make it any easier for yourself by pretending there aren't any evil people.'

'I never pretend that. But I also try never to forget that I am a minister of Christ.'

He wanted then to break out of her embrace, but she held him firmly; so his mother had done, forty years ago, when he had tried to run away from a lecture, say, on the disgrace of dirty ears.

'You can never get it into your head, Archie, that God leaves people to make of their lives what they want.'

'Well, it would seem He certainly didn't interfere overmuch in the lives of the parents of these boys. Or perhaps, looking at it in another way, He did. Perhaps His was the hand that lifted the hatchet, just as they're prepared to say His will be the thumb that will release the bomb.'

She shook him, firmly but gently. 'Keep to the point, dear. What are you talking about? What hatchet?'

'Their father killed their mother with it; that's all.' She let him go at last, pushed him off rather, in a kind of revulsion. At that moment he represented humanity that murdered, fornicated and wallowed in filth.

'How utterly horrible,' she whispered.

He felt like saying: 'Yes, you're right to shrink from me, Sheila, because I'm partly to blame for this murder, and you're right, too, to feel this disgust at your own human self, for you are to blame also. We all are, every one of us.' But he kept quiet.

206

'I see it now,' she said. 'They want to send the boys away, and you don't think they should.'

'Do you think they should?

She turned on him, fiercely; it was as if she was defending her own child; as perhaps she felt she was, from the foulness and brutality of the world represented, however innocently, by John and Tom Sneddon. 'Of course I do. It's not enough to be sorry for the boys, or to say that they are not to blame. If there has to be suffering, and surely it's inevitable in such circumstance, then they must bear their share. It would be wrong to let them stay here, poisoning not only the McArthurs' home, but the atmosphere of the whole island.'

'You can't mean that, Sheila,' he whispered.

'Yes, I do. It's what the majority of people would say too, if they were honest. I'm glad to see Mary McArthur has that much sense.'

He held her hand, and again began to stammer. 'I'll tell you this, Sheila. If those children are sent away, then none of us on this island will ever enjoy a moment's peace of mind for as long as we live, and we wouldn't deserve to. I should consider Christ remiss if He allowed us to settle down in our miserable self-sufficiency after such a betrayal. For that's what it would be, Sheila, a betrayal.'

She kissed him. 'There you go again, Archie,' she murmured. 'I won't say you exaggerate, dear; but you do make everything so urgent and dramatic, as if every day was a Day of Judgment. I mean, surely Christ for His own reasons more often than not keeps out of it, leaves us to decide for ourselves?'

Then as they waited, for what neither was sure, they heard bagpipes start up and begin to play, somewhere close out in the garden.

Sheila laughed. 'Good for Dugald. He must have smelt the tea.' She went to the door to look out. 'My goodness. He's in all his glory.'

The old piper was in his full regalia of silver-buttoned velvet jacket, kilt and plaid of Stewart tartan, shoulder belt with three large thistled silver clasps, red stockings, skean-dhu, and on his straggling white hair a balmoral with cairngormed and feathered badge. Though all this finery was grimy, tattered and tarnished, he wore it as proudly as he held the faded bag of his pipes, and as he blew his fat red cheeks were balloons of joy. He marched up and down, and occasionally stamped, no doubt to disturb the midges pasturing in thousands on his naked hairy thighs.

Fascinated, they watched and listened.

At last he stopped. With his usually squeaky voice oiled too much with saliva he cried: 'That's it. What do you think of it? The choon, I mean, the choon; not the playing.'

'It's very sad, Dugald,' said Sheila.

'Sad? But, Mrs McNeil, it's not meant to be sad; well, not altogether. You see, it was written for your man. I wrote it last night. It came into my head. "Salute to the Minister." That's what it's called. Wait now. I'll play it again; though, mind you, the midges are fair savage.'

This time as Sheila listened she found her eyes filling with tears. The music seemed to her sadder than ever. She felt afraid, and remembered a conversation she had had with Archie not long after they were married. 'Well, anyway,' she had said, 'my man's not got a dangerous occupation. Look how long ministers live.' 'Dangerous enough,' he had answered. 'Don't just count when our bodies die.'

Nineteen

On her way to the McArthurs' Jessie Ogilvie went by the path along the shore, so that she could pause often to listen to and be advised by the birds. Rock doves, oyster-catchers, plovers, red-throated divers, and even a corn-bunting called and warned her not to let this crisis which had arisen among her friends the McArthurs involve her and so weaken her authority, not as a schoolma'am merely, but as an aloof, independent woman. A sybil, she said, smiling like one, and began to imitate the various bird cries in her uttering of the word, crooning it like the doves, piping it like the oystercatchers, and chirping it like the stonechats. Just as well it was Sunday afternoon, with no one about; so she was thinking when, looking down at a small bay below, she saw hundreds of gulls motionless on the sands, and approaching them at the sea's edge, Flora McArthur and Hugh McEachern hand in hand.

As she hesitated, reaching out to touch with her own empty hand a rough warm boulder, she felt, beginning slowly in some small, secret part of her being and ending by possessing her wholly, an envy of the black-haired girl so soon to be married. It was not, God knew, a malicious envy, and at its climax, while she trembled under its stress, the great flock of birds, startled, rose as one and flew above and about the heads of the lovers, obscuring them in a great exhilarating flutter of white wings and wailing cries.

But Flora was not exhilarated. She did not run amidst them and jump and sing and wave her arms, as a young woman in love might have, even on a Calisay Sabbath. Dourly reaching the water, she stood gazing out towards Sanda, near and green in the sunshine. Hugh spoke to her, was ignored, spoke again, was ignored again, tried to embrace her, was shrugged off, and so, sadly, he walked apart to where there was something lying on the beach.

He poked at it with his foot, and then, stooping carefully, lifted it up by a black wing-tip, for it was a dead bird, a gannet, Jessie saw, from its great size and long neck. He shouted to Flora who turned, unwillingly, to look at it; but she did not go to him.

It was not the first time Jessie had seen a gannet with a broken neck. Perhaps in its daring perpendicular dive into the sea the bird had miscalculated by a fraction, or had mistaken for shadow a submerged weed-covered rock.

Flora turned to the sea again, leaving Hugh and the dead bird isolated. He continued to examine it, waggling its neck and prodding its breast. As he did so he happened to glance up and catch sight of Jessie on the high path. He rose eagerly, shouting her name.

Instantly Flora spun round, looked, cried 'Jessie!' and began to race towards her. At first near the sea where the sand was firm she came swiftly, but then where it became soft and deep she floundered in spite of her haste. In a few yards, thought Jessie, she has gone from youth to age. Behind her her footprints were like memories, the more distant ones faint and perfect, the nearer ones broken and deep.

'Jessie!' she panted, when she was under the cliff. 'Jessie!'

Jessie crossed the strip of heathery rock to the edge. 'What is it, Flora?'

Dressed for Sunday, in a dark costume, Flora stood, frowning, her breast heaving. She was not after all, thought Jessie, so very bonny: mouth too big, brow too bony and freckled, cheek-bones too high; but, beauty denied, goodness, vitality, and compassion, all better qualities, had to be conceded, more than ever.

Hugh, rubbing his hand against his dark-blue trousers, walked slowly towards them. He too was dressed for Sunday, and looked a little raw and uncouth. His hair stuck up as usual like a lark's crest; but he was in no singing mood. He stopped about ten yards behind Flora.

'Hello, Jessie,' he called.

'Hello, Hugh.'

'Did you see the gannet?'

210

'Yes.'

'I think it must have broken its neck.'

'Likely enough. What is it, Flora?'

Tears were running down the girl's cheeks. 'You've heard that Johnny and Tommy are to be sent away?'

'Your mother mentioned it to me at church this morning.'

The gulls were settled again, quiet and attentive, like a congregation.

'But my father didn't?'

'No.'

'He couldn't, could he, Jessie? What was there for him to say, especially near the church? The minister's spoken to him, too; but it's no good. He won't even explain. He just shakes his head, as if that was enough. I feel as if it was my fault. I told mother—about their father and mother, I mean—and then when she asked me should she tell father I said, yes, why not? You see, I was sure he was as fond of them as any of us. It would be a pity for us, wouldn't it, Jessie, if we were to be held responsible for everything our parents did?'

Yet, as Jessie saw, she felt responsible for what her own father was doing now.

Hugh ventured to intervene. 'I've been trying to tell her, Jessie,' he said, 'that she's being a bit unfair to her father. I'll admit he's old-fashioned in his ideas, with the Bible and all that, but a lot of men would feel the way he's feeling. My goodness, murder's a terrible thing.'

Flora turned on him furiously. 'Who said it wasn't?' she cried. 'Don't be a bigger fool than you can help, Hugh McEachern. So a lot of men would feel the same way? Yes, yes, of course you're right; and yourself are one of them.'

'She won't believe me, Jessie, when I tell her I think her father's wrong.'

Flora clenched her fist and shook it at the sky. 'Oh, I feel so ashamed, ashamed.'

'Have they been told yet?' asked Jessie.

'They hadn't been an hour ago. But the letter's written. Jessie, if this happens I'll go away from Calisay, and never come back, never, never.'

211

'But that's silly. Isn't it, Jessie?'

Yes, it was silly, thought Jessie; granted the reason for getting rid of the children was ignoble and perhaps cowardly; but to be realistic were they not just two out of millions of ill-treated children? Good island sense advised that to renounce one's home for their sakes would be to add to the folly and suffering in the world. Yes, it was silly, but as Jessie gazed down at the young girl guilty of such silliness she understood and loved her. She herself had chosen to stand aloof and watch; but she was prepared to honour those who remained at the heart of the struggle, provided they did not encase themselves in callousness, which could take many forms.

'He'll maybe change his mind,' she suggested.

'No, he won't, Jessie. This isn't the first time. Ask my mother.'

'It is not my business, Flora.'

Hugh pointed to himself, as if to indicate that that was how he felt, in the circumstances. As he was doing it Flora looked round and saw him.

'If it isn't your business, Hugh McEachern,' she cried, 'then I'm not your business, either. I'll tell you something. If we do get married, and have children of our own, I'll be ashamed to look them in the face.'

Sobbing then, she raced back towards the sea, raising the snowstorm of gulls again.

Hugh came nearer. 'What am I to do, Jessie?' he asked, desperately. 'She seems to blame me.'

'Because she loves you, Hugh.'

It had occurred to him. He smiled, and turned to look at Flora now at the sea's edge. 'But do you think she meant that about her own children?'

'I think she did.'

He nodded. 'Aye, that's right.' But instead of petulance or disappointment it was love and pride his face showed. Yet Jessie would never have called him sensitive or even more than normally intelligent.

'If you've got a heart as good as Flora's, you're going to get hurt, often, and hard.'

212

'I know that, Jessie.'

'She'll need protecting, against herself.'

'I know that, too. She refuses to speak to her father.'

'She'll get over it.'

'Not altogether. Are you going there now?'

'Yes.'

'Do what you can, will you?'

'You heard me say, Hugh, it's not my business.'

He scratched his head, doubtfully. 'That's really what I feel, but Flora says it should be everybody's business. You know, Jessie, in a way she's right.'

'She may well be.'

Hugh grinned. 'Donald's a bit afraid of you, Jessie. Maybe if you did talk to him he might change his mind.'

'Just why is he doing it, Hugh?'

'Ooch, I think it's some religious prejudice. I've been thinking. You see, Jessie, before he found this out about their father and their mother, he wasn't happy about having them. Now he keeps saying he's not surprised to know what their father did. He expected something of the kind. So if he kept sheltering them here he would be acting against God's purpose. That's what he tried to say to me, in private, when neither Flora nor Mary were there. I asked him what he thought God's purpose was. Do you know what he said?'

'I think I could guess. To punish the wicked.'

'Yes. In other ways too, he's so reasonable. I don't understand it.'

She thought she did. From her own observations, and from hints dropped by Mary, she had come to look on Donald McArthur as a man undermined by a long, corroding frustration. After the war he had returned to Calisay, but he had found few opportunities to feed the conceit that his medals had bred in him.

'Well, Jessie, I'd better go to her.'

'Aye, Hugh, you'd better.'

She watched as he ran towards his sweetheart. Once a man, as young as he, and handsomer, had hurried towards her, just as eagerly. And what had the world in its wisdom done with him? Left him a sun-scorched corpse in the Africa desert. As she walked steadily on, she imagined now that the birds, the sea, and the very beatings of her heart, were calling his name. John McDougall, John McDougall, John McDougall, busily chirped the little stonechat, as it bobbed from stone to stone in front of her. J-o-h-n Mc-Dou-gall called the curlew from somewhere along the coast, prolonging it until she felt she could bear it no longer. Dry-eyed she spoke it herself, curtly: John McDougall. As tall as Hugh, with dark hair, lively blue eyes, and a mouth as quick to smile as his mind had been to see the fun of living and loving, he had thought her beautiful, had said so often, laughing but sincere, and had written it too, from the hot sands where he had been killed. If he had come home and if they had got married, their children today would be older than the Sneddon boys, but not, she warned herself, any more deserving of love. Almost, looking back, she felt as ashamed of them, as Flora did of hers, looking forward.

'But why should I be?' she asked. 'I'm only their school-teacher. My job was to try and teach them to count and read. Well, I did it, as well as I could. Now all I have to do is to fill in their report cards and send them, with their medical cards, to Glasgow Education Authority, who will forward them to their school. As a teacher I have lost dozens of children I cared for more.'

The only objection to that path by the sea was that it led past the back of Angus McArthur's cottage. If he was about, with his impudent blue eyes, she had decided to be coldly polite and pass on, certainly not to stop and talk, not even to berate him again for being what he was, evil, and a spreader of evil. Perhaps he could no more help it than a hoodie crow could. Mary had told her it was he who had threatened to tell Donald about the boys' parents. So astute was he in his wickedness that Mary had been disposed to defend his right to interfere. Jessie had almost blurted out what she had so far told not even the birds that fed from her hand in her garden.

'Why not, Jessie,' he had murmured that winter's night, with the sea crashing on the rocks, 'you are a woman, and I am a man, responsible only to ourselves, both of us lonely, both of us above our companions in intelligence and imagination; if we should wish to comfort each other in the way God, or whoever it was fashioned us, intended, why not? Whose business is it but our own?' Filthy words enough, despite the silkiness of the voice uttering them, but not so filthy as her own whispers of acquiescence; and filthiest of all had been, not his hand creeping up her thigh, nor her allowing it to remain there, but the pleasure it had given her. Yes, that had been filthier even than her subsequent desperate lying down to be made love to, or used as she afterwards thought of it. For, in the midst of it, confused by shame on her own and John McDougall's behalf, she had become aware that her partner, for all his endearments, enriched with classical allusions, and for all the delicacy of his caresses, had in reality been laughing at her, as no doubt he had laughed at the big woman from Glasgow when he had enticed her over to Sanda, and at all the other women he must have beglamoured in his day.

Yet when she saw his cottage ahead she could not deceive herself into believing that this sudden excitement which had her trembling was caused by loathing alone. No, anticipation was a far more hateful cause. Nevertheless, she did not slacken her pace or give the house more than two glances, enough to see that he was not about. All the same, it was with a shock of disgust and delight mingled that, a little past his house, in a sheltered nook where a wild rose bush grew, she came upon him seated on a knoll of grass and moss, smoking a cigar and going out to sea. A book lay open by his side. It was, she thought, as good a place for contemplation as it would be for lovers, secluded, fragrant, and commanding a view of the mighty Atlantic beyond Sanda just below.

Putting down his cigar, he leapt up and greeted her with a grace that no other man on the island, not even the laird or any of his fine friends from London, could have outdone. How blue his eyes were: the forget-me-nots she had noticed in a marsh along the path were not more innocently coloured. Again she wondered if she had been unjust to him.

Though so gracious, he seemed subdued and thoughtful,

215

with what struck her as concentrated concern; for himself, she tried to believe; and yet how sincere and impressive his smile.

She could have stood in front of him, weeping, tormented by a sense of happiness killed like that gannet on the beach. Even if he were evil, could she not have redeemed him? It was the sourness of her womb that had condemned him, not her heart.

'Ah, good afternoon, Jessie,' he said. 'This is a pleasure.'

'Good afternoon.' She made to walk on, but was easily stopped by his hand as light as a bird upon her shoulder. She shrugged it off, but waited.

'Are you for Mary's?' he asked.

'Where I'm for's my business.'

'True, Jessie; but I shall consider it a pity till the end of my days that you weren't able to let it become my business too.'

She felt her cheeks go redder than the roses on the bush. 'You'll oblige me by never, never, never, using such talk to me.' Had she repeated the word, with such passion too, because Flora had used it so recently?

He looked hurt. Agitated, she realized it was possible she had wronged him more deeply than Donald McArthur ever could wrong the two boys. She tried to remember John McDougall, but he had gone, or rather Angus was he, twenty years older.

'I'm deeply sorry, Jessie. I know you don't believe me, but for you I have more respect than for any other woman I've ever met.'

'You have strange ways of showing it.'

'When did I ever treat you with disrespect, Jessie?'

Her cheeks burned.

'Your spite's not against me, lass, but against nature.' He was silent, and they heard beneath them the splashing of the sea and the crying of birds. 'Jessie,' he went on, 'I've been sitting here for the past hour wondering about this unfortunate business of Donald and the two boys. I think Mary has mentioned it to you?'

'Yes.'

'If you've spoken to her, no doubt in her grief and

216

disappointment she'll have blackened my name because of my share in it.'

'She said you had a right to say what you did.'

He seemed sincerely and simply grateful. 'That was very decent of her. Mary's always been a fair-minded woman. Yes, Jessie, I had that right, just as Donald had the right to know; but what's troubling me now is whether he has the right, for the reasons he gives, to send the bairns away.'

'You ought to know that if a body wants to do a thing, he can find a hundred reasons for justifying it.'

'It applies to nations as well as to individuals, Jessie. But the rest of us have a sacred duty to look very clearly at the reasons given for an act like this one, say, which undermines— I don't think I am exaggerating—the very foundations of civilization.'

'Yes, you're exaggerating.'

'No, Jessie. I am not. The trouble with most folk today is that they have no horizons left.' He gestured towards the vast horizon on the Atlantic, and, fascinated, she had to turn and stare at it too. 'They're shut up in their narrow minds. They grab what material satisfactions they can get. But they're never appeased. How can they be, Jessie? Every day their minds get narrower; their horizons shrink still more. I think you'd find that most folk, on this island and off it, if asked about this business that's between Donald and the boys, would want to shrug it off. What does it matter? they'd say. Why worry about a couple of bairns, the offspring of a murderer and a whore, when the whole universe is in daily danger? I tell you, Jessie, they'll never realize in time that the universe needn't be in danger if their horizons were wide enough, if they understood that—yes, accuse me of exaggerating again—that these little boys are civilization. Cherish them, and in the end you cherish it.'

'Yes, you are exaggerating, Angus McArthur. Worse than that, you're laughing at me, at yourself, at the boys, at Donald, at Mary, at God Almighty Himself. You never had any feeling for anybody in your life.'

'If that is so, Jessie, God help me.'

'I'm not judging you. I'll leave that to your Maker. But don't expect me to believe you have that much—' she stooped, snatching a blade of grass and breaking off a piece as small as a fly—'of compassion in you. As for talk, oh, as for that, we'd need the Atlantic itself to measure what you have.'

He looked from grass to ocean and back again.

'So keep out of Donald and Mary's business. You can't help, so don't defile.'

'Defile, Jessie? Well, I'll soon defile none of you much longer. I'm leaving Calisay.'

She was startled, and couldn't help showing it; more than that, she was dismayed, and this too her face revealed. 'It's not before time,' she said, but seldom had her voice sounded less convincing. Dear God, she was thinking, if he does this or that, takes my hand, touches his moustache, turns his blue eyes towards the sea, anything, I'll drop on my knees before him, and plead with him not to go. Then afterwards I should have to throw myself over the cliffs. 'And where are you thinking of going? Canada? Australia? Or hell itself?'

He laughed. 'Glasgow, just. You see, Jessie, I'm thinking of marrying again.'

Shock gripped her by the throat. She gasped and couldn't speak. She must have turned pale too, for gentlemanly and solicitous, he had stepped forward and was taking her arm.

'Sit down, Jessie,' he murmured. 'You look tired.'

'No.' She flung off his hand. 'Who is she this time? Somebody who can't know you, that's certain.'

'Who can know anyone else, Jessie? Men and women have been known to share bed, table, and children, aye, for more than fifty years, and in the end not know each other.'

'She'll not know you, I'm sure of that. Do you know why? Because there's nothing to know.' She had a vision of a quiet pool on the sands; one day it had been empty, the next it had dozens of dead jelly-fish in it. Such was his mind, his nature, his inmost soul. Yet was she not now, in hers, regretting that she was not the woman he was going to marry?

'It's no secret, Jessie. You know her. She's Miss Mathieson, who brought the boys here.'

'The one you had out on Sanda?'

'That's right.'

'She must have liked what you showed her there.'

'I think she did, Jessie.'

She could not accuse his smile of lewdness as he said that; her own thoughts were lewd.

'It hasn't taken you long to find out how much money she's got.'

'Don't be bitter, Jessie. She's a good woman. In many ways she reminds me of yourself.'

'Except that she's twice the size and ten times the fool. I hope she doesn't think her size is going to save her from a sore heart. When is it to be? We'll have to get Dugald to compose a tune.'

'There's no hurry. Nothing's definite yet.'

'You mean she's still got her doubts?'

'No. I've still got mine. It could be, Jessie, that fond of her though I am there's someone I'm fonder of still.'

She turned from him, trying to laugh contemptuously, but sobbing instead. As she hurried along the path her face was pale again. She was thinking how much more striking-looking as a woman Miss Mathieson was, and how much wiser in her submissiveness. She had not seen his caressing hand as an insult, but more truly as a tending of her womanhood, which in all likelihood had now flowered, whereas Jessie's own went on withering.

She kept telling herself she would not, must not turn, but she did, with a wrench of her whole being, and saw him standing where she had left him, with the immense blue sea beyond. So magnificently did he command his background that, knowing she had lost him, she felt for one dizzy moment of despair that she had indeed thrown herself over the cliff. Her mind whirled, her body was sick, the precipice rang with her cries and those of the sea-birds, as down she fell, headlong, to break in a moment on the sharp rocks.

He waved. 'Oh, by the way, Jessie,' he called, 'I'm thinking of coming to your picnic tomorrow. Is that all right? I'd be glad to help.'

She muttered, too low for him to hear: 'It's not my picnic. Come if you want.' Then, as she went on again away from him, she sought refuge in wondering what book it was he had been reading.

A few minutes later when she reached Mary's cottage in its green hollow she felt her whole body bruised and painful, and her mind desperate. Below the house, reached by a long flight of steps cut in the rock, was the small pebbly beach where Donald kept his boat. Discreetly playing there were the two Sneddons. They were throwing a small ball to each other.

She watched them for a minute or so, without their knowing, and during it pretended she was not their teacher but their mother. The pretence steadied and calmed her.

When she called down, therefore, her voice was very much their teacher's; so much so that Tom, the smaller one, whose turn it was to catch the ball, at once thrust it under his jacket.

They should not, of course, have been playing with it on a Sunday.

'Come up here,' she cried. 'I want to talk to you.'

They climbed up slowly and demurely, as became discovered transgressors.

'Why aren't you at Sunday school?' she asked.

'We've been,' replied Tom.

'It was early today,' explained John.

As proof Tom took out of his pocket a small text, which showed Christ, a lamb, and two curly-haired children, and bore the text: The Lord is my shepherd. 'I got this,' he remarked. 'Johnny got one too.'

As she looked at it the flavour of her own childhood sweetened and saddened her mind.

'Was it Mrs McNeil who took you today?' she asked.

'Yes,' said John. 'Mrs Lindsay was there as well.'

'She's going to Glasgow tomorrow,' cried Tom.

When Jessie herself used to superintend the Sunday school Janet had sometimes helped.

Forgetting, Tom unbuttoned his jacket. The ball dropped and went down in a series of high bounces into the sea. With a yell of dismay he scampered after it.

Jessie held John to prevent him from following. 'I'm talking to you,' she said. 'I'm not finished.'

'Be careful, Tommy,' he shouted. 'Don't go in.'

'He won't. You know why I'm here? It's to ask Mr and Mrs McArthur's permission to take you on the picnic to Orsay tomorrow. You want to come?'

'Oh yes. Can Tommy come too?'

'If he wants to, and if Mr and Mrs McArthur let him.'

'He does want to, miss.'

'Well, he should know he can't always get what he wants.'

He nodded, but hope in his eyes was bright and splendid.

'What's this he said about Mrs Lindsay going to Glasgow?' she asked. 'Did she tell you she was going?'

'Yes, miss. She wanted to know what she should take to Jean.'

Jessie had heard of Jean; in fact, she had had the little girl pointed out to her in the photograph, by Janet herself.

'So she's going to visit her?'

'Yes, miss. She said maybe, some day, she'd bring Jean here, to stay with her.'

'Did she?'

'Yes, miss. Tommy and me hope she does.'

'Tommy and I, you mean.'

'Yes, miss.'

He was smiling as she had never seen him smile before. It was like the sun breaking through black clouds and striking distant water. He was being utterly reckless at last about revealing his tremendous need for love. What Mary had given had apparently not been sufficient; or perhaps Donald's subtle and steady subtractions had left it inadequate. Flora, too, busy at the hotel and taken up with Hugh at present working there, had lacked opportunities to reassure him with her warm love. As for Jessie herself, she had scrupulously doled him out his portion of magisterial attention; that was all.

'So this girl was a special friend of yours?'

'Yes, miss. Jean will like it here.'

'Do you think so?'

'Yes. She likes flowers and climbing trees and running and

221

living in a house, not a Home.'

In an anguish of her own she remembered John McDougall, and Angus, and her own empty house.

'Don't build up your hopes,' she said. 'Mrs Lindsay might not bring her back. Besides—' She stopped herself in time. Whoever's duty it was to tell him that he must soon leave the island, it was not hers. How ironic, and how fit subject for an Angus jest, if as the girl arrived the boys left!

'Why, Miss Ogilvie? If Mrs Lindsay wants Jean to come, and Jean herself wants to come, why shouldn't she?'

'I don't know. Perhaps she might. But often it's not so simple as that. You just don't go into the Home as you do into a shop and say, "I'll take that one." There are papers to sign. There are lots of things to be done first.'

He nodded, accepting all that necessary bureaucracy with trust. 'I think she'll come,' he said, 'in the end.'

She paused, not knowing what to say. Then she noticed that Tom had taken off his shoes and socks and was wading into the sea.

'I can see you were right about your brother,' she said. 'He's in danger of drowning himself. You'd better go and help him. If the ball's too far out, don't try to get it. Understand?'

'Yes, miss.'

She let him go and watched while he went leaping down the steps. His brother, still full of ideas, was swinging a long stem of seaweed like a rope. It was useless as far as recovering the ball went, but it smacked the water importantly. Doubtless his trousers were soaked.

She noticed for the first time that Roy the dog wasn't with them. Of course not, this being Sunday, when even dogs, in Donald McArthur's view, ought not to be heard expressing their joy.

*　　　*　　　*

Roy was lying in the sun at the front of the house. Sheep grazed and rooks with iridescent feathers strutted yards from him. She wondered if by some instinct he was aware that his

222

friends were to be sent away, and so had lost heart. When she called him he got up slowly, not much interested in her, but prepared to obey. Tail trailing, he slunk across the glittering grass and accepted her pat on his head with whimpers of gratitude and, she imagined, appeal.

'If they fell into the sea itself,' she said, 'you'd jump in after them. But for this other sea they're in, there's nothing either you or I can do about that.'

He wagged his tail forlornly, as if he understood.

She had heard it said that a dog grew to look like its owner. Now it seemed to her that the long jaw, the whiteness round the mouth, the faithful yet shifty eyes, the big, wary ears, and the damp nose, gave it a strong resemblance to Donald. Even the grins that came and went, humble and hangdog, were like his. Others thought Donald quite a humorist. Jessie had never found him so, but then most folk considered her to be over solemn, too unwilling to see cause for laughter. Well, was she expected to laugh at this latest drollery of his? Some would, she felt sure, as she crossed the held to the open door of the cottage. Elspeth, Morag and their like would, with silly pious sniggers. Mrs McNeil might smirk in her bedroom, with her yellow hair about her like Delilah, and her thick-headed husband wishing he was back at his ship's engines, with a spanner in his hand rather than a Bible, and nuts to tighten instead of souls. Isa McGilvray would smile, but not with pleasure or appreciation. Big Annie McBirnie would laugh loudest of all, with scorn, for she considered that Donald McArthur and all narrow-minded sabbatarians like him were frauds. He had once reprimanded her for hanging out on a Sunday bedclothes that her father, old Tam, had soiled in his final illness.

In the shaded parlour, on a chair upholstered in faded red plush, with his big hands tranquil on his black-clad knees, Donald looked far less troubled in his conscience than Mary who, seated opposite, could not keep her hands still; they kept twisting round each other. The Bible lay on a stool beside Donald, but whether it had already been consulted or was still to be, she couldn't say. It too was black, like his suit and

Mary's dress. Jessie's own was dark purple. What in God's name, she wondered, are we all mourning?

'It's yourself, Jessie,' said Donald, with hospitable smile. 'Come in and sit down. I saw you having a word with Roy.' There was a window screened by curtains and geraniums; out of it a glimpse could be had of the bright grass and sky. 'I was thinking it was the birds you got the name of talking to. Those rooks now, the proud fellows, they always have a look in their wee eyes as if they knew a lot that other folk don't.'

'One thing you can be sure of, Donald,' she said, 'whether it's rooks or ravens or skylarks or hoodies, I'll never get an evil word in return.'

Humorously he considered her claim. 'I'm not so sure about the hoodies, Jessie.'

'It's nice of you to drop in, Jessie,' said Mary. Her voice was firm enough, yet surely she had been crying. What had happened to her lately? She had broken down at the party for Hector's going away, and had sobbed her heart out on the jetty as the motor boat at dawn had carried him out to the steamer. Now she had been expending tears again. Few women in Jessie's experience had been less lachrymose. Was it simply, bitterly, degradingly, that she would be fifty soon, at the change, with her body betraying her daily? Or was it, as Jessie had sometimes suspected, that fidelity to Donald, not as his wife merely, but as some kind of Old Testament hand-maiden, had become too great a strain? There certainly had been trouble between him and Hector before the latter had gone off to Canada.

'Did you walk up along the shore?' asked Donald.

'Yes. I saw Flora and Hugh.'

'They said they would be going for a little walk.'

'And I saw the boys. They're down at the boat.'

'They like the boat.'

There was a silence.

'I'm here to ask if it's all right for them to come to the picnic tomorrow.'

He nodded, not to give consent, but to show he was considering.

'As you know, it's over to Orsay this year, for a change. There will be carts for those that can't walk the whole way.'

'Tomorrow's a good day for Orsay. The strand will be clear for, och, four and a half hours at least.'

'That's why we've chosen tomorrow.'

'Is the laird's wife going?'

'Yes.'

'Angus was saying he was for going with you, if you didn't mind, Jessie.

'It's not *my* picnic, Donald. It's the children's. Whoever wants can come. Are you for coming yourself?'

'My days of picnics are past, Jessie. The minister and his wife will be there?'

'I think so.'

'He'll see to it, of course, that you'll not be having the games and races in the priory held itself, where the Cross is.'

'That's the best place, Donald. I see no reason why we shouldn't have them there.'

'But it's a sacred place, Jessie. Is not the Cross holy?'

'I suppose it is, but sheep rub their rumps against it every day. I don't think the children's games will desecrate it. Besides, Donald, I'd have thought it a bit on the papist side for you, with Christ in His agony carved on it.'

Mary nodded, with her lips tight and her eyes bitter.

'That is true, Jessie,' he said placidly. 'But still, it is a sacred spot surely; it would be wrong to turn it into a playground. I know I am old-fashioned, Jessie, but my guide is aye the same.' He placed his hand on the Bible.

No man's horizons, she thought, had shrunk more than his. Yet his eyes were wrinkled with staring at great sky and sea distances.

'I take it, though, you've got no objections to John and Tom coming with us? They want to come.'

Mary leant forward. 'How can we object?' she asked. 'It is the children's picnic. Are they not children? If the rest can go, why can't they? Is there anybody else objecting to them, Jessie?'

'On the contrary. Everybody is expecting them to go.'

He was nodding, as if sagely and sympathetically consent-
ing to everything they were saying; but it seemed to Jessie his
eyes were cold and mad.

'If they were my own children now,' he said, carefully, 'I
could not really find it in my heart to give them permission;
not if it was to be held in the field with the Cross.'

'If they were your own children,' said his wife, grimly, 'they
would be mine too. I would have a say. But these two you
have just been proving to me out of the book are neither mine
not yours; nor, it would seem, anybody's.'

'Until the big woman comes for them they are in my care.
I signed the paper.'

'Has he written?' asked Jessie, of Mary. It seemed pointless
to put the question to him. Had he been deaf or unconscious
he could not at that moment have been less communicable.
Somewhere, far within the dark labyrinth of his mind, he
could be reached, if the searcher had patience and love. It
was scarcely worth her own while to try. Besides, once
reached, he would be found, like most people pee-heeing to
God, insufferably ordinary and conceited.

'The letter's through in the kitchen, against the tea-caddy,'
said Mary.

The tea-caddy, once a box of caramels, showed antlered
stags on purple heather. Often enough Jessie, a guest, had
watched the companionable tea taken from it with the spoon
that had the crest of Oban on its handle.

'I will say only one word about this,' said Donald. 'It was
a mistake in the first place. We should never have taken them.
Mary will tell you that from the minute I set eyes on them
I have never been happy in my mind about them.'

'It is not my business,' said Jessie, rising. 'If they are to come
with us tomorrow, let them be at the hall at two o'clock, wet
or dry. See that they have with them cups or mugs and big
spoons. Good day.'

His smile was such then that she wanted to hurry out and
apologize to the dog.

'Good day, Jessie. Consider the matter in the light of God's
teaching, and you will see that I am in the right.'

'If I was to think that, Donald, I would be wondering if God's teaching was fit for Christians.'

'I'll see Jessie out,' said Mary, jumping up, and going out with her friend. 'You gave up very easily, Jessie.'

They stood in the sunshine outside the door.

'I said, Mary, it is none of my business, and neither it is.'

'You'll say that once too often, Jessie. It *is* your business. You'll find one day—'

'What will I find, Mary?'

Mary was silent. Tears gathered in her eyes.

'Don't threaten me, Mary. Did you know your brother-in-law was thinking of marrying again?'

'Angus! It's not you, is it?'

They heard Donald call: 'Mary!'

'No, Mary, it's not me. Your husband's calling you.'

'I'm sorry, Jessie. God forgive me. I said it to hurt you. But I have thought, whiles, there was something between you and Angus. I'm sorry. What is it, Donald? I'm thinking of walking part of the way with Jessie.'

'No! No!'

The two women exchanged glances. The words had been bleats. Indeed, as they waited, they heard similar from the young sheep in the field, complaining to their mothers.

'I need some air and light, Donald. Come on, Jessie. Are you going back by the same way?'

'No.'

'By the road, is it? Well, let's go.'

They were under the gean-tree, now blossomless, when Donald appeared at the door. He had the Bible in his hand. Clutched like that, thought Jessie, it too was without blossom.

Twenty

Awake, but keeping very still so as not to waken Tommy, Johnny for a minute or two pushed aside the fear that for days now, ever since he had learned the picnic was to be on Orsay, had come creeping into his mind, or rather out of a dark place in it into the open where he could see it. He lay and listened to the sounds he had come to love and trust: the cocks crowing, not only their own near at hand, but others in the distance; Roy barking, and being answered by dogs on other crofts; the rattle of the milk cans being loaded on to the hotel's van, voices, laughter, and then the van driving away; sheep bleating, cows mooing, and far away on a hill a bull roaring; sea-birds screeching above the house; and the sea withdrawing with long roars from the pebble beach. He could distinguish them all now, and there was comfort in being able to do it. Some of the children at the school had warned him weeks ago when he had first come, not to be so sure he would be staying; others whom they could name and describe had come and gone, very quickly, nobody was quite sure why. Now everybody, even Peggy Blair who was always crying, thought he and Tommy must be safe. He at last believed it himself.

Tommy had believed it from the very beginning; the first lick Roy had given him had been enough. But remembering those who had left the Home only to return in a short time, as Jean McDonnell had done, Johnny had listened to the warnings in the playground; he knew they weren't meant just to frighten him but to prepare him too. Now, surely, the danger was past. Having given his love to Flora, especially, but also to Mr and Mrs McArthur, he was confident they would not suddenly hand it back, like money they had been keeping for him.

He had tried very hard not to offend anyone, and he had done his best to make Tommy take care too; though, to his

228

surprise and joy, Tommy had made people laugh here, whereas before in the Home he had made them cross because he was always complaining and sniffling. Even women like Mrs McDonald, of whom he was himself still a little nervous, had been kind to Tommy and given him things. At first he warned Tommy not to speak so much, but later when he had noticed how people liked to listen to his brother he had decided to let him say whatever he wanted.

One thing Tommy never spoke about now, and Johnny was grateful for it: he seemed to have lost all his curiosity about their father and mother. In the Home he had kept pestering about them. Johnny had been afraid of those questions. They had seemed to be a kind of trap; trying to answer them, he might remember other things he did not want to remember; whether he had really forgotten those, he wasn't quite sure and never tried to find out. Some things he did like to remember and tell Tommy about: their father and mother at Rothesay, with Tommy in his pram; and the visit to Kelvin Hall, when their father had taken Tommy, wrapped in a shawl, and Johnny, on to the Big Dipper. Their mother had refused, because it would make her sick; but she had waited for them, and was still there when they had come off.

But this fear, in connection with the picnic on Orsay, had nothing to do with his father and mother. Robert McDiarmid and Jean Fairlie, who had been to Orsay before, had been describing it. First, they had said, there was the great stretch of white sand to cross; then, just as you climbed up on to Orsay, you saw a cross of stone covered with seaweed, lying on its back. In the old days, Miss Ogilvie had explained, this had been kissed by men fleeing from enemies, because if they kissed it and got on to Orsay no one could harm them while they remained on the island. After a year on it all their crimes, even murder, had to be forgiven. In the old priory, which had no roof and where nettles grew as high as a man, there were long, thin slabs of stone, not properly in place now, so that under them and through cracks human skeletons could be seen. In corners everywhere, like birds' eggs, glimmered skulls. In the darkest place of all, where part of the roof still stood and a door had to be gone through, were more slabs, thicker and immovable, on which were carved the figures of knights of old, with shields and swords. Before you saw all this you had to pass another Cross, still upright, with Christ nailed to His crucifix sculptured on it.

All that had frightened Johnny a little; but what had caused the recurrent fear had been the small bit of pure white bone that Robert had produced from his pocket. No, it hadn't really been the bone itself, which could have been a sheep's or bird's, but his living hand disappearing into the mystery of his pocket to come out again, closed, and remaining closed while Johnny was asked to guess what it contained. His throat had been too dry to speak, and as the hand slowly opened into his heart had leapt that fear.

As he lay now, his bare feet touching Tommy's, the fear showed itself, unexpectedly, like a rat he had once seen poking its head out from a dyke. What it represented, and what it might do to him and Tommy, he did not know, and did not want to. A rat could race and bite, could jump up and sink its sharp little teeth into your throat, as Robert had said, but this thing in his mind could likely do far worse than that: it was more terrible in its threat than a hundred rats, all hungry.

Tommy awoke. He opened his eyes, saw the sunshine, and at once sat up, yawning.

'This is the day of the picnic,' he said. 'Good.' Scrambling out of bed he crossed to the window. 'There's a huge big cloud,' he reported, anxiously. 'It's going to swallow up the sun.'

Almost as he spoke the sunshine went out.

'But it's still shining on the water, in places,' he said. 'Maybe it's shining on Orsay.'

'The picnic's not till the afternoon,' said Johnny. 'The clouds will all be away by then.'

'Maybe it'll be the sun that'll all be away, Johnny. There's a ship,' he added in excitement, as he caught sight of the dot in the immense blue expanse. 'That's thirteen. Unlucky.'

He was right, it was the thirteenth they had seen since they had arrived, but Johnny was ready to tell a lie: 'It's fourteen,

Tommy. You missed one.'

'When?'

'Yesterday, I think.'

'Was it a trawler?'

'I think so.'

'British?'

'Yes. But we'd better get dressed, Tommy.'

'Read the letter first, Johnny.'

This was the letter from Jean that Uncle Angus had brought. Tommy himself wasn't very much interested in it, but he knew Johnny liked to read it.

'All right,' he said, 'but I'll have to read it quick.'

He got it out of the drawer, and read it while Tommy put on his clothes.

*   *   *

As they were taking their breakfast Mrs McArthur stood by the table. Usually she went on with her housework, or sat and had a cup of tea with them. This morning she made them feel a little uneasy by just standing and staring.

'If you want that letter posted,' said Tommy, pointing to it on the mantelpiece, 'Roy and me will take it to the box.'

'No. We'll give it to postie when he comes. There's no hurry.' Then she bent and spoke very quietly. 'I want to tell you something.'

They waited, spoons arrested.

'If Mr McArthur asks you to go with him in the boat this afternoon instead of going to the picnic, you've to say you're sorry but you'd rather go to the picnic. That's true, isn't it?'

They nodded. Johnny was surprised, for he was sure Mr McArthur knew they wanted to go to the picnic.

'I like going in the boat,' said Tommy, 'but the picnic's just once a year. We could go in the boat tomorrow, or the next day, or the next after that, if he liked.' He spoke solemnly, for he had been led to believe, by Donald himself, that he was very useful in the boat. Sometimes he was allowed to hold the tiller. He loved too to peer into the creels as they came

231

dripping out of the sea. If they contained lobsters he was usually so delighted and amazed that he had nothing at all to say, much to Mr McArthur's amusement.

'In any case it looks like rain,' she said.

They were worried by her bitterness.

'Johnny said the clouds will all be away before the picnic starts,' said Tommy.

Johnny smiled and nodded, but when he had said that he hadn't seen how enormous and dark-centred those clouds were. Like gigantic roses they were, growing out of the Atlantic. They threw shadows a mile long on sea and land. There was a breeze too, strong and warm. The sky really was like the big garden of roses at the Big House, all being tossed about by a wind.

'Mind now,' said Mrs McArthur sharply, 'you're going to the picnic.'

They heard Mr McArthur come in. He looked into the kitchen before going into the scullery to wash his hands. 'Having your breakfast, boys? Sleepy-headed fellows. But eat well. Sailors have got to be strong.'

They heard him in the scullery humming to himself.

Tommy, his brother noticed, was frowning at his boiled egg before cracking it with the spoon.

'I want to go to the picnic,' he said, as if it was a final decision.

Mr McArthur came in. He was very jolly. 'Bless me!' he cried, looking at Tommy's egg. 'It's almost as big as your own head, boy.'

Tommy grinned; this was the kind of jocularity he could handle so well. 'I think I know the hen that laid it,' he said. He giggled. 'Do you know what we call her? We call her Matron. You see, she's fat and she's got red feathers and she's always bossing the other hens.'

Mr McArthur sat down. 'Pour me out a cup of tea, wife,' he said, laughing. 'Matron now, is it?'

Johnny felt that perhaps it would be thought Tommy wasn't being respectful. 'We made jokes,' he murmured, 'but we liked her.'

232

Tommy paused in the excavating of his egg to ponder over what, with a sigh, he decided was the kind of lie people had to tell to be polite.

'She liked Johnny better than me,' he said.

'Now why was that, boy?'

'Because I was always crying, maybe,' he admitted, and paused again, to consider those many occasions when he had wept, for no reason except merely for unhappiness. He could not help shuddering and sighing.

'Were you now? That was a pity. Why was it, do you know?'

Tommy nodded, with another sigh. 'I think I was frightened.'

'Frightened? Och, I'll not believe that. A lad like you that's not afraid to steer the boat so near the cliffs you could hit the birds with a stone.'

'That's different. I like boats.'

'Of course you do; and so does John, though he isn't saying very much. Now how would you like to go out with me all this afternoon? I've got the creels in a new place. Maybe there will be dozens of lobsters. I could do with two keen lads like you to give me a hand.'

Johnny glanced up at Mrs McArthur. She nodded. He got ready to speak, but waited first to see if Tommy would do it for him, so much better.

Tommy did. 'If it was tomorrow,' he said, 'we would go. If it was any day but today. You see, it's the picnic this afternoon. Everybody's going.'

As Mr McArthur drank his tea he made the same sucking noises that Matron had so often scolded children in the Home for, Tommy especially.

Tommy noticed too, and grinned indulgently.

'So you would have me go out alone?' asked Mr McArthur. 'What if a storm blows up? Would you desert me?'

'We're sorry,' said Tommy, 'but it canna be helped.'

'We promised Miss Ogilvie we would go to the picnic,' said Johnny, cautiously. 'She said she wanted all the children to go.'

233

'Even Douglas Munro's going,' said Tommy, 'and he had mumps last week.'

'Of course they're going to the picnic,' said Mrs McArthur. Her voice trembled.

'Mary, please, I am talking to the boys.' He looked at her for what seemed to Johnny a long time.

She looked back. Neither of them smiled. It was the first time Johnny could remember them looking at each other without one of them smiling.

'Women do not understand,' said Mr McArthur, suddenly smiling as he looked at the boys. 'I shall be frank, as men should be with one another. It is like this: I do not want you to go to the picnic.'

Tommy stopped chewing.

'Donald, please,' whispered Mrs McArthur, as if she was going to cry. 'Remember, for pity's sake, they are only children.'

'I am the one remembering that, Mary. Please do not interfere.'

'But all the boys and girls are going,' pointed out Tommy again. 'Miss Ogilvie said we had to go. It's the holidays, but she's still the teacher.'

'It does not matter if all the boys and the girls in the world were going, Tom. I do not want you and John to go, and I shall tell you the reason.'

'There wouldn't be room for them all,' said Tommy, but his grin was uneasy. 'Robert McDiarmid says Orsay's not very big.'

'It is not very big, but it is very holy.'

'Donald, for God's sake!'

'There's a church,' admitted Tommy, 'but Robert McDiarmid says it's all broken and has got no roof. He says—' he paused, and decided to censor what Robert had said— 'seagulls sit on the tombstones inside it.' His own tactfulness made him chuckle. Robert had really said 'shit', which was a rude word.

'That is true, Tom. There is no roof and sea-gulls sit on the tombstones. God wishes it to be left alone.'

'Jean Fairlie said there's a man goes about in a long white

gown, at night, ringing a wee bell. A ghost. Is that true?'

'It is not true. It is a foolish superstition.'

'She said that if you go there when the moon's shining you're sure to see him. But you can sometimes hear his bell in the daytime.'

'Yes, yes. No doubt the wind among the loose stones makes noises that sound like a bell to foolish folk. It is all superstition. It is better not to go to Orsay at all, but if people do go surely they ought not to sit on the grass beside the holy Cross, and eat, and laugh, and sing, and play games?'

Tommy, frightened a little now, looked up at Mrs McArthur and then at his brother. 'I'll not sing,' he promised. 'I canna sing. And I'll try not to laugh.'

Johnny could not understand. He knew Mr McArthur read the Bible every day, and would not let anyone play on Sundays; but everybody else approved of the picnic to Orsay, including Mr McNeil the minister and Miss Ogilvie the teacher. Even James Buchan and Andrew Elliot were to be allowed to go; yet Mrs McDonald with whom they lived sang loudest in church and wouldn't let them take comics into the house.

'Leave the children alone, Donald,' said Mrs McArthur. 'Don't you think you've forfeited your rights over them?' She turned, snatched the letter leaning against the tea-caddy, and held it in front of her husband.

Johnny, stabbed by terror, tried to see what the address on it was. Had Mr McArthur written to Matron complaining about them? He could not think of anything he and Tommy had done wrong, and then remembered that Miss Ogilvie had seen them yesterday playing with a ball. She must have clyped.

Mr McArthur took the letter and placed it on the table, with the address beneath.

'There is a special reason, boys, why you should not go,' he said, quietly.

'Is there going to be a storm?' asked Tommy.

'There is, boy: a storm of God's anger.'

It occurred to Johnny that perhaps Mr McArthur was drunk. Other men on the island got a little bit drunk on

235

Saturday nights, so Roderick McDiarmid had said. They went home singing. Uncle Angus had once or twice called in on his way to his own cottage; he had been at the hotel, and had sounded drunk. But Mr McArthur drank only tea. Besides, how could he go out in his boat that afternoon if he was drunk?

Perhaps he wasn't drunk; perhaps he was ill; which was why Mrs McArthur looked so worried.

'In the Bible,' whispered Mr McArthur, with a queer smile, 'it says: honour thy father and thy mother.'

Tommy nodded; he remembered that bit. So did Johnny; it was one of the Commandments.

Suddenly, taking them by surprise, Mrs McArthur grabbed hold of them both and rushed them out of the house into the warm sunshine.

'Go and play,' she cried, and went in again, slamming the door shut.

Roy came bounding and barking up to them. Shouts were coming from the house out of the window open at the top. Memories began to stir in Johnny.

He seized his brother's hand. 'We'll go down and look for crabs,' he said.

'But what's up, Johnny? I wasna finished. She put us out. Have we never to get in again? What are they shouting for? Is she greeting? What's up? Will we have to go back to the Home?'

'I don't know. Never mind. We'll go and look for crabs.'

'I'd rather play at pirates in the cave.'

'Then we'll play at pirates.'

'But the picnic, Johnny?'

'It's in the afternoon.'

'Are we going? What did he mean? He said God would be angry.'

'I don't know.'

'What's up? What have we done?'

'Maybe it was because we were playing with the ball yesterday.'

'But we lost it, Johnny.'

236

'That doesn't matter.'

'But nobody knows, Johnny. Nobody saw us.'

'Somebody did.'

Tommy remembered, in dismay. 'Jings, the teacher. Do you think she's told?'

'I don't know.' He didn't really think she had, but what other explanation could there be for all Mr McArthur's questions and Mrs McArthur's worry? Dimly he realized there could be other reasons, connected with the letter, with the Home, and with their father and mother.

'What's up now, Johnny?'

He became aware Tommy was tugging him. He must have stopped. He looked round. They were still in the field in front of the house. Sheep grazed all round.

'Are you frightened of the sheep, Johnny? Roy's with us. He'll chase them away.'

Tommy himself was still a little scared of them. Often he would whisper: 'Which one's the ram, Johnny? The one with the horns? But they've all got horns.'

The devil's got horns. Who was it that once had said that? Johnny, pale, resisting his brother's pull, tried to remember, tried hard, frantically, desperately; it was so necessary that he should remember. The sheep, every black face horned, went scampering as Roy, urged on by Tommy, barked at them. Was it Matron? No, she had never spoken about the devil. Agnes, perhaps? Maybe, for she was a Catholic; but he didn't think so. Jean McDonnell? No, because she would have laughed, and in his recollection it had been murmured in terror. Then suddenly he remembered. It had been wee Jackie Cameron in the Home. They had climbed over the wall into the field. This time Jean wasn't with them; perhaps she had had a sore throat. Cows were in it, at the far end. The boys, alarmed, had crouched behind a hawthorn bush. One of them whispered that cows' horns were sometimes very sharp. Then it was that wee Jackie had said: 'The devil's got horns.' It had been a sunny day like this, with huge white clouds and sky blue. There had been a smell of cow dung, and afterwards, when they were safely out of the field back in the Home

237

grounds, they had discovered that Jackie's boots were covered with it.

Twenty-one

'I think, Maud, we can start now,' said Jessie. 'By the time we get to the strand the tide should be out.'

'But, Jessie, they aren't here yet, those two little chaps, Mary's boys,' cried Mrs Morton-Home. 'Our latest. Not to mention Angus himself. We can't walk the sea-bed without our Viking.'

They were standing outside the schoolhouse, near Maud's Land Rover. Along the road, at the village hall, were gathered the children for the picnic, with the horses and carts. Some boys were taking blows at old Dugald's pipes. The minister was there too, and two or three women helpers; among these was not his wife. Rather shamefacedly, he had brought her usual excuses: she wasn't feeling very well. 'Not much of a loss,' Maud had muttered. 'Insipid creature, far too damn sorry for herself.'

'I don't think they're coming,' said Jessie.

'Why? Are they sick too?'

'Donald's taken it into his head that Orsay's not a fit place for Christians to play games on.'

'Oh my God, not another dose of the drearies! And Donald McArthur of all people, so bold a sailor. Hasn't Mary talked sense to him? And Flora?'

'With no effect.'

'But what about Angus? Don't tell me he's turned holy too?'

'He's one that'll never be missed. Shall we start?'

They climbed into the Land Rover and drove up to the carts, horses, children, men, women, and piper, to the accompaniment of cheering, neighing and piping.

Jean Fairlie ran forward. 'Tommy and Johnny aren't here yet, miss.'

'I don't think they're coming, Jean.'

'But they wanted to, miss.' The girl turned away, her face bitter.

'Are we going to the Hangman's Rock as well, Miss Ogilvie?' shouted some boys.

'You'd better ask Mr McNeil that,' she replied.

Maud chuckled as she drove on. 'I suppose the man's just doing his job, Jessie. Maybe it would be unchristian of us to take the kids to see what after all is a relic of barbarism.'

'It's as well to remind them we're still barbarians.'

'But without sanctuary.'

'There never was sanctuary.'

'So you say, Jessie. But I don't want to believe you. I want to believe that once, however long ago, a man, a murderer even, God help him, if he got across the big strand and kissed the Cross on Orsay's shore, was safe from his pursuers.'

'Even if he was guilty?'

'God forgive you, Jessie, for stripping me of my illusions. If we can't afford them here, where in God's name can we?'

'Nowhere.'

'Look about you, woman.'

Earth seemed as immense and airy as sky. Sea-birds piping reminded that the sea beyond those hills red with bell-heather was vast, too.

Then, approaching, down a path through those hills, a tall man was seen, astonishingly tall, for on his shoulders was perched a child whose head bobbed among the white clouds. Another child trotted in front.

They were Angus and the two Sneddon boys.

'Wonderful!' cried Maud, stopping the Land Rover. 'Has Donald relented? Or has our Viking abducted the innocents?'

Both children had obviously been weeping, and looked as if they might weep again at any moment. On the older one's face, too, was a kind of desperation that shocked Maud, it was so peculiarly childish.

'Good afternoon, ladies,' cried Angus.

'Are you for the picnic?'

'We are, dear lady. Our little scout from his eminence has reported that the carts are coming. So do not let us detain you.'

'No. Come with us. We're laden, but you can squeeze in.'

'The boys would be happier with the other children,' said Jessie.

'Not this boy, Jessie,' murmured Angus, meaning himself. He lifted the children in among the utensils and hampers at the back, and then climbed in himself between the two women, bringing with him that scent of myrtle, good cigars, and Drambuie which always delighted Maud. He was dressed too with customary elegance and gayness: a white sweater, open-necked lilac shirt and fawn slacks.

As the car went on, he murmured: 'Sorry we were late. Had to carry out some running repairs at a burn.' He showed his wetted handkerchief; it had been used to wipe off the marks of tears.

'What's this about Donald's idiotic bigotry?' asked Maud.

'Ah yes. But I'm sorry to say it's more than that.' He looked to Jessie for support, but she kept staring grimly in front where the wide strand could now be seen, with Orsay on its far side. The tide had not yet fully receded, but hundreds of patches of pink sand were appearing. The sun flashed on many pools.

'Later,' he murmured, 'I'll explain later.'

Soon Mrs Morton-Home ran the car on to the firm sea turf. 'Right, boys,' she said briskly, 'hop out and catch grass-hoppers.'

Angus helped them down. Like released animals, they raced for the shelter of the sand dunes.

'Now, Angus,' said Maud, as she stood with legs apart and face lifted to the sun, 'what the devil did you mean?'

He pointed. Even with the naked eye they could make out in that marvellous clarity the strange projection on the distant rock face, though from that angle they could not see the hole through which the rope had been threaded. 'The symbol,' he said, 'reminding us for ever that man's justice must inevitably take precedence over God's forgiveness.' Now his finger pointed towards Orsay.

'And what the hell does that mouthful mean?'

Again he pointed, this time towards the two small boys

241

crouching among the sand dunes. 'Their father, you might say, stands suspended between man's justice and God's forgiveness.'

'What are you havering about? I understood that both their parents were dead.'

'She is. *He* stands in need of such a sanctuary as Orsay yonder was hundreds of years ago.'

'D'you mean he's a criminal?'

'Yes.'

'What'd he do?'

'Murder.'

'My God. Is this true?'

Hand on his heart, blue eyes upward, he looked like St Orsay himself. Even Jessie stared at him with grudged admiration.

'Whom'd he murder?' asked Maud.

'His wife. Their mother.'

'Why?'

'She was unfaithful.'

So smoothly did he say the word that Maud had to laugh. For decency's sake she made it a bark of incredulity. 'Kings, dukes, film actors, company directors, landowners, nowadays accept infidelity with composure. Who was he that didn't?'

'A cobbler.'

'You mean, a shoe-mender? One of those little men in striped aprons, with their mouths full of nails?'

'Yes, one of those.'

'Did they hang him?'

'No. They decided he was insane. So he crouches in Perth prison, cobbling at his broken wits. I doubt if he remembers he ever had children.'

'Dear God, yes, the children. Poor innocent creatures. Is this what's turned Donald against them? You'd think that a man who sees God sitting like a cormorant on every second rock would know where to go for good Christian advice. What's the point of being proud of Orsay as a sanctuary long ago for the guilty, if we can't make Calisay one today for the innocent?'

'That is the question shaming us all, Maud.'

'It doesn't me,' said Jessie. 'I have never deceived myself I'm better than other folk.'

'But, Jessie,' cried Maud, 'they're innocent.'

'I don't know what innocence is. Let Donald send them away. In our hearts we'll be grateful, though with our mouths we'll condemn him. A challenge we're not fit to face will have been removed.'

'You're too bitter, Jessie. Good Christ, it's not the lack of work, or a craze for city pleasures that will empty our island in the end and leave it for the birds and seals. It's the lack of faith in ourselves.'

Then they heard piping and singing. The Sneddon boys went racing to meet the carts.

'You'd think looking on this would cleanse our minds.'

It was an inspiring-enough view, he agreed: the strand itself, a mile across, more pink sand now than pools, Orsay low and green, in the distance the hills of Islay, eastwards Jura with its great bare purple Paps, and to the west the mighty Atlantic, green till far out, and then turquoise to the horizon.

'Indeed, Maud, in a way I think it does, you know.'

He smiled, for what he was wondering about then was whether his nephew in Canada had received the letter he had sent him, enclosing another addressed to Nell in Oban, which Hector was to stamp and post. In it Angus had told her he had fled to Canada to escape her, and how, serving him right, he had fallen out of luck. He had even hinted that if she could spare him a pound or two they might well save his life; and he had given her an imaginary address to write to. There, in that mythical abode, dwelt the guardians of innocence.

*   *   *

As he led the children across the strand on foot, it seemed to Archie McNeil, the minister, that the sea-birds which every day waited for this miracle of the withdrawal of the sea were complaining against the intruders, in shrill mimicries of his wife's protests. Looking up, he answered them as he had tried to answer her: 'No, Sheila, I don't expect everyone to be perfect. I'm not such a fool as that. But as Christ's minister I do expect those who profess belief in Him and attend His church to seek His guidance and follow it, even if it means, as it mostly will, that the world has to be defied.' She had screamed, 'Why was my child refused?' and now these gulls, with diabolical insistence, kept echoing her.

He turned to his little band of barely accepted children, and cried: 'You know, since Orsay has always been a holy isle, and still is if we choose to make it so, we ought on our way to it to sing a hymn or two, like pilgrims. What do you say?'

Since he was the minister they said yes, but not very enthusiastically.

'Dugald canna play hymns on his pipes,' said little Tommy Sneddon, adding cautiously, 'I think.'

They all laughed, Archie too.

'No, but he's out of puff anyway. A good rousing tune to start off with. One we all know. What about "Yield not to temptation"?'

He noticed the two oldest, Roderick McDiarmid and Jean Fairlie, exchange quick, knowing grins, which said of course: Just like a minister; here we're on a picnic, enjoying ourselves, and he wants us to sing hymns. Had it been, say, one of the laird's wife's superior London friends, he would not have minded so much; but to see Christianity derided, no matter how respectfully, by these children daily becoming more and more infected by the world, dismayed him. As a consequence his leading of the singing was perhaps at first too aggressive; but when he saw the younger children join in with enjoyment and simplicity his own voice grew triumphant and joyful.

Maud, walking beside Jessie (one of the men had driven the Land Rover across), was startled and at first displeased by this outburst of pious fervour. Then it seemed to her to suit the situation, especially as the two Sneddon boys were singing dutifully, and Angus's rich voice was ringing out. She began to sing herself.

Jessie, though, kept her mouth tightly shut, in a grimace of scorn. Yet, despite herself, she pictured Angus, clad in white

244

and bearing a jewelled cross, at the head of a great procession. The refrain was sung with gull-scaring gusto:

'Ask the Saviour to help you,
Comfort, strengthen, and keep you.
He is willing to save you,
He will carry you through.'

'It's damned embarrassing really,' said Maud. 'After all, why come to Calisay if you're thirsty to save souls?'
'Aren't they here for the saving, Maud?'
'Dammit yes, but only a hundred or so; in the heathen cities there are millions. Just listen to him bellowing.'

'Shun evil companions; bad language disdain;
God's name hold in reverence, nor take it in vain.
Be thoughtful and earnest, kind-hearted and true;
Look ever to Jesus, He will carry you through.'

Not so presumptuous as to look to her Creator, Jessie looked instead to the boys whose father—her blood glittered in her with horror—had killed their mother, in the small room in the great dark city. When she saw them, the peculiar appropriateness of where they were and what they were doing struck her as just too perfect, so that she wanted to shout a warning that however it was to be done, it could never be so pat as that. The parson had them by his side. When he wasn't waving his hands at the gulls or God, he was lavishing blessings on the boys' heads. Then in a moment there seemed nothing mawkish about it after all; it was as simple as sea and sand and gulls. The minister was a good, not very intelligent man who believed in what he was singing: 'Ask the Saviour to help you, and He will carry you through.' He could be right.
They reached Orsay. On its threshold the great broken cross lay half-buried in the sand, barnacled, and slimy with seaweed. Sandflies hopped about it. It stank of the sea.
In the old days, when it was upright, pilgrims used to kiss it. Maud thought she'd as soon kiss a rotting whale.

The children were frank. They leapt about, yelling and holding their noses and making wishes.

As if drunk or frantic with faith, the minister scrambled about it, lifted the fronds of weed with worshipping hands, and almost rubbed his nose on it trying to decipher the inscriptions long since scoured away.

'You've got to remember, boys and girls,' he cried, 'this making of a wish is just a silly modern superstition. When the ancient pilgrims kissed it they did it out of gratitude, not selfishness. They made no wishes, unless you can call the favour of our Lord a wish.'

'What else?' murmured Maud.

'Is it true, Mr McNeil,' asked Roderick McDiarmid, 'that if a murderer kissed it he was pardoned?'

Maud looked for the Sneddon boys; they were, with others, poking at sea-anemones in a pool. She was reminded of blobs of blood.

'In a way, yes, Roderick,' replied the minister. 'They believed, you see, that God was on this holy isle. Once in His presence you were absolved from every crime and every sin.'

It was again little Tom Sneddon who put the question all their eyes were asking. 'Is God no' everywhere?'

'Yes, Tommy, of course He is; but in some places even He finds more peace than in others.'

'Like in a church?'

The minister was delighted. 'Exactly. Like in a church. And also on this lovely sacred island.'

Then Angus, in his best Viking voice, shouted and pointed seawards: 'Yonder they wait on their wild white horses, the great blue warriors of the Atlantic.'

The boys cheered and galloped about, splashing through pools. They were those great blue warriors. The two Sneddons were as valiant as any.

'It's time we got on our way to the priory,' said Jessie. 'If we're not back here by half past five we'll have to sleep on the shore.'

'Like Robinson Crusoe,' cried Angus.

Again the children cheered, and as they went racing on

ahead, up the track that led across the island to the priory, they imagined themselves to be the famous lonely castaway.

'I don't think I'll walk, Jessie,' said Maud. 'That damned varicose vein is beginning to hurt like hell. You'll be walking, though, with Angus?'

'I'll be walking,' said Jessie drily, and went on alone.

Soon Angus was by her side. 'I hope you don't mind, Jessie?'

'Haven't you heard, this is God's island, not mine?'

'Well, Jessie, what did you wish for?'

'Nothing.'

'Ah Jessie, don't spoil the sport.'

'Did you wish?'

'My head's as full of wishes as the sky is of clouds.'

She glanced up. 'I hope it doesn't rain. There's my wish.'

He laughed tenderly. 'You're as Scotch as heather.'

'And what was yours? I saw you put your mouth to the stone.'

'Don't they say that if it's told it's never granted?'

Then Tommy Sneddon, red-faced with happy excitement, came rushing back to show them a treasure he had found. It was a pebble shaped like a heart, sky-blue, with tiny specks of red and green. 'Is it a jewel?' he cried.

'It's just a stone,' said the schoolmistress.

'But it's as bonny as any jewel,' said Angus.

'What's it worth?'

'Nothing,' she said.

'Nothing!'

'In money, laddie, that's about all,' said Angus. 'But just you give it your brother, as a keepsake, to remind him of this picnic to Orsay, and it'll be worth more than all the money in the world.'

'That's what I'm going to do,' he shouted. 'I'm going to give it to Johnny.'

Off he raced, yelling his brother's name.

'Well,' murmured Angus, after a pause, 'they'll have it to remember us all by.'

'You think, then, that Donald will get rid of them?'

247

'Let's be fair, Jessie. One day of high wind when I mentioned to Donald that it was dangerous going out alone in his boat, he replied: "Angus, in my boat I am never alone." What right had I not to believe him?'

'Aye.' Then she was silent. A worse madness, a more destructive illusion, than Donald McArthur's was often at work in her. She too felt a presence, even in her bed at night; but in her case it had a recognisable human shape, and sometimes, as now, could be seen, touched, smelt and desired.

His hand was resting on her shoulder. In front the children shouted and shrieked. Everywhere, in grass, heather, whin bush and dyke, the wind laughed. In the west boomed the Atlantic. Among the heather sheep bleated, and in the skylarks sang: it might have been the other way round, so intermingled were the sounds, and so whirling her mind.

'Were you in earnest,' she said at last with difficulty, her mouth dry, 'about what you said yesterday, on the cliff?'

'I said many things, Jessie. I meant them all.'

'About marrying this woman in Glasgow?'

'Ah yes.'

'What does that mean?'

'I think so, Jessie.'

She smiled, revealing her shame and humiliation. 'You think so? Wouldn't you be sure about such a thing?'

'Sure enough, I suppose.'

Far away then a curlew, her favourite, called, and surely it was her own heart fleeing in shame and sorrow?

'Wouldn't you say I had a prior claim? If I wanted to assert it, that is.'

'Just what is this you're saying, Jessie?'

His voice was low with respect and wonder, and his face serious and noble.

She felt so grateful to him that tears almost came into her eyes. She was stripping her very soul, and he was not sniggering. To give him his due, he never sniggered. When he had seen part of her body naked no man could have been more tender and respectful.

'Never mind,' she said.

248

'But I do mind, Jessie. What is this you're trying to tell me, lass?'

'Don't "lass" me. I'm over forty, and look it. I'm no beauty, and never have been.'

'Beauty's not just a lucky arrangement of features, or a skin like rose petals. It's principally in the mind.'

'You're laughing at me. If anything, my mind's bleaker than my face.'

'You're unfair to yourself, Jessie.'

'That's true enough, and it makes me unfair to other folk. You're the one that's suffered most.'

'Aye, Jessie, you've had me as empty of feelings as that old priory down there.'

They had diverged from the main track and now stood on the stony hill above the bright windy field where sheep grazed about the standing cross, and where, deep in nettles, lay the broken walls of St Orsay's priory. Children crept with caution and awe among the ruins. Under slabs glimpses were being had of skeletons; and in niches skulls were being found, two or three at a time, like birds' eggs.

'Let's sit on this rock for a minute or two, Jessie.'

'We're exposed to the world here,' she said. But she sat down.

Humility struggled to possess her soul and make her face lovely. Moved, he took her hand.

'There's really nothing for us to say to each other,' she said, 'except that maybe I owe you an apology.'

'For what, Jessie?'

'For condemning you. For seeing you as blacker-hearted than any murderer that ever tried to find safety here.'

He remembered Margaret weeping that first night in her flat in Glasgow, and himself feeding on her surrender and humiliation.

'Just let me say this much in my defence, Jessie. I sinned against you; I soiled an innocence as pure as any bairn's; but I did it, God help me, out of a warmth of affection, and a depth of admiration, such as I had never felt before for any woman.'

'You couldn't say that now. You've met somebody you think more of.'

He remembered now Margaret's transfiguration into loveliness, through her love for him. Pity for her, for Jessie, for himself, and for all humanity entrapped by the relentless compulsion of love, caused in him a sadness so profound as to be prophetic. He almost wished he had been able, like a Moslem, to marry them both in public. As it was, one of them must be sent off into lonely bitterness and unfulfilment.

'It would have to be done properly,' she said. 'I mean, if, after all, you were to prefer me.'

He was astonished and alarmed.

'I thought that would silence you.' Yet she still seemed to be waiting for an answer.

He could not say: 'But, Jessie, she says she's pregnant. Most likely she's wrong, she's so new-fangled with her body since it blossomed with love. But suppose she isn't, don't you see that the child she'd be carrying would be mine, Jessie, mine, boy or girl? You'll say, everybody on the island will say, even Flora will say, that I'm not fit to be a father. I'll say it myself. Yet somehow I like the thought, Jessie; I like it enough almost to marry the woman. Maybe it's because I've discovered I'm alone too, and that the only bridge across which I could step among humanity would be a child of my own.'

What he did say was: 'Jessie, if you'd only told me this two months ago.'

She had her eyes closed. Now she opened them, to reveal a bleaker, bitterer hatred of him than she had ever done before. He realised that she had been certain he would marry her if she found the humility to say she was willing. She left her hand in his, but only through its trembling to communicate more and more hatred.

Never had he been so much at a loss. There was absolutely nothing he could say.

Then, in the silence, they heard from beyond the ruins a child's scream of terror.

Maud and the others, unloading the foodstuffs in the field below, heard it too. They looked about them. She made a megaphone of her hands and shouted up to the two on the hill. 'Has somebody been bitten by a seal?'

'Somebody's found a skull,' muttered Angus.

Then they saw the children appear from among some huge boulders down by the shore and hurry towards the priory field. They were led by Jean Fairlie. She had her arm round someone.

It was John Sneddon.

Jessie threw Angus's hand from her as if it was filthy, and hurried down the steep, rocky hillside. He came after, anxious to help. She ignored him.

By the time they reached the Cross Maud and the minister were tending the elder Sneddon boy. As Angus approached, he thought for a moment, from their alarm and helplessness, and from the boy's stillness, that he must be dead.

Maggie McLennan, the district nurse's sister, was comforting his brother, but she could not answer his shrill questions.

Jessie pushed past them all. 'What's the matter?' she demanded, as if annoyed.

'He seems to be in a kind of fit,' said Maud. 'Has he had this before?' Then she whispered into the schoolmistress's ear: 'Can it have anything to do with his father?'

Jessie rose and looked for Jean Fairlie. 'Jean, come here,' she cried.

As they waited for the white-faced girl to come forward, Angus bent over the stricken boy. Diagnosis was simple: he had just seen his father kill his mother again. Had the saint's ghost appeared, then its face could not have been more remote than this small pale one, with the teeth chattering, and the head shaking, as if to deny what was still in the haunted eyes. The body itself seemed in a curious way absent: far from joy at that moment, from human touch, it was just as far from pain or feeling of any kind.

Jessie had seized Jean Fairlie by the shoulder. 'And just what was it he saw behind the rock?'

The girl was reluctant to say. It had to be shaken out of her. 'A man and a woman.'

'And what were they doing?'

251

Crouched over the boy, rubbing his cold hands, Angus marvelled at Jessie asking so artless a question. Maud's voice clashed with the minister's in ordering the other children out of earshot. They went with dreadful unwillingness. From earliest infancy, thought Angus, until the most drivelling senility, we are fascinated by the dirt in our minds.

'And what were they doing, Jean?' repeated the minister.

'Nothing, Mr McNeil. I didn't really see them.'

'Had they their clothes on?' asked Maud.

'I think so. I think they were sunbathing. The man had something in his hand; it looked like bracken.'

'Don't you see?' whispered Angus. 'In some way they must have reminded him of his father striking his mother.'

'You say that,' said Jessie, bitterly, 'because you want it to be that. It pleases the blackness of your heart.'

She pushed past to crouch over the boy and shake him.

'Gently, Miss Ogilvie,' said the minister. 'He's not malingering, whatever else.'

'What were you saying to her up there?' whispered Maud, to Angus.

He could not answer.

'Listen to me, John Sneddon,' Jessie was saying. 'This won't do. Wake up. Pull yourself together. You're upsetting everybody. You'll make yourself really ill. Look, you've got your brother crying.'

Three or four of the other children were crying too.

'He looks as if he'd just been lifted out of the sea,' said Maud.

And that's just what's happened, thought Angus. He's been washed up on to this human shore where none of us speaks his or indeed one another's language. Let no one be surprised, or weep: this incommunicableness is nothing unusual; on the contrary, it is our fate from the womb to the grave; here in this boy we see it in its primeval starkness, that's all.

Then he and the others looked up when Roderick McDiarmid shouted: 'Here they are, Miss Ogilvie, the man and woman who gave him the fright.'

Shyly coming through the gate was a couple, middle-aged,

obviously married and ludicrously commonplace, he grey-haired and small, carrying a red-and-white striped picnic bag, she with her hair kept blonde by dyeing. Angus recognized them as hotel guests. He had had a drink with them in the lounge. They were a Mr and Mrs Murtrie from Liverpool.

Both looked frightened and concerned. Her brow was lumpy with cleg-bites, some of which were bleeding. She kept dabbing with a handkerchief soaked in eau-de-Cologne.

When they reached the group at the Cross they stared in horror at the boy on the grass, and then around, in self-exculpation, at the other children, whose eyes seemed keenly to accuse.

'How is he?' asked Mr Murtrie. 'God knows what happened. He let out such an awful yell. Molly and I will never forget it. We hadn't time to find out what it was all about before the girl rushed him away. We were doing nothing wrong, you must understand.'

'If it wasn't that the poor kid looks so bad,' said Mrs Murtrie, 'we're the ones who'd be looking for an apology. When Mr McGilvray brought us here in his boat this morning he said we had a right to be here. Is the kid one of the boarded-out ones? I would just say this, if he's half-mad or given to fits, he oughtn't to be allowed to roam around.'

'Nobody's blaming you,' said Maud. 'Just tell us what happened.'

'Bert and me were sunbathing behind a rock. He had his jacket off, and I this cardigan; nothing else. The horse-flies were bothering us, me especially. I must have sweet blood, Bert says. Look at these lumps.'

'I was trying to keep them off with a bit of bracken,' said her husband.

'I was half asleep. Then there was this horrible yell. I got up to see the kids running away.'

'All right,' said Maud. 'We're sorry you've been disturbed. Angus, we'll have to take him home and see what Annie McLennan says; maybe we'll have to telephone for the doctor. Jessie, you stay and get on with the picnic.'

'Mrs Morton-Home,' called Maggie McLennan, who was

trying to comfort the younger Sneddon, 'what about this little fellow? Will you take him?'

'Better not, Maggie. It's up to you all to cheer him up. Well, Angus, the sooner the better.'

As Angus lifted the boy it was almost a surprise to himself not to see falling from his arms the white folds of the saint's robe.

Twenty-two

During Sunday school, when Mrs McNeil was telling the story of Jesus as a boy, if she had been asked how many children there were listening, she would have answered, rather crossly—for she had a cold and a headache—that of course there were eleven, Chrissie McFadyen being the only absentee. Anyone else would have counted the same number. But for Janet Lindsay, the minister's wife's assistant, there was, as indeed always nowadays, one more, seated between the Sneddon boys. This was the girl Jean McDonnell, whom she had almost made up her mind to adopt. The tiny doubt was permitted, not because she hadn't the courage to get rid of it, but because its presence in her mind produced excitement and suspense. Now, though, in the church this Sunday, listening to the sniffed account of the boy-God driving out the money-changers, that doubt suddenly grew enormous and savage, threatening to devour all her meek confidence. In terror she heard, as if from above, the angry admonition that a living child was not to be treated like some unsaleable piece of merchandise and pushed to the back of a shelf where it would lie till wanted. No, at this very moment the child was suffering from loneliness and want of love. God being merciful, especially to children as the Bible said and Janet believed, He would not wait for ever before sending someone else, less cautious and niggardly, to take her away from the Home. Indeed, He would not wait one single day longer.

After that Janet could hardly wait for Sunday school to finish. She almost ran home, surprising Neil not far from the house, for they had arranged that he would meet her near the kirk. He thought at first she was ill, and made her sit down on a bank of red bell-heather until she got her breath back.

'Don't try to stop me,' she gasped. 'I'm leaving tonight.'

'Leaving for where, wife?'

'For Glasgow. For the Home. I've got to see her, Neil. We're going to lose her, that's what; we're going to lose her.'

Worried, he sat too and put his arm round her.

'Look, Neil, I'm swearing it on the Bible. Don't try to stop me.'

'I'm not trying to stop you, Janet. But Glasgow's not just round the corner, you ken.' As he gazed about him, he wished it was: these hills were bonny, and he liked the sea and the birds singing as much as any man, but they were not after all to be preferred to the cheerful crowds. 'There's no steamer till Tuesday morning.'

'There's one that leaves Port Ellen tomorrow morning.'

But that was in Islay, far enough away too. He said so, gently.

'Isn't the *Islesman* at the jetty now? And isn't it sailing for Port Ellen this evening? What time is it now?'

'Ten to four.'

'It's sailing at six. I've got time. Captain Murdoch's a friend of yours; he'll take me.'

'Aye. Geordie would, wife, but—'

'But nothing. I'm going, I tell you. It's my last chance. I feel it in my heart.'

Jumping up she rushed homewards, almost too fast for his fatter legs and lazier lungs to keep up with.

She kept saying: 'Don't try to stop me, Neil.'

He thought of sensible arguments, but kept them to himself. If she went and got the girl, and liked her as much as she dreamt she would, then there would be happiness for her, and for him too, for the rest of their lives; but if things went wrong and she lost her, she might very well, at this rate, destroy herself, and him with her.

Once she stopped, and turned. Fear made her face strange and old. 'Laugh if you like,' she whispered. 'In the church today, I heard a voice. As sure as that stone's standing there, I heard it. It warned me I had wasted too much time already. If I wasted another day even, it would be too late.'

They were almost opposite the great Standing Stone, put up thousands of years ago by men, like himself at this moment, by no means disposed to deny God's interference.

'You know I'm with you, Janet,' he said. 'Haven't I been advising you to do something about it? But we've filled no forms, wife. We've made no application. There's an official way of doing these things.'

'After I've seen her I'll bring back all the forms that are needed. She's got to see me, too. That's what you forget. We've been thinking, will we like her? But what if she doesna like us? That's to be faced too, forms or no forms.'

'She'll like you, wife; a bairn has an instinct that tells it. But the *Islesman*'s so damned slow. It'll be nearly midnight before you get into Port Ellen. And where will you spend the night there?'

'With Peggy Thomson. You know we're welcome there any time.'

'That's so.' He was glad of it, and grateful too. Peggy and her man Dick were, like the Lindsays themselves, shopkeepers and also incomers from Glasgow.

'So my mind's made up. If you try to stop me I'll never forgive you for the rest of my days.'

'No, Janet, I'm not going to try to stop you. What I'm going to do is to take a walk down to the jetty and have a word with Geordie.'

The old captain of the puffer was in an irascible mood. Since he was having to sail on a Sunday, he was making the gesture to the God of his fathers of not smoking all day.

'Yes, yes, Neil man,' he answered testily, 'it will be all right for Janet to come with me. It will be more than all right, it will be a pleasure. She is a God-fearing woman. What is her opinion of that slippery dog-fish, Angus McArthur? I hope it is the same as Miss Ogilvie, the schoolmistress's. He was here this morning, if you like, speaking to me as if he was the Lord God Admiral Himself and me a lascar coolie. He is a man— wait and you'll see, Neil my friend—sure to be struck down in his insolence and pride by the hand of God. And I would not be at all surprised if this, look,' and he held up his own huge fist, 'was the shape of that hand, for the time being.'

So Neil, on his return to the house, warned Janet to expect

to have to pay for her passage by listening to much abuse of Angus.

'I hope not,' she said. 'He's not half as bad as he's painted.'

He laughed. 'True enough, I've noticed that the women who have so much to say against him have eyes for nobody else when he's there. Jessie at the school's as bad as any of them. I wouldn't be surprised if you turned out to be right, and they got married in the end.'

'Jessie could do worse. They say he's not genuine to the core. Which one of us is? But I'll always say this for him: he makes a woman feel somebody; even if she's mucking out a byre, or down on her knees scrubbing a shop floor, he greets her as if she was a lady. Those who call him false would do better to take a lesson from him.'

Neil supposed he was included. Never rude, as befitted a shopkeeper, he also was never ready with compliments that transcended the needs of business. Like most of his country-men, he hid behind the belief that delicacy and graciousness of speech, especially to women, didn't suit the Scottish tem-perament, which preferred bluntness and candour. Now, listening to Janet's strangely passionate gratitude towards Angus, he felt ashamed.

When the *Islesman*'s siren sounded, he carried her suitcase down to the jetty. She gave him instructions sharp with sympathy and affection. He was aware that she, too, found the soft word hard to manage; but he did not want to cast it up to her, or remind her not to condemn others for a fault she had herself. On the contrary, as he listened to her voice and watched her face, both of them protected by the familiar harshness, he loved her all the more.

'I'll be fine, Janet,' he said. 'Don't worry about me. You're the one that's to take care.'

'Because I'm doing something daft and reckless? Is that what you mean?'

'I was referring to the Glasgow traffic; that was all.'

'Am I a child, then, not fit to cross the street by myself?'

Since there were a few neighbours about, chatting to the crew, and waiting to see the puffer off, they did not kiss, but held hands firmly for a moment. Then she went on board, and he stood on the jetty, scratching his head with one hand and waving with the other, until the little boat had cast off and was far down the Sound. Janet kept waving, stiffly. Jura stood behind her, vast with its purple mountains; but it, and the rest of the world, did not matter.

He felt very lonely.

'Well,' he murmured, to a large, arrogant-eyed gull on top of a barrel near him, 'am I going to be a father when she comes back?'

It blinked its fierce amber eyes.

'I take it,' he added, with a sad chuckle, 'it's nothing to you, you'll likely have been one a hundred times over.'

He thought of its eggs on some high, spray-splashed ledge, and also of the quick hop on and off of successful, heedless procreation. Then he thought too of his own many failures, with Janet more and more tender towards him.

As he stood staring at the gull, it occurred to him again how timorous and old-fashioned Janet and he really were. Other couples unable to have children went from specialist to specialist. Janet and he had gone, shyly, to one, who had assured them there seemed to be no physical reason why they should not have a child. If they did not, he had implied, it was because of God's will.

*　　*　　*

When, on Monday evening, after the long sunny journey, by sea most of the way, Janet came out of the Central Station into Union Street to wait in a queue for the tramcar, she found herself giving little smiles to everybody whose eye she caught: the one-armed man from whom she bought the *Evening Citizen*, the fat woman in front of her, and especially all the folk back from their holidays, tanned and eager, carrying heavy cases.

Hearing the Glasgow voices all round her was delightful and reassuring. To hear her own, as well as out of an irrepressible feeling of kinship, she spoke to the fat woman, despite the latter's sulky double chin and glazed tired eyes.

'There's something about Glasgow,' she said, 'that makes you glad to be back.'

Just to show how people, and particularly Glasgow people, oughtn't to be judged from their appearance, the fat woman at once laughed cordially. 'Why, hen, where have you come frae?' she asked. 'India it could be, you're so black wi' the sun.'

'Not just as far as that; though far enough. Calisay.'

'And where in the name o' the wee man's that?'

'It's in Scotland; a sma' island off the west coast, not far from Islay. We went there two years ago. We bought the only shop that's on it. We like it fine, Neil and I, but it's terribly quiet, compared wi' Glasgow. We miss the noise and the cheeriness.'

The fat woman cackled. 'Rather you than me, hen. Islands are a' right for a holiday, in the summer. My God, in the winter, do you just pu' the claithes ower your heids and try to wake up in the spring, like the squirrels?'

'No. You'd be surprised. The winter's all right. The weather's much better than it is in Glasgow. There's never any fog, and often it's as warm in December as if it was spring. We have happy times too, in one another's houses. Then we've got a grand hall, with films and dances, and badminton for them fit to play it. But it's true there aren't enough young folk. As soon as they can, they leave. It's a pity.'

'I thocht they were awfu' clannish in thae ootlandish parts, and werenae very keen to welcome interlopers.'

'Well, they are a wee bit like that.'

'Still, if you're freendly wi' them, ye leave them nae alternative but to be freendly wi' you. That's my motto. But here's my tram, hen. Guid luck. Your weans will like it fine yonder?'

Janet called after her: 'Wean, not weans. Just the one. But you're right, she likes it fine.'

It did not seem to her a lie, because whenever she thought of any place on Calisay that she liked there Jean always was, sometimes with her, sometimes with her and Neil, sometimes with Neil himself even, and sometimes alone. In the field on the way from the shop to the hotel was the Standing Stone, freckled with lichens, like a giant's fist clenched against the sky. Though it could be seen from every window at the back of the house, and from the garden, it was not more vivid in her recollections than the little red-haired girl she had still to meet.

Later that evening, after high tea in the respectable boarding-house near the Mitchell Library, when she put a call through to Neil she almost, to appease the ache in her imagination, asked first of all how Jean was.

A moaning and surging as of the stormy sea came over the wires.

'This is me, Janet.'

He chuckled, like one of the sea-monsters that used to live, so they said, off Calisay, and come creeping ashore to eat any child left unguarded.

'What's so funny?' she demanded.

'Sorry, wife. You sound like old Ewan McCuish.'

'Well, that's a compliment, I'm sure. It's worth spending the money just to hear that.'

'You know what I mean.'

She did, and smiled. This indeed was how the old bed-bound sailor gasped for want of breath and frailness of heart as he told his stories of wild adventure.

'Did you have a nice trip?'

'Nice enough. Sunshine all the way. Lots of folk on holiday at all the places, Tarbert, Tignabruaich, Rothesay, Dunoon.'

'I hope you threw Highland Mary a kiss for me as you were passing.'

She smiled again. In their young married days they had often spent a holiday at Dunoon, and had walked arm in arm past the statue of Burns's sweetheart.

'It's raining here now,' he said. 'In fact, it's quite a wild night. It's been a fine day, though, windy a bit, with big clouds. About an hour ago it came on to rain, and now it's fairly pelting.'

'But it was all right for the picnic?'

'Aye, as far as the weather's concerned. I mean, it seems there was some sort of accident.'

'To one of the bairns?'

'It seems so.'

'Which one?'

'Now, wife, don't get excited. Because we're going to take one on ourselves doesn't mean we've got to take them all on.'

'No, that's right. Who was it? Andrew Elliot?'

'As far as I know at this moment, it was one of Donald McArthur's little boys; the older one, I think.'

She let out a cry of dismay. 'But he's Jean's friend. He knows her better than we do. What happened to him?'

'That's what nobody seems to know. I haven't been over the door myself all day. You know Monday can be pretty busy. Jim McFadyen was in about half an hour ago and mentioned about this accident. He said as far as he knew the lad took some kind of fit.'

'A fit?'

'Aye. But don't start imagining things. He's going to get better.'

But Janet was staring in horror into the unknown. No one had known John Sneddon was subject to fits. No one knew what Jean McDonnell, another mystery, might be subject to.

He understood. 'If we take the lass, Janet, we accept every responsibility. You know that.'

'Are you trying to put me off?'

'Never in the world. I'm holding your hand. I'm saying I'm with you, at the beginning and to the very end. You've got more faith saved up in you than anyone else in the whole world. Now's the time to spend it.'

The pips went.

'Will you be back on Wednesday night?'

'Aye. That's still my intention.'

'I'll be waiting on the jetty. If you can find time, give Williamson's a look in, will you? It's as well to keep in touch. Good night. Mind, I'm with you, all the way.'

'I know that, Neil. Good night.'

As she put down the telephone her hand was shaking.

Miss Rowan, the white-haired, pleasant-faced proprietress, came out into the hall. 'I hope you gave Mr Lindsay my regards,' she said.

'I'm sorry, Miss Rowan. I forgot.'

Miss Rowan laughed. 'I was joking, dear. I'm sure you had more to do with your precious minutes than chatter about me. But you will be sure to give him my regards when you get back? I always like it when your husband pays me a visit; he's so cheery.'

'No' like me.'

'Now I never meant that at all.'

'I know you didn't, Miss Rowan. But it's true all the same.'

'There was no bad news?'

'There's been an accident.'

Miss Rowan knew the couple were childless. 'I'm sorry to hear that. To some neighbour?'

'It happened at the children's picnic. Mrs Morton-Home, that's the laird's wife, organises one every year. Well, it's really Jessie Ogilvie, the schoolmistress, that does all the arranging, but the laird's wife supplies the food. She's very generous. This year it was over to Orsay they went, across the big sands. Something happened. Neil's not sure yet what it was. A boy I know. But how could anything bad happen to a bairn in such a place? They say it's a holy isle, and has been for centuries. There's a Cross; there's two, but one's buried under the sea most of the time.'

Miss Rowan had her hotel to attend to. She patted her guest's arm. 'I'm sure you'll find, Mrs Lindsay, that it was nothing very serious. After a good night's sleep, you'll feel more cheerful. It's a long tiring journey from Calisay.'

'Aye. But maybe it'll be a longer one back.'

As Miss Rowan went off, shaking her head sympathetically, she was thinking what a gloomy sober-sides Mrs Lindsay was. Her husband might have the whole lounge laughing with his stories of Calisay, but she would sit puzzled and anxious. It could never have occurred to Miss Rowan that childlessness might be the cause. How could it have, seeing that she herself had never married, and after more than forty years of pink-

263

cheeked spinsterhood still slept cosily and contentedly alone?

Before going to sleep that night Janet stood in front of the dressing-table mirror and forced herself to listen to some home truths and also to watch them being spoken: 'So this is you being a mother, Janet Lindsay? This is you, who pretended to be horrified by Mrs McNeil's attitude to adopted children. Yours is worse, much worse. If this girl, once you've signed for her, took ill or was hurt, you'd spend your last penny and sit up every night for months, to get her better and ease her pain. It's true enough you would do that, and I'm giving you the credit for it. But just because the Sneddon boy's been found subject to fits—and you don't know for sure he is— you're turning against her, you're telling yourself she might have worse, be syphilitic, diseased in her brain, infected with wickedness. So you're for burying her before she's even been born. Tomorrow you'll not go anywhere near the big woman, or the Home either; you'll go instead to Williamson's the wholesalers, and complain in person about those tins of sausages they sent, half of them bad and stinking; and you'll be thanking your lucky stars that it's not the girl you're going to complain about, because after she's yours, after the forms are signed, nobody will take her back, nobody will allow you discount, nobody will listen to your complaints, she'll be yours even more permanently than this hand, which could be cut off, if necessary. I think, and I'm sure you agree, that it would be a greater kindness to the girl to leave her in the Home, where somebody not so timorous or treacherous as you will find her in the end.'

'So what are you going to do?'

She did not know, and went to sleep, eyes wet and hands clasped, still not knowing.

*　　　*　　　*

Next morning, the rain that Neil had said was falling on Calisay had reached Glasgow. She could not help taking it as a bad sign, although as she gazed out of the window at the dreary, dripping sky she remembered mornings on Calisay, after a night of storm, when the blue of the sky, the whiteness of the clouds, and the green of the earth had been as bright as the first day of the world. So it probably was that morning, and she could picture Neil coming out, his own grey hair rimmed with radiance, to feed hens whose beaks and claws glittered; the cock would be crowing as if he, iridescent and proud, had brought the splendour. At every croft, including the McArthurs', would be the same happy, innocent scene.

When she had tried to imagine her first meeting with Jean, it had been like a memory of her own childhood rather than a foreseeing of something still to happen; sunshine had blessed it, and God had approved. Now this reality of rain and dreichness confronted her, of folk saving their friendliness for a benigner day. All the boats on Calisay would be putting out this morning, to visit lobster grounds or set new lines. Hers should stay on shore; only a fool would risk drowning in this bitter weather of truth.

When she left the boarding-house, under an umbrella borrowed from Miss Rowan, she had decided not to seek out the big woman, but to go to Williamson's instead, and attend to the business that earned Neil and her their bread and butter. At the tram stop she kept telling herself that was the sensible thing to do. Jean could wait. Maybe God had indeed spoken to her on Sunday in the kirk, though more likely she had just imagined it; but even if He had, could not this rain and these glum folk be His way of suggesting He had changed His mind, or had withdrawn His interest? Even as she was nodding, she let a tram go past that would have taken her to the whole-saler's; and a minute later, still nodding, she was climbing on board one that would take her into the district where the big woman's office was.

As she sat in the tram a young woman came in carrying a baby that smelt of wet rubber, and accompanied by a girl of about six or seven. The weight of the baby, the discomfort of soaked clothes, and the shaking of the tram caused her to be bad-tempered. She vented most of it on her daughter, who suffered it stoically, as if accustomed to it, and even returned the smile Janet gave her.

'There's just one blessing,' said another woman, grimly. 'We're no' on holiday at the coast. Think of a' the poor folk there paying exorbitant rents to sit and look oot at the rain.'

Though Janet nodded, she was remembering the pink cheeks of the Sneddon boys that day when, gleaming in oilskins, they had come into the shop and told her about Jean.

It took her half an hour to find the office, but when she did she walked straight in. Had it been sunny, she thought, she might well have hesitated and in the end have gone like a coward away.

*　　*　　*

With the new dainty pen that still looked a little silly in her big hand, and with her legs carefully closed and uncrossed, Margaret was adding a paragraph to a long letter to Angus when Molly the office-girl came in, huffy as usual, and said: 'Somebody to see you, Miss Mathieson; somebody from Calisay.'

Certain it must be Angus, Margaret leapt to her feet, about as gracefully as a hippopotamus clambering on to a river-bank to meet its mate, as Molly later described it to the clerks. For of course they all knew about Angus and the approaching marriage, though some of them still couldn't believe it, in spite of the bride-like gaiety of costume that Margaret now affected.

'A woman,' added Molly, with a grin.

Margaret laughed. They tried, but none of them these days could hurt or belittle her.

'Did she give her name?' she asked.

'Lindsay, I think she said.'

'Lindsay?'

She knew at once what Mrs Lindsay was here for, and for a moment felt like telling Molly to go and say she wasn't available. Up to a point she sympathized with women hesitating about adopting a child, but beyond that point the hesitation struck her as ghoulish. She wasn't sure if Mrs Lindsay had reached it yet. In any case, she thought, it was

266

up to her to be tolerant; her attitude ought not to be that of an official any longer, nor even of a woman merely, but of a mother.

'Shall I tell her you're out, Miss Mathieson?'

'No. Certainly not. Ask her to come in.'

As Molly went away, her scowl was one of admiration and envy.

When Mrs Lindsay came in Margaret hurried forward to welcome her with sincere joy. This rather dull woman was from Calisay, Angus's island. Perhaps she had seen him only a day or two ago.

'Good morning, Mrs Lindsay,' she said. 'How nice to see you.'

At first Janet didn't recognize her, and when she did she visibly lost heart. It was obvious she thought that the big woman she remembered, with the man-like way of talking and doing things, would have been far more likely to help her than this tall, proud lady in the expensive mauve suit and blouse, with the gold brooch on her breast and her fingers twinkling with gems.

'You bring a breath of the thyme and the tangle with you,' went on Margaret, laughing at her visitor's rather comic dismay. 'Please come in here, Mrs Lindsay. We'll be more private.' She ushered her into the small room used for interviews of this kind. I am the one that smells of thyme, she thought; she smells only of damp. 'Would you like to take your coat off?' she asked.

'No, no. I'm not wet. You see, I've got an umbrella.'

'Did you bring it from Calisay?'

'No, I got a loan of it from Miss Rowan; she's the owner of the boarding-house I'm staying at. It's quiet, but very respectable. I'm sorry if I'm wasting your time, miss.'

'You're not doing that. Is there any special reason you've come to see me, or is it just to keep me in touch, with Calisay, I mean? You see—but perhaps you know already—Mr Angus McArthur and I are getting married.'

Janet frowned. 'No, I didn't know that.'

'I thought it would be all over Calisay by this time. I

267

thought even the sea-gulls would be crying it.'

'They may well be, miss, but none of the folk are, so far as I know.'

Margaret felt disappointed, indignant and a little afraid. She would have forgiven surprise, but not sullen incredulity like this. 'Don't you approve?' she asked, trying to sound amused.

'It would be impertinent of me to say whether I approved or not. It's not my business.'

'Perhaps it's Mr McArthur you don't approve of?'

'If I was to say that it would be a lie. Nobody's ever heard me say a word against Angus. I hope you don't mind me calling him Angus? Almost everybody does.'

'Why should I object?'

'I was just saying to Neil—that's my husband—before I came away that Mr McArthur has got a rare gift in a man: even if a woman's on her knees scrubbing out a shop, he treats her as if she was a lady.'

'Yes, he is like that.'

'There's some, though, not very willing to give him credit for it.'

'You find people like that everywhere.'

'Mind you, I always thought it would be Jessie Ogilvie, the schoolmistress, that he would marry.'

Margaret, in sudden agitation, found herself sitting forward with legs wide apart and her hands wrestling with each other. This other woman, for all her thin, solemn face and flat bosom, was by nature more feminine.

'But of course it's no business of mine,' said Janet sullenly, 'and I shouldn't be speaking about it. So I'd better explain what I'm here for. You mind that girl Jean McDonnell you wrote to me about? Well, I've come to see her. If I find she takes to me, and I take to her, then I'll make up my mind to adopt her, outright. I wouldn't be interested in taking her as boarded-out. If I want her, I want her for life. That's possible, isn't it?'

'Yes, it's possible,' said Margaret, drily. This woman seemed in some obscure way to be insulting her.

'I thought so. I've prayed for it. My man's willing. He sees he'll never get any peace from me until I get her. But don't mistake me. Neil's got a good heart, and he'll make her as good a father as I will a mother; better, maybe. Ever since the Sneddon lads mentioned this girl and showed me her in a photograph she's never been out of my mind. I know there must be lots of forms to fill up, and investigations to be gone into, means tests and such like. We're prepared for all that. But I was hoping you'd be so kind as to take me out to the Home so that we could meet each other. I'm well aware the girl has her rights too. If she doesn't want me, then that'll be that.'

Though Margaret kept listening, it was with a professional politeness only. The dreary, selfish, whining, vulgar voice set her nerves on edge; and how unutterably impertinent of it to speak about her and Angus. The little girl McDonnell surely deserved better than this pair of shopkeepers who seemed to be expecting a profit of some kind out of the transaction.

'I've got my bank-book with me, to show you if you like, as a guarantee.'

Margaret could not keep gruffness out of her own voice, nor dislike either. 'It is important of course that you and your husband can prove financial capability, but you will appreciate that money's by no means the chief thing we look for.'

'I'm glad to hear that. That's been one of my fears; that somebody with more money might outbid us. If it's a matter of affection, I'm afraid of nobody's competition. This girl, I feel she's mine already. I've got into the habit of seeing her about the house. You'll think I'm daft; but it's true.'

'I'm afraid this request of yours to go out to the Home and meet the girl is out of the question.'

'I thought you would say that. But why should it be? I'm a woman, so are you who would be taking me, and so's the Matron who would be there to see to the lassies's interests. What other authorities need come into it at this stage? They'd be men, anyway, wouldn't they? But here's me arguing, which I know I shouldn't do. Neil says when I'm nervous I argue too much and give folk a bad impression. God knows I've got no unfair advantages with which to win over the girl. Children as a rule don't take to me at first sight. Later it's different; not always, but most times. I've got to be fair to myself too.'

'I'm sure no one wishes to be unfair to you, Mrs Lindsay. But to tell you the truth, I doubt very much if Miss Montgomerie, the Matron, will allow you to call until all the preliminaries have been completed.'

'I never expected it to be easy. Bringing a child into the world, this way or the ordinary, is bound to be hard. But you could at least try.'

Margaret considered. Part of her urged that she should tell the woman it was impossible and send her away, back to her fat, sniggering husband who would help her to decide in the end that an adopted child was more trouble, expense, and danger than it was worth. But another part kept remembering that praise of Angus; this part also rather wanted to get into touch with Helen again, to find out if the latter's gibe about tears and jewels had been withdrawn.

Besides, was it not more than likely that the little girl, who had looked as shrewd as she was courageous, would reject a foster-mother so parsimonious of emotion? No child would care to be welcomed home with a grim nod. Jean was not the sort to expect tears and hugs, but even she would hardly be satisfied with an attitude more suitable to the buying of potatoes.

'Very well, Mrs Lindsay,' said Margaret, 'since you have come such a long distance, I shall telephone Matron. I won't be long.'

'I've waited twenty years, surely I can be patient for a minute or two longer?'

Yet the hands on the damp lap, as still as Margaret's own were restless, did not somehow suggest patience. Gazing at the grave, workaday face, Margaret suddenly saw in it devotion, suffering, and unappeased love.

'I'll do what I can,' she said, as she went out.

Yet as she dialled with her long, jewelled finger, it was not Mrs Lindsay's hands she was remembering, but rather the schoolmistress's, so plump and stern. It was ridiculous to think of her as a rival. Angus might be imagined in bed with other women, but scarcely with the dour, buck-toothed, flyter of children.

Helen's voice was as dry and efficient as ever. 'Miss Montgomerie, Matron, speaking,' she said.

Margaret made hers cordial. 'Good morning, Helen. This is Margaret.'

'So I hear. Good morning, Margaret. This is an unexpected pleasure. Is it in order to congratulate you? Has the devout consummation taken place?'

'What do you mean, Helen?'

Helen laughed. 'I have got used to thinking of you with ear-rings, my dear. I don't think I could ever get used to thinking of you as coy. I meant, are you married?'

'Not yet.'

'Why all this self-denial, my dear? At our age waiting is deadly. It hasn't been cancelled?'

'No.'

There was a pause. 'Remember I shall wish to send you a present,' said Helen at length, with a strange cheerfulness. 'I believe it's customary, in these rather shameless times, for brides to suggest what they would like, so as not to be presented with, say, half a dozen coffee percolators. Of course I could let you have your pick of eight or so of the bonniest babies you ever saw. It's hardly likely that anyone, even the Almighty Himself, would duplicate such a present.'

Margaret felt her belly for reassurance; there her own child might be protecting her against the whole world. 'This is really a business call, Helen,' she said.

'Do you expect to have a family?'

'Yes, I do. Helen, a few weeks ago a Mrs Lindsay of Calisay wrote you a letter about Jean McDonnell. Do you remember?'

'The shopkeeper woman?'

'Yes. Well, she's here in my office. She wants me to bring her out to see Jean.'

'The woman's a fool. Didn't you tell her I wouldn't entrust a dog to her?'

'That's unfair, Helen.'

271

'There is a procedure. I would have thought you'd be in favour of observing it.'

'Yes, I know.' It would be a relief to fall back on that impartial reason for refusal. But, remembering her own hope of happiness, Margaret felt she must make another effort to secure Mrs Lindsay's. 'She's come a long way, Helen. Another thing, she'll be able to talk to the girl about the Sneddon boys. She appears to know them well. I'm sure Jean would be interested in hearing about them.'

'Is there anything in particular to hear about them?'

'I suppose not. But it's pleasant to listen to somebody talking about people you knew and liked.'

'Do you think so?'

'Yes, of course. We like to feel we're one of the circle.'

'What circle's that, Margaret? It's a long time since I played ring-a-roses.'

'What about it, Helen? Shall I bring her?'

'What is she like?'

'Not very prepossessing, I'm afraid. But I'm sure she's got a good heart.'

'It almost sounds as if you were describing me, Margaret. Very well, bring her.'

'Don't try to set the girl against her, Helen.'

Helen laughed. 'But, Margaret, surely you know that if I were to do that it would have the very opposite effect? Jean and I don't usually admire the same things. If I really wanted to spoil the woman's chances, all I would need do would be to let Jean think I approved of her.'

'You know you love the girl, Helen,' whispered Margaret. 'Why torture yourself by pretending otherwise?'

'Shall I tell you why, Margaret? You will laugh at it as you lie in bed with your man. I am the mother of, at present, forty-two children, but, do you know, I cannot remember a single one of their fathers.'

Margaret frowned. 'We'll be there in half an hour, Helen. How is the girl, by the way? Is her throat all right now?'

'Yes. You may find her a little thin and pale, but no doubt the fresh butter and eggs, not to mention the loving air of

Calisay, could soon mend that.'

'In half an hour then, Helen.'

Almost in tears, and sick with an inexplicable presentiment, Margaret put down the telephone. Before she could face Mrs Lindsay she had to go into the little lavatory and dab her eyes with cold water. It was too early yet for the sickness of pregnancy. But this would probably come, and what if she were still unmarried then? Who in that case would be the most unlucky, she, or Helen, or Mrs Lindsay deprived of Jean?

When she saw the car Janet was reluctant to enter it. 'If it's not convenient to take a tram or bus, I'm willing to pay for a taxi,' she said, dourly.

'There's no need, Mrs Lindsay. It's much more convenient to go by car.'

'Then you'll have to let me pay for the petrol.'

'No, no. I can call this an official journey. I get a petrol allowance.'

When she got in Janet sat in a way that seemed to show that she regarded the journey as a duty, an expedition of danger, rather than as a pleasure. Tense and awkwardly straight, she was also, especially in contrast with Margaret herself, workworn and drab. Coming from Calisay where the rain was always clean, surely she could have chosen a more interesting colour for her raincoat than this muddy khaki? And why in God's name did she wear that black, close-fitting hat that made her look like some elderly, unsuccessful nun? Beside her Margaret felt rather too gorgeous. The schoolmistress, the ornithologist, looking in, would have taken them for a bird and its dowdy mate.

'I'd prefer to pay,' said Janet, 'especially if it's the Corporation I would be cheating.'

Margaret felt irritated. Only a tiny sum was involved. The woman's mind was as dreary as her clothes. 'You're cheating no one. It isn't important.'

'It is to me. Right from the beginning I want to pay our way, as if she was mine already.'

'She isn't that yet, Mrs Lindsay.'

'Do you think I don't know, miss? Every nerve in my body

knows it. I'm not always like this. If I was to be going through an operation, for cancer itself, I couldn't be more worked up and anxious. I feel that if I don't get her, I might as well not live.'

'It's not wise to take up that attitude, Mrs Lindsay. There are other little girls; any number of them, I'm sorry to say.'

'It must be her. Others might be bonnier and more biddable; but she's mine. Mothers don't disown their bairns because other bairns are in some ways superior.'

Margaret could say nothing. The poor woman's belief that Jean was already hers was quite mad. Disillusionment would be cruel. Margaret preferred to leave it to circumstances.

She decided she ought to say something about Helen. 'The Matron's my friend,' she said. 'You'll appreciate she's got a very responsible position. About forty children at a time are under her care. Every child that's born deserves consideration, but these deserve it more than most; either they've been abandoned or given up, or their people have died. Helen—the Matron, that is—naturally feels towards them as any right-hearted woman must.'

'Was she ever married herself?'

'No. She's got to remember that most of them will only be in her charge for a year or so at most. She must therefore try not to become too attached to them, and also not to let them become too attached to her.'

'You're not trying to tell me she's got too fond of Jean to let her go?'

'No. She can't hold on to a child if the authorities have decided it has to be boarded out, or put out to adopt. What I'm really trying to say, Mrs Lindsay, is that if you find her a bit sharp, harsh even, you must realise it's not against you personally. Here's something I'll tell you in confidence.'

'Is she old?'

'No.'

'Somehow I got that impression.'

'She's not much older than we are ourselves. Or than the schoolmistress. What I want to tell you is that, for some reason, she was particularly fond of the Sneddon boy.'

'Wee Tom?'

'No, his brother.'

'That's odd. Tom's the talkative one. Everybody's fairly taken to him. Not that anybody's got a word to say against John. He's on the quiet side, that's true; but being the oldest he's likely had to carry the burden.'

She had made up her mind to say nothing about the accident. It wasn't her business, and in any case she didn't know yet what had actually happened.

Do you, wondered Margaret, know just what that burden has been, and still is, and always will be? Do you, for that matter, know that Jean's mother was a prostitute, and her father any one of a hundred furtive, lust-driven anonymities? No, you do not. And when you do, will you still be so desperate to take the child, and her associations?

'Matron won't ask you about him,' she said, 'but if you can manage to bring the talk round to him she'll be delighted. She'll maybe not look it, but she will be.'

'Is she like me then, often belying her looks? Often they say I'm looking angry or sad, when inside I'm feeling peaceable and happy enough. Will I get seeing the girl in private?'

'I'm afraid that will be up to Matron.'

'You're not meaning to, I know, but you're making her out to be a bit of a tyrant. I suppose she just can't help it in her position.'

'She's not a tyrant.'

'If the bairns like her, that's the main thing.'

Both knew it was a question, but were agreed to leave it unanswered. Nothing more was said until they passed through the gates of the Home and saw the children, wearing capes, playing in the park among the big trees. The rain had stopped. There was a watery gleam in the sky.

Janet gazed out at them strangely. 'You would think,' she murmured, 'that I'd never seen a bairn before.'

Margaret stared out too. 'I don't see her,' she said. 'The grounds are large, and I understand she's a wanderer.'

'Calisay will give her all the scope she wants.'

'It would.' And myself too, thought Margaret. She had

spoken to Helen about the circle of humanity; how real and close it was! Who would ever have thought that this little girl and she might find homes on Calisay, that remote island? It could be that Jean in time to come might take out her baby in its pram, and show it the swans on the loch.

To Margaret's surprise Agnes, as gallous as ever, met them in the hall. 'You've to go right up, Miss Mathieson,' she said. 'Matron's expecting you in her office.'

Margaret would never forget the compliment the servant had paid her in this very hall. 'I'm glad to see you're still here, Agnes,' she said.

Agnes laughed. 'Ach, you ken me and Matron, miss. We gie each ither notice a dozen times a year. Oor barks are worse than oor bites.'

'Agnes, this is Mrs Lindsay, from Calisay.'

'You don't mean that back o' beyond whaur they took wee Tommy and Johnny?'

'Yes.'

'God bless them! So folk can come back frae it. It's no' juist in outer space, as I was given to believe. How are they, Mrs? If ever bairns deserved a break, they did.'

'They're very happy,' replied Janet, a little worried lest, after the accident, it might be a lie. 'They couldn't have landed luckier than with Mary McArthur; not to mention her daughter Flora.'

'Whit age is she, this Flora?'

'About twenty-five, I would think.'

'Ah then, she'll not hae done wee Jean's eye in yet.'

The blood sang in Janet's ears; she felt weak. 'And who is wee Jean?' she managed to ask.

'She'll no' admit it, nor would he, but she used to be Johnny Sneddon's girl-friend. If ye ken o' onybody yonder wi' a hert o' gold, wha wad like a bairn wi' one, you tell them aboot Jean. Mind you, though we'd a' be mair than pleased for her sake, for oor ain we'd be hertbroken. Look, there's the sun coming oot. Do you hear the bairns yelling mair happily? Weel, that's Jean; she's like the sun coming oot.'

'She sounds a favourite.'

Agnes followed them to the foot of the stairs. 'They're a' favourites, Mrs, but Jean's a special one.'

'Well, when I get back I'll start enquiring for someone with a heart of gold.'

'There's nothing she'd like better than to be wi' Tommy and Johnny.'

'You'd think,' whispered Janet, as she crept up the stairs at Margaret's side, 'she'd been put there deliberately to interest me in the girl. As if it was needed!'

They passed the busts of Walter Scott and Augustus.

'Fancy having things like that in a house full of children,' she said. 'Enough to frighten them out of their wits, I would think. And he's not much better, with his funny wee eyes.' This was the ex-Provost, the benefactor, in his ermine robes, leering down at them from the wall.

Poor soul, she's almost drunk with anticipation, thought Margaret. Should I try to sober her, or should I leave it to Helen?

'Mrs Lindsay,' she said, stopping her for a moment outside Matron's office, 'don't take it for granted. There's nothing settled. It's not safe to build up your hopes too high. It could be that someone else will have an application in before you, and the authorities could easily decide to give her to them.'

'Then they would make the biggest mistake of their lives.'

'Perhaps. But it could happen. Please keep that in mind, for your own sake.'

'And it could happen, too, that when she sees me she won't want me. Don't worry, miss, I never was one for building my hopes too high. Neil said I had more faith saved up than anyone else; it was time I spent some of it, he said. But faith's like money; once you start hoarding it, you never want to spend it. So don't worry about me.'

Helen was waiting for them at her desk. She wore her full Matron's uniform, cap and all. It was the first time in years Margaret had seen her in it. She looked curiously younger, in spite of her grim mouth and whiter hair.

Margaret introduced them. Mrs Lindsay was surprisingly self-possessed. Helen was icy.

'Please sit,' she said, in her Matron voice. 'I had better make it clear, at the outset, that I do not approve of this visit, and also that I am not in sympathy with its purpose.'

'For nearly twenty years my husband and me were Glasgow ratepayers,' replied Mrs Lindsay, quietly.

Helen glanced at Margaret, as if to say: wasn't I right, the woman's a fool?

'I meant, we're neither strangers nor interlopers.'

'I understand you are thinking of adopting a child?'

'That's so.'

'There is a procedure to be followed.'

'And I'll follow it gladly, once I've made sure the girl is willing to have me.'

'What girl?'

'I think you know the one, Matron. Her name's Jean McDonnell. I wrote to you about her.'

'I got your letter. I do not apologise for not replying to it. In my opinion it deserved no reply. It really will not do to insult children by making them the subject of sentimental dreams. You know nothing at all about this particular child. You've never set eyes on her. You have no knowledge of her antecedents.'

It seemed to Margaret then that Mrs Lindsay, eyes closed, was spending a great deal of faith.

'Jean McDonnell is no dream-child; she is very much flesh and blood. Let me be frank with you, Mrs Lindsay. In my view she is troublesome, inclined to disobedience, naturally dirty, and basically very common.'

'Common?'

'Considering her antecedents, that ought to surprise no one.'

Mrs Lindsay tried to smile. 'That's twice you've used the word. Are you trying to frighten me with it? I take it, you're referring to her mother. As for common, I'm common enough myself, God knows.'

'Yes, I was referring to her mother; and to her father, too.'

'I thought they weren't known?'

'You were wrong.'

278

'Well, what was so terrible about them? They were human, at least.'

'Barely. They are still alive.'

Again she tried to smile. 'But they've given up all their rights?'

Before Helen could answer the telephone on her desk rang. She picked it up calmly, while Mrs Lindsay, like a child when the teacher has looked away, turned towards Margaret with an appeal to which there could be no response, except a pitying shake of the head: Jean's parents were what they were, and not all the faith in the world could alter that.

'It's for you, Margaret,' said Helen. 'Mr Gilliespie.'

'Oh.' Margaret took the telephone. 'Yes, Bob, it's me. A telegram? My God. Yes, I do. She's Mrs McArthur's daughter. Yes, I think I should. Tomorrow, if I can possibly manage it. I'll explain when I get back to the office. In about half an hour. Thanks for letting me know.'

As she put down the telephone she said: 'I've had a telegram from Calisay.'

'From Calisay?' cried Mrs Lindsay, turning pale. 'It's not about Neil, is it?'

'No, no.' Margaret decided it was time Mrs Lindsay knew. By this time probably everyone on Calisay did. Here, with Jean within call, was the best place for her to be told, before all her faith was squandered. 'It was from Flora McArthur. It said: "It has happened. Quite ill."'

'Did she not say who she was referring to?'

'She didn't have to, Mrs Lindsay. She was referring to John Sneddon.'

'Has it to do with the accident?'

All this time Helen's hands on the desk were rejecting each other.

'What accident?' she whispered, her voice hushed with bitterness.

Mrs Lindsay was taken aback, but went on bravely, faltering a little: 'I don't know if there was anybody to blame. Neil didn't say; he didn't know. You see, he told me about it last night over the telephone. He just said there'd been an accident to one of the Sneddon boys during the picnic to Orsay. But what did Flora mean? Did she expect it to happen?'

'Yes,' said Matron, in that same quiet, terrible voice, 'she expected it.'

'Let me explain, Helen,' said Margaret.

'No. I shall do it.'

Mrs Lindsay looked from one to the other. 'Explain what?' she asked. 'What's all the mystery? Has it to do with his antecedents too?'

'Yes, it has,' whispered Matron. 'John Sneddon's father killed his mother.'

'You mean, murdered her?'

'Yes.'

'In God's name, why?'

'She was sleeping, as the saying goes, with other men.'

More and more faith was desperately spent. 'When was this?'

'Three years ago.'

'Does the boy know?'

'He saw it happen.'

'Dear God.'

'And now it seems that all his life he's going to keep on seeing it.'

'You think that's what's happened on Orsay?'

'Yes.' It was Margaret who spoke, anxious to break into this conversation between the two tortured women. 'But it may not be as bad as we think.'

'But how could it have happened there? It's supposed to be a holy island. Long ago, they'll tell you, criminals were safe once they reached there and kissed the Cross. Orsay himself was a saint. Some say he can still be seen walking among the ruins, ringing a little bell. True enough, there are bones to be picked up there, as easily as you'd pick flowers; and skulls too. You'd think, though, that a saint, and a monk, who'd never so much as looked at a woman in his life—in that way, I mean—would have protected the boy. No wonder he was so quiet; John, I mean. I used to blame him for it, God help me. I suppose, when you come to think of it, all the children here must have backgrounds that, well, couldn't be called respectable.'

'To take one other example,' said Matron. 'This girl, Jean McDonnell.'

Faith, then, was all spent. Margaret thought she had never seen a human face so destitute; and when it turned towards her, seeking a loan, she found herself shaking her head, she had nothing to spare, hadn't enough even for her own needs. Helen, who also had saved so much up, never gave any away; she did not even use it to sweeten her own griefs; she was not falling back on it now.

'Her mother was a prostitute, and her father a prostitute's customer.'

'Let's be fair,' said Margaret. 'That doesn't mean the girl's bound to turn out bad.'

'It wouldn't seem to give her much of a chance, though,' whispered Mrs Lindsay.

So Margaret left her to bury her hopes. She spoke to Helen instead. 'I wonder just what "quite ill" means?'

'Will you go?'

'Yes. As soon as I can. Tomorrow, if possible.'

'I suppose it will eventually mean his leaving the place?'

'Not necessarily, Helen.'

'It's a small place, and small-minded. Everybody will know. They'll point to him as some kind of freak. They'll have him seeing it, not once in three years, but every minute of the day and night. They'll have him beside his father before they're done.'

'Wasn't his father hanged?' whispered Mrs Lindsay.

'He's rotting away in a criminal asylum.'

'Poor soul. But you're not being fair to the Calisay folk. Maybe they're slow, and cautious, and a bit suspicious of incomers; but once you reach their hearts you'll find none warmer. Isn't that the case with most folk everywhere? Lift every newspaper, and it's full of terrible things, all over the country, and abroad; yet in my experience, and I'm forty-six, I have often been surprised by the kindness of people. I mean, there was no reason why they should have been kind to me;

but they have been, many's the time. Why should I forget it? Why should I believe the newspapers? When all's said and done, I'm a Christian. I'd be greatly obliged, Matron, if I could see the girl now.'

Margaret was astonished and moved. She felt suddenly that into the little room faith was pouring like sunlight, and into her too, and Helen, who sat amazed and transfigured. Its source, there could be no doubt about it, was the drab figure in the silly black hat and khaki-coloured raincoat.

'I see now,' said Mrs Lindsay, 'that all the time what I've been frightened of is that she wouldn't want me. I've never really been worried about her antecedents, as you called them.'

'Very well,' said Helen, and pressed the bell.

None of them spoke during the half-minute they waited for the young nurse to appear.

'Nurse,' said Matron, 'would you please fetch Jean McDonnell?'

'Jean?' Nurse Sutherland glanced at Mrs Lindsay, instinctively antagonistic; but she could not maintain it, and grinned cheerfully. Whatever her criteria, thought Margaret, evidently Mrs Lindsay judged by them was more than satisfactory. She herself once again had the feeling that there must be riches of humanity enjoyed by others but not so far by her. She had spoken to Helen, rather hopefully, of the circle; yes, it existed, closer, wider, and stronger than she had thought. Now this sense of deprivation and exclusion didn't sadden her; on the contrary, she felt glad that in time, with Angus and their child to help her, and many others such as Mrs Lindsay, she would find all those resources available to her, so that she in her turn could make them available to others. With a little luck, she could look forward to a lot of happiness.

'Where are you going to stay on Calisay, Margaret?' asked Helen. 'When I wrote I was told the hotel was full up until October.'

'Mrs McLennan, the district nurse, might be able to put me up. It's always a problem visiting these places in the summer.'

'Annie's got her sister and a friend staying with her,' said

282

Mrs Lindsay. 'If you've no objection, I'd be pleased to have you.'

'Thank you, Mrs Lindsay. Certainly I've no objection; indeed, I'm very grateful.'

'And I'd be pleased to offer you hospitality, Matron, if you wanted to visit the island.'

'Thank you. It is very kind of you. But I have arranged to wait until October.'

'October? That's the month of chestnuts. We have some of the best chestnuts you ever saw. Folk think there are no trees on Calisay. There's a lovely wood round the big house. It can be very nice in October. The heather's still out, and often the sun's warm enough to sit in. Maybe it's on the cold side for bathing, though.'

'I'm not likely to be doing that.'

'No, nor me.'

Margaret smiled, loving them both. She would be bathing, and swimming, and running along the sands, like Juno, Angus had said. At home was her new costume, green and white; in it, in the small mirror and in the small room, she looked clumsy and massive; but on the wide white sands of Calisay she would be in place, like the seagulls and seals.

'Did you never have any children, Mrs Lindsay?' asked Matron.

Janet blushed. She couldn't help it. Was having no children something to be ashamed of? Surely not, if one had tried, and tried again? Or was that fruitless trying itself, after so many times, shameful? Some men, exempt through physical defect, had not fought in the war. Ask these what service they had been in, and they were inclined to feel this same kind of shame. Poor Neil, for instance.

'No,' she whispered.

'Why do you want to adopt a child as old as eight? Wouldn't it be better to take one that's only months old?'

'That's what my friend Isa McGilvray says; she's the wife of the hotel-proprietor, you know. She says that whether it's a cat or a dog or a child, best to take it when it's very young so that it can be trained in the way you want it.'

283

'Yes, and also so that you can accept each other more easily.'

'There's that to it,' admitted Mrs Lindsay.

Helen turned and smiled towards Margaret, with affection, it seemed; yet she said: 'Miss Mathieson's getting married soon. Did you know?'

'Well yes, as a matter of fact, she told me just this morning. I was very interested because, you see, I happen to know the gentleman quite well; for that's what he is, a gentleman. And I don't think I've ever seen a handsomer man, either.'

Margaret stood still, smiling, like a wax figure in a shop window. This conversation concerned her intimately; yet she felt helpless either to take part in it or to stop it.

'Is he from Calisay?' asked Helen, in surprise.

Mrs Lindsay looked at the wax figure for permission to go on, and apparently found it in that artificial smile. 'Oh yes. Mr McArthur was born on the island. True enough, he only came back to live there about a year ago; before that I think he lived here in Glasgow. He worked on one of the cargo boats that connect Glasgow with the islands. Some call him Captain McArthur, but I don't think he was ever just that.'

Helplessly smiling, Margaret could not call her liar, nor prevent the circle turning harsh and hostile, resisting her entry into it.

'Margaret has told me nothing about him,' said Helen.

'Goodness, he could pass for the captain of the *Queen Mary*, he's so tall and dignified, and talks in such an educated way. I don't know where he got his education from, because like me he left school when he was fourteen; and look how I talk!'

Yes, like a human being, and so like a liar and calumniator. You poison with your tongue; you defile with your every breath. I hope, I hope to God the girl when she comes hates you at first sight. And why should she not, you being so human?

Mrs Lindsay laughed. 'But it's not right for us to talk about Mr McArthur like this, in front of Miss Mathieson.'

'Don't mind me.' Strangely, she was able to say it, almost

merrily.

Helen, though, wasn't deceived. Mrs Lindsay, the source of faith, the simpleton, the shopkeeping madonna, was: she smirked, as Margaret remembered having seen the Mother of Christ smirk in famous paintings.

'Wasn't he married before?' she now asked. 'To some widow woman here in Glasgow? They say she left him comfortably off when she died. That was why he was able to retire so young.'

'Young?' asked Helen.

'Well, in a manner of speaking. He's not quite fifty, I would say.'

But, thought Margaret, what if, fool though she is, everything she's saying is true? She speaks as if she had a licence to speak the truth. And was I ever wholly convinced by his stories of far eastern ports, or for that matter by anything he ever told me, in or out of bed? Am I sure even now that he is going to marry me? Might he not marry the schoolmistress instead? She already has one eagle in her house; he would be another. For, let him be proved to have betrayed her in everything, she would still think of him as magnificent and soaring. Miss Ogilvie as his wife would clip his wings and chain him to her threshold; that, even more than Margaret's betrayal, would be the great pity.

His child, she then remembered, his eaglet in my womb; and it began to hack and rend with its beak, as if to get out.

There was a knock at the door, and in came the young nurse, with the little red-haired girl. The latter had eyes, and eager eyes they were too, only for Mrs Lindsay; no doubt the nurse's preparation of her had gone beyond a hasty washing of face and hands. It seemed to Margaret, her perception sharpened by that pain in her womb, that everything which made motherhood so beautiful and so deserving of poets', painters', and even God's own homage, was absent from that obscure face under the black, out-of-date hat. Yet the child saw it there.

Twenty-three

They were safely across the ford and less than half a mile from the house when the boy, supported in the back seat of the Land Rover by Angus's arm, began at last through rigid lips to try and speak. The bumping on the rough track and the rattling of the empty boxes at first made it difficult to make out the mewing sounds. Then, with his ear held close, Angus recognized them as attempts at Flora's name. Scenes associated with his own boyhood lurching past outside, including cottages whose past occupants were either long since dead or gone as far afield, caused him then to remember his own mother at Flora's age, like her, too, black-haired and bonny, with the same power to subdue, in one miraculous moment, troubles and griefs that to the lonely boy creeping home in the dark had seemed about to destroy him. The tall, thin father had sat in the corner stroking his moustache, waiting with lordly patience for this little thief to be deprived of the limelight he had so impudently stolen. So she had had him to humour too, as well as her sons to console and give faith to. In Donald's keeping, after a war's stress, that faith had got warped and tarnished. Angus had taken care to lay his aside, deep in his mind, for safety, just as in his cottage, in a drawer, wrapped in silk, lay the small gold-edged Bible she had left him.

They stopped outside the cottage. Roy came barking, and Mary appeared at the door, anxiously.

Angus lifted the boy down. He was still whimpering for Flora. To everyone's dismay, Mary's most of all, he shrank back from her at first. It was as if she had already beaten him cruelly, and he was terrified she would do it again.

She shrank back too. 'What's wrong, John?' she asked. 'What's happened to you?'

'Get him to bed, Mary,' said Angus. 'He's as cold as death.

286

I'll tell you about it in two or three minutes.' He turned back to the car. 'If you'd be so kind, Mrs Morton-Home,' he said, 'as to fetch Nurse McLennan, and Flora too.'

'Certainly, Angus. I'll have them here in no time.'

He glanced up at the sky, and saw a darkening in the clouds. There would be rain soon, perhaps storm. It already felt cooler than it had been all day. The sea would come racing into the ford. He hoped the carts would get across safely, and wondered if Donald was out in the boat alone, save of course for the Lord.

As the Land Rover went away it had to swing aside to let Sandy Campbell the postman pass on his bicycle. He stopped beside Angus, and rummaged in his bag. 'What's she in such a great hurry for?' he asked. 'She damn near knocked me down. And what's the matter with Mary's boy? Is he hurt?'

He had seen Mary help John into the house.

'He had a little accident at the picnic over on Orsay,' replied Angus, taking the two letters handed to him, one his, and the other Mary's; hers was from Hector in Canada. He knew she would be overjoyed, even in the midst of this worry about John. His own was from Nell. He had thrust it into his pocket before he realised it was addressed to him here on Calisay, not care of the Shipping Company in Glasgow. It had been inevitable, of course; even to stupidity, encouraged by greed, a bright idea came at last.

It was surely a sentence of exile. In the old heroic days a man would be handed such a letter from his king or queen. Today it came from an obtuse boarding-house proprietress with rolls of lard on her belly, and her grey hair in paper curlers.

'What kind of accident?' Sandy was asking. 'Nothing serious, I hope?'

A small burly man with big leathery ears, he was curiously sensitive; he had been known to go into a huff for a month because a letter had been taken from him without thanks or a smile. He represented as well as anyone the intelligence and conscience of the island.

Angus held the handle-bars. 'I'll tell you, Sandy.' He stared

287

into the smaller man's face, seeing in it the imperfections that made it human, though in God's likeness. It was not Apollo's, but it wasn't one of Cerberus's, either, for all its heathery moustache.

'Well, get a move on, man, for I want to get my round over before the rain comes on.'

'You think it's going to rain?'

'Aye. And so does my Nan's rheumatics.'

'These boys that Donald and Mary have taken, you know them?'

'Certainly I know them. Fine, cheery little fellows.'

'You think so, Sandy?'

'Everybody thinks so; well, except one, maybe.'

Angus considered: Nan, Sandy's wife, so often cross with her rheumatics? No, she had brought up a family herself and liked bairns. Elspeth Morrison, maybe? Her sister Morag? Nobody else really, and he wasn't sure about them. They didn't like him, he knew, but that was different. It struck him, even with that letter in his pocket, that people were better than he had ever given them credit for.

'If you can't say right out,' said Sandy, 'then you don't know; and I'm not going to say.'

'Their father, Sandy, killed their mother, with a hatchet.'

After a few seconds of gaping Sandy took off his postman's cap and studied the brass letters on it, as if trying to understand what they meant. His thin grey hair stirred in the strong breeze, like creatures in a nest uncovered.

'Well,' he said at last, 'that was about as bad a thing as could happen to any family.'

'The elder of the two lads, him you saw Mary with a minute or so back, saw the blows struck, the blood splash. Today, over on Orsay, there was a couple—Mr and Mrs Murtrie, staying at the hotel—lying behind a rock. He, it seems, was keeping the clegs off her face with a stick. The boy burst upon them, and in less time than it takes a gannet to hit the water he'd been changed from a happy bairn playing I-spy into the kind of creature they used to say the wee folk were responsible for with their spells and curses.'

288

Sandy's grandparents had believed in those wee folk and their malice. He was not completely sceptical himself, even now. 'Give it what name you like,' he said cautiously, 'you mean he's had a shock?'

'A bad one.'

'He's young, he'll get over it. But he'll need help.'

'A doctor, you mean? Annie McLennan's been sent for.'

'A doctor, maybe. But not just that kind of help. Now I'm as ordinary a man as you'll get.'

Angus could not deny it.

'Nan says I'm a good sample. I'll tell you what I'm going to do. Next time I see these boys, will I give them any less cheery a greeting than the last time? I will not. Will I give them a more cheery greeting perhaps, because of this? No. What did he kill her for?'

'Sleeping with other men.'

'Did he hang?'

'No. He's still alive, if you could call it that, in the mental prison at Perth.'

Sandy put his cap on again and became a postman. 'Mind you give Mary her letter,' he said. 'I see it's from Hector.' Then he mounted his bicycle and rode away, more reassuring, Angus thought, than larks in the sky. Who, though, was that one person on the island who did not approve of the boys? Who was it could not find it in his or her heart to love innocence?

He saw his brother Donald come up from the sea, carrying a great load of fish on a piece of rope. There would be time to glance at Nell's letter.

Dear Angie,

Youve been silent so long I made more enquirys now I know where you are hiding not so very far either I felt it in my bones. They creak for you every night, Angie. Its not money I want now, its you. Belive me I am losing weight worrying. Come back to me, lover. Do you mind that's what I liked to call you and you pretended not to like it? Lover. A woman has no pride when she seeks the man she

289

wants she'll enter hell to drag him back to her. There's deep water between us but I'll drown myself in the attempt a womans instinct will smell you out should you go to hide in the deserts of Australia among the kangaroos. I lie at night with a bolster beside me pretending its you, but its got no moustache of silk. A reply inside a week, lover, or I'll come in person.

Donald was as calm as an apostle. Fish-scales glittered iridescently on his blue jersey. 'Good news, Angus?' he cried.

'Indeed,' replied Angus, laughing. 'From someone who loves me.'

Donald held up his fish. 'A good potful. The boys will like these. Where are they? Did you come back early with the laird's wife? I heard her car.'

Angus tried not to be irritated by that exalted smile. Was Donald going to become one of those who used religion as a substitute for whisky?

'Before you say another word, Angus,' he said, 'I have to tell you that I have made my peace with the Lord.'

'I'm glad to hear it. Just what does it mean?'

'I am to keep the boys.'

'You've got permission?'

'You may put it that way. This afternoon, under the cliffs.'

Where it was, of course, dangerous for a man alone in a boat, with the swell rising twenty feet at least up the great whitened walls, and where all that ordinary ears could hear at any time was the screaming of hundreds of thousands of birds. Well, it was as convenient a place as any to listen to Christ telling you to do what your brother and wife and daughter had already told you you ought to do. Still, Donald, while He was telling you that, in one of the magnificent corners of His creation, in another He was terrifying innocence with a vision of evil. Not to mention that yesterday, in a prim boarding-house in Oban, He was tripping up mendacity by inspiring a fat, grey-haired woman to write a letter.

Therefore, reporting the accident, Angus pretended he was God's agent who had brought it about. Anyone else's eyes would have glazed like those of the dead fish; but Donald's on the contrary kindled, so that Angus learned again what he had learned many times before, that those who could hear the authentic voice of God calling out of a tempest of bird-cries and snowy wings, or in the din of dropping bombs, were always able to interpret it to God's glory and their own advantage.

Donald had visibly to prepare his mouth for what he was going to say: 'The bairn has been asked to suffer, for my sake.'

Those last three words especially were uttered with such an unctuous sadness that Angus realized Donald was not merely his fellow-creature, but his blood brother. Both of them had learned it at their father's knee. Whenever they used it their mother, asleep among the spotted orchises, was shamed.

'For all our sakes, Donald,' he said, cautiously.

Donald merely grinned, but not even the fish staring up at the sky seemed more mysterious.

Then the Land Rover came roaring back. Flora, wearing her maid's uniform, leapt down and ran past them into the house. She had time, though, to glance at her father as if, whatever anyone might say, he in her opinion was to blame.

Nurse McLennan had to be assisted down by Angus. Stout, she had rheumaticky knees; but she was conscientious and, carrying her bag, hirpled quickly across the grass after Flora.

The laird's wife was left alone in the car. She called the two brothers over.

'Well, Donald,' she said sternly, 'I hope you're proud of yourself. Have you seen him yet?'

Donald held his cap tucked under his arm. 'No, I have not,' he replied, respectfully. 'But no one need worry.'

'What d'you mean? What do you care anyway? Aren't you sending him and his brother away?'

He shook his head. 'It was not I.'

'Who was it then, for heaven's sake? Mary?'

'It was the Lord.'

She could not restrain a cry of indignation.

Suavely he went on: 'But this afternoon He let me know He had changed His mind.'

291

She stared at Angus, who glared back as if to say, Well, madam, are you trying to deny that God never speaks to His creatures any more? Is religion mere superstition to you? Some of the arrogant incredulity left her eyes, and for an instant wonder, timid rather than glad, flickered in them.

'So if the boy recovers,' she said, 'he'll be staying on?'

And that, thought Angus, is more than you or I will be doing. During the winter she went south; long before it he would go much farther.

'It is the Lord's will,' said Donald.

She decided to get down from the car. 'Let's see how Flora and Annie are getting on,' she cried.

They found the little parlour empty. The three women were upstairs with the boy. Soon Mary and the nurse came down.

'Well, Annie,' asked Maud, 'how is he?'

'He's had a bad shock, and no wonder.'

'But he'll get over it?'

'Yes. But I would say it depends not so much on him, as on the rest of us.'

'It depends on the Lord, working through us, as always,' said Donald.

Angus looked for and saw the strange look Mary gave her husband. There was no doubt that she, like Angus himself, suspected another cog had slipped, and so she was going to have the Lord in her very tea for the rest of her man's life.

'I gave him a sleeping pill,' said Annie. 'But it would be as well to send for the doctor.'

'Listen,' said Angus.

They were silent. Upstairs the boy had begun to rave. They heard Flora comforting him in a voice so deep with love and sympathy that they felt thrilled and moved. The hairs on their heads tingled as he shrieked that his father had killed his mother, with the hatchet used for breaking sticks. It had always been kept in the bunker. There was string round the handle, blackened by the coal. A coloured streamer had got caught in it. That frenzy of the green and red paper seemed to terrify him most. Then as suddenly he was quiet again.

In the parlour they heard the clock on the wall wheeze and

tick, and the kettle on the hob sing. Someone's stomach rumbled; Angus thought it was Maud's. The smell of the fish in the sink in the scullery was strong and recalled the sea, so close and fresh, with its limitless horizons. Soon he might be beyond those horizons. The wind made the open door creak. Outside a sheep bleated.

'Wheesh,' they heard Flora say, 'wheesh. It's all over and finished with. They're with God now, both of them; that's where they are. It's just you and Tommy now, and me, and Roy, and my mother who's your mother too, and my father.'

Donald rubbed his chin; the noise roared in all their ears, like the sea.

More quietly then, with painful sighs, the boy spoke about his brother.

'Don't worry about Tommy, either,' said Flora.

'But what am I to tell him?' he suddenly yelled.

'You won't have to tell him anything. I'll tell him. I'll tell him it was an accident.'

'But it wasn't.'

'It was, you know.'

She said it in such a voice that the adults listening downstairs, avoiding one another's gaze, knew that in a sense impossible to explain it really had been an accident.

Maud Morton-Home tried to explain it: 'Well, God help us, it's hardly the way He meant a man and his wife to live; so it was, from that point of view, an accident.'

They heard the boy say sleepily that Peggy Blair had lost her father and mother in an accident; they had been drowned at sea.

In another minute Flora came down. She was trembling and exhausted. 'Well, he's asleep,' she said, trying to smile.

'Good for you, Flora,' whispered Maud, embracing her and making up her mind to give the girl a really handsome present when she got married in a few weeks.

'I could do with a cup of tea,' said Flora.

'Well,' murmured her mother calmly, 'the kettle's on the boil.'

293

Twenty-four

Later that evening, after he had walked back in the wind and rain to his own cottage, and was sitting in the dark with glass after glass of whisky in his hand, Angus found himself visited by someone whom up to then he, like everyone else, had looked upon as a kind of guilty source, not as a man at all: the boys' father, the ex-cobbler, crouching in prison and holding on his lap the tattered lump of grief and suffering that not all the nails of remorse or penitence in his mouth, for three or thirty years, could ever make whole. What had he looked like before he had turned that corner and found himself hacking at his wife's face with the hatchet he had so domestically mended with string? According to Margaret, just ordinary: small, brown-haired, stooped, patient as butter; but more disturbing even than that ordinariness—which ought surely to have protected him, that being its natural purpose—were his less than thirty years. Hitherto when thought about, in odd half-minutes, he had seemed to Angus no human age at all, but rather as old as wife-murder. Now in the dark cottage, with the sea angrily pounding the human island and the wind howling at the door like a homeless beast, he was seen to be young enough for the redemption that he would never ask for.

Why he had come there, Angus could not say; he was not interested even in reassurances about his sons, nor in suggestions that on the Day of Judgment he would find God, Himself male, understanding and merciful. He just sat in the striped apron that Maud had given him and went on with his hopeless cobbling. His presence was somehow never frightening, but in the end it became too persistent, he would not go even when the light was put on, and this roused in Angus a craving for living human company.

Angus tried to read, but though he opened volume after

volume of the encyclopaedia that he had bought twenty years ago and knew almost by heart, he could not tonight find any solace either in the weirdness of nature or the ingeniousness of man. His hands shook; was it with the whisky, with foreboding, or with sexual desire? He stared at the couch and pictured Sheila McNeil stretched out naked on it; all he felt was a kind of priest-like disgust. Even Margaret's splendid, tender body did not allure. As for Nell's, it sent him to fill his glass again and empty the bottle.

All the time he knew whom he wanted, but was unwilling to admit it, not for his own pride's sake, but for hers, Jessie's.

It was her company he craved, not to make love to her, but to confess to her longings that until recently he had not known he possessed, and that even now he could not clearly describe to himself. As he remembered her that very day, beside him going across Orsay to the priory, and afterwards among the ruins, he had a sensation of richnesses that he knew could never be his to spend. He was like a thief confronted by a safe too strong for him to break into; or like young Sneddon in that one peaceful instant after the hatchet had struck for the last time.

He had drunk, he noticed, a full bottle of whisky; yet he still felt surprised and angry when putting on his oilskins turned out to be a long, difficult task. Someone must be trying to hamper him: the vindictive cobbler, for instance. He found himself shouting at that interferer, whoever he was. Then, ready at last, he crossed to the bureau in which his mother's Bible was kept. As tender-fingered as if it had been an egg, he lifted it out and placed it in his pocket.

As he put out the light he murmured and gestured goodbye, to the cobbler, yes, but to someone else almost as woebegone; himself yesterday it must have been, he thought, as he shut the door and staggered away from the shelter of the house into the howls and buffets of the wind. It was not quite dark. A watery moon gleamed, often hidden by huge swift clouds. The sea thundered against the cliffs and swept along the beaches. If he stumbled into it, it would sweep him away as a woman might brush away a cockroach trying to cross her threshold.

It would have been safer to take the path inland, but he somehow needed the menacing presence of the sea, as a believer caught in apostasy might need the presence of his God. Soon in fact he found himself off the path altogether, trudging across the beach to where his boat, *Aphrodite*, was drawn up. He stood beside her, patting and comforting her. The breakers, twice as high as white-plumed, helmeted horse-men, kept charging in, to die in glory and gleams of moonlight on the level sands. Once he began to heave madly at the boat, as if to get her into the water and do battle with those arrogant warriors; but he could not move her an inch.

About an hour later, soaked, exhausted, bruised, and humble, he emerged on to the road less than fifty yards from the schoolhouse. The front windows were in darkness, but he thought she would be sitting in the little kitchen at the back. She was not alone that night; she had little Tom Sneddon as a guest. Flora, on her way back to the hotel, had called in to report on John and also to give to Tom the explanation he must have been desperately waiting for.

When he crept round to the back of the cottage he saw all the windows there were dark too. He felt as desperate as any child. He could not face the journey back to his own house, though it was less than two miles; he, too, needed an explanation. Yet within this small, closed, dark cottage lay only a child of six and a spinster of forty-odd years; they could explain nothing. Caught between the two useless courses, either returning or entering the house, he stood for a minute or two in despair, listening to the wind in the trees and hearing the rain rattle like spit against his oilskins.

As he knocked on the door he tried to keep his fist as calm as it should be, since it was in search of friendship and hospitality; but he could not restrain it, it beat desperately, and his other fist came up to help it.

Almost at once a light went on in a bedroom upstairs, the blind was raised and the window opened. Jessie looked out.

'Who is it?' she asked, as wide awake as if she had been lying waiting for him. 'And whatever your business, there's no need for all that clamour.'

He stood back. 'It's me, Jessie. Angus.'

'So I see. What is it? Has the boy taken a bad turn?'

'No, no. Nothing like that, thank God. He's all right, Jessie; still sleeping. One or two folk called in to inquire. You'll know too that Donald's changed his mind.'

'So Flora told me.'

'What about the other one, Jessie, him that's with you? Flora was going to try and explain it to him, God help her. How did he take it?'

'As a nestling takes a worm.'

'Ah yes.' He laughed in delight at the similitude. What sight on earth was more consoling than that of a mother-bird feeding its young in the unharried nest?

'He's asleep now, sounder than you or I can apparently manage.'

'Were you not able to sleep then, Jessie?'

'You're drunk. You'd better get back home before you catch pneumonia.'

'I want to speak to you, Jessie. I came through the storm to do it.'

'We spoke enough today to last us for the rest of our lives.'

'Don't say that, Jessie. We've got long years ahead of us. We've just begun.'

'Do you know what time it is?'

He laughed. How foolish clocks seemed, with the sea roaring and the clouds racing across the moon. 'Does that matter, Jessie?'

'To me it does. It's after midnight.'

'I'm in trouble, Jessie. Only somebody that's truly fond of me can help get me out of it.'

'You'd better send for the woman in Glasgow you're going to marry.'

'It's you I need, Jessie.'

'You've never needed anyone in your life.'

'I do now, Jessie. Look, I'm on my knees.'

'Get up, and don't shame us both.'

'Let me in, Jessie.'

'Tomorrow maybe, at a proper time.'

'I thought you were fond of me, Jessie. Didn't you admit as much today, on Orsay? Didn't you say something about claiming priority?'

'I wondered when you would cast that back in my face. It hasn't taken you long.'

'I'm not casting it in your face, Jessie. I'm repeating it, in wonder, in gratitude, in fondness. I'm here to offer myself. God knows it's a poor bargain you'd be getting. I'm here to explain just how poor.'

'You're drunk.'

'For hours I've sat in my house yonder on the edge of the sea, and do you know who I had to keep me company?'

'That new maid from the big house, I wouldn't be surprised.'

'No, no. No woman at all. No man, either. A ghost, Jessie. The boys' father. All of us keep forgetting, Jessie, that he's not dead, that he's still amongst us, poor miserable bastard.'

'If you use that kind of language to me, I'll close this window.'

'I meant no disrespect, Jessie; the opposite rather. If there is a moral, Jessie, surely it's this: let's have pity for one another.'

'You're certainly drunk. How much did it take to get you into this state?'

'The state I'm in is humility. Don't mock, Jessie. I'm not surprised you can't recognize it in me. I know I've never been a very humble man.'

'You'll wake the boy.'

He tried to speak more quietly. 'It's likely, Jessie, I'll be getting an opportunity to show my humility; in jail.'

'Why? Is it true then, what some of them have always said, that you stole the money you've got, that you weren't left it at all?'

'I was left it, Jessie. Poor Peggy, she would never have kept me out on a night like this.'

'They say you cheated her into leaving you her money.'

'I was guilty of a greater sin than that, Jessie. I cheated her into believing I loved her.'

298

'But you were married to her?

'I was.'

'You slept with her?'

'I did.'

'So it's possible to lie with a woman night after night without having a scrap of affection for her?'

'I didn't say that, Jessie. You're too uncompromising. Human beings aren't sums that always come out even.

'Don't think I'm as innocent as all that. Poor woman. You must have done it with her scores of times, with me just the once; yet I feel so defiled that that sea, for all its roaring, could never cleanse me.'

'Jessie, you're leaving no room for pity. I was wrong. Give me the chance, and I'll make it right with you.

'What was that nonsense about jail?'

'It wasn't nonsense, Jessie. While I was married to Peggy I went through a form of marriage with another woman.'

'Good God.'

'Jessie, if not for my sake, then for your own, please let me in. You'll catch cold at that open window.

'It's easy enough to shut it. So you're blacker-hearted than I thought.'

'You've got a right to call me that.'

'There would be others too.'

'There were others, yes.'

'Not to mention me, and the big woman. No wonder you've always looked like the cock o' the north; you've had hens enough round you. Does she know?'

'Not yet. Let me say this in my defence, Jessie: they were all mature women. I deceived no young girl, ever.'

'Mature women that have been lonely are easier to deceive than young girls. Haven't you found that to be so?'

He was silent.

'I wouldn't raise a finger to help you,' she said. 'Is this woman you falsely married threatening you with the police?'

'Yes.'

'Good for her.'

He was genuinely appalled. 'You can't mean that, Jessie.'

299

'I never meant anything more in my life.'

'You want me to go to jail?'

'It's where you deserve to go.'

'That's true. But it would be a bitter world if we all got only what we deserve. Leave room for mercy, Jessie, and repentance.'

But while he was speaking she closed the window, pulled down the blind, and put out the light.

For another minute or two he stood there, picturing her climb resolutely back into bed, turn on her side with her face to the wall, and shut her eyes.

'Jessie,' he murmured, 'it isn't just me you've decided against; it's the happy life you and I could have had together, here on this island. You've condemned us both. You've tried to make it come out even.'

He turned and walked wearily away. Only when he was almost back at his own house did he remember the Bible in his pocket.

Twenty-five

As leader, Roderick McDiarmid had sent word round that there would be a meeting in the Pirate's Cave at two o'clock. It was called that because it had a high entrance through which horses laden with contraband could have entered. Inside the floor was dry, and the ceiling was lofty enough for echoes. Other caves had to be entered by wriggling through on one's stomach.

Only the boarded-out children had been summoned, because, as Roderick pointed out to Jean Fairlie, his second-in-command, Johnny Sneddon was boarded out. All seven turned up on time. Wee Douglas Munro, wearing the kilt he detested, reported that he had had a hard job preventing Tommy Sneddon from coming. Eyes solemn, he recommended that a guard be posted at the mouth.

A guard was always posted, he was told.

'Aye, but usually there's nothing to watch for,' he said, 'except sea-gulls.'

'Tommy's scared of the cave,' said Nancy Dewar. 'He always shouts if he's alone.'

They looked at one another and nodded. Indeed, listening to an oyster-catcher outside, they could almost imagine it was their small friend. One or two of them shuddered, and tried to grin bravely. They knew the meeting was about Johnny. All their lives they would remember what had happened yesterday on Orsay.

They sat on planks of driftwood, except for Roderick whose seat was a small keg.

'Well,' he said, 'you all know what happened yesterday.'

'You mean at the picnic, Roddy?' asked James Buchanan.

'Yes.'

'I just know Johnny Sneddon got a terrible fright,' cried Peggy Blair. 'But I don't know why. When I asked Mrs

301

McKenzie she just snapped my nose off.'

The others nodded; their inquiries had got the same reception.

'It's a secret,' said Andrew Elliot.

As usual, James sought to contradict. 'How can it be a secret,' he asked, 'if everybody knows it but us?'

'We don't know it.'

'I don't think there's a secret,' said Douglas. 'If it was a secret Tommy would have told me. Johnny just got a fright. A fright's not a secret, is it? I get lots of frights, but I've got no secrets.' Even when he'd found a bird's nest he had shared it with someone, especially with Tommy.

'Roddy knows,' said Jean.

Roddy nodded.

They stared at him in wonder and fear.

'Who told you, Roddy?' asked James.

'Mrs McBirnie.'

They nodded. Mrs McBirnie would have. She had the loudest voice on the island, and the loudest laughter. It would be impossible for her to keep a secret. They liked her, but weren't sure she had done right to tell Roderick. After all, though he was now thirteen and next year would go to Oban High School, he was just a child like them.

'Why did she tell you?' asked Nancy.

'Roddy's older,' said Jean. She, almost as old, and feminine, turned and looked at the younger children beside her: Peggy, ten, but as weepy as six; wee Douglas, sturdy and brave, but so nervous inside he still wet his bed; Nancy, fair-haired and sweet; James, serious and thin; and Andrew, the only one bold enough to hear a really important secret without being terrified by it. Of course, it all depended on what the secret was. Judging from Johnny's scream yesterday, and the whispers of the grown-ups afterwards, it must be terrible enough. Now here was Roddy's face, fat and greedy with sensation. She had not noticed before how fat he was getting. At Oban they would call him Fatty, if he wasn't careful.

She rose. 'I would like to ask you something first, Roddy,' she said.

'Are you going to ask him what the secret is, Jean?' asked Nancy.

'She thinks,' said Andrew, 'we're too young to know.' Yet she was little more than a year older than he.

Roderick rose too. According to his own rules Jean had a right to consult him. They went towards the back of the cave.

Douglas crept towards the mouth to look out for his friend Tommy. He had nothing to report, except that there were eight sea-gulls seated in a row on Angus McArthur's boat. 'They must be having a meeting too,' he said.

At the back of the cave the light was curiously green. Voices were hollow.

'Well, Roddy?' asked Jean. Her face was keener than ever with responsibility.

He noticed that sign of maturity, and also those two others, her breasts, beginning to show under her thin green jersey.

'What is it?' she asked. 'Is Johnny mad, or something?'

'Mad?' He grinned, and hunched his shoulders.

'Does he go mad like yon often, every two or three months? Is that the secret?'

He shook his head; then realised he didn't know. 'I don't think so. Maybe he does, though.'

She looked towards their companions chattering at the mouth of the cave. 'They're just kids, Roddy,' she said, and added, though it almost wrenched the heart out of her breast: 'And they've got no real parents.'

Masculine and callous, he jeered: 'Neither have you, Jean, nor me.'

'We're older. Wee Douglas is just five. Peggy too, you know how nervous she is.'

'But, Jean, if Johnny and Tommy are going to stay here, everybody's bound to get to know.'

'Why, do you think they're going to be taken away?'

'Mrs McBirnie said she thought they might.'

'Then there wouldn't be any need for our kids ever to know.'

'How are they ours, Jean?'

She blushed. 'I think of them as my brothers and sisters.'

303

Then Andrew Elliot, pale-faced and black-haired, marched up to them. 'Well, have you made up your big minds yet to tell us your silly little secret?'

'We're still consulting,' said Roddy.

'Consulting!' He put his hands to his mouth and began to yodel the word sarcastically, so that it went ricocheting from wall to wall.

The others came running to join in the fun. All five danced about, yelling the word.

Roderick and Jean stood in their midst, he frowning, she smiling.

'You see,' she cried, 'they're just kids.'

He snatched up a bit of wood and beat furiously on the wall with it, like Sneddon's father, he thought, striking Sneddon's mother with the hatchet.

'Shut up,' he shouted, 'shut up.'

Laughing, they rushed back to the sunlit entrance.

'Wouldn't it be better to let Miss Ogilvie tell them, whatever it is?' asked Jean.

He shook his head. The secret mustn't be told as if it was a grammar lesson. It would be ruined. He felt obscurely that the grief and suffering for them all that it represented would in some way be cheapened.

Jean seemed to sense that too. 'Mr McNeil the minister, then?' she suggested.

'No.' The trouble with the minister would be that he would try so hard to take the horror out of it.

'Or Angus?'

He almost consented. Angus McArthur could tell a story well; he kept everything in it, grief and suffering and horror; indeed, he heightened all these, but he also could leave a calmness in the mind at the end. That most of the women, especially Miss Ogilvie, didn't like him, made him all the more suitable.

But Jean was shaking her head, rejecting her own suggestion. 'No, not him,' she said. 'He doesn't care. Flora would be best.'

'I don't know what you're saying all these names for, Jean.

I'm going to tell them. If you don't want to listen you can be sentinel.'

'Tell me what it is, and then I can judge.'

He was about to refuse when he realized that she was almost a woman herself; he had heard Mrs McBirnie say so recently. Well, Mrs Sneddon had been a woman.

'All right.' He bent closer and whispered: 'Johnny's father killed his mother with a hatchet. Like this, look.' He tapped her forehead with the bit of salt-smelling wood. 'Only harder, with all his force. He killed her.'

She had her hands clasped and could hardly speak: 'What did he do it for?'

Fascinated, he noticed the faint impression left on her brow.

He hadn't quite been told why the murder had been done, but he had guessed. 'You can guess,' he whispered.

She nodded, with an awareness in her eyes clearer than his own. Her face seemed much older.

'But I'm not going to tell them that,' he said. 'There's no need. They'll not ask.'

'They will.'

'Then I'll say he was mad.'

She closed her eyes. 'Poor Johnny, and poor Tommy. Did Johnny see it? Was that why he got a shock yesterday?'

If he wasn't careful she would spoil it all. Suddenly he pushed past her and shouted: 'Back to your seats. Meeting's resumed.'

Mocking him, they scampered in and sat down. One of them had put a dead crab on Roddy's keg. He poked it off with his bit of wood.

At first Jean wouldn't come and sit down. She stood in the shadows, frowning.

They stared at her curiously.

Then Peggy Blair stood up. 'I'm not going to listen if Jean's not going to be here,' she said.

'Me too,' said Nancy.

'What's up?' demanded Douglas.

'It must be a terrible secret,' said Andrew. 'Jean thinks we're too young to hear it. Never mind her, Roddy. Tell us.'

305

Jean changed her mind. She went and sat down. Nancy took her hand.

'It's really nothing,' said Roderick, grinning at them all. 'I mean, it's about something that's past, long ago.'

Douglas gazed up at the ceiling. 'Like pirates?' he asked. 'Sure, like pirates.'

Jean suddenly remembered she hadn't asked if Johnny's father had been hanged. She too looked up, as if to see him dangling there.

Roderick paused. Outside they heard another oyster-catcher, and then a sheep.

'Johnny Sneddon's father killed his mother—' he lifted the bit of wood and slowly let it fall again— 'with a hatchet.'

They were at first more embarrassed than shocked.

Andrew asked: 'Whose mother? Johnny's? You just said, his mother. Was she an old woman?'

'I meant Johnny's mother. She wasn't old. She couldn't have been.'

'What age was she?' whispered Nancy.

'I don't know. About twenty-six, I think.'

'Like Flora McArthur?'

'Yes, just like Flora.'

So that the name, always a happiness and reassurance to them, couldn't be so any more.

Douglas was clenching his fists. Jean was almost sure he had wet his underpants. 'What about Tommy?' he asked.

The others waited; they did not know who would or could answer, in that cave or on the island or in the whole world.

'He was just a baby,' muttered Roddy. 'He didn't see it.'

'But Johnny saw it?' asked James, eagerly.

'Aye. That's why he got the fright on Orsay yesterday. The man was keeping clegs o his wife's face with a stick. He hadn't done it very well, for one had bitten her and there was blood on her brow. Wasn't there, Jean?'

'Not much.'

'But there was some.'

She had to nod.

'So Johnny remembered, you see, and got a fright.'

306

They nodded. It was very easy to understand.

'Will he always get frights like that?' asked Nancy.

'Maybe.'

'I'm glad,' muttered Douglas, 'I never had any mother.'

Peggy Blair was sucking her thumb. Her eyes were strangely cunning. From that moment, indeed, no one was ever to hear her speak about her parents who had been drowned.

'Was he hanged?' asked Andrew, sharply.

As if he knew it might be a disappointment, a failure, as it were, of the horror to culminate, Roderick hesitated. 'No,' he said at last. 'They said he was mad.'

'It's not important,' said Jean.

Their faces showed they thought it was.

'Where is he?' asked James, looking round as if he might be there, among them, hatchet lifted.

'In prison,' said Roderick.

'What's important is that we've got to help Johnny and Tommy,' insisted Jean.

'But it happened, Jean,' said Peggy. 'We can't make it not have happened, can we?'

'No, but we can pretend in our minds that it never happened. If we don't, maybe they'll take Johnny and Tommy away.'

'Who will?' asked Nancy, although she knew.

'The people in Glasgow.'

They frowned: however well-intentioned those authorities, their jurisdiction could never be wholly acceptable.

'But if Johnny and Tommy don't want to go,' asked James, 'will they still take them away?'

'They'll say it's for their own good.'

For their own good: that was another mystery to ponder.

Then they heard, no oyster-catcher this time, but Tommy Sneddon, almost as shrill and sad. As they listened he called all their names in turn: 'Roddy. Douglas. Jean. James. Peggy. Nancy. Andrew.'

They rushed to the entrance. He had halted in the midst of the sands, about fifty yards away. His red pirate's hankie was round his head, his wooden sword in his hand. He glanced apprehensively towards some birds standing near the water's edge. Once he turned and stared back at his own footprints.

Jean was the first to run, and though the others came whooping after, she reached him before they did and, unable to control her emotion, sank down on her knees to embrace him.

He was pleased enough, but puzzled, especially as the rest also pressed round him, laughing and shouting his name and even touching him, as if they hadn't seen him for a year.

'What's up?' he kept crying. 'What have you done?' He thought maybe they were playing a joke on him, and in the cave a trap was waiting.

'Nothing, Tommy,' said Jean, 'we're just glad to see you, that's all.'

He could have believed her more easily if she hadn't been crying. Douglas too, and Peggy Blair, were in tears.

'How's Johnny?' asked Roderick.

'He's better. The doctor's just been. He's to stay in bed for a day or two; that's all. But I thought we were going to play at pirates?'

'So we are,' they cried.

'Well, what are you not wearing your hankies for?'

They took out their handkerchiefs and solemnly tied them round their heads.

Twenty-six

That night, when Angus learned from Flora at the hotel that Margaret was coming to Calisay next evening, it did not change his plans, but accelerated them. He would have to leave, not in three days, but in one; tomorrow he must be gone, in all likelihood for ever. Certain places, such as his mother's grave, would still have to be paid a special last visit; but everywhere else would have to find its farewell in his ordinary everyday glance; and this applied of course to the hotel bar.

Unfortunately Neil Lindsay, gross and stupid, came in, drunker at first with pride than later with beer. He had just come from telephoning his wife in Glasgow, and announced to the few present that he was afraid he was going to become a father, since Janet had been to the Home and had taken to the girl she had been determined all along to adopt. The others didn't quite understand, but congratulated him politely enough. McDonald, a wag in spite of being Elspeth's man, called on him to stand a round, and he did so, not at all reluctantly, though he just couldn't keep calculation out of his eyes. Angus was persuaded to join in.

Whether bemused by the joys of imminent and ready-made fatherhood, or by the beer, Neil then took it into his big round head that Angus was particularly thoughtful that evening, and sitting down beside him in his private corner said so; and added with beery sibilance that it wasn't because of the unfortunate accident on Orsay, either. No, Janet had told him why, in secrecy of course, hence his lowered voice and lifted beer mug. She had told him that Miss Mathieson, the Child Welfare Officer—a handsome woman—was arriving with her tomorrow evening, and in fact was going to put up with them as the hotel was full. She had also told him that Miss Mathieson was engaged to be married to someone well known

309

to Angus, very well known indeed, someone tall, with ruddy cheeks and a white moustache.

Listening to and watching this display of human intimacy, the beery lips and eyes dim with maudlin lubricity, Angus felt a fortifying scunner. What he had planned to do had seemed objectionable, on the grounds that it was mean. Now, confronted by this exhibition of true pettiness, he saw that he had been unfair to himself. Tomorrow, to leave Calisay for ever; to go in his own not quite seaworthy boat as far as Islay, if he was lucky; to say sudden farewell to scenes he now loved and needed for his soul's refreshment and possible regeneration; to abandon Margaret and his unborn child, not out of treachery only, but out of a desire to protect them both from him if that regeneration—as was more than likely—failed; and finally, at his age to set out for Australia to squander all his, or rather Peggy's, money in a year or two, and thereafter, unless he had been successful in finding some rich and comely widow, to sink as elegantly as he could into the gutter, and die there with as much style as hunger, old age, self-contempt, and inward erosion left him: no, no, such a programme, condemnable from many points of view, could not with justice be called petty.

Neil must have interpreted his long, sighing silence as huff, because, with a wink that was in itself a recapitulation of all his previous inanities, he murmured that he was well aware of the danger of interfering between a man and his wife, or a man and his intended; wasn't there a terrible example before them all in the case of the father and mother of the Sneddon boys? Encouraged by further silence, the fat shopman then, with another wink more offensive than the other merely because it was a repetition, whispered that he hoped it would not be taken amiss if he were to say that once or twice he and Janet in their marital conversations (very private, of course, no customers being by) had agreed they wouldn't be at all surprised if one day, despite what others said, Angus and Jessie Ogilvie made a match of it. Chuckles as of an accomplice concluded the performance.

A minute or two later Neil went off, looking a little hurt

and surprised that he hadn't been thanked for his interest and solicitude. Indeed, when he hurried back a minute or so later, Angus thought he had returned to demand it. His purpose was worse. It was to whisper into one of the iciest ears he must ever have had an inch from his lips that tomorrow night, when the steamer brought the two ladies, there would be dinner at the shop house for them, and also, of course, for the two men needed to make up the celebrating quartet. A hand then flapped on Angus's shoulder, once, twice, three times, with a canniness that only years of self-interest at the scales could have achieved. He hurried off after that, as if every extra half-second had to be paid for.

'Man, Angus,' said Rory the barman, 'Neil's been filling you with words tonight.'

Minutes later Angus took his own leave. It would be for the last time, he realised; but the very ordinariness of his departure had more pathos in it, for himself, than if he had made a dramatic speech and shaken hands all round. 'Good night, Rory,' he merely said. 'Good night, all.'

They wished him, sincerely enough, good night too. Yet, he thought, as he made for home under the bright moon, they had been as sincere as he deserved and wished.

He went to bed after the moon had gone down into the sea. His preparations were made; tomorrow all that remained to be done was to have petrol put into the boat, hand over to Flora what he had decided to leave as legacies, say a few goodbyes, and visit one or two special places. He hoped to be able to leave the shores of the island soon after midday. With luck he should be at Port Askaig by six, in time for a meal at the hotel before the steamer arrived. He did not know yet whether he would try to catch a last look at Margaret while it waited at the pier; he thought not, but it was possible that after six hours alone in a small leaky boat sailing down the Sound of Jura he might have changed his mind, though never to the extent of abandoning the whole programme and returning on the steamer with her.

Next morning was again bright and sunny, with the air like silk between the fingers. His shoes were yellow with pollen

311

from the wild flowers in the machair as he carried his luggage down to the *Aphrodite*, ready at the little jetty near Pirate's Cave. When the two small boys, Tommy Sneddon and Douglas Munro, accompanied by the dog Roy, offered to help, he accepted briskly and gave them to lug between them a suitcase so big and heavy that they were both as red as poppies and glistening with sweat like seals when at last they staggered with it to the motor boat.

'Are you flitting?' puffed Tommy, feeling he had earned the information.

'I am that.'

'Where to?'

'Far enough.'

'America?' asked Douglas, staring towards it across the shimmering sea.

'No.'

'Are you never coming back?' asked Tommy.

'Never's a long word, boy. How's your brother this morning?'

'He's all right. But he's to stay in bed yet.'

'Maybe I'll look in and have a word with him before I leave. Do you think he would like that?'

Tommy's nod indicated that at least the visit wouldn't be forbidden.

'Will there be anybody staying in your house?' asked Douglas.

'Likely enough.' As he turned to gaze up at it he wondered himself who those occupants might be. Perhaps one of them might be his own son.

'Are you going in your boat?' asked Tommy.

'As far as Islay, just.'

'What will you do with it there?'

'I'll look out for a couple of wee fellows, with tongues as big as that anchor there, and give it to them.'

They grinned and looked at each other's tongue.

'I wish it was us,' said Tommy. 'I would like a boat.'

But Douglas was more cautious; he stared at the water in the bottom of the boat. 'Does it let in?' he asked.

'I believe it does.'

'But what if when you're in the middle of the sea it gets flooded?'

Angus smiled; the thought had already crossed his mind. 'Would it sink?'

'It would.'

'And you'd be drowned?'

'I would.'

Douglas, as satisfied as Socrates, turned to his friend. 'Maybe it would be better, Tommy, to wait for another boat.'

Tommy agreed. 'My boat,' he said, 'will be red and white.'

Then off they raced, the dog with them, no longer interested in Angus or his boat.

Rejection upon rejection, he thought; first, Jessie; then the men in the bar; and now these children; and not rejection either, nothing so positive as that, just a withdrawal of interest that had only been there for politeness' sake. Keeping humanity at a distance had more than one consequence; no doubt he had preserved himself from contamination, but he had also been deprived of what up to now he had thought well worth doing without, a sense of involvement, not in humanity's joys—these he had had in plenty—but in its sorrows and dangers. He was still by no means sure he wanted even a taste of these; yet as he watched the two little boys, one murder's get and the other lust's, he felt a flicker of uneasiness at not being involved, however slightly, in their fates.

A quarter of an hour later he was in the cemetery, seated on a warm bank of heather, and smoking a cigar. His parents' headstone, green with moss, and nodded against by wild flowers, lay below. In a corner by the tumbled-down dyke was the grave of Duncan, Mary's brother, drowned almost forty years ago. At first he carefully did not try to resurrect these who had loved him, and whom he in his turn had surely loved. He was content to relax near them.

In the heather under his hand love was made and murder done; also in the sea sparkling so amiably beyond the dyke. Butterflies twinkled by in an airy dance. Red-bottomed bees hummed round him. One alighted near him, and by looking at its nose he recognized it as one of boyhood's 'fuggies', which instead of a painful sting in their behinds had only a pair of useless pincers. As he had done long ago, to impress the girls, he reached out and caught it in his fist. It buzzed furiously and tickled, but did not sting. When he opened his hand it flew away.

With the sun so warm on his face and hands, he found himself turn drowsy, and he began to half-dream, half-fancy that he was on board the liner, crossing the Indian Ocean, and beside him on the shady deck lay a woman in a white dress, widowed, wealthy, white-haired, buxom, and pleasant-faced. She laughed at his every jest. Often she glanced aside fondly at his mature handsomeness. Already he had been to her cabin.

He awoke, with a start of guilt; true, all he had done was dream of what he intended to do and was confident he could do, but perhaps he ought not to have dreamt about it there. The living could be deceived, and deserved no better; but the dead, whether smirking in Elysium or groaning in Hades or just mouldering under the peat, surely they should have the truth told them? If they clyped it could only be to one another, and all were 'fuggies', stingless; or to God, who knew in any case. Some of them had loved him; yes, but did love last in Heaven, Hell, or under the peat?

You see, he murmured to them, I've told you the truth, I've let you see what lies in my heart in spite of what my tongue might say or my head think; I've shown you what I really am, so that as you lie there you can be unanimous about this, as you must be now about so many other things, chief among them being, surely to Christ, the inescapability from self. If I wanted to change you know I couldn't. You think Jessie was right to reject me; married to her, and so lacking opportunity for the kind of conceit I need as those butterflies need sun, I would, like them, have soon lost what splendour I have. Married to Margaret, with a child as a complication, who knows that in a year or so I shouldn't have become suffocated by the domesticity she would have wrapped round me, or humiliated by the legitimate sexual demands, amounting to

314

revenge, she would have made? Let her come tonight and talk it over with Jessie. She'll soon learn what a scoundrel she just avoided marrying; and if at first she weeps and says she would willingly have married me, were I six times as wicked, soon enough she'll dry her tears. It was never really me she loved, it was that in me which released her femininity. Now that she's as feminine as Flora, almost, she'll not want for men to fondle her, despite the child.

But none of them, not even his mother, answered. They were not there. He was alone, with insects, slabs of stone, flowers and grass. A stonechat chirped and bobbed for an instant, a sheep bleated, a boy shouted. It made no difference. He was still alone. He always had been, and always would be; the hands that had helped him from the womb had not touched him, and the hands that would lift him into his coffin wouldn't touch him either.

As he rose, carefully, so as not to disturb that loneliness, and slipped away, he had another vision of the little ex-cobbler, crouched in his cell, trying hopelessly to mend not only his own misery, but all mankind's. Let him keep trying all the same.

*   *   *

Less than an hour later, yachting cap on head, he had, with the help of the children playing there, brought the *Aphrodite* successfully into the jetty, and filled her tank with petrol. Then, feeling and looking at his most splendid, he went striding up the road to the hotel to leave the legacies with Flora and say goodbye to her. Guests came to peep at him as he passed, especially a couple of middle-aged women, English schoolteachers, who had already cast admiring eyes at him. One, the taller, might have done, he thought, out of the corner of his mind. Indeed, for his kind of entomology, every hotel was a stone ready to upturn; an ocean liner, first-class, ought to prove the most fruitful field so far.

In spite of these thoughts, he was gracious and gallant enough towards his niece to flatter and amuse her. She was in the dining-room setting the tables for lunch.

'I haven't got time, Uncle Angus,' she said. 'Did you see Johnny this morning?'

He had not looked in after all. The omission made him realise afresh that within half an hour he would be sailing down the Sound, never to return. All over the island were people he had not said goodbye to: Donald and Mary even, old Ewan and Kirstie McCuish, the minister and his wife, Maud Morton-Home, Dugald who might have piped him off, and others whom he had known all his life.

'No, I'm afraid I didn't, Flora; but I was talking to Tom, and he told me John's going to be all right.'

'You think so?'

'Don't you?'

She nodded, but for a moment her dark eyes were fey. 'There are times when I wonder. It must be terrible for a child so young. But when Jean comes, she'll help.'

'Jean?'

'Aye. The wee girl Janet Lindsay's going to adopt; the one in the photograph.' She laughed. 'I was hearing things about you too.'

'From Big-head Neil?'

'Aye. Oh, I got it awful secret, as I'm one of the family. Am I allowed to congratulate you?'

'If you like. But not on that; on my imminent departure.'

'Why, where are you going?'

'Away.'

She laughed. 'Where to?'

'Limbo.'

'Where in goodness' name is that? Africa, somewhere?'

'Beyond Africa.'

'You're joking?'

'I am not.'

'Are you running away?'

'Put it that way if you wish. Everyone else will say so. Here are a few things I'd like you to hand over for me, Flora. First, this is for yourself: a wedding present, with my most sincere best wishes.'

316

She took the envelope with her name on it. 'Thanks, Uncle Angus.'

'This is for Jessie.' It was his mother's Bible, also in an envelope. 'And this is for Miss Mathieson.' For Margaret the key to the cottage, and a letter of explanation. 'I'm going as far as Port Askaig in the *Aphrodite*,' he said. 'I shall tell them there it's for Hugh, if he cares to go and collect it.'

'But it's a good boat, worth hundreds! Of course he'll collect it; he'll be delighted. He'll look after it till you come back.'

'I am not coming back this time, Flora. Only one thing I'd like to ask: don't change the name. My cottage and everything in it I'd like to leave to Miss Mathieson. If she doesn't want it, I would like you to have it, Flora.'

'Can I look to see what's in here?' She was now almost in tears. It had struck her he was old, twice her age anyway, and his eyes were bloodshot and unhappy.

'Why not?'

She opened the envelope and took out the cheque: it was for a hundred pounds. 'But you can't afford all this, Angus. Won't you need it where you're going?'

'I want you to have it, Flora. Tell Hugh I'm sorry I didn't have a chance to say goodbye.'

'Why? When are you leaving?'

'I am on my way.'

'Now, you mean?'

'In five minutes I shall be waving farewell to Calisay.'

She laughed and wept. 'I'm sorry, Angus. But it's so hard to believe.'

He took her hand. 'Will you remember me, Flora?'

'Goodness, none of us will ever forget you, you can be sure of that.'

For his notoriety, she meant. Even those under the peat would talk scandal about him. Those burning it in the winter would burn him too.

'I mean,' she said, still laughing and weeping, 'you've been so different from the rest of us. Look at you now. Half the folk in this hotel think you're a millionaire visiting us on your

317

big yacht.' Her voice softened. 'But I don't think you've ever been very happy.'

He was surprised, and a little indignant. 'Happy? I've been happy enough.'

'You haven't had folk to talk to. We've all been too heathery and ignorant for you. Maybe you'll find them where you're going.'

For a few moments he let himself remember the great rhododendron in the schoolhouse garden, the cave the children played in now and in his day, the quiet nook with the wild rose bush above the cliffs, the road at night home from the hotel, the great strand, the sacred ruins on Orsay, and the Hangman's Rock.

'Well, Flora,' he said, a little huskily, 'give my warmest regards to your mother and father.'

'You haven't even said goodbye to them?'

'No. Nor to many others. I'm just slipping discreetly away. No hearts will be broken. To you and Hugh, Flora, all the luck in the world. Bring your children to Calisay, as often as you can.'

'I've to get them first.'

'You will. Wherever I may be I'll want to think of them playing in the places where I used to play. Our island mustn't be allowed to die, Flora.'

'Mother thinks it's sure to. First, Hector left; then I'm leaving too. And you, Angus.'

'I don't count.'

He could have prolonged the conversation for hours, but in the end he might not have had the courage to go, at least with the jauntiness he intended. Besides, she had already looked three times at the clock as a hint that, whether his destination was Timbuctoo or the bottom of the Sound, the work of the hotel must go on.

'Goodbye, Flora,' he said, and went.

'Oh no. Wait. Surely I'll come and wave you off.' She came running after him, tears in her eyes.

'There's no need.' But he could not hide his pleasure.

In the vestibule they passed Isa McGilvray. She looked

astonished and displeased.

'I'm just going down to the pier with Angus,' explained Flora. 'You see, he's going away.'

'Going away where?'

'That's a secret, Isa,' he said. 'But what's not secret is that I'm not coming back this time.'

'You're leaving for good?'

He nodded.

She laughed. Was there envy in her laughter? Was she betraying a desire to go with him? It could well be. No eligible woman had striven harder to resist him. Yet he had not tried even once to seduce her.

'I can't say I'm surprised,' she said. 'I always knew you'd go like this, quick and sudden. I never thought you'd stay. Good luck.'

'Thank you, Isa. And good luck to you, and Ken.'

She followed them out on to the road and stood staring after them as they went down to the jetty.

The children were guarding the boat, or so they said. They were eager to help him cast off and shouted advice. In spite of them, and of his own nervousness, he made a good enough departure, backing out and turning without scraping against the wall.

'Where is he going?' asked Roderick McDiarmid.

Flora shook her head. She was too busy waving and weeping. Seated like a Viking in the boat, but very lonely, Angus was waving back.

The children gathered round her.

'What's wrong, Flora?' asked Jean Fairlie.

'He's going for good. He's not coming back.'

'Ever?' asked James Buchanan.

She shook her head.

'He's lucky,' murmured the boy, and running to the very end of the jetty he began to shout with a peculiar longing that confused Flora's sadness and chilled her heart.

'Isn't James happy here?' she asked the others.

'Not very,' replied Roderick.

They all stared at her with pity and affection, but none

disapproved when their leader added: 'None of us is, really. We'd all prefer to be back in Glasgow.'

The motor boat was now too small to make out Angus in it, even if her eyes hadn't been blurred by tears and a new understanding.

Twenty-seven

About two months after Angus's departure from the island Janet Lindsay paid her third and final visit to the Home.

'Just wait here,' she said proudly to the taxi-driver. 'It doesn't matter how long. This is one day when I'm refusing to count the expense.'

He grinned at her as she went up the steps of the Home carrying the suitcase. Then he picked up his *Noon Record*, to study the horses running that afternoon. If there was one with a name like Orphan or Adoption he would risk a half-crown on it whatever its form.

She was met by Agnes in the hall.

'I'll carry your case, Mrs Lindsay,' said the servant.

'Thank you. But I am quite capable of carrying it myself.'

Agnes smiled. More than the other servants and some of the nurses she was willing to make allowances for Mrs Lindsay. Even she couldn't deny that the dour-faced woman was in some ways unsuitable as a mother for so merry and high-spirited a child as Jean McDonnell; she was too glum, unimaginative, and ridiculously conceited; but it was in her favour that she was fond enough of the girl to have gone into a tigress's cave after her; as indeed she had done, Matron being the tigress, with claws these days at their sharpest. Better still, Jean returned the fondness; and Agnes was satisfied that though some children's desperate need for love might deceive them into seeing it where it really wasn't, Jean's never would.

'You see,' added Mrs Lindsay, 'her clothes are in here: a complete rig-out from the skin outwards. When she leaves with me not even the ribbon in her hair will belong to charity.'

Agnes could appreciate that pride, but she also saw its dangers. If it could be kept below the surface and have its effect without being shown, it would do no harm and might do a lot of good; but if it kept breaking out, in many little

321

things, such as this matter of the ribbon, it might end, not with Jean spoiled, which struck Agnes as impossible, but with Mrs Lindsay herself so possessive as to be a torment to everybody.

'It's no' for me to shove in my oar,' said Agnes, with a grin. 'I'm only a skivvy here.'

'My girl's told me you've been a good friend to her.'

Agnes blushed with pleasure. 'I'll no' deny I'm fond o' Jean,' she said. 'So I'd like to say, meaning nae offence, for her sake maistly—' Then she found she didn't quite know what it was she wanted to say, or rather how to put it. She couldn't very well blurt out: 'For Christ's sake, woman, you've got a gem. Don't spend all your time polishing it. There's no need, it'll shine bright enough if you just gie it an odd dicht noo and then. But don't, for sweet Jesus's sake, try to keep it to yourself. A lassie like Jean belangs to us a'. You've just got the privilege o' looking after her.' So she said nothing at all, just grinned, and looked, Janet thought, good-natured enough, but very coarse.

Matron, as always nowadays, was dressed in her uniform. 'Agnes,' she said pleasantly, 'please fetch Jean. I think you'll find her in the nursery.'

'Helping to look after the babies?' asked Mrs Lindsay.

'Yes. She likes that.'

'But ought she to be doing it, Matron? Isn't it the nurses' job? Besides, these babies, coming from goodness knows where, are they free from infectious diseases?'

Matron, to Agnes's surprise, remained pleasant and calm. 'Yes, I think they are, Mrs Lindsay,' she said. 'You see, the other children are at school, and Jean was lonely. She asked to be allowed to help in the nursery.'

'If you saw her wi' the weans, Mrs Lindsay,' butted in Agnes, 'you'd be prood o' her.'

'I'm not complaining,' said Mrs Lindsay.

She had reminded them whose daughter Jean now was, and was content.

'Please tell her Mrs Lindsay is here,' said Matron.

'Tell her her mother is here.'

Matron smiled. 'Yes, of course. You must excuse me, Mrs

Lindsay. I'm not accustomed to the new relationship.'

'Neither am I, really. But I'm determined to start as I mean to finish. I'd be obliged therefore if everybody recognized what's legal, after all.'

As Agnes went out it was Matron she felt sorry for. The old girl was bound to feel lonely, surrounded by children whom she couldn't get near to. Mrs Lindsay certainly did lack imagination.

She didn't have to go all the way to the nursery. She met Jean on the stairs, gazing up at the painting of the provost in his red robe.

'Your new mither's come for you, Jean,' she said. 'Are you saying goodbye to a' the funny faces?'

Jean chuckled and nodded.

Agnes bent down. 'Here's anither, hen, the funniest o' the lot. Gie it a kiss.'

Jean promptly kissed her; it was a typical, full-hearted smack.

'Bless you,' muttered Agnes, wanting and yet not wanting to warn the child against this reckless giving of her full heart. Maybe Johnny Sneddon had been wiser, in always withholding a little.

'I was nursing wee Sambo,' said Jean.

There was a smell of baby damp and talcum powder on her. Sambo was the name Agnes herself had given to a black baby brought in a few days ago.

'You're happy you're going, hen?'

'A wee bit of me is, a big bit isnae.'

'Ah, but a big bit o' you should be. They tell me that the daffies on this island Calisay are like the Chinese army, in millions.'

Jean laughed, and with a forefinger at each side of her face made her eyes narrow.

'Think of us, lassie, at times.'

'Often, Agnes.'

'I believe you will, God bless you. But whit are we blethering here for, wi' auld Wattie, the clype-clash, straining his lugs.' This was a Home joke, that the two busts told tales to Matron. 'Your mither's waiting for you. She's got a case full of new claithes. You're going to be the toff, I can tell you.'

It was maybe lucky, thought Agnes, as they went upstairs and along the corridor hand-in-hand, that Jean was too much of a tomboy to be dainty about dress; Mrs Lindsay's own was so drab that she was hardly likely to be good at choosing it for anyone else.

In the office both Matron and Agnes stood back, smiling at each other like enemies in a truce, while Mrs Lindsay and Jean kissed. The girl was warm and spontaneous, the woman had to struggle against an awkwardness that by no means suggested insincerity. They would do, decided Agnes, in tears: the girl's warmth would thaw out the woman's stiffness; in a year or two—yes, it might take as long as that—there would exist between them as deep-rooted and bonny-flowered a love as grew between any mother and daughter.

Matron saw the tears and widened her own eyes, as if to emphasize their dryness. 'Agnes,' she murmured, 'would you be so kind as to take Jean along to her room and help her put on these clothes Mrs Lindsay has brought for her?'

'No,' cried Mrs Lindsay. 'That's what I won't allow anyone to do. It's my duty, and my pleasure, as her mother.'

'I would like to have a little talk with you, Mrs Lindsay, while Agnes and Jean are busy putting on the new clothes.'

'In that case,' said Mrs Lindsay stubbornly, 'without disrespect to your servant, who's been very kind and to whom I'm properly grateful, shouldn't it be one of the nurses who should do it?'

Bless you, thought Agnes; if ever a woman needs blessing more than cursing it's you, Mrs Lindsay; but if you're not careful it's the cursing you'll get mostly. No, it isn't going to be daffies all the way for Jean. But oh, to hell, who had ever thought it would be? Certainly not the spunky little girl herself; she knew how to make one daffodil go a long way.

'It's all right, mother,' said Jean, clasping Mrs Lindsay's hand. 'I'd prefer Agnes to help me.'

'Prefer her to me, you mean?'

'No, she doesn't,' said Agnes. 'She means she prefers me to

the nurses. Don't forget, Mrs Lindsay, your Jean and me's great pals. This is our last chance of a natter together.'

Reluctantly then Janet nodded, and watched them go out, with Agnes carrying the suitcase. She heard them laugh as they went along the corridor.

'She's got a good heart,' she muttered, 'but I wonder if she's a good influence.'

'Please sit down, Mrs Lindsay. Surely a good heart is always a good influence.'

'You know what I mean. It's the way she talks; she's so common. Is she a Catholic?'

'I believe so.'

Mrs Lindsay nodded, as if it proved something.

'In a few minutes you will be taking Jean away from us all. You can start getting rid of our influence and make her as uncommon as you like.'

Mrs Lindsay stared defiantly across the desk. 'I know what you're hinting at, Matron. You said it once before, in this very office. There's no need to remind me. I remember who her antecedents were. I remember it all the time.'

'Wouldn't it be wiser to forget them?'

'I'll forget them all right, in my own way and in my own time.'

'Yes. We have only a few minutes for our little chat, Mrs Lindsay. Last time you were here I didn't get an opportunity to speak with you alone.'

Officials had been present then.

'What is there for us to say in private to each other, Matron? I don't want to hear anything about my girl, either in her favour or against. I'll find it all out myself.'

'It isn't Jean I want to talk about. It's Miss Mathieson.'

'Oh. But she's your friend, Matron, not mine.'

'I haven't seen or spoken to her since she came here with you about two months ago.'

'She's still in her old job, I understand.'

'Yes, but she seems not to want to come here. I am anxious about her. Tell me, please, what actually happened when she went with you to Calisay. From what I could gather, something went wrong; things didn't turn out as she expected.'

Janet put on her dourest, least intelligent expression. From behind it she was better able to assess what other people meant; thinking her stupid, they were inclined to speak as if to a child, revealing more than they intended.

'If you're referring to the business that took her to the island, Matron, then nothing went wrong. The very opposite. She found John Sneddon greatly improved; brighter than he had been for weeks. It was as if a great weight had been lifted off his mind, as of course it had.'

'He was a bright enough child when he was here. But I was not referring to him.'

Janet frowned as if in surprise. Inwardly she was laughing and saying: 'Fine I know you weren't. It was Angus McArthur. Well, speir away. I don't have to tell you what I don't want to.'

'Margaret Mathieson has been my close friend for many years. I loved her. I still do. I want to help her, if I possibly can.'

'That's up to you and her, Matron. It's none of my business.'

'He jilted her, didn't he?'

Something in Matron's quiet voice then, a kind of quiver, not of relish, or spite, or gloating, but of desperation, caused Janet to drop her mask of obtuseness and search, with sincerity, the soft bland face and unblinking grey eyes under the white cap. She realised that it must be a mask, too. Perhaps most people needed one, to face the world. At first her impulse was to put hers on again, but the knowledge of the happiness in store for her caused her to soften, in mouth, mind, and heart, and she found herself smiling in pity and understanding. Matron had never had a husband and never would have a child. No wonder she needed this jilting, as she called it, to feed her imagination.

Yet it was true that Margaret Mathieson and Angus McArthur were none of Janet's business. She had said so that unfortunate night when they had arrived to find him fled. Her opinion had been that a man who had deceived a woman with

326

lies and then had run away from her like a coward was not worth a single tear, but she had expressed it only to Neil. As for Margaret's claim, uttered with queer pride in a storm of weeping, that she was pregnant by him, she hadn't been able to credit it, and still couldn't. Now, however, gazing at Matron, she saw that her disbelief had been based simply on resentment that this woman, so big and mannish, unmarried, and without the delicacy to keep her legs together when seated, should have succeeded in achieving in a few weeks and one or two attempts what she, Janet, had failed to do in twenty years and a thousand attempts. There had been times when Janet, in despair, had hardly been able to believe in the orthodoxy of any woman's pregnancy. Confronted by the swollen belly, and later by the red wizened morsel in the shawl, she had felt that here again must be what had caused all the commotion when it had happened to the woman in the stable at Bethlehem. What was wrong with her and Neil's love and their mingled seed, that they should not be able to do what, once a miracle, was at all other times as common as, yes, as people?

'That is what I have heard,' said Matron, 'that he jilted her.'

'Well, I suppose that's what it amounted to. When she got to Calisay she found he'd gone. He left her his cottage, and a letter.'

'A letter?'

'Aye. I don't know what was in it. She never said, and I never asked.'

'Where has he gone to?'

'Nobody knows that. He used to talk of going to Australia.'

'That's far enough away.'

Was it compassion for all women, or jealousy of those with fruitful wombs, that made her say what she did then? Afterwards Janet was to ask herself that many times. 'Not so very far,' she said, 'if what she said was true.'

Matron smiled, pretending to be patient; her fingers trotted, mild as a piano-player's, along the edge of the desk. 'I don't understand, Mrs Lindsay.'

'She claimed she was pregnant.'

'By him?'

Some loving friend you are, thought Janet, if you think she's been lying with various men. Yet had not the question been breathed out in a kind of wonder? There was more than one way of looking at it. The woman as usual had been left with the shame and responsibility of the baby; that was how Janet up to now had seen it. Another way was: the woman had got rid of the treacherous and selfish man and had the joy and glory of the child into the bargain. Which way, though, was Matron looking at it? Judging by her eyes, some other way altogether.

'But is it true?' whispered Matron.

'I just had to take her word for it. She could have been mistaken, of course. She wouldn't be the first. That was weeks and weeks ago. It might be beginning to show now, unless she's got rid of it; but I don't think she'd do that.'

'Why not?'

It occurred to Janet that Jean had been got rid of, though not in the womb. 'I think she was fond of him.'

'She loved him?'

Janet seldom used the word. In future she might not distrust it so much. 'Aye. Just that.'

'But what went wrong? She is a beautiful woman, and you told me yourself he is a handsome man.'

'Few handsomer. But those who said he was black-hearted would seem to have been right. Trust Jessie, she had the right instinct.'

'Jessie?'

'Miss Ogilvie, the schoolmistress.'

'Has she got protruding teeth?'

'Well, they do stick out a bit. I thought at one time she and Angus would make a match of it. I don't know why I should have thought that, mind you; maybe because Jessie took every opportunity to miscall him. Apparently she was right. You see, it turned out he had more admirers than Miss Mathieson. There was a woman in Oban, for instance, with whom he'd gone through a form of marriage, while his real wife was living here in Glasgow. It seems she threatened him with the police.

328

No doubt there were others.'

'Do you blame him, Mrs Lindsay?'

'Certainly I do. What right had he to go about making women unhappy?'

'Perhaps he made them happy too. If I had been a man, tall and handsome like him, I would never have got married and been tied to the one woman. I would have had dozens, hundreds of them.'

Janet stood up, puzzled, affronted and apprehensive. Was the woman mad? Was it a consequence of never, all her life, having slept with a man? She was at the age when a woman as fallow as she could be plagued with delusions.

There was a knock on the door, and in ran Jean, transformed: no longer Jean McDonnell, the sad, shabby, orphanage child, but Jean McDonnell Lindsay, gay and happy in her blue coat, red dress, pink socks and brown shoes, and with the green ribbon in her red hair. She rushed at Janet and embraced her. Over her head Janet stared at Matron, who also had risen and wore a smile as cold and sane as charity.

'Quite the wee peacock, ain't she?' cried Agnes.

Janet turned on her. 'Peacock?' she asked, indignantly.

'So many colours, I mean. Wee Josephine, I was calling her. Of course it'll be fine on this place Calisay where the heather's purple, the sea green, the sands white, and the sky blue. Don't heed me, Mrs Lindsay. I'm just excited. I'm auld enough to be her mither, you ken. I'd be a prood woman if I was. The coat's maybe a shade too long, but everything else's fine.'

Interfering besom, thought Janet. There will be lots of her kind—Sheila McNeil the minister's wife, for instance, Isa McGilvray, Elspeth McDonald, the laird's wife, and others. Well, I shall deal with them as I'm going to deal with her.

'Fine or not,' she said, 'it's as I've chosen it, and I'm her mother. I know it's the fashion for little girls' clothes to be short, but I don't approve of it.'

'I wouldnae care if it was doon to my ankles,' said Jean, 'except that I don't think I'll be able to run very fast.'

'You'll find, dear, you'll have suitable clothes for playing in.'

329

'Little girls like me,' cried Agnes, with a cackle, and pulled up her own skirts until a glimpse was had of fat thighs bulging out of tightly gartered pink knickers.

Vulgar and hysterical, as well as interfering, thought Janet. It's a blessing we'll be far from your sort on Calisay.

'Well, Matron,' she said, 'we'll be going now. I've got a taxi waiting. Thanks for all you've done. If you come across Miss Mathieson, be sure to give her my regards. It's possible, of course, she'll come and stay in the cottage. Jean, thank Matron.'

Jean marched sturdily across and held out her hand. 'Thanks,' she said. 'I'm sorry I gave a lot of trouble. Before I go there's something I've got to tell you. There's cotton wool in Sir Walter Scott's ears; and in the other one's ears too, him wi' the curly hair. It was me put it in. I don't want somebody else to get the blame when I'm gone.'

'And why did you do that?' asked Janet.

'Blame me,' said Agnes, laughing. 'I called them the clype-clashes. I said they carried stories to Matron. So Jean here goes and stuffs their ears wi' cotton wool.'

'Whose ears?'

'Those white monstrosities on the stairs.'

'I see.' Janet smiled. It was just a child's prank, with no badness in it, and the maid had put her up to it. 'You'll take it out, though, as we go down.'

Jean, eyes twinkling, nodded demurely.

Matron remained in her office, but Agnes accompanied them downstairs, and took the little balls of cotton wool as souvenirs. Other servants and some nurses were gathered in the hall. Jean scampered from one to another, as delighted as a puppy. There was laughter as well as tears. Presents were pushed into her arms.

Standing by, Janet said to herself: I should be proud, not jealous. They would never make such a fuss of a child they weren't genuinely fond of. This is fondness, not just sympathy. As for the presents, well, I was determined not to let her leave here with as much as ribbon belonging to the place, but these are different. Affection paid for these, not charity. It would ill become me to try to save her from affection.

Yet in the taxi as she sat with her arm round her daughter she was wondering how she could save her from the two little Sneddon boys, who surely loved her best of all. Not from themselves, but from the shocking predicament in which, to be truthful, God had chosen to entangle them. Everyone on the island knew their father had killed their mother; even the bairns at school knew it. Jean still did not. She would have to be told, about this now, and later about other things. Janet resented bitterly the necessity forced on her so soon to take her innocent and courageous daughter and baptize her in the world's terror and filth. 'If you like, wife,' Neil had said, 'leave it to me, I'll tell her.' God forgive her, she could have struck his fat, fond, earnest, male face, so furious had she felt at his interference, even though its purpose had been to try and spare her a great unpleasantness.

She would have to take care to give Neil his place as Jean's father.